JOY
AT THE DISMAL RIVER

LLOYD WARNER

THE COZY BOOK CLUB

One of the first ladies to read the unpublished manuscript of my first book, Faith at the Dismal River, defined it as being 'cozy.' And so, it has been my intention that each book in the Fruit of the Spirit series be considered as such. If you are considering reading this book, but have not read the first in the series, which is Faith at the Dismal River, I strongly urge you to read that book first, as it holds the key to the early life of Miss Laura Martin throughout the rest of the series.

Faith at the Dismal River is available for purchase at www.lloydwarner.com.

The Fruit of the Spirit series consist of the following books:

Book I   Faith at the Dismal River (Published June, 2011)
Book II   Joy at the Dismal River (Published March, 2012)
Book III Peace at the Dismal River (Pending October, 2012
Book IV Goodness at the Dismal River (Pending March, 2013)
Book V   Love at the Dismal River (Pending October, 2013)
Book VI subtitled The Ghosts of the Teasdale Cemetery

Joy at the Dismal River

ISBN: 978-0-865459-18-2

CHAPTER 1

A NEW DAY, A NEW YEAR AND A NEW HOPE

The whistle of the train frightened Miss Laura Martin, shattering her thoughts, as she trudged through the snow. The winter sun was making its appearance on the eastern horizon as the morning train was blowing its whistle for the crossing east of Summit City in the Sandhills of Nebraska. Shortly after the train and the sun had made their grand entry, Laura entered the Holliday residence to begin preparing the first meal of the day. She had left behind in her tiny upstairs apartment, Tylor, her three-month old son in care of her former student, sixteen year old Hannah Williams. They would come to the Holliday residence later, after the others had been fed. The first to arrive for breakfast was Ken, the master of the house and owner of the local bank. His brother Darren and wife Diane followed after him. Ken's mother, Joan Holliday came downstairs later, but she only wanted coffee. The absence of Stella, Ken's wife was most noted. Yesterday, Friday, December 28, 1951, she had been laid to rest in the Summit City cemetery.

Laura had been Stella's companion and caretaker for almost three months. She had been a widow in England when Ken married her while serving with the Army during WW II. She had suffered extensive lung damage in England as a result of the bombing. Stella and Ken had arrived in Summit City in 1946, along with her two children. Todd is now fourteen years of age and his sister, Tara is nine.

When they were all gathered around the table, Laura cleared her throat to get their attention. She spoke in a quivering voice. "While everyone is here, I think that this would be a good time to discuss meeting the needs of the household. Stella and I had discussed this earlier, but were unable to reach a decision."

3

Joan Holliday immediately spoke up. "You seem to be quite capable. I see no reason for your not continuing as you have done in the past." Darren nodded in agreement, as did his wife Diane. Ken remained silent. Laura thought, *apparently I am the only one to bring this to some conclusion.*

"Thank you for your vote of confidence." Laura continued, "However, this is a small community and I am not sure that they would approve, despite my capability. I have been living in the home for almost three months, but the situation has changed. Stella and I discussed this rather thoroughly three weeks ago. We were blunt with each other. She asked me if I would marry Ken, following her death. Let's face it. Ken and I are not social equals. My past is not compatible to that of the local banker. I am somewhat younger and have very little in the way of earthly goods. Sometimes when two people are in close proximity of one another, their emotions have a tendency to override common decency. I will not leave the family without proper domestic assistance, but I would urge that an effort be made to secure an older woman who loves children. I shall continue to live outside of the home until a replacement can be found."

Ken spoke up. "But Laura, this is full employment. I presumed that you were living from hand to mouth when you started here. With the expense of Tylor's birth, is it a wise decision to forgo fulltime employment? Also, I have heard that you help out with Hanna's care."

Laura replied. "Yes, you are right. It was a difficult decision because of my obligations. But, I am quite frugal. Also, as I have placed my finances before the Lord, He sent you to me when you were seeking help with Stella. What started as one day a week became daily and eventually as a live-in. I have saved my money and I am looking forward to what the Lord has in store for me. Living in this home has truly been a blessing and

I will miss being here with the family. However, I don't have peace about remaining beyond the appointed time."

Ken's mother asked, "Do you have any recommendations for a replacement?"

"Ideally," Laura began, "I would look for the grandmotherly type, preferably one who is widowed, looking for security for herself as well. The three families represented here today must have someone among their acquaintances that would be available. This is a very pleasant place to work. The children are well behaved and Mr. Holliday is not demanding. Take your time, but find a good match for this family." Laura checked the coffeepot. Turning to leave the room, she said, "I will leave you to your ideas. There is ample coffee. I presume that everyone is staying for dinner, so I will need the kitchen by ten o'clock."

As Laura was leaving the room, Joan called after her. "Wait a minute, Laura. I need to speak with you alone. The rest of you go into the living room where you will be more comfortable." After the others had left, Joan went to the door and closed it. She turned to face Laura. "Young lady, stop being a martyr for my son or this community! I know when I see a woman in love! Bide your time in this home. At this point, Ken doesn't know what he wants, but he will after the shock has worn off. I know that Ken will not seek another wife until the customary year has gone by. I know my son and I believe that he will be honorable towards you. Don't worry about not having any money. My philosophy is 'marry for love, but love money.' Ken has enough for both of you. Laura, when you talk about your past, I don't see you as being promiscuous. I don't know what has happened in your past, nor do I want to know, but let it go! You can't change it. Forget about asking the community for permission to marry whomever you choose. I see you as a refined, educated lady from New England. Probably being from the East is a greater stumbling block for the people of the Sandhills than your character. My advice to you is to continue on here, but live in your own home until the year has passed. Think this over before making any rash judgments. These months as a caregiver have taken a lot out of you and Ken. If either of you think that by marrying you are betraying Stella, you are wrong. I know what Stella's wishes were for the two of you." Joan then went and opened the door. As she went to join the others, she turned to Laura. "I know you are a stubborn woman and I admire you for it, but let your heart speak to you instead of your pride."

Leaning against the kitchen cabinet, Laura was speechless as she watched Joan leave the room.

After a few moments, she experienced such a pain in her chest that she thought she could not breathe. Rushing out of the kitchen, she saw Hannah and Todd in the foyer. She said, "Hannah, would you please look after Tylor? I need to run an errand. I'll be back by ten o'clock to begin dinner." Not waiting for an answer, she went to the hall closet. Putting on her red coat and grabbing her purse, she ran to the door, sucking in the cold morning air. It was as if she couldn't satisfy the needs of air for her lungs. She continued to hurry along, oblivious of her destination. Only when she came to the Dismal River did she cease running.

It was then that she began to cry out! "Oh, God, why, why did you have to take Stella? Everything was all right as long as she was in the home. I loved her so and now she is gone! What am I to do? I don't know if I love Ken, or if he even loves me. Why did his mother have to say what she said? Now, I don't know what to do. Speak to me God, speak to me! Show me your way." Laura sobbed as she looked out over the Dismal River.

Drying her eyes, she turned to retrace her steps. As Laura came to the Cattleman's Bank, she was drawn to go into the bank. Greeting Mrs. Stahl, she asked, "May I get into my safety deposit box?" Mrs. Stahl quit her typing and ushered her into the area where the deposit boxes were kept. It was disturbing, as she had never seen Laura act as she was this morning. Laura spent little time as she took an envelope from the box and returned the box to its slot. Turning the key, she left, not bidding Mrs. Stahl goodbye.

Walking the few blocks, Laura came to the small Episcopal Church that she had attended since moving to Summit City. As she entered the sanctuary, she took note that the midmorning sun filtered through the stained glass window. Sitting on the pew near the altar at the front of the church, she opened the envelope. Taking out several sheets of paper, she began to silently read.

After a time, Laura returned the papers into the envelope. As she continued to sit at the pew, she began to rehearse the events that took place almost one year ago. *Perhaps I failed by not demanding some sort of a settlement from my son's father. However, I will not be beholden to any man, no matter how much I might love him. I loved Tylor's father dearly, but he was weak. I loved David Riggs, the newspaper editor, but I knew that he could not accept my pregnancy or the thought that I could have loved another before him. And Ken, dear Ken. I fear that I love him, but I am not sure. Perhaps it is that we have been so close during the time of Stella's illness. However, I will not pursue him. I shall let him deal with the gossip and social morals of the community. If he is not willing to initiate his pursuit of me to show his love, he is not worthy to be my husband. Time will tell, time will tell.*

Laura returned to the bank with her envelope, which she replaced in her deposit box. As she crossed the bank lobby, she was unaware that she was being watched by the young man standing in line at the teller window. Chase Adams recognized her as the lady in the red coat that had been on the train from

Madden about a year ago. He saw that she was as beautiful as the first time that he had seen her. However, today he was able to see her hands without her gloves. There was no wedding band! He did notice her eyes exhibited a show of peace as she left the bank, contrary to the fear that he had witnessed a year ago. As Laura Martin left the bank, she then continued to make her way to the Holliday house to begin the dinner preparation.

Laura was thankful that she had asked for Hannah's assistance following Stella's death. As Laura had earlier reflected on the events of the past year, she remembered her first meeting of Hannah. *I had been hired to teach school at the Good Hope School. At the open house at the teacherage, I met Hannah, a shy girl of almost sixteen. She was a student in the eighth grade and certainly not capable, or desirous of entering high school. After she moved in with me, she began to blossom under my mentoring by winning the County Spelling Bee, as well as placing second academically among the eighth graders in the county. Her mother, Virginia had died last summer and she is now living with Maude, proprietor of Maude's Café. I love her as the sister that I never had!*

With the additional visiting families, it was an unending task of providing meals and housekeeping chores in the home. It was almost as if Laura was a surrogate wife. Fortunately, having been in the home for the last three months, she was able to meet the demands of the inhabitants of the home, as well as the guests. After dinner, Joan Holliday asked Laura, "Do you have a moment later in the afternoon that we could discuss your replacement? Say, about three o'clock. I am rather exhausted, so I will take a nap before we meet. I will be ready for my afternoon tea at that time. Is that good for you?"

Seething inwardly, Laura wondered when she might get her own nap; perhaps after she did the dishes, cleaned the kitchen, straightened up the dining room and fed her son. Being gracious; realizing that this too will pass, Laura answered her. "That will be fine. I will see that the tea is hot at that time. Will anyone else be joining us?"

"Not likely," replied Mrs. Holliday. "I was the only one to come up with a possible replacement for you during our meeting. Ken is still in shock and Darren and Diane had nothing to bring to the group. Perhaps we could meet in the study. Incidentally, I will be leaving in the morning and driving back to Lincoln, so don't count on me for lunch tomorrow." Laura was glad for that bit of news. *That will be one down and four to go. I expect that Darren and Diane will be leaving on New Year's Day, along with their two young children. It is interesting that Joan Holliday refers to the noon meal as lunch rather than the Sandhill's dinner.*

Laura had a tray with the teapot and some fruitcake setting on the coffee table when Joan came into the study. As Laura began to pour the tea, Joan started the meeting. "When I get home, I will be in touch with Leah Andrews, the lady I had in mind. I have known her for some time and I am sure that she will be a good fit for this family. Tell me, what has Ken been paying for your services? I need to know this in order for her to make her decision."

Laura replied, "I think you need to discuss that with Mr. Holliday. Perhaps he may want to pay her more or less than what I was getting. You realize that part of my time was spent caring for my own son. Also, my inability to drive an automobile was a hindrance as well. Mr. Holliday was always more than fair and oftentimes my duties fluctuated from time to time."

Joan Holliday stiffened, "What you are telling me, it is none of my business what he is paying you!"

"Oh no, Ma'am," Laura hastily defended. "I meant no hostility toward you. I have no problem of Mr. Holliday revealing to you what he was paying me, but I would rather that it came from him instead of me."

Mrs. Holliday still was not satisfied. "Let me put it another way. How much do you think Ken should offer a woman to do those things that you are doing?"

She won't let it go! Laura paused a moment before answering. *Let her think that I am giving serious consideration to her question.* "I'm not sure, Mrs. Holliday. I don't know what Mr. Holliday will expect of the lady. I was a bit of a novice in my ability to cook when I came here three months ago. We did very little entertaining in the home, whether that was because of Mrs. Holliday's condition or my amateur culinary skills, I was never told. If Mr. Holliday pays the next person more, I have no problem with that. All I know is that he gave me ample pay."

Not getting any further information from Laura, she dismissed her with a nod. "I will be leaving about eight in the morning. Coffee and toast will be sufficient for me at that time. Thank you for the tea and fruitcake and meeting with me."

"Yes, Ma'am," said Laura, as she gathered the cups and saucers on the tray. *Perhaps I was being too presumptuous by my taking tea with her. I was used to sharing tea and cookies with Stella. I seemed to have forgotten my place. I'm not sure that she would be a good mother-in-law to have if the opportunity should arise.*

As Laura was making her way to the kitchen, Ken stopped her. "I wanted to remind you, everyone will be here tomorrow except for Mother. She will be leaving after breakfast. If you need to do some shopping, I will be glad to help, or take you to the store. Darren and his family will leave early New Year's Day. How are you doing, Laura? I wish I could be of more help to you, but I am at somewhat of a loss. Probably do more harm than good."

"I would appreciate a ride to the grocery store. We should go right away before they close. Thank you for offering your assistance and I appreciate your entertaining everyone. Diane has been good with the children. I know it isn't easy for her, now that she is in the latter stage of her pregnancy. Let me get rid of this tray and I will get my shopping list. Then, we will be on our way."

Arriving at the store, at first glance, one would take that here is a man and wife doing the weekend shopping. As they went from aisle to aisle, there was a familiarity about them, as if they shared a marital intimacy. Laura was the first to speak. "Mr. Holliday, is there anything special that we need? Monday is New Year's Eve. Do you do anything special, or have a traditional food for the occasion?"

"Not really." He then asked, "Do you have anything in mind? It is difficult to be in a festive mood at a time like this. And yet, I sense that Stella wouldn't want us to grieve and be morose."

Laura was unsure of herself, *but I must venture some way to get through the coming days.* "Mr. Holliday." Ken touched her arm before she could say anything more.

He said, "Laura, I want you to stop being so formal. We are in this together, so let's be on a first name basis. Agreed?"

"I will agree, but this formality will not begin until your family has left." Laura looked at him for his approval.

"That will be fine, but can't we be informal while we are away from the family, like right now, in the grocery store?" Ken had a smug smile on his face, knowing that he had bested her in their negotiations.

Laura laughed, "All right, Ken, if that makes you happy, having the final word in the matter."

11

Ken smiled, "Now I am happy!"

Laura looked over her list. "Ken, I am going to revert to my childhood. Grandma Martin wasn't much for splurging for food, unless it was the necessities of life. However, the Holiday Season was a bit different. I never and I mean never had soda pop during the year, except for this time of the season. If I can find it, I would like some eggnog too. Let's pick up some cheeses and a bit of lunch meat and we will eat differently on New Year's Eve." As they continued through the store, Laura suddenly stopped. "Ken, am I on a grocery budget? Look here, I have found a container of pickled herring. If I forego my weekly pay, may I have them for our party? Also, some small crackers would be good."

Ken answered her, "Laura, buy what you want. When everyone has gone home, I know it will be a tremendous let down for all of us, especially the children. I remember when my father died. It was difficult to continue for some time."

Laura added a few more items that were not on her list. Finally, she said to Ken, "I think that we have what we need and a bit more. We need to go, as they are about ready to close. Thank you, Ken, for allowing me to indulge myself."

The joyous mood at the grocery store was short lived. Arriving at the house, Hannah met them at the front door. She was holding Tylor, as he was wailing at the top of his lungs. Angrily she asked, "Where have you been? Tylor wants fed and I don't know what to do. Here, you take him."

Taking him, she said, "Don't panic. I am not the only source of milk for him. You know that there is milk already made up for him in the refrigerator. Todd and Tara are also aware of this as well. I'm sorry if I have upset you. It is not intentional, but I can't hold this family together by myself. Now, do you want to get supper ready, or do you want to feed him a bottle while sitting in the rocking chair?" She paused. "Please say, 'I want to get supper ready.' The choice is yours."

Hannah was somewhat subdued, as she said to Laura, "I'm sorry. I'll feed Tylor his bottle."

"Thank you, Hannah. I'll hold him until you get the milk warmed." Laura then looked down at Tylor, "And you, young man, you can be a bit more patient as well."

It was after nine before Laura was able to leave the Holliday household. She had sent Hannah and Tylor home right after supper. She sensed that it would be a long evening and she knew that Hannah was getting tired of the routine. Arriving at her little apartment, she found that Hannah and Tylor were sound asleep. In the turmoil of things, Tylor had deviated from his regular feeding schedule. Laura knew that once things settled down, she needed to get him back on schedule. She set her alarm for six a.m. and anticipated that tomorrow would be another long day. It was only after going to bed that Laura, tired physically and emotionally, cried herself to sleep.

At six, the alarm went off. Laura's first thought was of Tylor! *Why didn't he awaken me!* Getting out of bed, she went to his crib. He was sleeping soundly. *Has he slept all night? I am hoping that was the case, as I wanted him to forego his two o'clock feeding, which seems to be his favorite time to eat. Was I so tired, that I fed him and didn't know that I had?* Getting dressed, she roused him, so that he might nurse before she went to the Hollidays. He did not seem overly hungry, so evidently he had nursed at two o'clock.

Laura hurried through the crusted snow on her way to the Holliday home. Joan Holliday was the first one to arise. Laura had her fed and out the door before any of the family was up. *That is strange! Evidently, she had said her goodbyes the night before. Perhaps it is not nice to say, but I am glad to see her go.*

I sense that she is a bit manipulative.

Breakfast was almost like eating at a café. There was no organized manner of eating. Laura greeted the individuals as they made their way to the table. Regardless of what they ordered, she was prepared to fix what they desired. For some it was bacon and eggs, while others, it was cereal, or just coffee and toast. Laura did forewarn them that the noon meal was to be sandwiches and salad. However, what Laura called 'snacks,' was what they were to expect for the evening. She had planned games for those that would stay up to see the old year out and the New Year in. She had also prepared a punch to drink as a toast.

When Ken learned that some were staying awake until midnight, he insisted that Laura and Hannah stay overnight instead of going back to an empty house at such a late hour. The room vacated by Ken's mother was now available. Laura had agreed and sent Hannah back to the apartment for their nightclothes.

At the usual suppertime, Laura told the group, "Tonight, we are going to have something different to eat. Hannah and I have popped some corn and earlier, we even made some popcorn balls. There is soda pop and eggnog to drink, as well as our punch. However, if you want punch to drink as a toast to the New Year, you might go easy on that, as we have cleaned out the refrigerator. We added about everything that was liquid to concoct a different drink. There are games, chess and card games. The adult Hollidays have promised me that they would teach me how to play bridge."

Hannah tasted the eggnog. Carrying a glass as she stopped by the table where the bridge game was getting underway, she said to Laura, "Miss Martin! This is so smooth that I could drink a glass of this every morning for the rest of my life."

"When we bought that, I had you in mind. Don't drink

too much of it the first time. It is quite rich and I don't want you to get sick. Save some for tomorrow. Did you try the pickled herring?"

"Miss Martin, if you still have the list of things that I don't like, add the herring to the list."

Diane and her two children, along with Tara, were tired and went to bed. However, the rest of the celebrants stayed up until midnight. Laura encouraged them to go outside, even though it was now below zero on the thermometer.

As Laura stepped out into the cold, it was so refreshing that she yelled at the top of her lungs, "Happy New Year!" The others did the same. They could hear others across town, answering back.

Stepping back inside, Laura had the wineglasses set out and she ladled punch into each one. Passing the glasses to Hannah, Todd, Darren and Ken, she asked, "Who would like to offer a toast to the New Year?"

Ken said, "If I may? May this be a toast to those who have preceded us in death? It is to Hannah's dear mother, Virginia and our dear Stella, wife and mother. Both of these ladies left us much before their time. We also offer a toast to Tylor, who has given us the assurance of new life. We would be remiss if we didn't offer a toast to our new friends, Hannah and Laura. Without them, life would certainly be dull." Lifting his glass, Ken said, "To life."

They each lifted their glass, and said, "To life."

Everyone was moved with emotion from the toast offered by Ken as they left in a solemn mood to retire for the evening.

Laura was awakened in the night. Hannah was ill. Evidently topping off the eggnog with the citric acid of Laura's concoction, referred to as a 'punch for the toast,' had not set well

15

with her stomach.

Darren and his family left midmorning on New Year's. Wednesday, the children were back in school. Laura was trying to establish her routine. She got up early to fix breakfast for the family and see the children off to school. She fixed dinner for Ken, but he was a heavy meat eater, so Laura made sure that it was to his taste, preferably beef. He also enjoyed coleslaw or potato salad as a side dish. His coffee wasn't complete without some type of a sweet dessert. She was usually home by ten and then didn't return until about three in the afternoon. It usually depended on how much housework there was, but she made it a point to be home to greet the children when they arrived from school.

The first week was difficult, as Laura was often expecting to sit down with Stella to share a pot of tea and a plate of cookies, but she wasn't there. The gloom that hung over the house also hung over Summit City. The clouds were dark and dreary, but refused to snow. Strangely, even Tylor missed being rocked by Stella. When he fussed, Laura would have to take time to console him. Neither was the family spared. Laura would linger later in the evening after supper, so that the period before bedtime was filled with activity. She desired to seek the comfort of Maude during the day to salve her loneliness, but the days were too short for her to go to the cafe.

On Sunday, Ken and the children had started to attend the Good Hope Church south of town. Ken and Pastor Don began to develop a friendship as a result of Pastor Don ministering to Stella in the latter days of her life. Ken had asked Laura to ride with them, as he knew that she missed the people of Good Hope. She was tempted to ride with the family, but this was contrary to what she had deemed as proper. She would continue to attend the Episcopal Church, however, she promised Ken that she would have the usual beef roast for them when they returned. Laura was concerned that they might not get home in time to turn off the roast, so she promised that she would be there to eat with them. They had an understanding, that if they were not home by 1:00 p.m. she was to eat without them, unless they called.

The first Sunday of the New Year, Ken and the family had attended the Good Hope Church. Ken said it was a sad day, as Peggy Barnes' father had died rather suddenly the day before. Laura remembered Peggy's mother, Carol Baker. Peggy was an only child. *I must remember to send a sympathy card. I will give her a call in about a week after she gets back from Kansas.*

Previously, after observing Laura Martin at the bank on the Saturday morning of December 29, 1951, Chase Adams had written in his journal that night:

A dove of peace flew from the tree

Slowly she walked, as she came to me

With tilted head, she began to coo

As if to ask, just who are you?

Suddenly, she flew away. She flew away

Will she return another day?

Will she return another day?

CHAPTER 2
THE HAUNTED HOUSE

Laura was busy doing the laundry when the phone rang. She was still reluctant to talk on the phone, but she would answer, hoping that the call was unimportant. She always answered, "Holliday residence, how may I help you?"

Ken said, "Stella, will you--. I'm sorry, Laura. Will you stop at the bank on your way home? I need to talk with you." Then he hung up, not waiting for her response. Perhaps calling her 'Stella' had upset him.

Laura was at the bank a little after ten o'clock. She stopped to chat with Mrs. Stahl. "Mr. Holliday called at the house and wanted to see me. Would you tell him that I am here?"

"Certainly. I'll be right back." Mrs. Stahl was gone a short time and returned, saying, "Mr. Holliday will see you now."

Ken looked up as Laura entered the alcove. He didn't look happy. She was the first to speak. "What is it, Ken, is something wrong?"

"Yes," he said. "It is Mother. She is sending a housekeeper on the morning train."

"Isn't that what you wanted?" asked Laura.

"Yes and no." He looked grim. "My delaying tactics has spurred her to action. I was content to continue as we were. I'm not sure that I have much faith in my mother's choice. Leah Andrews will be here unless I can derail the train."

"It can't be that bad. I'll help her get settled. Do you know the woman, or anything about her?" Laura was trying to be positive.

"No, I don't know anything, except that she is nice, according to Mother. We will see how much time you will need to get her started. I will give you a month's severance pay, beginning the last day you work. I'm sorry, Laura." Ken was downhearted.

"Ken, let's see how things go tomorrow. I will be at the house early, so that you can have your breakfast before meeting the train. I am confident that things will work out. As far as the severance pay, I certainly don't expect a month's pay. If you think you must, two weeks will be sufficient. If you think of anything more, we can discuss it this evening. Look on the bright side, as you won't have to eat my cooking anymore. As a token gesture of good faith, there is a roast beef sandwich awaiting you, along with an abundance of potato salad. Good bye." Laura picked up Tylor and left the bank.

The next morning, Laura and Tylor arrived early at the Holliday home. It had snowed a light snow overnight. The gloomy clouds had yielded a miserly amount of snow, considering how long they had lingered over the city and how heavy they were. Laura's stomach was in a knot, awaiting the new arrival. Now she had second thoughts. *Did I do the right thing by insisting that I be replaced? I need to trust that this is right.*

Laura had the coffee ready when Ken came to the kitchen. "Good morning, Ken. Did you see that we received snow last night? Not much, but some. Do you have anything that you would like for breakfast? There is plenty of time to have a good breakfast before meeting the train."

"No thanks, just coffee. I don't think my stomach can handle anything at this time." Ken slouched in his chair, as he sipped the hot coffee.

Laura sat in a chair near him. She reached out and touched his hand. "Ken, you make me feel sad when I see you in this mood. I am not abandoning you and you are not abandoning me. We need to move on. It is a part of life." Laura got up and went to see about Tylor. She didn't return to the kitchen until she heard the door close and he was on his way to the garage.

Tara and Todd came down for breakfast and left for school. Still, Ken had not come home. Laura wondered if the train was late, as she didn't remember hearing it. Usually, on a cold morning like this, it can be heard. Laura had the dishes washed and the beds made up. She was straightening up the living room when she heard Ken drive up. She went to the door to see how she could help, when Leah Andrews, carrying her purse, met her. Ken was following after her with a suitcase in each hand. Laura was trying to size her up. *She definitely was not the grandmotherly type which I had requested. Late fifties, coal black hair, but it could be dyed. She is a little taller than me, but not much heavier.* Laura introduced herself, "I am Laura Martin. Welcome to Summit City. Can I get you some coffee, or even some breakfast, if you haven't had anything to eat?"

"I could use some coffee. I thought we would never get here. The train hit a cow and the crew didn't know whether to eat it, or bury it." Ken came in with two more suitcases and placed them with the first two.

Ken said, "I didn't expect to be this late. I need to get to the bank. Laura, can you help Leah get organized and settled in and I will see the both of you at noon? I will put the bags in the bedroom before I leave."

Laura poured coffee in a mug for Leah and added coffee to her own as well. Also, she added cookies to those already on a small plate. Laura said, "Leah, do you have any questions before I show you around the house?"

"Honey, Joan has filled me in and has given me all the information I need, right down to any phone number I might want to call. You don't need to stay around for my benefit. The quicker you leave, the better it suits me. I don't mean to be rude, but I can handle whatever comes up."

Laura stood up. "That is refreshing to know that I won't have to spend my time training someone to replace me. If you will excuse me, I will get my son and be out of your way. Good bye, Leah." Laura went into the living room and wrapped Tylor in his blankets. She stopped to put on her own coat and was out the door in less than fifteen minutes after Leah's arrival.

After leaving the house, Laura went to *The Sentinel* office. She was unable to find anyone there, so she left a note for David. 'Please run the same ad as you did last fall. I am now unemployed.' She signed her name, Laura M and left $2.00 on the counter. She thought, *I'm glad that he is not here. I'm not up to talking with anyone just now.*

As Laura made her way to her apartment, she remembered that at one time she thought that she was in love with David. She decided to go see Maude after lunch. She thought, *I need to vent my anger, but on second thought, I will stay home and rest. It has been a long time since I have rested. I will feel better after a nap. I might even be able to laugh at the arrogance of that woman. Why did Joan Holliday send her out here? Was it to deliberately sabotage me or to have Leah fail miserably? Then Ken would have to ask for my return. Was Joan Holliday a friend or a foe?*

Laura remained sequestered in her apartment for two days. Thoroughly rested, she took Tylor with her to visit Maude. *If I go this afternoon between the dinner trade and the late afternoon coffee drinkers, I might find her idle long enough to have a good visit with her.* The day was one of those rare winter days when the air was crisp, but the sunshine was most welcome. Laura was glad to have moved to the Sandhills. *The weather is varied, but not as severe as that in New England. I*

21

have been so busy with the Hollidays that I have neglected my beloved Dismal River.

On her way to Maude's, she stopped at the Dismal River. *She marveled how true you have been to me; you continue to flow, whether I am here watching you or not. I could never depart from you.* Suddenly, Laura questioned her sanity. *Here I am, talking to a river. I have been shut up too long.* As she hurried along the street, she came to Maude's café. Opening the door, the bell welcomed her. Stepping inside, she removed her coat and Tylor's blanket, but she didn't see Maude. Vera was at the counter, talking to two early afternoon coffee drinkers. Vera saw her and said, "Well, Laura, how are you? I haven't seen you for some time. Maude went to the post office. She will be right back, I hope." Laura thought *that is the most words I have heard from Vera for a long time.*

Maude entered the café, huffing and puffing. Even though Maude put a lot of hours in at the café, she still battled with her weight and shortness of breath. "Good afternoon. I thought you might have run off with some no-good cowboy. I haven't seen you, and it appears that the Hollidays have a new housekeeper. What have you been doing?"

Laura sighed before answering. "I have been resting. I didn't realize how tired I was. I haven't had a day to myself since Tylor was three days old. It has been three months since I have watched the Dismal River flow past this glorious city. I have missed our visits Maude, so I have come to visit with you this afternoon, that is if you have the time? How is Hannah? She was such good help during the time of Stella's death." Reaching into her purse, Laura brought out a twenty-dollar bill. Handing it to Maude, she said, "Give this to Hannah and tell her that I'm sorry that I was short with her the last day that she was with us."

Maude was pleased that Laura had asked about Hannah.

She smiled and told Laura, "Hannah is doing well in school. She is setting the pace for the freshmen class. It pleases her when she can best young Holliday in a test. When he does better than she, then she is goaded to do even better. You have cultivated a real jewel. Also, having experienced the death of her own mother earlier, I believe that she has been able to help Todd cope with his mother's death. They have been good for each other." Maude grabbed two mugs and filled them with coffee. "Hannah will appreciate the money. This will give her some independence. She may possibly spend some of it for clothing, which will be good."

Laura asked, "I should question you before I accept this coffee. Is this free, or am I obligated to pay?"

"Had you stayed away any longer, I would have required payment, seeing that you are a stranger. Fortunately, you arrived in the nick of time. Tell me, what is the new housekeeper like at the Holliday house?"

Laura blushed, not wanting to say the wrong thing about Leah Andrews. She began, "Her name is Leah Andrews. We didn't have much of an opportunity to chat about her personal life. Really, if you have seen one housekeeper, you have seen them all."

"What you are telling me is, that you are not telling me."

"You're right! My prayer is that this is a good match." Laura paused, "Mrs. Andrews, that is if she is a Mrs., exhibits confidence, so I am sure that she can handle the task." Laura remembered her visit to the newspaper office. "Incidentally, I have placed an ad in *The Sentinel* advertising that I am looking for work. It is exciting to anticipate what the Lord has for me in the days to come." Laura noticed that *Maude is not comfortable when I talk about spiritual things. I don't want to offend her, but it is real to me.*

Reaching out, Maude said, "Let me hold that boy to see if he has grown. Are you sure that you have enough milk? I question if you have enough time for this precious child if you are taking on the burdens of the community. Slow down and enjoy him."

"I am slowing down, in fact, I am almost at a standstill. If I don't find work soon, I may have to put him on the auction block. You seem to have most of the money in this town. Would you care to place an opening bid?" Laura admired her son, as he snuggled himself in Maude's arms.

Maude asked, "Have you heard from Peggy Barnes since she returned from her father's funeral?"

"No," said Laura. "I sent her a sympathy card. When did she get home?"

"I'm not sure, but I presumed that she would be home to get the twins back in school." Maude laughed. "You should see that Karen. You remember how Sharon always spoke for the both of them. Now Karen does the same thing. She is a little faster on the thought than Sharon, so now she is the spokesman." Maude jumped up and handed Tylor to Laura. "I almost forgot, you like something sweet with your coffee. I will fetch a sweet roll and warm up your coffee. It has been so long since I have had a bit of company that I totally forgot my manners."

Maude and Laura had a good visit. Laura wanted to stay until Hannah came home from school. After a time, Hannah came into the café. When she saw Laura, she rushed over and took Tylor from Maude. She gave him a kiss on the cheek and he laughed. She turned to Laura, "See, someone loves me."

"I love you, Hannah," said Laura, "but sometimes you don't heed my advice. Tell me, Hannah, do you still like eggnog?"

"Yes, but that horrid concoction is what sickened me. You need to clean out the refrigerator more often and throw most of it away." She then made a terrible face.

Laura was getting ready to leave, when Ken Holliday came into the café. He motioned Laura over to a booth and invited her to sit down. He handed her an envelope and said, "Laura, I expected you to stop in at the bank for your money. What happened between you and Leah? I got home at noon and you were gone. Have I made you unhappy over this situation?"

I sense that you are unhappy with me, were her thoughts regarding Ken Holliday. *I need to limit this conversation to as few words as possible, lest I lose my temper.* "No, Ken, you have not made me unhappy. What did Leah tell you, when you came home that first day at noon?"

Ken thought a moment, "Basically, you told her to handle whatever comes up and that you would get your son and be out of her way."

Laura had to remember her earlier thoughts and not get angry. "Ken, I am not going to get into 'I said, she said.' I was in your home for three of the most grueling months of my life. Do you think those are the words that I used? Tell me, does she call you Honey?" Laura got up, leaving the envelope on the table. She went over to the counter. Pulling her coat on, she reached down and got Tylor out of Hannah's arms. As Maude later described it, Laura 'marched' toward the door and was last seen walking up the street to her apartment.

Ken got up from the booth. Picking up the envelope, he determined that *now was not a good time to approach her again. Laura has her moments of indignation, which later turn to remorse. That is when she is the most approachable.*

Laura stayed close to home in hopes that someone might wish to contact her regarding employment. *I am sure that the community is aware of my faithfulness to the Holliday family during Stella's illness.* The second issue of *The Sentinel* was delivered. Laura placed it before the Lord, that she would have direction before the next issue was published. She wasn't the only one in the community that was struggling.

Monday morning, about nine o'clock there was a knock on Laura's door. She had finished with Tylor's bath and had him wrapped in a green terry cloth towel. It was his favorite and whenever Laura used it, he would utter a little giggle and grab it with both hands. She was playing a little game with him and his towel. As she heard the knock, she offered a prayer that this was a job offer. Going to the door, she saw that it was Peggy Barnes, holding her daughter Rebecca in her arms. Opening the door, she hugged Peggy. In doing so, the two infants were pressed together in the hug. "Oh, Peggy, I am glad to see you." Immediately, Laura remembered about Peggy's loss of her father. "I was sorry to hear of the loss of your father. The suddenness must have been a shock to you. Sit down and let me get some coffee started. I must admit, since I am no longer working at the Hollidays, I get up later and later each day. And, how is this Rebecca? Does she walk yet?" Laura remembered that she had offered coffee and went to start it, after laying Tylor in his crib.

"Oh, Laura," Peggy replied to Laura. "You always ask so many questions in a row, I will try to answer them, if I can remember them. Coffee would be great. Rebecca has taken her first steps, but she prefers to hang on to the furniture and prance around and around. Regarding my father, yes, it was sudden. We were totally unprepared, even though he was. That is why I came to see you today, to seek counsel regarding our family. Mother is not doing well. You may recall, I am an only child, so much of the burden falls upon Carl and me regarding Mother's welfare."

Laura stood up. "Don't let me interrupt. I will fix the

coffee as you continue. I do have one question. Why seek counsel from me? I'm certainly no winner."

Peggy was almost pleading, "But, Laura, you are. I admire you. You have the patience to persevere and to accept how and where the Lord leads you. Look what happened with Karen. We were all willing to accept that Karen was unable to talk, but not you. And Hannah, nobody wanted to get involved, or seemingly cared about Hannah's welfare. Even Stella Holliday is an example of your caring ways. Are you aware that in all these, you were the one in the middle, exhibiting your love. And you ask, why? Those people are why." At this point, Peggy was almost in tears, as she clutched Laura's hands.

Laura was surprised by Peggy's words. "I don't know what to say, other than I will do what I can. What is it you want from me?"

Peggy dried her eyes. Taking a sip of coffee in order to compose herself, she started over again. "One of the reasons that mother is not doing well, is not physically, but financially. She will do well if she sells the farm and has enough to pay the debts and the funeral expenses. They have had some tough years and were deeply in debt. She doesn't want to leave the community that they have been in for years. She is still too young to receive social security. Unfortunately, she hasn't held a paying job for years, as the last time was before she married. Carl and I have tried to help her with a solution. Here is where we differ. Carl is for bringing her to live with us."

Pausing to sip her coffee once again, she continued. "Laura, our home is not big enough for one more adult. We have three bedrooms. It would mean that the three girls would share one room and each year they are getting bigger. Laura, I love my mother, but I don't want to revert to being the child. Carl doesn't understand that you cannot have two females in the kitchen.

When Mother came to stay with me after Rebecca was born, she rearranged my kitchen. It is funny now, but at the moment, I was furious. The girls wanted cinnamon toast for breakfast and I reached into the cupboard where my spices were. I had put sugar on the toast and I was going to sprinkle the cinnamon on top. She had alphabetized my spices and I sprinkled the toast with paprika. Why should she care how my spices were situated?"

Peggy sighed, as she continued. "Carl maintains that he and his father worked side by side without conflict. I have to remind him that he told me that as a young man on his father's ranch, he never remembers tying the horse in the manger, but that his father would correct him that he had tied the horse either too long or too short. It was only after Carl had his own ranch that his father ceased to correct him. I'm thankful that I have a husband that is concerned for my mother and willing to share our home with her. Many husbands wouldn't be so generous. His parents are gone, so Carl sees her as the only living grandparent. I come off as the selfish one by not willing to share my home." This brought more tears.

Laura asked, "How soon does your mother need to make a move, or make a decision?"

"The farm sells in two weeks, with immediate possession. She may be granted some time to vacate. At this point, we don't know how much to retain of her furniture and personal items as family keepsakes." Peggy could only shake her head, when she considered the enormity of the task that lay ahead.

"Does Carl know that you have come to see me?" Laura was cautious of causing a rift in the family.

"No, I told him I was going to Summit City to pick up some groceries. I didn't lie to him, as I will get groceries before I go home. I do need to get home before dinner."

"How do you think Carl would react, if he knew that

you came to see me for counseling regarding this problem?" Laura was testing, to see if she should be involved in this family problem. She certainly didn't want to compound a situation that could become volatile.

Peggy looked up, somewhat surprised. She thought a moment before answering Laura. "I imagine that he might be hurt. Sometimes I think that he feels he can solve the problems of the family without any outside help."

"Peggy, what I am about to say may surprise you." Laura poured more coffee in the mugs, giving herself time to form her words. "Let us continue to let him have that feeling. This may surprise you that I take this stand. My usual pattern is to wade into a problem like I was killing snakes with a hoe. Keep from making any rash decisions that you will regret. This problem did not happen overnight and neither will it be solved overnight. You and I must be committed to prayer. In the finality of this, we do need for you to honor your husband. He may not make the right decision in our eyes, but he is the one that will have to live with that decision. With authority comes responsibility. Do you have any questions?"

Peggy shook her head. She took Laura's hand. "Thank you for listening to me. You have given me comfort and assurance that when we pray, we will see answers. Laura Martin, I love you. Now, I do need to go get those groceries. A final question is what should I buy?"

Laura quickly responded, "It doesn't make any difference, as long as it's chocolate."

After Peggy left, Laura was perturbed with herself. She was so taken up with Peggy's problem that she hadn't completely dried Tylor after his bath. He was lying in his crib, playing with his green towel. It was now time for his feeding and then a morning nap. Laura considered herself blessed. Tylor was such a joy, as he rarely exhibited crankiness. He would soon be five months old. It is amazing, when Laura considered that she had lived in the Sandhills for more than a year now. The question for her at this time is when will I have some direction in my life? Except for the time spent teaching at Good Hope School, there has been no thought of a lifetime career. She realized that it has been three weeks since placing the ad in *The Sentinel* with no response. The thought came to her; *perhaps now is the time to move on. Have I worn out my welcome in the Sandhills? If I don't get some response soon, I may return to Maine, or at least the New England area. If so, I need to make the decision soon, while I still have funds to begin anew.*

After Tylor had been fed in the afternoon, Laura took a nap. It was as if she could not get enough sleep, since her time at the Holliday home had completely depleted her stamina. At a few minutes after four, she was awakened by a knock on the front door. Laura had trouble getting awake, as she staggered toward the door. Opening the door, she was met by a little girl, quietly crying, trying to hold back the tears. Suddenly, Laura realized that it was Tara. Bringing her into the house, she asked, "Tara, what is the matter? Are you hurt? Why are you here?"

Bravely, she said, "Miss Martin, I want to live with you. I have brought my pajamas and my toothbrush. I won't eat very much. Can I stay?"

If she hadn't looked so pathetic, it was almost comical, as she made her plea for asylum. Laura asked, "But what about your father and Todd; won't they miss you?"

"Miss Martin, can they come too? I want to be with you. They are sad, but they are too scared to come and ask you."

"Does anyone know that you are here? Perhaps they are looking for you and wanting to know where you have been."

Tara made one last plea. "Nobody cares about a little girl

like me. Let me stay here and they will never miss me."

Laura took her by the hand. "Sit here and have some milk and two cookies. I will get Tylor dressed and we will go for a walk. It is such a nice afternoon that I think we need to get some exercise."

With Tylor braced on her right hip and holding Tara by the left hand, the trio walked down the street. They crossed the street where The Mercantile was located and after a time, they were walking on the sidewalk in front of the Cattleman's Bank. Tara spoke for the first time since they had left Laura's apartment. "This is where Daddy works. This is where he keeps his money."

Laura asked, "Does your daddy really work here? Should we surprise him and go in to say hello?"

Tara nodded her head, as they entered the door. They walked past Mrs. Stahl and Tara said, "Hello, Mrs. Stahl. We are going to surprise Daddy." Laura pulled her hand out of Tara's and brought her own hand to her mouth in a hushing motion.

Entering Ken's alcove, Laura spoke up before Tara had an opportunity to speak. "Mr. Holliday, I have a young lady that knocked on my door, requesting me to let her live with Tylor and me. She even brought her own pajamas and toothbrush. What is taking place at your house to cause her to run away from home?" Ken had been busy working on a report and didn't know that they were in his office until Laura had spoken to him.

For a moment, Ken was speechless, as he had not fully comprehended what Laura had said. "What did you say? Tara, why are you with Laura?"

Laura whispered to Tara, "Please go sit with Mrs. Stahl. I need to talk with your father alone." Tara left the office area, leaving Laura still holding Tylor. Laura reached back and finding a chair, she slid it closer to Ken's desk before sitting down.

Laura repeated, "What is taking place at your house to cause Tara to run away from home? She came to my home, requesting to live with me. She even had her toothbrush and pajamas with her. No one packs those unless they are serious." Ken was stunned, not realizing fully what Laura was relating to him. "By your silence, Mr. Holliday, I am presuming that it meets with your approval that Tara can come live with me. That is fine. I will stop by the house and get the rest of her clothes."

"What happened to the agreement that we would be on a first name basis?" said Ken, as he pushed back from his desk.

What started as a surprise visit had suddenly escalated to a full-blown conflict. Laura was trying to remain calm, but finding it difficult by Ken's reaction to the news that his daughter had run away."I find the fact that I failed to refer to you as Ken, instead of Mr. Holliday, is immaterial to the crux of the problem. Your daughter no longer wants to live in the same house with you. Let me rephrase that. Tara told me that you and Todd want to come live with me also, but are too scared to ask. Are you?"

"Of course not!" denied Ken.

Laura smiled. Now she was beginning to enjoy herself after she had calmed down. "Ken, you answered that awful fast. Grandma Martin always said, 'only children, fools and drunks tell the truth.' I trust Tara because she is a child. It is a big step to run away from home and it takes a lot of courage. Did you ever run away from home, Ken? If not, did you ever want to run away?"

Ken was uneasy. "Laura, you ask too many questions. Things are not good in our household. Todd tolerates the situation and I ignore the problems that arise. But, not Tara! No, she will say, 'Miss Martin did it this way, or that way.' I have talked to her about it, but she puts great faith in what you say or do.

This irritates Mrs. Andrews. She also objects to any reminders of Stella. I'm sure that she detests Stella's portrait. Namely, because you painted it and also, it is a reminder of Stella. Now that we are back to a first name basis, I will answer your question about running away from home. No, I never did run away from home. Did I want to? Yes! Now you are getting ready to ask the next question, as to why didn't I run away? I was scared. Even now, I am scared."

"Then Tara was right! You are scared." Laura reached across the desk and took his outstretched hands in her own. "And, I know why! Leah Andrews was your mother's choice. In respect of your mother, you will not cross Leah Andrews. I know something of what you are enduring. She dismissed me rather promptly. I anticipated several days of getting her familiar with how the house functioned. I was informed, the quicker I left, the happier she would be. I have one more question for you. What are you going to do about it?"

Ken had an impish grin, as he looked at Laura. "Before I answer that question, I need an answer from you. Will you come back, if I fire her?"

"By the look on your face, I knew that was going to be your question." Laura thought a moment. *Don't be too quick to answer.* Laura had withdrawn her hands from Ken's and placed them both around Tylor. Looking down at her son, she said, "Yes, but under the same basis as before, until such time as a replacement is found. However, I would suggest that you and I do the interviewing of the next applicant."

Laura saw by the look on Ken's face, that he was happy. "I will tell her tonight and put her on the late afternoon train. I will also need to inform Mother. She won't be happy, but at least the Holliday home in Summit City will be. Laura, we need to protect our witness. Can she stay with you tonight and will you

33

see that she goes to school in the morning? After all, she did bring her pajamas and toothbrush to your house."

"After Leah leaves tomorrow afternoon, I will stop by the house to begin the supper for the family. What do you have in mind for supper tomorrow night?"

"Laura, I remember the first meal you made for us that was such a hit! Do you remember the spaghetti dinner with the fruit cocktail? That is what I want for our second supper. Tomorrow night, we will celebrate by eating at Maude's. Do you know how long it has been since we have eaten out as a family? Tomorrow night is the night." Laura could see that Ken was almost jubilant with anticipation of Leah's return to Lincoln.

Laura left and found Tara sitting at Mrs. Stahl's desk, using her rubber stamp and pad. Once again, shifting Tylor to her right hip, she took Tara's hand and said, "Let's go to my house. If we hurry, we will have macaroni and cheese for supper. We will also have time for one story before your bedtime." Tara giggled, as she knew that it was going to be a fun evening.

As soon as Laura and Tara left the bank, Ken called the house to inform Mrs. Andrews that Tara was staying overnight with a friend and not to fix supper for her. Ken was late leaving the bank after the interruption by Laura. He didn't mind the loss of his time, but replayed the events of the afternoon. *That Laura Martin has a way of getting under a person's skin, but while doing it, she is bringing the problem to the surface. I wish the bank was able to come up with a position for her. She is quite capable. In fact, she would make a good loan officer.* He smiled at the thought. *I would like to see some of those tough old ranchers come up against her. We are not ready for that now, but maybe someday the bank would have a female loan officer.*

When Ken arrived at home, he was actually nervous, as he wasn't looking forward to a confrontation with Mrs.

Andrews. Going into the kitchen, he asked, "How soon will we have supper? Do I have time to make a phone call first, or should I wait until later?"

Leah Andrews quickly replied, "Dinner was ready fifteen minutes ago. It is already dried out. Take your choice. Do you want it dry, or drier?" Ken took note that she insisted it was 'dinner,' if he referred to it as 'supper.'

Ken decided that he was not going to be intimidated by her this evening. He smiled, "Sounds like my best option is 'dry.' I'm now ready to eat."

The meal was not only dry, but it was also cold. Mrs. Andrews was not the best of cooks, despite Joan Holliday's lavish recommendation. Todd asked his father, "Who is Tara staying with tonight?"

Ken said, "All I know is that she is her best friend."

Todd was displeased when he replied, "Don't you think that you need a little more information than that? What if something happens that we need to find her?"

"Todd that is a good thought. Why didn't I think of that? Sometimes, it would be better if you were the father and I was the son. We need to pick one day to switch rolls. If that were the case, what would be your first decision? I know, you would say Son, don't worry about going to school tomorrow. Forget about having your homework assignment finished. Am I right?"

Todd said, "Never. I would say, Son, be sure that you have your homework finished before going to bed."

Ken laughed and said, "Son, be sure that you have your homework finished before going to bed. See, leadership always requires responsibility, no matter how distasteful."

After supper, Ken went to the study and closed the door. He was not looking forward to his phone call to his mother.

He was not sure which would be worse, breaking the news to his mother, or to Leah. *Tonight, I am going to disregard the formalities and use the Laura Martin approach, which is head on!* When he dialed the number, as soon as he heard the phone click, he started talking. "Hello, Mother, this is Ken. I am calling about Leah Andrews and I wanted to let you know that I am discharging her. It is not working out, so I will be getting her a ticket on the afternoon train tomorrow. Unfortunately, it will be near midnight before she gets into Lincoln. Can you arrange for someone to meet her?"

"Well, that was well rehearsed." The laughter on the other end was his brother Darren.

"What are you doing, answering Mother's phone?" Ken was upset*, as he wasn't sure if it was his brother's laughter at knowing what he was trying to accomplish by the instant message, or the fact that he will have to do it over again.* Before he could say anything more, Darren interrupted him.

"I am her son and after that news, there is no doubt, her favorite son." Darren was having a lot of fun at Ken's expense. "I had a meeting in Lincoln, so decided to stay at Mother's rather than spend the money on a hotel room. I am alone, as she had the evening at a concert that she was attending with a friend. I'm glad that I was here to take your call. Before you even ask, I will not give Mother the message. However, I will tell her that you called. I take it that things are not going well with Mother's choice of housekeeper."

"No," Ken sighed. "I still have to meet with her to inform her that she will be leaving. I haven't been happy with her, but I didn't want to upset Mother regarding her choice. But, it came to a head today when Tara ran away. Of course, you know where she went, she went to Laura's. It was downhill from that time on. Tara was serious, as she had her pajamas and toothbrush with her. Then she told Laura that Todd and I wanted to run away too, but we were too scared to do so. Once Laura was involved, decisions had to be made. Leah will be leaving after I meet with her. Laura insisted that the witness must be protected, so Tara is spending the night with her. Laura will be back here, but still on a temporary basis until she and I can find a replacement. Have Mother call me when she returns. It was good talking to you. I feel better after relating the day's events with you. Bye."

Hanging up the phone, Ken left the study to see if Leah had finished in the kitchen. She was almost done and he asked her, "Mrs. Andrews, when you are finished here, I will be in the study. Could you stop in for a moment?"

"Is this about the dried out dinner? If it is, maybe you need to find another cook, which will tolerate your being late. I am fed up with living in this haunted house. I have washed my last dish and vacuumed my last rug! I quit!" Leah slammed the dishcloth on the counter and turned to leave the room. She paused to remove the apron from her waist.

Ken was shocked at her outburst. "What do you mean, this haunted house?"

With her hands on her hips, she faced Ken. "Haunted! I said haunted! Most haunted houses have one ghost, but this one has two. One is living and one is dead! Your dead wife roams this house day and night, particularly the living room where her portrait hangs. I go in there, and her eyes follow me, watching every move that I make. And at night, she is keeping watch in the hallway, fearful that I will steal out of my room and into yours."

Ken was curious. He asked, "And the second ghost, the one living. I didn't know that ghosts were living? I thought they had to be dead to be a ghost."

Leah was angry now, as Ken saw the anger displayed

upon her face. "The live one is the worst one of the two! Every other sentence that Tara says is about Miss Martin this and Miss Martin that! The only peace I get from her is when Tara goes to school. I do believe that Laura Martin haunts the school when Tara is there. I can't wait to get out of here. This is my last night in this house!"

Ken was surprised by her anger, but not disappointed by her decision. "Mrs. Andrews, if you are disturbed about staying here any longer, we have a small hotel in town that could accommodate you until the train leaves tomorrow. I will take you there tonight. Tomorrow afternoon, I will purchase a train ticket for your return to Lincoln. I can contact my mother to arrange for someone to meet you when the train arrives and escort you home. Tomorrow we can settle up for what wages are due, along with two weeks' severance pay. I will pay for your lodging tonight and your meals tomorrow. I think it best that you not endure another night in this house if it disturbs you so. Is all this satisfactory?"

Leah started for the stairs, all the time muttering, "I will pack my bags, and be down in five minutes. I won't stay any longer than is absolutely necessary."

True to her word, Leah Andrews was packed and ready to leave within the five minutes. Ken took her to the 'Dismal River Hotel.' When he took her bags in, he told Leah, "I will pay for your meals at Maude's Café. Stop in at the bank at 3:00 p.m. and we can settle up and I will take you to the railroad station. By that time, I will have called my mother to arrange for someone to meet you, as it will be almost midnight when you reach your destination. Good night, Mrs. Andrews." Ken left, realizing that Leah ignored his salutation.

Ken had been home only a few minutes when his mother called. "Ken, darling." Fear struck as he heard his mother's voice. "Darren said that you called while I was at the concert. I hope it isn't bad news."

Ken was hesitant. What should I tell her? "Mother, I fear that I have upset Mrs. Andrews to such a point that she quit this evening. She is so distraught that I moved her out of the house for her own benefit. She thought--." That is when Joan interrupted the conversation.

"Ken, I handpicked her among my friends. Were you decent to her? Why on earth would she leave?" It was now to the point that Joan was blaming Ken for Leah quitting.

"Mother, let me explain, without you jumping to conclusions. I was late for supper, not much, but a little. She thought that I was being critical about her cooking when I wanted to visit with her after we had eaten. When you see her, don't mention this, but because of Stella having died in the home, Leah thinks the house is haunted. That is why I moved her away from the home tonight. She will be returning tomorrow, but she will not arrive in Lincoln until near midnight. I would count it as a personal favor if you could meet her, or arrange for someone to meet her and see her home. Unfortunately, the Sandhills takes some getting used to and I am sure that she misses her friends in Lincoln. I'm sorry that it didn't work as planned, as I know you put in a lot of time in getting us a housekeeper. I thank you for that time and effort."

Ken could hear his mother sobbing. "But, Ken, how will you manage? You know absolutely nothing in managing a household, or finding a housekeeper. I will keep looking for you. In the meantime, do you think that you could have Laura help you out in a pinch?"

Ken was elated. "Why, Mother, that is a good idea. Why didn't I think of that? She hasn't found any work that I know of. Perhaps she is ready to swallow her pride and earn some much needed money; but only temporary. I may have Mrs. Stahl help find a housekeeper locally. After the experience with Leah, I think it is best to have someone raised in the Sandhills to look after the children. I fear that our cultural life is rather lacking to that compared to Lincoln."

"Tell Leah that I will meet her at the station. I won't mention our conversation. Let me know how your search for a replacement turns out. I love you, Ken, and good night."

"Good night, Mother. I love you and the children send their love also. This is a school night and they are in bed at this time."

Ken felt good and he felt bad. He was glad that the dismissal of Leah went as it did. He felt bad in deceiving his mother. *I trust that Darren says nothing in regard to our conversation.* Ken was exhausted after the events of the evening, so he turned in early, knowing that he would have to fix his own breakfast. Sleep did not come easy for him that night. He was remorseful in his dealing with his mother, but he didn't want to hurt her, or Leah. His dreams were troubling, as he couldn't remember exactly what took place, but there were two ghosts roaming the house.

CHAPTER 3
THE RETURN TO THE PROMISED LAND

Laura woke up at six, feeling rested for the first time in days. *Perhaps I am regaining my* strength. She looked over at Tara, sleeping soundly, with the look of innocence peeking out from under the locks of her dark hair. Tara was a much better bed partner than the Barnes twins, but one must understand that there were three in the bed instead of the two last night. Laura's first thoughts were of Ken. After returning from the bank yesterday, *her prayers were with Ken throughout the evening. Arrogant as Leah was, Laura did not wish her harm. Also, that she would accept the dismissal with grace. Even when Laura knew that Leah was coming to Summit City, she feared that the divergence of cultures, urban vs. rural, might be more than Leah could overcome. One must keep in mind, it is the newcomer that submits or bends to the majority. Laura had learned this lesson early as the teacher at the Good Hope School. The community and the school board were tolerant, but Laura learned not to push them too far. A sweet smile and a demure look can carry one only so far.*

Laura went to Tylor's crib. He heard his mother's footsteps and when she arrived at the side, he was looking up and stretching forth his arms. He was looking forward to his mother's first kiss and his first meal of the day. Laura changed him and he began to nurse. He was cuddled in her arms as she sat in the rocking chair, occasionally giving the chair a rock. After Tylor was fed, she returned him to his crib. Now, Laura was ready for her sustenance, as she drank a glass of milk. She then reached for her coffee mug. As she filled it, she enjoyed the aroma and warmth of the beverage. She toasted herself two slices of bread, realizing that she needed to be eating more, now that

Tylor was requiring more nutrients from her milk. She promised that when she returned to the Holliday home, she would eat a larger breakfast with the family. Opening her 'working Bible' as Pastor Don called it, she read from the Book of Proverbs. *I like Proverbs, as it is so logical and forthright. I guess that is the way that I am.* She thought of her experiences which sometimes caused her heartache. When she finished with her reading, she prayed once again for Ken and the children. She also prayed for Peggy, that she might give her wise counsel.

Laura awakened Tara to get her ready for school. When Laura was in the home, Tara never gave her any problem in getting out of bed in the morning. She was always prompt and eager to get to school. Todd was totally different. After a time, Laura learned not to fight with him to get him out of bed. She called once and left the rest for Todd and Ken to work out the problem of his getting to school on time.

Tara got out of bed and was straightening the sheets and blankets. She was folding her pajamas and said to Laura, "I will put my pajamas under the pillow. Then I will be able to find them tonight when I go to bed. Also, I will leave my toothbrush in the bathroom. Miss Martin, will you be able to get me some clean clothes? I forgot to pack any clothes. I guess I was in a hurry to find you."

"That will be fine, but I hope that you will be able to sleep in your own bed tonight. Mrs. Andrews may be leaving today. I will stop at the bank this afternoon to ask your father if she has left." Laura admired the seriousness that Tara was showing. And to think, it has only been a little over a month since this little girl lost her mother. *Sometimes the children have to grow up too fast, much too fast.*

Tara left for school. Laura gave her a hug and promised her that she would be at the school to walk her home. Laura was looking through Tylor's clothes, sorting those that he had already outgrown. She had stopped for coffee when a blue car drove into the driveway. Laura recognized it as the Barnes' family car. Peggy got out and was carrying Rebecca up the stairs to Laura's apartment. She had the door open when Peggy got to the top of the stairs. "Come in and share a mug of coffee with me. It is always good to see you, even though it was only yesterday that you were here."

"Oh, Laura," Peggy began, "I let it slip that I had been to see you. And now, Carl and I are hardly speaking to one another. What am I going to do?"

"Here, sit down and have some coffee." Laura pulled out a chair for Peggy and poured the coffee, setting the mug before her. "Peggy, I don't know what took place between you and Carl, but why don't you tell me what you think you should do."

Peggy looked at Laura as if she had been slapped. That is not what she wanted to hear. She wanted a sympathetic ear. Peggy reached in her purse for her handkerchief to wipe away her tears. "I should apologize. I have been unyielding in this conflict. I have never had stress like this before. I need to go back to Carl and tell him that I have been selfish." She started to get up to leave.

Laura stopped her. "Finish your coffee. I need to ask some questions of you regarding your mother."

Peggy sat back down. She set Rebecca on the floor so that she could stand by her chair. Laura asked, "Has anything changed since we talked yesterday?" Peggy shook her head. Laura continued, "What is your mother capable of doing? Let me rephrase that to what is your mother willing to do, that she is capable of doing?"

Peggy thought for a time. "Mother isn't lazy. She will

43

work, that is if she knows what needs to be done. All she has ever done is to keep house for my father. She would help in the field whenever she could, but not a great deal. I think that she could clerk in a store, but I'm not sure that she could put in an entire day being on her feet. With that in mind, what do you think are her possibilities?"

"I may be missing something in all this conflict," said Laura. "Perhaps we should be asking Carl, what does he think Carol is capable of doing? What does he expect her to do, if she comes to live with you? I know that you love your mother, but once she moves in, if things don't go well, it is difficult to make other arrangements without a lot of heartache. What if you worked outside of the home? What would be Carl's reaction to that suggestion?"

Peggy responded instantly to the question. "Carl wouldn't tolerate anything like that. His idea of the head of the family is to provide and the wife is to be in the home."

Laura replied, "What do you think Carl sees as the responsibility of his wife's mother in the home? What must she do to be a fruitful contributor?"

Peggy threw up her hands, almost knocking Rebecca to the floor. "I just don't know. Help me, I guess. But I don't need help and I don't want help. It would be great if we had four single men to cook and clean for, but we don't. Then I could use some help."

"One last question and then we will quit discussing this for the day. I see this is causing you a lot of distress and we haven't yet arrived at a solution. Perhaps, we need to settle back for a time and see how things will work out. The question is, would your mother see this as too demeaning, if she was to do housework in another person's home, other than her daughter's?" Laura tried to see if she could determine any facial response

44

from Peggy relative to this question. There was none. "Another question, if you please. Is your mother expecting a free ride in your home? Is she looking forward to retirement from the struggles of life? No more worries, no more cares."

Peggy responded at once, "Mother is not looking for a life of ease. She certainly kept busy when she cared for me. However, she and I had our silent conflicts. As I mentioned yesterday, she was intent upon restructuring my kitchen. She might have trouble accepting orders from another woman, particularly if that woman is younger. I'm sure that she would be quite faithful and accepting from an older person, that is if she was caring for them in the home. Why do you ask?"

"Don't get your hopes up," said Laura, "but if everything went well yesterday, Leah Andrews is no longer employed at the Holliday home. Ken and I will be looking for her replacement right away. I will be filling in, starting tomorrow morning until a permanent housekeeper is found. Now, Peggy, I can see by your facial expression that you think your problem is solved. I hold your friendship in the highest regard. However, I will not let our friendship interfere in the finding of a housekeeper for Ken and his family."

"I understand, Laura," Peggy said. "I trust you to do what you deem best. With your permission, may I pray to that end? Not because she is my mother, but I believe she would do well in that family. Also, she would still be close by. It isn't as if we have abandoned her. How soon do you want to fill the position?"

"We want to as soon as possible. I have run a personal ad in *The Sentinel*, seeking employment for myself and I have been praying for some response. To date, I have heard nothing. I know that your mother has a number of loose ends to see to in the next two weeks. I promise you, Peggy, we will not make a decision without first interviewing your mother, that is if she is interested. Perhaps she has other plans not yet revealed to you. Share this with Carl if you like. And, please make peace with him. I do want to emphasize, unfortunately, your problem is not my first priority. The Holliday household has first priority at this time. They have a need of continuity in their life."

Peggy stood up to leave. Taking Laura by the hand, she gripped it, "Thank you, Laura, for being a friend. You have given me hope and right now that is what I needed. I need to get back home and make peace with Carl. I also need to get in touch with Mother to see what she has in mind. Carl and I need to realize that we can't solve Mother's problems, as she needs to take some responsibility for them herself." She thought, *oh, so many needs.*

As Peggy and Rebecca descended the steps of Laura's apartment, Laura waved goodbye and returned to see what Tylor was making such a fuss about. Tylor insisted it was time to eat and Laura remembered that she had promised to meet Tara at the school to accompany her home. Also, they were to eat at Maude's tonight. She was anxious to hear how things went with Leah.

As it neared time to meet Tara at the school, Laura left her apartment. She stopped at the bank to see if Ken was in his office. Mrs. Stahl greeted her and said, "Oh, Miss Martin, you have just missed Mr. Holliday as he has left to take Mrs. Andrews to the train station."

"That is fine," said Laura, cheered by the news. "Please tell him that I was in and I will be meeting Tara at the school. We will await his arrival at home when he finishes his work here. Thank you for telling him. Good bye, Mrs. Stahl."

Laura had brought Tara's pajamas and her toothbrush in expectation that Mrs. Andrews would be gone. Also, she wanted to survey the house to see if she needed to straighten up after

Leah's departure. The beds were unmade, but she would see to those after she and Tara came home from school.

Tara was pleased to see her. She hugged Laura and asked, "Is it safe to go home?"

Laura laughed, "Yes, Tara, all is safe. You will be sleeping in your room tonight. Your father also has a special surprise for you tonight. We are going to your home and make up your bed. Then, you may dress up in a dress of your choice and we will await your father's return home from the bank. Then you will know what the special surprise will be."

"Miss Martin, can't you tell me now," Tara begged. "I can't wait until Father comes home. Tell me now!"

"Sorry, if I told you, then you wouldn't be surprised when he told you." Laura was firm in her decision not to tell.

They arrived at home and Laura had Tara involved in watching Tylor as she made the beds. She determined that things weren't too bad. In a few days, things would be back to normal.

Todd arrived home and greeted Tara and Laura with sly a grin. "Well, I see the deserting rats have returned to the sinking ship."

Laura turned to Tara, "After a snide remark like that, we won't tell Todd about the upcoming surprise that we will be having." Laura put her finger to her lips to indicate that they were hushing up about the surprise.

Tara asked, "Miss Martin, what does 'snide' mean?"

"Tara, snide means 'sarcastic,' or poking fun at us. What he fails to realize that if the rats hadn't left the ship, the crew wouldn't have known that the ship was sinking and they would all go down with the ship. We have saved his life and that is the thanks we get."

Turning to Todd, Laura said, "Please dress nice for supper tonight. This is a special occasion at the Holliday house. I am expecting your father will be home early this evening."

A little after five o'clock, Ken drove up the driveway, and as he came into the house, Tara ran to him and asked, "Daddy, Daddy, what is the surprise?"

Ken feigned ignorance, "What surprise? I know nothing about a surprise. Who told you there was to be a surprise? In fact, the surprise was last night, but you were gone, so you missed any surprise."

"Miss Martin had a surprise for me last night. She made macaroni and cheese, and she read me a story and I slept in a big bed with her. That was the surprise last night! What is the surprise tonight?" Tara was pulling on Ken's arm, trying to make him tell his secret.

Ken said, "All right, Todd is going to drive the car tonight and we will stop at Maude's café for our supper. Everyone is a winner tonight, as Todd gets to drive, Tara can order whatever she wants from the menu, Laura doesn't have to cook and I don't have to eat Laura's cooking. Everybody wins!"

Tara said, "Daddy, that is a snide remark, saying that about Miss Martin's cooking."

"Where did you learn that word? Did you learn about 'snide' in school today?" Ken was amazed that she even knew the word, let alone using it in the right place.

Tara blushed, "Miss Martin taught me that word. Is it a good word for me to use, Daddy?"

Now it was Laura's turn to blush. "Ken, did she use it correctly? Is it a good word?"

Ken was flustered now. "How can I answer that question? If I say yes, it was used correctly, then I am admitting to saying

48

a snide remark about Laura's cooking. I can't win. Here are the keys, Todd, take us out of here before I get into any more trouble."

Todd drove the family to Maude's. While they were getting out, Laura commented, "That was a fine job of driving. I sense that you are a cautious driver. It is good that you learn at a young age. Should I ever purchase a car, I may have to ask you to teach me to drive. Have you been driving long?"

Todd beamed at her commending him for his driving skill. He answered, "Only about a month. Father has me drive to the Good Hope Church, that is if we get started in time. I enjoy driving and hope to have a car of my own by the time I graduate from high school."

Maude was surprised to see Laura with the Holliday family. She had some insight of the departure of Leah Andrews, as she had her breakfast and dinner at the café. She had them sit at a table near the rear of the café. It was quieter and avoided the draft of the winter air by the opening and closing of the front door. As Maude brought the water to the table, she gave Laura a wink to let her know that she was pleased to have them and Laura back with the family.

Maude didn't have menus to give to the customers to study, but rather a blackboard listing her specials. However, her regular customers knew that they could deviate a bit from the specialties. Maude would prepare what they requested, that is if Maude was in the mood to do as such. The specialty for this evening was pork chops.

Laura was the first to order. "It has been some time since I have had pork chops. That sounds good to me, but only one with the mashed potatoes and gravy. I do believe that Tylor will enjoy the potatoes and gravy. Is there a vegetable that comes with that?"

49

Maude said, "I have cooked carrots tonight. Hannah peeled the carrots after school, so they aren't out of a can. I imagine that Tylor will like the potatoes and gravy. I will bring him a highchair, so you can enjoy your meal without wrestling him on your lap. We may have to tie him in with a dishtowel. Now, what will the rest of you have?"

Not having any comment, Todd said, "I will have the same as Miss Martin."

Tara ordered next, but not seeing what she wanted on the blackboard, she asked Maude, "Could I have macaroni and cheese?"

Before Maude could answer, Ken said, "Tara, Laura said that she fed you macaroni and cheese last night. Why don't you order something different?"

Tara asked, "Spaghetti?"

"When Laura asked me what to fix for supper tonight, I chose spaghetti as my second choice, following eating out tonight. I believe that Laura is planning spaghetti for tomorrow night. Why don't you order the pork chops?" Ken was trying to finalize Tara's order.

Laura spoke up, "Ken, I try not to interfere in your decision making when it comes to you and the children. Oh, all right, there are times that I do and this is one of those times. If that is what she likes best, please let her order the macaroni and cheese. If she had her choice at home, she would order it every night for supper. That is, if Maude will fix it?"

Maude laughed, "After all this, how could I refuse? Macaroni and cheese is the order for Tara. Mr. Holliday, could I interest you in the same?"

Ken knew when he had been bested. When it came to Tara, he knew that Laura would come to her defense, using her charm to override Ken's decision. Unless of course, if it was a major decision. To date, no major decision has arisen. "Maude, the potatoes and gravy sounds great, but I will have a steak with that, cooked medium rare."

Laura had taken a sip of her water at the time Ken was ordering, but when he had ordered a steak instead of the pork chops, she choked on her water. Between coughing and laughing, she barely uttered, "Didn't you tell me that Leah cooked you a steak last night? Couldn't you order the pork chops off the blackboard tonight?"

Ken started to blush, "But the steak was dry and cold. Oh, all right, give me the pork chops."

"Don't give up so easily, Ken," Laura pleaded. "In all fairness, I do come to your defense. Inasmuch as you will be paying for our supper and you will be giving Maude a generous tip, it is only fair that you have your steak. Given the opportunity, steak would be your choice for supper every evening. Only Todd and I are willing to conform and make it easy on the cook. Please bring Ken his steak, medium rare and make it hot."

Maude smiled as she returned to the kitchen. It looks like the Holliday household is back to normal.

The family sincerely enjoyed their meal. Little Tylor smacked his lips when Laura fed the mashed potatoes and gravy to him, with a minimal amount of spills. Tara was entertained by how he tried to get his fingers in the bowl and grab the spoon. Everyone was relaxed and in a festive mood, it almost reminded Laura of the family's last Christmas together. *If only Stella could have been with them tonight.*

As they were finishing, Laura asked, "Would it be appropriate if we had a bit of pie? I have the craving for a small slice of cherry pie and a mug of coffee. Maude makes the best of pies."

Every one ate pie. Ken and Laura lingered over their coffee, as Todd and Tara told of some of the things happening at the school.

As they left, Maude waved and told them, "Come back again. I'll let you know the next time our supper special is pork chops."

Todd drove the family to Laura's apartment and she and Tylor climbed the steps to her little home. She enjoyed the Holliday household, but she also cherished the privacy she shared with her son.

Early the next morning, Laura was back at the Hollidays. She and Ken shared over their morning coffee his ordeal in dismissing Leah and his conversations with his mother and with Darren.

Laura told Ken about the visits that she has had with Peggy Barnes and the possibility that Carol Baker might work as a housekeeper. Laura said, "I'm expecting that I may hear from her, or if she is intensely interested, she may suddenly show up. I only met her once, so I have little knowledge of how she would fit in the home, or if this is what she desires. I am well acquainted with Peggy. However, if mother like daughter is any indication, she would work out well."

Ken was silent. Laura sensed that Ken was deep in thought. He was pondering as how to put those thoughts into words. Finally he spoke, "Laura, I don't know how to say this, but sometimes you frighten me. Not that I am afraid of you, but you are so feminine, I don't know how to react to you. It is hard to explain. You are so gracious to me, but I'm not sure as how to respond to that, as you are gracious to everyone else. I am unsure if you have any feelings for me. Therefore, I am hesitant to show feelings toward you that might be misunderstood. Perhaps it appears to you that it is too soon after Stella's death for me to even consider such things. However, once I received the word that she was dying, it was as if that was the day of her death. That was when my sorrow of bereavement began. I continued to love her, but I had lost all hope of her recovery. Instead of one month to be reckoned to her death, it has been four months for me. This may seem as macabre to you, but I need to be honest with you." It was then that he got up from the table. "I don't know, this doesn't make sense and I can't explain my feelings for you." It was then that he grabbed his hat and coat and rushed out the door. Laura heard the car as he backed out to the street. Laura was at a loss to know how to react to his words. *Was he trying to tell me that he loves me? Or, was he questioning my love for him? I fear that my absence from the home while Leah was here has raised some serious doubts. And now, my bringing up the thought of bringing Carol Baker into the home has created the fear that I will leave him? It appears that as long as I am in the home, there is no fear of him losing me. Apparently, he is willing to bide his time. Now he has created doubt in my mind. Am I in love with Ken, but refuse to acknowledge that love?*

Laura continued to remain at the table, thinking about their conversation. Tara and Todd came down the stairs for their breakfast and interrupted her thoughts.

Laura was washing all of the bed linens to insure that they were fresh. It was almost noon before she was able to leave the house. She had fixed Ken's lunch, but she wanted to leave before he returned at noon. She was uncertain how to handle their conversation this morning, but thought it best to say nothing more unless he brought it up.

The morning sun had been covered by the clouds that rolled in about ten o'clock and it was starting to turn colder. Laura hurried home, hugging Tylor to her bosom to keep him warm. Her apartment felt comfortable despite the outside cold. She decided that this was a good soup day, as she warmed the soup and toasted some bread to go with it. It was then that she remembered that tonight she was to fix the spaghetti supper for the Hollidays. I will need to go to the grocery store to get the meat for the sauce. The cold air had tired Tylor. After he was down for his nap, Laura thought it was the kind of day to encourage a nap for herself. In a matter of minutes, she was asleep in her rocker.

A light rap on the door awakened Laura. Looking at the clock, she realized that she had been sleeping for almost an hour. Going to the door, she opened it and there was Peggy and Rebecca, with flakes of snow dotting their coats. "Come in. I see that you have brought the snow with you. Are you alone, or did Carl come with you?"

"No," Peggy replied, "just the two of us. I did want to touch base with you regarding the housekeeping position at the Hollidays. Is there anything new with you?"

"Not really," answered Laura. "I visited with Ken about your mother, but we were of the same mind that we would want a personal interview before making any decision. Ken's mother sent Mrs. Andrews to us. We were of the same conclusion that she would not have been hired, had we met her personally. Have you contacted your mother? If so, what is her thinking about moving to Summit City?"

"I called her last night while Carl was at a board meeting." Peggy paused, not sure how to express the rest of her thoughts. "I didn't want Carl to overhear our conversation, but I felt that I could be more frank with Mother if Carl was not in the room and only hearing one side of the telephone conversation. She was somewhat apprehensive about working in another person's home. In fact, I see her confidence in her ability is so low that she is fearful of working anywhere. I know it sounds terrible, but I told her, 'Mother, I think it best if you didn't live with us at this time.' This left the possibility that she could live with us should she be old, or disabled. She cried and tried to make me feel guilty. I told her that there was not enough work for both us and that she was too young to simply quit being productive. Maybe she would want to get some education to learn a new occupation. I did tell her that we would help, but we wouldn't support her totally. After a time, she began to realize that I was serious and it was necessary for her to accept responsibility for herself. My father made all the decisions, so she has been at a loss to know what to do. What would Mr. Holliday be paying for a housekeeper?"

"Peggy, you would need to discuss that with Ken. Perhaps you could give him a call as he is aware that you and I have been in discussion regarding your mother's employment. When might she be able to come and interview? Ken is seriously considering her, based upon your integrity in the community."

"I would like to know where she stands now as it will help us if we need to make other decisions. She has a little less than two weeks before the farm sells. I could have her here in three or four days, make a decision and have her home before the sale of the farm. We would buy her ticket, here and back. Should we have a job for her, we would then know what to do with her personal items and furniture."

Laura was thinking, "Peggy, just a thought, but it might be best should she take this job, that she rent a small house. That would give her privacy and she would be able to keep some of her furniture and personal items. It isn't necessary that she live in the Holliday house twenty four hours a day. I don't do it now, however, I am available to stay overnight if need be. Right now, I go in at six and stay until ten. I usually go to work by three to prepare supper and am there when Tara comes home from school. I then leave after I have cleaned up in the evening. I usually eat breakfast and supper with the family. I have been cooking a roast on Sunday and they serve themselves." Laura paused, "Incidentally, how are you and Carl doing, if I might ask?"

Peggy replied, "It is much better. I apologized and then he began to understand my position as well. We are still speaking and sleeping in the same bed, so it is good!"

Laura stood up. "Let's have a quick cup of coffee and you can help me run one small errand. Would you care to stop in and see Ken and ask him about the wages and see if he is open to an interview within the next five days? Then you will have something to tell your mother and go from there."

"Good idea," said Peggy. "Laura, you are a genius. I think this may work. It would give my mother some dignity and also save my marriage!"

Laura laughed, "I know I am good, but I don't think that I'm that good."

Peggy drove Laura to the grocery store, where she picked up the meat for the spaghetti that she was preparing that night.

The two ladies met with Ken and he was welcome to the idea of meeting with Carol Baker. Inwardly, he would have preferred to delay the inevitability of Laura leaving. Peggy talked privately with him regarding the wages.

After leaving the bank, Peggy drove to the Holliday house. Laura had the meat in one arm and her son in the other, conveniently placed on her hip. Peggy said, to Laura, "Thank you for all your help. Are you sure that this is what you want, leaving this home?"

Laura didn't answer as she bid Peggy good bye.

Two days later, while serving Ken his breakfast, he remarked to Laura, "Peggy Barnes called last night and asked if her mother could meet with us on Friday. She would arrive on the morning train and we could meet in the afternoon. Friday afternoons are usually slow here at the bank. What is your thought of our meeting here at the house? That way, it would give her an opportunity to see where she would be working? As I thought about this, I would like to have the children meet her. I don't know, but there is something about a child, particularly a young child, as they seem to have a sixth sense when meeting a stranger."

"That is an excellent idea," Laura exclaimed. "We learn from our mistakes. After Leah Andrews, we are certainly more cautious. I feel bad that we were unable to work with Leah, not only for her sake, but your mother's as well. Perhaps, had we more time to acquaint ourselves with Leah and as you mentioned, to have the children interact with the housekeeper, we would have been able to avoid a disaster. Just an idea for you to give thought to, would you want me to prepare supper and have Mrs. Baker eat with us? Perhaps the grocer still has some pork chops available." Ken gave her a startled look. Instantly, Laura clarified her statement. "No, no, I'm only kidding with you. As the head of the house, you may choose the menu, right down to the dessert. I usually learn more about a person when eating with them than merely meeting together. When you consider it, many occasions in the New Testament records Jesus eating with people, saints and sinners. So that you might be aware in my visiting with Peggy, I did suggest that if her mother was your choice, that she might consider renting a small house and not live full time in the home. That would afford her the option of bringing her own furniture and personal items. It would allow her privacy and the opportunity to entertain family and friends in her own setting. Personally, it was needful for me to be here during Stella's illness. However, I do enjoy the privacy of my apartment, humble as it may be. Because of Tylor, it did work for my benefit to live in the home. Stella was able to care for him while I was seeing to the needs of the family. No situation is perfect, but it can be made to work."

Ken remarked, "Laura, this has been good! We have laid the groundwork for our interview. Let's plan to have supper together. As far as the menu, I have no interest to tell you what to cook, or how to cook. From that first spaghetti and fruit cocktail supper, to this breakfast, I have never had a bad meal. I did get a bit tired of the leftover turkey, but it was never bad. There is one other thing regarding Peggy Barnes. Perhaps you might indicate to her in a subtle way that we don't want her present when we interview Mrs. Baker. The manner that I said it now is not the way to do it, but you have the ability to say it in such a manner that Peggy will think it was her idea. If Peggy wants to bring her, that is fine, and I--." Ken stopped there. "I mean we will see her home after supper." Jumping up from his chair, he said, "I'm running late, as I need to get to the bank." Brushing by Laura, Ken kissed her on the cheek, and said to her, "Bye, Hon." When he got to the door, with his hand on the knob, he turned and looking at Laura, he whispered in a voice barely audible, "I'm sorry, old habits are hard to break. That is how I would leave Stella when I was late and needed to hurry to the bank. I'm sorry." Opening the door, he rushed out. As Laura heard the car go down the driveway, she was still holding her hand to her cheek where Ken had kissed her.

It was then that the tears slowly rolled down her cheeks. She was uncertain as to why. *Was it remembering Stella, or her feelings for Ken?* Only when she heard Tara coming down the steps was she able to stop the flow of tears. Drying her eyes, she greeted Tara with a smile and a hug. As Laura anticipated, Peggy arrived at Laura's apartment a little after one with Rebecca in tow. Laura greeted her, "I have the coffee hot. For some strange reason, I thought perhaps Peggy Barnes would be here to see me this afternoon. Sit down and I will pour you some of the best coffee in Summit City."

Peggy could scarcely contain her enthusiasm. "I'm excited. Mother is coming and she will have a job interview. As a surprise, I have made an appointment at the beauty shop to have her hair fixed. I only wish that she was as eager as I am about all this."

Laura, wanting to encourage Peggy, said, "I am sure, as the time draws near that she will be looking forward to this new opportunity. You must realize, Peggy, this is totally new to her. Things have changed dramatically within the last six weeks. She has been experiencing so many unknowns. Many people of her background might give up and not proceed. Fortunately, she has you to help and guide her as she seeks to make the adjustments in her life."

"In our phone call this morning, she indicated that she has confidence in being able to do what is required for the position." Peggy stopped there. "However, she is uncertain how she will handle the interview. She wants me to be with her through the interview. She is afraid that she may say the wrong thing, or appear too unsure of herself. What do you think, should I be at the interview?"

How do I handle this, was Laura's thought, as she prepared to answer her? "Peggy, look at this from several different angles. If it was your interview, would you want your mother to sit in? Would you be comfortable to be involved with your mother's interview? Or, look at it from the point of the interviewer. Is it appropriate for the daughter to be there when the interviewer is asking the questions?"

"You have answered my question. Mother needs to answer for herself. I can go see Maude for a time until the interview is over. Yes, that is what I will do." Peggy appeared to be satisfied by answering her own question.

"Let me tell you what Ken has in mind," said Laura.

"If we met at three o'clock, we would discuss the details of the responsibilities and tour the house. At some point the children would be included also. Ken was planning for Carol to join us for supper and then we would return her to your home. That way you need not kill your afternoon. Have you approached your mother about renting, or buying a home in Summit City? I don't know how much she knows about the town, but it shouldn't take long to tour it. Houses certainly are not very expensive as compared to the urban areas. David Riggs at *The Sentinel* might know of any vacant houses, or perhaps Sheriff Morgan for that matter. I'm not sure if Ken is aware of anything, but I will ask him. Something is sure to come up."

Peggy sighed, "I don't know why I am so nervous, as you and Ken seem to know what you are doing. However, Mother is planning to return Monday afternoon. Will you have come to a decision by that time? I'm sorry to be pressing you with all these questions, but I do want to get her settled. A week from this Friday is the day of the sale. The neighbors are helping to line up the machinery and gather up all the small items. We are still uncertain as to how much furniture to retain. Oh, I just wish it was all settled."

Laura clutched Peggy's hands. "The Lord has His timing for all things. He tells us to be anxious for nothing, or for 'no thing.' It is easy for me to say this, for I am also guilty of running ahead of the Lord. I am looking forward to see how He will work out all these questions that we each have." It was at that time that Tylor crying from his crib interrupted her. She brought him to the table, not knowing why he cried out. He looked at Peggy and Rebecca and was content to be held in his mother's arms.

Peggy looked at her watch and commented, "I should be going home. I don't know what to do with myself. I know you have things to do, so I will stop interrupting you." She laughed. "I may stop at the hospital to see if they have a 'straight jacket' that I could borrow until Friday. Bye, Laura." She picked up Rebecca and went out the door.

Friday morning dawned bright, just as Laura expected of a February morning. She was at the Holliday house when she heard the morning train blow its whistle for the crossing east of Summit City. Laura said a silent prayer for Carol Baker and Peggy Barnes and this day. Laura remembered a verse. She was not sure, but she thought it to be in Psalms; *'This is the day that the Lord hath made, we shall rejoice, and be glad in it.' Laura was overwhelmed, that the Lord had put those words in her mind today. 'Rejoice.' How often we fail to rejoice. Jesus said, "Rejoice, and again I say, rejoice." Laura expected God to touch her today, even as he had touched her this morning with His precious Word.*

Ken came into the kitchen and remarked to Laura, "What are you so happy about?"

Laura turned from the counter where she had been pouring Ken's coffee. "I am happy because I am rejoicing in the Lord. I am expecting great things from Him today." She handed Ken his mug of coffee.

Ken grinned, "Well, I hope the first great thing He did was start with the coffee."

With her hands on her hips, Laura said, "Let me assure you, if there is a better cup of coffee in Summit City this morning, then it came from God and no mere mortal."

Taking a sip of the coffee, Ken nodded his head. "He did well. But, what can we expect for supper, and will that be great as well?"

Laura was just warming up to the greatness of God. "Let me assure you, just a few days ago, the master of this house assured me that he had never had a bad meal at the hands of Miss

Martin. You shall not be disappointed. Neither shall you know the menu until it is served."

Laura continued with the breakfast preparation. Ken was an easy man to cook for, in that he was consistent. His early morning breakfast consisted of two eggs, over medium, bacon and toast. Occasionally, Laura would fix sausage and if for some reason Laura deemed it necessary to bribe him, she would fry a small steak with his eggs. Saturday was the time for pancakes as they were the favorite menu of Todd and Tara. Naturally, Ken tolerated them in deference to his children.

As Ken was working on his second cup of coffee, Laura was explaining her thoughts on the interview with Carol Baker. "I will come early this afternoon to begin preparing for the meal tonight. I am positive that Peggy will have her mother here promptly at three o'clock. I have no idea how long the interview will take, but while I am putting the finishing touches on supper, Tara can show Mrs. Baker around the house. Tara is good at entertaining, as she is a great conversationalist. It might be well if Todd and Tara help me in the setting of the table, as that way she will know that they are capable of helping when needed. Before taking her home, I will clean up in the kitchen with the children's help. You and Mrs. Baker can have some time alone. Am I missing anything?"

Ken chuckled and shook his head. "No, Laura, it appears to me that you have it well orchestrated."

"There is a problem as to when we make a decision? And when do we tell her what we have decided? While doing the kitchen cleanup, I can determine the children's thoughts. That leaves you and me, especially you, as I don't have to live with the decision." Laura thought, *that wasn't very well put, but I guess that is what it comes down to at this time.*

Ken grimaced at the thought of replacing Laura, but she

is determined to leave. *If only we had met at a different time and under different circumstances. And yet, I would not have changed meeting Stella and our shortened life.* "Laura, I will know your feelings regarding Mrs. Baker. In most instances, your face will reveal your thoughts. Not always, but many times I can discern your thoughts."

Laura blushed."Is it that revealing? I need to develop what is known as a 'poker face' when I am communicating with you."

Ken was ready to leave. "Don't worry about it, as everything will work out for the best." He started for the door, "Then I will see you at three."

As he closed the door, Laura thought, *what, no kiss on the cheek this morning?*

Laura was back at the house by two that afternoon, peeling potatoes and preparing the meat for the supper meal. Promptly at three, there was a knock at the door. Laura still had her apron on, so as she passed through the kitchen she pulled it off and placed it on the counter.

Opening the door, there was Peggy and her mother. Laura greeted her. "Welcome to the Holliday home, Mrs. Baker. Good afternoon, Peggy. Won't you ladies come in? Mr. Holliday has not yet arrived, but we can wait for him in the living room." As Laura was showing them to the living room, she looked back at Peggy, who gave her a strange defeated look. I know that look. Her mother doesn't want to be alone. "Let me take your coat, Mrs. Baker. I won't bother with yours, Peggy, as I presume that you have children to pick up at school. I won't keep you, as I remember; you never want to be late. We will see that your mother gets home, so don't worry." All the time that Laura was talking, she was ushering Peggy toward the door.

As Peggy reached the door, she said, "Bye, Mom; see

you later." Peggy then whispered to Laura, "Thanks."

Hurrying back to the living room, Laura said, "When you were here for Rebecca's birth, we never had that visit that you promised me when you and Carl picked up the girls at my house. Now is a good time to have that visit before Mr. Holliday arrives. He should soon be here. I have made some refreshments. Do you prefer tea or coffee?"

"Tea will be fine, thank you," said Mrs. Baker. As Laura was pouring the tea, she was impressed with her choice of clothes. She had chosen a blue skirt, with a matching jacket and a white blouse. She was wearing a string of pearls, which Laura recognized as belonging to Peggy. "Mrs. Baker, your hair looks nice. I'm glad that you have come to interview for this position. Mr. Holliday is a fine man to work for. The children, Todd and Tara are well behaved. They will be home in a few minutes and you will have an opportunity to meet them and visit with them as well." Laura thought, *did I note a bit of panic when I mentioned visiting with the children?* Laura was pouring herself a cup of tea when Ken came hurrying through the kitchen door. Laura called to him, "Mr. Holliday, we are in the living room having tea. Would you prefer tea or coffee?"

Coming into the living room, he said, "Coffee please. I'm sorry that I am a bit late, but what I thought would be a slow day turned out to be just the opposite. Mrs. Baker, welcome to our home." She had offered her hand and he shook it gently. "How was your trip this time? As I recall, the last time you came, you missed the connections and it cost you an extra day."

Mrs. Baker replied, "Uneventful, but shorter than the last trip." Laura noticed that she was apparently feeling more at ease.

"I had discussed the salary with Peggy," Ken began. "I had wanted you to know what to expect before you made the trip. Do you have any questions concerning the pay?" Carol shook her head, indicating that she had no questions. Ken continued, "Were you thinking of wanting to live here, or having a home of your own? You may have known while my wife was living, Laura came in one day per week. However, once that Stella became extremely ill, Laura lived in the home until Stella's death. Now she has returned to her own apartment, which has worked quite well. You must understand that I am a novice when it comes to running a home or doing anything in the home, especially the kitchen. I leave the menu choice to others. Laura understands my preferences and pretty much adheres to those, with an occasional deviation. Tell me, Mrs. Baker, did you have any preference as to living arrangements?"

"Should I find affordable housing, I would prefer to rent a small home. If a lot of time were required of me, it would be best for me to live-in. What hours would I be working each day? Also, what hours are required on the weekends as well?" Laura thought those to be good questions asked by Mrs. Baker.

Ken replied, "Laura, you would be the best to answer those questions, so I will turn it to you."

Ken noticed that Laura glared at him, as if she didn't want to answer Mrs. Baker. However, Laura began, "Keep in mind that when I come to work, I bring an infant with me to care for as well as to do housework, so I am spending more time in the home than you would. I come in at six in the morning and see to Mr. Holliday's breakfast as well as the children's breakfast. Mr. Holliday's meal is a standard Sandhills breakfast of bacon and eggs with his coffee. The children are less restrictive. With all the clean up and bed making and whatever laundry, I am gone by ten. I have spoiled the man of the house by fixing him a nourishing lunch. I return at three, as I want to be here for Tara when she returns from school. Supper is at six. Todd and Tara are good help and they will help with the table setting and also the dishes each evening, so I am gone by eight or shortly

JOY AT THE DISMAL RIVER

thereafter. Saturday is slower paced with a later breakfast and usually pancakes to please the children. I have been stopping by on Sunday morning on my way to church to put in a small roast and serving it up as I stop by. Now that the family is driving out to Good Hope for church, Sunday dinner is the 'iffiest' of all the meals. Menu preparation is your responsibility, as is the shopping. Everyone is quite tolerant, that is if they get their own way." Laura laughed at her last statement.

Laura heard the kitchen door and knew that Tara had arrived home. She called to her, "Tara, would you please come to the living room as we have a guest." Tara came into the room and Laura introduced her. "Mrs. Baker, this is Tara. Tara, please meet Mrs. Baker." Reaching out to Tara, Laura said, "Would you care to show Mrs. Baker your room. I need to check on the supper and then I will fix you some milk and one cookie. We have a special menu tonight, as it is my first time to serve it in this house. It is a recipe my Grandma Martin would prepare. The only difference is, she used venison, but I have substituted beef."

"Miss Martin, what is venison?"

"Tara, it is deer meat. Grandma Martin hunted deer in the woods. I was thirteen when I shot my first deer. It was good meat, but nothing compared to Sandhills beef like we are having tonight. People refer to it as venison, the same as the meat from cattle is called beef."

Tara was curious about Laura shooting the deer. "Miss Martin, is that anything like shooting the wild turkeys?"

"Very similar," said Laura. "But with deer, you must have a license before you go hunting."

"Miss Martin," asked Tara. "Did you have a license?"

"No, Tara, I didn't have a license. What Grandma Martin and I were doing was breaking the law. We were poaching, which is hunting deer without a license and out of season. With a license, you can only hunt deer at a certain time of the year. It is a sin to break the law. I didn't know that I was breaking the law, but I was still guilty of breaking the law." *This is getting deeper and deeper all the time. This is a good object lesson to portray the penalty of sin, and the ignorance of breaking the law. We need more time to expand on this, but unfortunately, now is not a good time.* Laura said, "You remind me of one of my students when I taught at Good Hope School. His name is John Wesley Schumacher and he wanted all of the details of every story, just as you do tonight. We will talk of this another time."

"I know John Wesley. He is in my Sunday school class. I like John Wesley."

"I'm sure that you do, but remember, you were going to show your room to Mrs. Baker while I looked about the supper." Not wishing any further conversation with Tara, Laura went into the kitchen as Todd was coming into the house. "Hello. Your father is in the living room. Check with him to see if he has anything for you to do. I'm busy at this time."

Tara and Mrs. Baker came into the kitchen and Carol asked if she could be of help. Laura said, "Todd and Tara are learning dining room etiquette, so they will be setting the table tonight. Please sit down and rest. I'm sure that with the travel and your other affairs that it has been exhausting. We will be eating in a few minutes. This is an average American family, with rural standards. With your years of experience, if I can manage this home, you should have no trouble whatsoever. Has Peggy had an opportunity to see if there are any houses for rent, or purchase in town? I was fortunate to find a furnished apartment, as I had no furniture, so I had no cash outlay to get started. Mrs. Baker, do you drive or own a car?"

"I own a car. It is three years old, so it is quite reliable and it certainly has afforded me a measure of independence after Peggy's father died. Should I take this job, I would bring the car with me. Also, I want my next home to be furnished with some of my older and better furniture."

"Now that there is just the two of us here, do you have any questions or concerns regarding this position?" Laura waited, as Mrs. Baker hesitated to respond.

"Miss Martin, this appears to be an ideal place to work, but if it is so good, why are you leaving? I don't want to pry, but I see you as a forthright person and I thought you might reveal some reason that employment here would be inappropriate for me. I don't want to come all this way and regret it."

"Mrs. Baker, it is difficult for me to answer that question. In your case, I see no reason for you not accepting employment with Mr. Holliday. I left once and only returned to fill in until a replacement was hired. At this time, if I don't find employment, I will probably relocate to another city."

Carol Baker had one last question for Laura. "Miss Martin, do you love Mr. Holliday? Is that why you are leaving?"

Laura was sliding a serving bowl out from under a smaller bowl. She was so distracted by Carol Baker's question that the bowl slipped from her hand and crashed to the floor, shattering as it hit the tile. Laura didn't bother to pick up the pieces. She stood there, looking at the shattered dish. Carol Baker started to gather up the broken bowl, being careful not to cut herself. "I'm sorry, Laura, I shouldn't have asked. Here, let me help you."

Todd and Tara came into the kitchen. Tara asked, "Miss Martin, if we helped set the table, could we eat early this evening?"

Laura responded as if nothing had taken place. "Absolutely! Everything is about ready and I'm hungry as well." Laura reached for another bowl and spooned the mashed potatoes into the dish. She handed the bowl to Carol. She started to open a small can of what she thought was a second can of green peas. As she removed the lid, she laughed, "Tara, how can we make your father believe that this was opened by mistake? I thought it was a second can of peas, but it is black olives. Will you be able to eat black olives tonight?" Tara nodded. "Well, we will be a bit short of peas tonight as that was the last can. Do olives count as a vegetable?" The first can of peas was already hot, so Laura added some seasoning and a dollop of butter and handed the bowl to Carol. "On second thought, Tara, please take the peas to the table. Mrs. Baker, I will entrust you with the olives." Tara laughed, as she knew why Laura made the switch.

The family and Mrs. Baker were seated around the table. Laura noticed that Carol said a silent prayer before eating. Ken took one look at the surprise entrée that Laura had prepared. He said nothing, but passed it on to Todd. He in turn passed it to Tara, without helping himself. Tara handed it to Mrs. Baker. Mrs. Baker took a small portion and seeing a ladle in the bowl, used it to pour some of the sauce over her meat. Laura spoke up. "I see that the family has some doubt concerning the main course. I would encourage everyone to take one bite. The meat is in a sauce, or you may call it gravy which can be ladled over your mashed potatoes. The meat is beef, actually it is round steak and the dish is referred to as 'Swiss steak.' The sauce is a tomato paste base. If you liked my spaghetti, you will like this even better. However, if you prefer, I will remove it from the table. You can add butter to your mashed potatoes and eat them that way. This is the only meat that I have prepared. The choice is yours. Evidently Mr. Holliday, now you will be able to say that you have had one bad meal at the hands of Miss Martin. On second thought, I may do as Grandma Martin did to me shortly after I went to live with her. She had prepared ham and beans for supper. I told her that I didn't like ham and beans. For the next seven days, we had ham and beans. Only ham and beans for supper, nothing more. I never told her I didn't like anything after that."

The bowl was now setting in front of Ken after it had made it around the table. "I'm sorry, Laura. That was rude of me as I passed judgment on it without tasting it." Using the fork that was in the bowl, he took a generous portion and ladled the sauce over his potatoes. He then handed it to Todd, with a nod of his head, he indicated that Todd was to help himself to the Swiss steak. Todd took a smaller portion than his father, but none of the sauce. He then handed it to Tara.

Tara said, "No thank you, but will someone please pass the olives."

That triggered a response from Ken. "Tara!" That is all he said, but it was sufficient as Tara forked some of the meat on her plate.

Laura had mixed some of the sauce with the mashed potatoes for Tylor. When he was fed the mixture, he smacked his lips and grunted for more. The family laughed at his antics as Laura said, "At least someone has healthy taste buds."

None of the Hollidays admitted to liking it, or asked for the Swiss steak to be passed, however, when the bowl was passed around, they each helped themselves to a second helping. At the end of the meal, there was none for leftovers which Laura had counted on as she enjoyed it warmed over.

"Miss Martin," Tara asked, "when will we have Swiss steak again? I liked it."

"I'm glad you did, Tara," Laura replied, "as I will be making it for the family for the next seven days." That brought a groan from the family.

Laura had baked a cherry pie and it was still warm. She offered that for dessert and ice cream for those that wanted it. Ken said, "I will have the pie and coffee. There is something so western about pie and coffee. Oftentimes, when the ranchers meet with me in the afternoon, they want me to go with them for pie and coffee." The adults had the pie and coffee and the children ate pie and ice cream.

Mrs. Baker and Ken remained at the table having a second cup of coffee, as Laura started washing the dishes and Todd was drying. Tara picked up the dinnerware and took it to the kitchen. It wasn't long before the table was cleared and after a short time, they returned to the dining room.

Carol Baker commented, "My goodness, that didn't take long. Todd and Tara, you are certainly a great help."

Tara spoke up, "Miss Martin trained us. Sometimes if we hurry, we have time for a game or a story before bedtime. Daddy is the only one that isn't trained." Mr. Holliday blushed and only nodded in ascent.

Speaking to Mrs. Baker, Ken asked, "Do you have any further questions for us or any need to look about the house any further?"

"Two questions for you," started Mrs. Baker. "I didn't see any pets around the house. Do you have any pets, or are they hid out for my sake?"

"No pets, Mrs. Baker," answered Ken. "When I married Stella, she was a widow with the two children you see here. I met Stella while I was stationed in England with the Army. When we moved here, we didn't see the need of having any pets. Most of the families that have pets in the Sandhills, house them outside. In answer to your second question, I am presuming that you will ask if I am a smoker and have I hidden that from you? No, I am a non-smoker and I will make an effort to encourage my children to be the same. May I ask the question of you, are you a smoker?" Laura smiled, making an effort to keep it hidden. That Ken, he is having fun with Mrs. Baker, as he knows that she doesn't smoke. He had specifically asked Peggy if her mother did.

"Oh, dear no," Mrs. Baker asserted. "And I'm glad that you don't either. It just makes it easier to keep the house clean."

"Good," said Ken. "Is everyone ready for a ride? I imagine that Mrs. Baker's granddaughters are wondering what has happened to her. You probably didn't get to see them before they went to school this morning and we had you most of the afternoon and evening. Would you mind if Todd drove this evening? We are trying to get him experienced with night driving. Then we will wait for a big snowstorm, so he can experience snow. He is doing quite well. I'm looking forward to spring, as I will have him drive and I can look at the cattle and scenery. I will feel like a millionaire with a chauffeur. I think that I'll buy a black suit for Todd to wear as he drives me around in my black limousine."

"Mr. Holliday," Laura said, "quit your dreaming and let's get started."

It took Todd about ten minutes to drive to the Barnes Ranch. Walking up the sidewalk, Laura lagged behind. She was carrying Tylor and he was wiggling under the covers. She stopped as Mrs. Baker was already at the door. Ken paused, waiting for Laura to catch up. When she was near him, she whispered, "Well?"

"Well, what?" he queried.

"What have you decided? What have you decided about Mrs. Baker?" Laura asked.

"I don't know, what are your thoughts about Mrs.

Baker?" asked Ken.

"This morning you told me that my face revealed my thoughts. What do you see now?"

Carl Barnes interrupted their banter with one another as he hollered from the doorway, "Is everything all right?"

Ken answered, "Yes, Laura is rearranging Tylor's blankets. We'll be right there."

Laura brushed past Ken and whispered, "Liar."

Peggy greeted them. "I know that you just finished one of Laura's exquisite suppers, but do you have room for a cup of coffee?"

Ken chuckled, "Yes, yes; after one of Laura's exquisite suppers, I do have room for coffee."

Carl said, "I must be missing something here, but Ken seems to be in a good mood tonight."

Laura answered, "How well he should as he knows what he'll be eating for supper for the next seven days."

The Hollidays and Laura stayed for about forty-five minutes before Ken decided to leave. The evening was spent in mostly idle chatter. Tara played with the twins and Todd listened to what the men had to say. Ken got up and said, "We should be going as someone has to get up early tomorrow and look after the cows and I'm glad it isn't me." Laura had wrapped Tylor in his blankets and Ken cautioned her, "Laura, be sure that you get Tylor folded in right this time." She gave him a strange look, as she tried to get Tylor to hold still.

When they got into the car, Laura asked, "Ken, what is your decision? You never gave Mrs. Baker any indication, one way or the other. I don't know where you stand on hiring her. Surely you aren't this indecisive with your banking decisions."

Ken knew that she was miffed, but he thought it was over his remarks about wrapping Tylor in his blanket. Todd started the car and had put the car in reverse to back out of the driveway. Laura said, "Please shut the car off until we get this settled." He looked over to his father. Ken nodded and Todd turned off the ignition.

Ken asked, "How do the rest of you feel about her? Do you want her or not?"

Tara said, "I like her. She seems nice and she asked about my room and my stuffed animals."

"We didn't visit much," said Todd, "but I sense that she will do her best."

"Laura," asked Ken, "you spent more time with her than the rest of us. Will she work out?"

"Let me see," Laura said. "Tara is now nine years old and will be in the home for nine more years. Mrs. Baker is capable of giving you nine years of service. She will be honest and loyal. Granted, she is no Laura Martin by any means, but I don't think you need another like Laura Martin. Mrs. Baker will accept without question whatever you say. She will be good for this family. What are your thoughts on her, now that we have expressed our ideas?"

"I'm satisfied," said Ken, "that she would be a good employee. I'm not sure how imaginative she might be, but after all, she is no Laura Martin. What can we expect, two Laura Martins in a lifetime? I don't think so."

Tara laughed, "Oh, Daddy, you are funny!"

"All right," Ken said emphatically. "We will hire her to be our new housekeeper. I'll call her in the morning to let her know that she got the job. Let's go, Todd, drive us home!"

Laura said, "No!"

"At first you said she was all right and now you say 'no.' Make up your mind, Laura!"

"I mean," said Laura, "no to calling her in the morning. She needs to know tonight. She is not going to get one ounce of rest, worrying about this job. She is a desperate woman and it would be cruel to have her wait until the morning. Here, Tara, hold Tylor. Ken, you and I will go in and tell Mrs. Baker that she has the job. Is that fair enough?"

"Laura, you are right." Ken said. "I never thought about it that way. You are so wise when it comes to dealing with people's feelings." Ken thought; *why can't Laura see to her own feelings as well as she does the feelings of others. It is always for others!*

Laura and Ken went to the door. Peggy asked, "What's the matter, won't the car start? I thought I heard it start up."

Laura said, "We need to talk to your mother."

Peggy motioned Laura to the kitchen. Ken stayed back to visit with Carl. Peggy said, "I don't think that is a good idea. Mother is in no mood for company at this time."

"What's the matter," asked Laura. "Did we upset her? I thought things went well this afternoon. She never gave any indication that she was unhappy."

"As soon as you left this evening, she started crying and went into her bedroom." Peggy dabbed at her own eyes. "She was pathetic as she started to rant, calling herself a no good old woman, not good for anything. Then she questioned as to why she even thought that she could do anything. I really got alarmed when she said that she wished she was dead and could be with Daddy in heaven."

Laura said, "Peggy, while we were in the car, we talked about her coming to work at the Holliday home. It was then decided that she was our choice. I encouraged Ken to come back

75

in and tell her that if she wanted the job, we wanted her as well. I feared that she would spend a restless night not knowing our decision, but I didn't think it would be this bad. With us being young, we have no idea of the fears and insecurity of the elderly. I'm sorry. Would it help if we went in and I assured her that she has a future at the Holliday house? I would like Carol to hear what Ken has to say. Ken isn't uncaring, but most men don't understand the frailty of our emotions as another woman does."

"I understand," said Peggy. "Mother will listen to you, as she knows the compassion you exhibited towards Karen. Let's give it a try."

Peggy knocked on the bedroom door. "Mother, it is Peggy. Laura Martin is here and she wants to talk with you. I think you will want to hear what she has to say. May we come in?"

Peggy and Laura heard a 'yes,' so they went in. Carol Baker was sitting on the edge of the bed, looking distraught and still crying some while dabbing at her eyes from time to time.

Laura went to her and put her arm around the lady. "Mrs. Baker, I'm sorry that we caused you undue grief. We came back to offer you the housekeeping position, but you will need to hear it from Mr. Holliday. Do you think you can go out there? It would make me feel better if Mr. Holliday could talk to you about your becoming the housekeeper. We discussed it in the vehicle before leaving here tonight, as we didn't have the opportunity to meet as a family this evening. Mr. Holliday wanted to hear what the children had to say. They agreed that you would be a good choice. Now, let's get a little cold water on those eyes so they will look excited when you hear the news. I'm an expert on using cold water on the eyes, as I have a tendency to be weepy; whether it is good new or bad news."

Peggy went to her mother, "Oh, Momma, isn't this great.

You'll be close and now you can see your granddaughters grow up. Here, let's get you brightened up. Go ahead, Laura, we'll be right out."

Laura went out and told the men, "Carol was rather tired from such a big day, so we had to get her presentable. She didn't want her future boss to see her in her nightgown."

Carol and Peggy come out and Ken apologized. "Mrs. Baker, I'm sorry we were unable to take a family vote any earlier, so we voted in the car before returning to Summit City. It was a unanimous decision that you come to be with us, that is if you will have us?"

"Thank you, Mr. Holliday," Carol uttered in a manner, indicating that she was choked up with emotion. "You don't know how happy this has made me. I'll start as soon as I can. Thank you for your kindness, Mr. Holliday."

Laura said, "Ken, we need to let these folks get to bed, so we will leave now. Good night."

Peggy followed Laura to the door and hugged her before she left. "Thank you, Laura Martin, I love you. You mean a great deal to me and my family."

As Ken and Laura were going down the sidewalk, he said to Laura, "Didn't want me to see her in her nightgown, did you? Liar! She was still wearing her pearl necklace!"

That night, as Laura lay in her bed, *she was reminded of her expectations she had expressed earlier that morning. It was to be touched by God. I can truly say that God has touched me! Oh, might others acknowledge being touched by Him today. Tonight, a destitute grandmother has comfort that she is not a burden to her daughter. And a daughter sees that her mother has worth, as she will minister to a widowed father and his children. It has been a good day, a day worthy of rejoicing!*

It was two weeks before Carol Baker moved to Summit City. The sale of the farm and equipment left her with a small amount of money. Carl and Peggy located a modest home near the Hollidays. They made the down payment. The payments were such that Carol would have it free and clear after a few years. Carol began working at the Hollidays with some help from Laura; but after a few days, she was able to handle it by herself.

Laura experienced a certain amount of sadness, but she felt more comfortable in the transition than when Leah Andrews took over. Right now, she was concerned with some type of employment. It had been almost two months since she had placed an ad in *The Sentinel.* She had not been selective as to the work that she would do, and still nothing. "Oh, Lord, what am I to do?" As she prayed, she remembered Gideon, who had placed a fleece before the Lord. *Am I so presumptuous to not accept a sign from the Lord?*

After a sleepless night, Laura got out of bed and dressed Tylor. The morning was beginning to dawn. *Tylor and I will walk through the city this morning!* Stepping out from her apartment, she felt a chill in the air, which was not unusual, as it was still late winter. That is, unless you are an optimist. Then you see it as early spring! As she and Tylor walked the city, she first paid her respect to the Dismal River. *Oh, flow on my beloved river, flow on. Only you are my faithful river. Would you think me unfaithful, should I leave this city?* Coming to the courthouse, Laura remembered when she saw it on her first morning in Summit City. A looming structure of stone! That is how she recalled it, as she presumed that all of the materials had been shipped in from a great distance. *This is where Hannah was freed from the dominance of her stepfather and placed in the custody of Maude Dunham.* Coming to the mortuary and cemetery, *I remember the two ladies that have been put to rest here, that were not here last year, Virginia Williams and Stella Holliday. Virginia Williams, I knew briefly, but she was a gentlewoman. Stella, my Stella, how I loved you in those three short months that we were together!* As Laura left the cemetery, she looked up and she saw the sign of the 'Summit County Hospital and Clinic.' Laura thought, *isn't it amazing, in a few short steps, I have moved from a place of death, to a place of life! This is where my beloved son Tylor was born. What a day of joy!* The lights were on at the school, as evidently the custodian was preparing the facility for a day of learning. *What memories! There was the spelling bee, and Hannah's graduation and her entry into her first year of high school. And who could forget those wretched dogs? And, who could forget that wretched woman with the willow switch?* As Laura moved on, once again, the whistle of the train interrupted her thoughts as it neared the crossing east of town. *In the silence of the morning, it sounds so sad, comparable to the playing of taps at a military funeral. Oh, God, send me a sign!* It was then that Laura came upon the 'First Episcopal Church.' She went in, expecting the morning light shining through the stained glass windows to fill the room as it did on her first visit, but there was none. Removing her shoes, she made her way to the altar. She kneeled down and prayed as she clutched her small son. Her prayer was simple as she cried out, "Oh, God, give me a sign! I ask of you, give me a sign! My heart is empty. Please touch me, God, please touch me." Getting to her feet, Laura went to the door and put on her shoes. Still clutching her son, she stepped from the church and returned home. Laying Tylor in his crib, she moved over to a small closet. Reaching in, she pulled her battered suitcase from the back of the closet and began to pack her clothes. As the tears streamed down her cheeks, she realized, *I came with one suitcase. Now there are two of us. After Tylor has his nap, we will get another suitcase.*

Laura reheated the coffee and sipped it, not realizing

what she was doing, it was as if she was in a trance. She got up to get herself some more coffee, only to realize that the pot was empty. Looking out the window, she saw large flakes of snow, drifting as if they were too light to fall to the ground. Laura decided to wait until after dinner to go to the Mercantile to purchase a suitcase. Suddenly, she had the answer to a difficult task. She was wondering how to tell Maude that she was leaving? It came to her that she would buy the suitcase and instead of bringing it home, she would stop by Maude's for coffee. Maude would ask about the suitcase, consequently, an opening for the conversation. I dread telling Maude that I am leaving and enduring the lecture from her as well.

A few minutes after two, Laura bundled up Tylor and left the apartment to go to the Mercantile. Laura was amazed at the snowfall and how slick it had become. Walking carefully, it wasn't long before she was looking at suitcases. There was not a great variety, but Laura found one that was similar in size to the one at home. As she left the store, Laura told Tylor, "Son, you now have your first suitcase. It will be known as 'Tylor's suitcase.' Take good care of it and it will last as long as mine has."

Arriving at Maude's, Laura paused at the door and took a deep breath. *Now, I have an idea how Daniel felt, when he was about to be thrown into the lions' den!* She opened the door and the aroma of the café struck her. It brought back memories of her first breakfast here.

Maude saw Laura coming in with one hand clutching Tylor stuck on one hip and the other hand in the handle of a new suitcase. "Well, well," she said. "Are you going somewhere?"

Laura took a deep breath, "Yes, we are. We are leaving tomorrow for Maine. I have come to say goodbye. However, I would like one more mug of free coffee before we go."

"It seems as if we played out this same scene over a year ago. You're running back to Maine. You didn't have anything to run back to last year and nothing has changed since. Face it! You are just running. Why don't you run to the next town. There is as much there as there is in Maine." Maude was moving about the counter, wiping it and then slamming the cloth back into the sink at the back of the room.

Laura remained calm. She had placed the suitcase by the coat rack near the door. Still holding Tylor, she went to the coffeepot and poured herself a mug of coffee. "Maude, I love you dearly, but I knew you would not understand. However, I knew that I must tell you that Tylor and I are leaving tomorrow evening. There is no employment here, so we are moving. I still have the apartment rented until the end of the month. I want you to have the bed linen and my kitchenware. You may dispose of them as you see fit. What are Hannah's needs at this time? I will take care of them before I leave. Also, I would appreciate it if Hannah would come to the apartment tomorrow right after school to watch Tylor, while I take the suitcases to the station. You are the only person that I have told. Please wait until Hannah comes home after school tomorrow afternoon to tell her that we are leaving. This is difficult for me and I only want to do it once. Perhaps you don't realize it, but I have no future in Summit City. I love you, Maude and it grieves me to leave you." Laura left her coffee untouched, as she cradled Tylor on her hip, stopping to take her suitcase and went out the door.

The next morning, Laura awakened to a severe headache as a result of a sleepless night. The snow had stopped during the night, but it was so wet that it created almost an ice-like surface on the streets and sidewalks. Laura visited with her landlord and informed him that she would terminate her lease at the end of the month. The morning seemed to drag on. Both suitcases were packed and waiting at the door. After lunch, Laura went to the bank. Mrs. Stahl was seated at her desk. Approaching her, Laura asked, "Mrs. Stahl, may I get into my two deposit boxes?"

"Yes," she said. "My goodness, it is certainly dreadful weather. The streets are ice coated. It seems unusual to have such icy weather this time of the year. I was hoping for an early spring."

Laura got into the boxes and retrieved her letters to Tylor from the one and her cash from the other. She recounted her money and compared it to her tally sheet of $360.00, which was correct. She also had her fifty dollar bill that had been in her Christmas stocking and Tylor's five silver dollars. She crammed all of this into her purse and returned the empty boxes to their slot. After leaving the bank, Laura went to the post office and purchased a stamped envelope. She placed the two keys in the envelope along with a note explaining that she no longer needed the deposit boxes. Laura sealed the envelope and dropped it in the mail slot.

Being extra careful, Laura returned to her apartment. She had cleaned and cleaned, making sure that it was spotless for the next tenant. Laura drank tea and paced the floor. Tylor watched his mother, while his mother watched the clock. Suddenly, Laura remembered her alarm clock. I didn't pack my alarm clock! Grabbing her suitcase, she placed it in one corner, disregarding what clothes she was wrinkling. She was careful to make sure that the alarm was not set.

Laura knew that school ended at 3:30, so Hannah will get here at no later than 3:45. That will give us 30 minutes to get to the station. That will be plenty of time. At 3:45, Laura wrapped Tylor in his blankets. And Laura waited and waited. "Where is that girl?" Laura said, as if someone was in the room to answer her.

At 4:05, Hannah rushed up the stairs. Gasping for breath,

she said, "Maude told me to get over here, as you were going to catch the train tonight. The teacher had me stay to help her. I'm sorry, Miss Martin."

"That's alright. Here, take this suitcase and this overnight bag. I will take Tylor and the other suitcase. If we hurry we can make it." Laura was closing the door, as she was finishing the last sentence. Running up the street, they saw the train pull into the station. Laura thought this is good, as we will make it. That is when she slipped on an icy patch of snow and fell to the ground. She turned loose of the suitcase and rolled, trying to protect Tylor as they fell together. The suitcase came open and her clothes were tossed in a heap. As she sat up, she saw that Tylor was unhurt, but her shoulder was bruised from cushioning the fall. As Laura struggled to get to her feet, they were close enough to hear the conductor yell "All aboard." The locomotive started to move the cars.

Hannah asked, "Miss Martin, are you all right? I'm sorry that I was late, but I didn't know, I didn't know. What are you going to do now?"

"Hold Tylor, and I will pick up my clothing," said Laura, as she handed Tylor to her. Laura made some effort to straighten her scattered clothing. She was thankful that the suitcase was not damaged beyond closing. Closing the suitcase, she said, "Hannah, we'll go on and I will leave our suitcases at the station so that I might claim them tomorrow. The train will run tomorrow and without the suitcases, Tylor and I will be here early. Thank you, Hannah."

They carefully walked to the station and inquired of the agent if she could leave the suitcases for tomorrow's boarding. When he heard of their struggles earlier, he agreed to leave them in the office area.

Laura and Hannah took their time returning to the

apartment. It was then that Hannah broke down and began to sob, "Please don't leave me, Miss Martin."

Laura hugged her, saying, "I must Hannah, I have no life here, I must."

Suddenly Hannah dried her tears, and laughed, "Miss Martin, I will always remember you as the lady that said everything twice."

Laura laughed too, "That's good, Hannah, that's good." Hannah left to go to Maude's. When she got to the corner, she turned and waved to Laura.

Laura was glad that she had the small bag with Tylor's necessary garments packed inside. She was beginning to feel some soreness from her fall, so she soaked in the tub before going to bed.

Laura slept late. She remained in the apartment until the time to go to the station. She and Tylor took their time and arrived safely with ample time to spare. In fact, the train was about fifteen minutes late. How ironic it is, as tonight I am anxious to leave and it is late, while last night I could have used the extra fifteen minutes.

Laura retrieved her suitcases and the conductor took them inside the coach where Laura had chosen to sit. A few seats back, Chase Adams was reading a newspaper. Glancing up, he noticed the woman carrying a small child as she entered the car. While she had a few minutes before the train was to depart, Laura and Tylor went to the back of the car. As she stood on the platform, she took one last look out over the city. *Oh, Summit City, a place of adventure, how I will miss you.* In the dusk of the evening, she thought that she saw a figure running up the street toward the station, waving their arms and hollering. It was then that the conductor yelled his usual 'All aboard.' Looking closer, Laura saw that it was Hannah, but she could not determine what she was hollering about. *Something is wrong! I need to get off this train!* She started down the steps, clutching Tylor to her bosom, yelling at the conductor. "Let me off this train!"

He was trying to stop her, telling her, "You can't leave now!"

Laura knocked his cap off and said, "If you don't let me off, I will jump!"

He brought his stool down and helped her to the ground, as he told her, "We won't wait for you!" He tossed his step on the platform. Picking up his cap, he signaled the engineer to start up.

Chase Adams heard the commotion to the rear of the car. As he stood to look out of the window, he saw that the woman and child had been left at the station. It was then that he saw the suitcases left behind. The one he recognized. It belonged to the beautiful woman with the red coat that had boarded the train at Madden over a year ago! *When will I see her again?*

CHAPTER 4
ONE FOOD, ONE PLATE, ONE PRICE

Laura was trying to get Tylor's blankets arranged, as Hannah came around the train station. Laura asked, "Hannah, what's the matter?" Hannah was so out of breath that she was bent over, gasping and trying to talk at the same time. "Take your time, Hannah. The next train won't be here for another 24 hours. The only thing that got on this train is our luggage. Now tell me, why are you here?"

"It's Maude. She was at the post office and fell." Still gasping, she continued, "They are sure that her leg is broken and they are checking for internal injuries. She hit her head and was unconscious for a little while. What will I do without Maude? Help me Laura!"

"We'll go into the station and see if I can get our luggage returned." Laura cradled Tylor on her hip and handed the small case to Hannah, as they went inside. The station agent agreed to telegraph ahead to the next station to pull the luggage off, so they might return it on the morning train.

"Let's go to the café. Right now we can help Maude that way and let Doctor Jessup do what he does best. Is Vera at the café?" Still out of breath, Hannah could only nod, indicating that is where Vera is, evidently taking care of the café while Maude went for her mail. "Now we can go help Vera with the evening patrons."

"Miss Martin," Hannah asked. "Why is it that you are so calm in all this and other times you get upset and tense? It's as if you are two different persons. Why?"

Laura was being cautious as they walked toward the main part of town. "Hannah, it is because I am two different persons.

Some things are difficult to explain, but this I see as self-evident. Yesterday, I was walking in my own strength. Because you were late, I was upset and consequently I missed the train. Had I been on that train, I would be nearing Chicago right now. Tonight, I was upset because the train was late and I was early. Had the train been on time, I would have been twenty miles down the line. All of your yelling and running would have been futile. I was trying to do things in my own strength. Right now, I am where God wants me. Yesterday morning, in my despondence, I asked God for a sign, but I didn't see one. Today, I have witnessed two signs. Now I am content to remain in Summit City to minister to Maude and help you through this until Maude recovers."

As they neared the café, Hannah rushed to open the door for Laura. Greeted by the tinkle of the bell, they entered the café. Laura noticed the first of the regular patrons had arrived for their evening meal. Vera looked up and exhibited the largest smile that Laura had ever witnessed coming from Vera, a rather stoic individual. Vera rushed to Laura, "Oh, Miss Martin, you are here, you are here. You have come to help us."

"Yes, Vera, I have come to help you and Hannah." Laura turned to Hannah and winked, "See, I'm not the only one to say things twice." Finding a comfortable and safe spot for Tylor, Laura asked Hannah and Vera, "What do you want me to do? Or, better yet, what do the two of you prefer to do? I am going to rely on the two of you to coordinate our efforts so that we can get through this evening without too much trouble. I'm sure that the customers will understand the situation when they find out that Maude is in the hospital. The other option would be to close the café for the evening."

Vera shrugged her shoulders, but Hannah spoke up, "It wouldn't be good to close up tonight. These people are counting on us to feed them. We may be a bit slower than usual, but they will understand. We don't want to send them to the other café in town. They might not return. Vera and I will handle the dining room if you will work the kitchen, Miss Martin. We understand the cash register, the order taking and the serving. Vera has spent more time in the kitchen than I, so if you get behind, Miss Martin, then Vera can help you until we get caught up. Let's grab an apron and get to work!" Laura was proud of the maturity that Hannah exhibited in this crisis.

They worked non-stop for three hours, with only a few mishaps. It was mostly a matter of Laura being unsure of the order. It was a little after eight and they had the kitchen and dining room cleaned. Hannah and Vera were in a mood of euphoria, having attained the impossible! Vera left to be with her family. Laura saw that Hannah was now feeling the let down of the earlier high. "Hannah, let's go to the hospital and see if we can learn of Maude's condition. We will sleep better, knowing how she is feeling."

"Oh, Miss Martin," said Hannah. "I do need to know how she is feeling. Can we go now, even before we have anything to eat?"

"We were so busy, that I forgot that we haven't had a bite to eat. But, let me feed Tylor, or once I stir him up, he will start to howl for his supper. And Hannah, now that we will be working together, you may call me Laura. When we are in a hurry, Miss Martin takes too long. Find yourself something to eat. Would you be so kind to brew me a cup of tea? I need to unwind slowly."

Hannah was excited as she fixed herself a peanut butter and jelly sandwich. "Here is your cup of tea, Laura," placing the cup where Laura could reach it. She gave Laura a big smile, realizing that they were no longer teacher-pupil, but equals.

As they stepped from the café, the night was clear and the snow cover made the night air cold. A full moon had made

89

its way past the eastern horizon and was now shining above the trees that lined the street. They were careful to make their way to the hospital. Laura and Hannah assisted one another to avoid a similar fall that had hospitalized Maude. When they entered the hospital, the nurse on duty stopped them. She said, "Visiting hours are over, so you will need to wait until tomorrow to come back. I'm sorry."

Tears came to Laura's eyes as she brought out her handkerchief to wipe the corners. "I understand the hospital policy, but I just got off the train this evening. I would have been here earlier, but it was late. I am Maude Dunham's daughter. Well, not by blood, but my sister and I would sleep much better tonight if we could see her for a few minutes."

The nurse hesitated. "I really shouldn't, but I understand how you must feel. She is in room 109, just to the left." Laura and Hannah started down the corridor and the nurse stopped them. "But the baby can't go in. Absolutely not!"

"No problem," said Laura. Handing Tylor to the nurse, "Would you please watch him for me? That way, we won't have to stay so long in the room. Thank you." Before the nurse could refuse, they were entering the room.

Maude looked up and saw Laura. She called out, "The prodigal child has returned! How kind of you to come and see your dying mother for one last time. And, I see that you have brought your sister as well. But, it is all for naught, for I have written you both out of the will." Holding out her arms, "Come, Laura, give me a hug." The nurse was still stunned by the brashness of the older sister. She hadn't returned to her desk, as she was straightening the blankets of the little tyke that had been handed to her. She could still hear the exchange of words as she returned to her desk.

Hugging Maude, she asked, "What have you done to

yourself?"

Doctor Jessup, entering the room, said, "Go ahead, Maude, tell her what you have done, or should I?" Not waiting for Maude to respond, the doctor proceeded to relate to Hannah and Laura, the extent of her injuries. "She has a fracture below the knee of the left leg. This will keep her off the streets of Summit City until the snow and ice has melted, or for three months, whichever comes last. She suffered a concussion, as she was still unconscious when admitted to the hospital. I don't think she has any broken ribs, but they are certainly sore. I am hoping not to wrap them, which would be uncomfortable. All of this is because she has been eating too much of her own cooking. Perhaps, if she would eat at her fellow competitor, she may lose a few of those pounds. Would you two 'daughters' see that she loses some weight in the next three months?" Leaving the room, he said, "Don't stay too long. She has had a rough day. Good night."

Laura turned to Maude and said, "We'll be going, but we wanted to let you know that the café is still open. One of us will be in to see you tomorrow."

"Wait a minute. I thought you and Tylor were going to Maine. What happened?"

"Until I give you more details, I missed one train and I jumped off the other. The main thing is that I am here. Tomorrow we will discuss how we will manage until we get you on your feet. Good night, Maude. We love you." Each of the girls kissed her cheek.

Laura stopped at the desk and retrieved her son. "Thank you for looking after him. I trust that he was a perfect gentleman."

"He was fine," the nurse said. As Laura and Hannah left the hospital, the nurse thought, *I have seen her before, yet it appears that she just came to Summit City tonight.*

After they got outside the entry door of the hospital, Hannah said, "I can't believe the way you lied your way to get in to see Maude. And that thing with the tears and bringing out your handkerchief, have you no shame!"

"Did I lie to that nurse? I told her that I had just got off the train this evening. However, I did fail to tell her that I was only on the thing for five minutes. And, I admitted that I was not a blood relative. Also, after working together this evening, are you denying that there wasn't a sisterhood established through our common cause? If anyone lied, it was Maude, when she called me a prodigal child and my bringing my sister with me. The only thing that I will admit to, the tears might have been a bit dry. I didn't see you offering to stay with Tylor while I visited Maude. If that is the night nurse, I don't want to see her again. She was the one that I had a bit of a run in with, when she was recording the data for Tylor's birth certificate. Oh well, it is done now. We need to figure out our sleeping arrangements when we get back. I don't want you to stay at Maude's alone. Tomorrow, we'll need to determine where to put Maude when she comes home, as she won't be able to climb the stairs. Tylor and I will sleep in Maude's room for the night. We'll get the crib from my apartment along with the linens and personal items. I fear that we have a number of decisions to make in the next day or two. I'm ready to find a good soft bed."

When Laura went into Maude's bedroom, she remembered that her trusty alarm clock was still in her suitcase, somewhere sitting in a baggage room of the railroad company. She located Maude's clock and set it at 6:00 a.m. This was early enough for a Saturday, as she knew that Maude didn't open until seven. Laura was exhausted. As she lay in bed, she prayed for Maude that she might have a restful night. She thanked the Lord for His direction in the events of the day. However, in thanking Him, she dropped off to sleep, only to be awakened by the alarm.

The last thing she remembered was praying. And now, it is time to get up. What a short night!

Laura hurriedly dressed. As she started down the steps, she saw that the lights were on in the dining room. As she went into the kitchen, there was Hannah, making the morning coffee. Laura thought *what maturity. Last year at this time, I was urging her along, trying to get her out of bed in the morning. I must remember, this is Hannah's domain. I will let Hannah be the leader.*

"Good morning, Hannah," Laura said. "What can I do to help you this morning?"

"Good morning, Laura. It would be good if you could start making up the pancake batter, while I work on the biscuits. Also, we have a number of people that order biscuits and gravy. I remember that you make excellent gravy, so you can start on that after the pancake batter is stirred up. I asked Vera to come in at seven to help us serve. Grab a cup of coffee, as we will be busy until nine o'clock."

At eight o'clock, Laura gave a start! "My son! I have forgotten my Tylor! What kind of a mother am I?" She went to the stairs, taking them two at a time. Tylor heard his mother and was eager to see her. He wasn't the least bit unhappy about being neglected. She changed him and fed him, knowing that he could have eaten more. After washing up, Laura took him downstairs with her. Her next thought was, *what am I going to do with him? I need to be working in the kitchen, but I need to be with him, too.*

Three elderly ladies sitting near the window saw Laura with Tylor. The one with a cane hooked over her chair asked Laura, "May I hold him? I see that you are busy and I would enjoy holding such a handsome baby."

"Certainly," said Laura, happy that she had found

someone to entertain him, if only for a short time. "His name is Tylor. He is five months old and he likes to be cuddled. Thank you for helping out. With Maude in the hospital, it is difficult to keep up. Already we miss her at the café." She handed Tylor to the lady. He looked her over, giving her a charming smile.

True to Hannah's prediction, they were busy until nine. Most of the morning customers had left, except for the three ladies that were entertaining Tylor. Laura had informed Vera to keep their coffee cups full, so that they might remain until the café had cleared out.

"I have an idea," said Vera. "We have kind of a playpen at home that we don't need any more. If you want, I could have my husband bring it over. If Tylor is left unattended, he could be in there. It has a soft mattress and he'll be able to look out."

"That sounds great, Vera." Laura was excited that Tylor wouldn't have to be left alone. "Vera, would your husband be able to stop at my apartment and get Tylor's crib. I have let my apartment go back, so I will need to get it cleaned out. I will pay him if he would bring it here."

"That's no problem. I'm glad to help out. Maude is good to me to give me work. We would be happy to bring the playpen and crib in one trip. Let me finish my coffee and we will meet you at your apartment at ten o'clock. What is the address?"

"127 River Street and it is upstairs. I will meet you at ten."

After the apartment was cleaned out and the crib and playpen were set up, it was time for the dinner crowd. Fortunately, it was light, as Hannah had expected. Laura was glad for the light duty, as she wasn't used to the café life. As they were finishing with the cleanup, Hannah said, "Vera, would you work this afternoon, as I will do the shopping for next week. Laura, this might be a good time for you to visit Maude and then I will go after supper. In all probability, you will not have to encounter the nurse that was on duty last night. Please be careful. I'm referring to your walk to the hospital and not your habitual lying."

"That will be fine, but you may want to go early tonight, as I will not be there to assist your entry into the hospital after hours." Laura picked up Tylor and then she remembered that he couldn't go into Maude's room. Laura said, "Vera, would you mind keeping an eye out for Tylor? I won't stay long and then if you need to go home for a while, I can relieve you."

"That's fine," said Vera, as she handed him one of his stuffed toys that he instantly put in his mouth. "We'll do fine. Just take your time."

Laura enjoyed her walk to the hospital. It was her first opportunity to be outside of the café. The sun was shining in a cloudless sky. It was still cold, but the rays of the sun warmed a person if they were fortunate to walk on the sunny side of the street. Laura thought, *wasn't there a song about the 'sunny side of the street?'*

Maude was awake and glad for the company. Her first question was not about the café, as Laura imagined she would ask, but she asked Laura, "Knowing your history, I need to know how it is that you are not in Maine, instead of the Sandhills? The last time I saw you, you were bent on leaving, as you felt that there was nothing here for you. What changed?"

"My last morning I was here, I walked the city, recalling my first morning here. I entered the Episcopal Church and begged God for a sign. I didn't want to leave, but as I had told you, I saw no reason for staying. I was a failure in the sea of love. I dearly loved Tylor's father, but that was a failure. I tell you this in confidence, but I was deeply in love with David Riggs. Unfortunately, that did not come to pass. Of all my loves, David and I were the most compatible. We were both educated and had so much in common. We were both outsiders, as we were not natives of the Sandhills. I have no doubt that David loved me as well." She paused a moment, as if she was collecting her thoughts before continuing. "And then there is Ken Holliday, yes, Ken Holliday. I don't know if I loved Ken, or just respected him. I so enjoyed his company. We were thrown together in the strangest of circumstances. He had Stella's blessing to take me as his wife. To this day, I don't know if Ken had any feelings for me. In another time and another place, yes, I could have made him happy. You must think I am fickle to have an interest in three men in a year's time. All I can say, I am a woman of passion. I desire the company of a man. I don't deem myself as immoral, for I respect the bonds of marriage, but I seek to have a man to hold me and tell me that he loves me. I ask myself, is that so terrible?"

Laura continued, "I was to leave on the evening train. I had my money and my bags packed. I don't know if Hannah told you, but as she was helping me catch the evening train, I fell. By the time I recovered, the train had left. I left my bags at the station so the next day I wouldn't be dependent upon anyone helping me. I arrived in plenty of time, but this time, the train was late. I was at the rear of the car, taking one last look at Summit City when I saw Hannah running and waving her arms. I knew that something was wrong, that I had to get off the train. The train left without me, taking my bags with it. Unfortunately, I have yet to recover my two suitcases. When I learned of your fall, it was then that I knew that God had put obstacles in my path to hinder me from leaving Summit City. I see that as a sign from God that I'm not to leave Summit City. Incidentally, I have moved into your bedroom until we find a suitable place for you."

Maude smiled, "I'm glad that you didn't leave. Call me selfish if you will, but I have never wanted you to leave.

96

I remember the story of the prodigal son and the father killing the fatted calf when he returned. Had I not been in the hospital, I would have killed the fatted calf for the return of my prodigal daughter. Laura, I have loved you since that first night you came into my home. Sometimes you irritate me to tears, but I can't help loving you."

Laura blushed, "Maude, you embarrass me. Speaking of daughters, the faithful daughter Hannah is amazing! She has taken over the café, giving orders left and right, however in a gentle manner. Right now, she is filling the grocery order for next week. I'm in the kitchen and Vera and Hannah are running the dining room. I'm proud of the leadership that Hannah is exhibiting. You have trained her well. Now, tell me, when are you getting out of here?"

"I'm still experiencing headaches from my concussion. However, I need to master the crutches. Once that is done, I can go home. Doctor Jessup anticipates that I will only need to stay about a week. I imagine that the hospital staff will be as glad to be rid of me, as I will be glad to get out of here."

"Maude," Laura began, "I don't want you to be mad at me for what I am about to ask, but do you have sufficient funds to pay for your doctor and hospital? I have some extra money and I would be glad to help pay what I have towards your medical bills."

"Laura," Maude started to respond before the tears began to make it difficult for her to speak. "That is what I just said, you irritate me to tears and now I have trouble thanking you. Laura, I hope that one day you have great wealth. For if you do have wealth, you will be a great philanthropist. For in your poverty, you are generous beyond all imagination. Thank you for your offer. The café has been good to me." Maude tugged at her bedcovers, mostly to regain her composure. "Laura, don't try to do too much at the café. If I can't run it, I may need to sell the building and the business. This is what happens when you get old."

"Maude, you are not old! Don't do anything rash until you have given some thought to what you have just said. Once you get out of here, the world will take on an entirely different perspective. Things will get better. In fact, the sun is shining and the snow will soon melt. Besides, Hannah, Vera and I will do our best. Count on it!"

Maude turned her face to the wall. She waved Laura off, as if she was dismissing her.

Standing by the bed, she kissed Maude's cheek "I love you. I will leave now and Hannah will probably be here after supper. Bye." Laura left the room, somewhat discouraged by Maude's mood. She realized that selling the café brought Maude's emotions to the surface. Selling the café is not what Maude wants, but she sees no other alternative at the moment.

As Laura stepped out onto the sidewalk in front of the hospital, she could feel the change in the weather. The wind had increased, but yet the air was cool, which surprised Laura, as she noticed that the snow was beginning to melt. It is near the time for the afternoon coffee trade. As Laura reached the door to go in, she noticed a new red pickup truck parked diagonally to the curb. *Let me guess, that must be a Ford.* As John Wesley Schumacher would say, 'Miss Martin, this is Ford country.'

As Laura shed her coat and hung it on the peg near the door, she went behind the counter. Grabbing her gingham apron, she fumbled with the strings as she tied them behind her back. She saw that Vera was with a customer to the rear of the room. As she looked up, she saw that the pickup occupants had come in and were approaching the counter. As they were sitting on the stools, she recognized them as Jim McCann and Tag Taggat of the 99 Ranch. "Good afternoon, Gentlemen, how may I help you?"

Tag was the first to speak. "Well, if it isn't the little school teacher! How about giving us some of that charm of yours?" He turned to Jim to see if his remark amused him. Jim gave a token smile to show that he was amused.

"Why, Mr. Taggat," Laura said, as she reached for the coffee mugs and started to pour their coffee. "I'm glad to give you my charm free of charge. However, I must insist that you order something from the menu. We can't have you sitting on our stools and resting your elbows on the counter, just to soak up the free charm. Now, I have poured your coffee and according to Sandhills tradition, when two cowboys meet at a café, they will order pie and coffee. What kind of pie would you like?" She handed them their coffee, making sure that the sugar and cream was nearby. "We have two kinds this afternoon, cherry and apple."

Cherry was their pie of choice.

As they each added the sugar and cream to their coffee, carefully stirring it, Laura asked them, "Are you two fellows still in the third grade, or has the school revised their advancement policy?"

Tag smiled and said, "Careful, your charm is running thin."

"I'm sorry. I didn't realize that you were touchy about your education." Laura was having fun needling Tag, as much as he enjoyed baiting her. "Tell me, have you had anymore 'wrecks' lately?"

Jim McCann jerked, spilling coffee down his chin and the front of his shirt. Tag got real red in the face. Laura was wishing that she hadn't brought up the incident at the Good Hope School when the horses were entangled and both men ended in the dirt.

Tag turned to Jim. "You told her, didn't you?" Jim was brushing his chin with a napkin and trying to dry off his shirt and shaking his head, indicating that he hadn't told Laura, whatever Tag was talking about.

Laura apologized. "I'm sorry for bringing up that unfortunate incident, but that has been almost a year ago." Laura stopped. "Or, has there been another incident that I need to hear about?" Now, Laura was being charming and showing interest in their mishap.

Tag bent over the counter, leaning closer to Laura. "I will tell you about our latest 'wreck,' but you had better not repeat it. That is why I am telling you, in the hope that you do. Then I can come back and wring your neck for telling. Is that fair enough?"

"That sounds fair to me! Let's hear all about it." Laura was excited.

Tag's demeanor had changed, as if he was glad to be telling Laura about his and Jim's latest 'wreck.' "Yesterday afternoon, Jim and I had been to Madden. We were taking the shortcut by the Carlin place and coming down the long hill to where we would cross the railroad tracks. I saw the train nearing the crossing and I had no intention of beating it there. The road was rutted, and with the ice storm of the previous day, I began to apply the brakes." Tag was now beginning to enjoy telling his story. He chuckled, as he went on. "I pushed on those brakes, but we continued on. The wheels were locked up, but we continued to slide. I then tried to turn the steering wheel, but we were in the ruts and sliding as if we were on a bobsled run. We weren't going fast, but it was as if everything was in slow motion. I was watching that train getting closer and closer to the crossing. I thought perhaps, it would pass before we would get to the crossing. I put the truck in low gear and turned off the motor, but we kept getting closer and closer. I hollered to Jim, 'jump,' as we were almost there."

Laura looked over at Jim and he was enjoying the recounting of the story, as well. Tag continued. "When you are wearing a heavy coat and overshoes, it is difficult to make a graceful exit. I ended over by the fence, with my coat snagging in the wire. I looked at Jim and he looked like a snowman. Looking toward the crossing, I saw our pickup truck sliding between the front and rear wheels of the last freight car. It sheared the front off, back to the motor. Then, the caboose had the last bite, crushing part of the motor. The engineer knew what was going to happen, but couldn't stop in time. He filled out an accident report. With the crew and us, we were able to get our truck out of the way. They gave us a ride to my cousin's ranch four miles east of the wreck. The conductor was upset, as it was going to make the train late getting to Summit City. We just picked up our new truck on our way home. We stopped here for pie and coffee. And now, we have been subjected to your ridicule, which certainly exceeds your charm!"

Suddenly, Laura leaned toward the counter with her fingers stretched forward. She placed them around his neck and pulled Tag forward, placing a kiss on his cheek. "Thank you, Tag, thank you. You have saved my life!" She then explained some of the events, leading to her desire to go to Maine and the need to be here with Maude. "The delay of the train is what made this possible. You have truly saved my life! Gentlemen, the pie and coffee are on the house. It is my treat."

Jim and Tag accepted her offer of the pie and coffee. Tag, in all his brashness, seemed somewhat embarrassed by Laura's kiss. Laura thought, *I might have kissed his forehead, but these Sandhills cowboys wear their hat all the time. I rarely see them without them, except in church. I wonder if Tag wears his hat to bed.*

101

Hannah visited Maude that night after supper. Laura was extremely tired, so she and Tylor went to bed early. Laura wanted to go to the Episcopal Church tomorrow. The café didn't serve meals on Sunday, which was good, considering that Laura needed a break from the kitchen cooking and cleaning. She made a special effort after her bath to lotion her hands and pull on her cotton flannel gloves. She didn't hear Hannah come home from visiting Maude.

Laura did awaken in the night to hear the wind, as it blew through the trees and rattled the windows. Awakening at dawn, she looked out, amazed that much of the snow was gone and the streets were flowing with the runoff.

At breakfast, Laura commented to Hannah, "When I looked out, I was surprised that so much of the snow was gone. When I heard the wind last night, I feared that a blizzard had moved in to give us snow on top of snow. I was expecting the worst. That was an unusual wind."

Hannah said, "The wind is referred to as a 'chinook'. It often occurs in early spring and is a welcome sight, as it melts the winter snow. Many people mistakenly call it a chinook wind, which is incorrect, as chinook means, 'a dry warm wind.' Consequently, if you refer to a chinook wind, in reality you are saying, 'a dry warm wind wind.' If you capitalized the word, it would refer to a member of a Native American people who once lived in the Northwest. The correct spelling of the word is c-h-i-n-o-o-k. Do you have any questions regarding the word chinook?"

"I think not," said Laura. "You covered the subject quite thoroughly, thank you. I was uncertain of the spelling and the meaning of the climatologically reference to the word. You are quite precise. Thank you."

Laura continued as she asked, "Hannah, what are your

plans for the day? Tylor and I are going to church at The First Episcopal Church. Would you care to accompany us? As for dinner, I am not particular, as probably a search of the refrigerator will be sufficient for us. Two days in the kitchen has damaged my taste buds, and especially if I have to do much preparation to make the food look edible."

"I have need of schoolwork to be prepared for Monday, so I will pass on going to church." Hannah continued to spoon her cereal. She poured herself a second glass of milk. Looking over at Tylor, she said. "I hereby appoint Tylor as my ecclesiastical representative for the day. If I am to miss school to help in the café, I need to work in advance as far as I can. Sorry, I won't be going with you."

"No, no, no!" Laura was emphatic. "There will be no missing school!"

"Miss Martin, oops, I mean Laura, you are serious. You said 'no' three times." Then Hannah laughed, mocking Laura.

"I am serious," shouted Laura. "Your education to date has come as a huge sacrifice. You are certainly not going to neglect it for the sake of a few people of this city and their appetite. We need to come up with a plan. The first few hours after Maude's mishap were spent in panic as how we might keep the café operating, regardless of the cost. Think, Hannah, think! How can we make a profit for Maude, with as little effort on our part as possible? While Maude is in the hospital and even those days while she is home, we can't expect much help from her. With you at school, how can Vera and I run the café?"

"Laura, you are asking me a question," Hannah said, "that you already have the answer to in your own mind. All right, what is the answer?"

"The answer is simplistic volume with one food, one plate and one price. The first night that I was at the Hollidays,

I was preparing to leave after my house cleaning duties were complete. Mr. Holliday asked if I could prepare something for supper, as he was at a loss as to know what to prepare, let alone how to prepare a meal. I found things in the refrigerator and made spaghetti with a sauce containing hamburger. For dessert I served fruit cocktail. As a side, there was bread and cheese. When I returned from tending to Mrs. Holliday, the spaghetti was gone and I accused the children of feeding it to the dog. Tara said that they didn't have a dog and the next time to make more of the spaghetti. Now it is a family favorite. What do you think Hannah, does that have merit? If need be, we could return to the menu for the evening meal when all three of us are available. Normally we would be charging more for the menu items, because it is more specialized than the 'one size fits all' noon meal."

Hannah nodded her head. "It sounds good. Do we need to clear it with Maude before we begin? She is a bit fussy if there is any deviation from the norm, particularly the menu items. If it isn't on the menu, don't ask. I would rather have you discuss it with her. I will beg off that I have homework to do. Besides, you have a way of bringing an idea to someone so that they think it originated with them. Consequently they express no objections to it whatsoever."

"All right," Laura said, "but you realize that I have been telling Maude how you are the one in charge at the café. Vera and I are the subordinates following your orders. If I see that the plan is failing, I will tell Maude that it is your brainchild and then she will approve. You are the favored child. Tylor and I will see her after church. We will be getting ready now, as we need to be on our way."

Laura's mood was much different than when she was at the church only a few days earlier. That morning she was troubled. This morning, she was at peace with God. Unless God directed her otherwise, Summit County was her home. *It is odd that this would come to my mind this morning, but I have lived in this county for more than a year. I need to register as a citizen, with the right to vote when an election is held.* Laura suddenly sat up. *What is the matter with me, here I am in God's house of worship and I am daydreaming about voting!* After her personal reprimand, she continued with her mind focused on the morning message.

Before returning to the café, Laura was planning to see Maude, when she realized that Tylor couldn't go into the hospital, so she continued to the cafe. Laura would return to the hospital after putting Tylor down for a nap. Hannah could listen for him, if he should awaken.

It was almost two o'clock before Laura was able to leave Tylor. It was good that she had been delayed as Maude had been napping after her dinner.

Laura entered the room and saw that Maude was trying to sit up somewhat, despite the awkwardness of her cast. Laura said, "Maude, you look rested. How are you feeling?"

Maude waved her hand, "So far, so good. The headaches have stopped and the ribs are not as sore. Now, if I could take the cast off, I would be ready to go home."

"Not so fast," said Laura. "We haven't finished renovating the place as yet. I left Hannah looking after Tylor, as they forbid his coming to see you. Right now, she should be studying for school tomorrow. I wanted to check with you first, but she wants to stay out of school tomorrow to help Vera and me at the café. What are your thoughts on her missing school?"

"Laura, why do you ask me a question like that? That is totally ridiculous. Knowing you, the question of her staying out of school has already been answered. What did you tell her?" Maude fussed with her sheet and blanket, as she awaited Laura's answer. Laura looked at Maude, rather innocent like.

"All right," Laura said. "I told her 'no, no, no!' As her guardian, I wanted to be sure that you would agree with me first. Maude, there is no way that I can fool you. You are too clever for me. I need to alter my strategy with you."

"Knowing now," Laura continued, "that there is no fooling you, I will hit you head on with my next idea. Originally, I was going to bring it forth under the guise that it was Hannah's idea. If it failed, then it was her fault. Now that your head no longer hurts, I will tell you of the plan to keep the café open, with Hannah in school, you in the hospital and Vera and me at work. I refer to it as 'simplistic volume. That is, one food, one plate and one price. Each day at noon, we feature one entrée. For example; Spaghetti and meatballs, with a side of a dinner roll and cheese, served with a small bowl of fruit cocktail. That would be the special for Monday. For Tuesday, ham sandwich and bean soup, with a brownie. Each meal would come with either coffee or tea. I could serve up the plate. Vera could do the serving and handle the cash register. What do you think Maude? Can it work? As it is, I am not familiar enough with menu meal preparation to keep up the pace, particularly with the two of us. I am the weakest link in the chain."

"Laura, sometimes it is good for a different person to come in and take a fresh look at the situation." Maude smiled as she pondered Laura's idea. She continued to give it more thought. "I have been babying everyone, trying to make them happy and in the meantime, I was wearing Vera and myself down. With me out of the picture, this is an ideal time to try it out. If there are any complaints, just tell them that with Maude out of the kitchen, you can't keep up and this is the best that you can do."

"Maude, can you come up with the menus and the pricing for five days? My thought was to be repetitive, so that our guests will know in advance that Monday is spaghetti day and so forth. I think that we can handle the breakfasts all right. The supper hour is sometimes extended and of course, Hannah will be there to help out. She is excellent help. It is a joy to work with her. Can you imagine that a year ago, she was so withdrawn? Now a leader in the freshman class at school?"

"Laura, I want you to make up the menus," said Maude. "You know what you will feel comfortable with cooking. You have cooked enough at the Hollidays to have an idea of what people might like and also that you are comfortable with preparing. Give me a list and I will do the pricing. I sense that we each have an idea of the serving size needed to provide a good meal. I like the idea of each day of the week being the same. That way, if they don't like something, they may choose to eat at home, or vice versa. If we have a favorite, they may choose to show up that day. Also, once started, it will give us a general idea of how much to prepare each day. If it works well, we may want to include Saturdays, or make Saturday a special day with a varied menu."

"I am happy that you like the idea," Laura said. "It isn't always that we agree with one another, but thanks for the support."

"What do you mean?" asked Maude. "What have we not agreed upon? Just tell me one thing that I have not supported you fully and been in complete agreement with you? I take that back. When it comes to your personal life, you have an extreme tendency to make bad judgments. You give excellent counsel to others, but at times Laura, your life is a disaster. If it wasn't for your closeness to God, you would self-destruct. I do believe that He looks after you so that you might minister to others."

"Maude, you surprise me! Then you acknowledge that God does work in our daily lives to guide and direct us." Laura

107

was encouraged in the direction of this conversation with Maude. Usually she brushed off any reference to God.

"He does in yours, but I don't believe that He does in mine. Laura Martin, in the eyes of God, you are special!" Laura sensed that Maude was getting serious, simply by the way she was moving about on her bed and smoothing her blanket.

Laura reached out and took Maude's hand. "You are right. God sees me as special. So special that He sent His Son, Jesus Christ to die in my place. He paid the penalty for my sin so that I would be able to share heaven with Him."

Maude withdrew her hand from Laura's. "That is enough of that religious talk. Go on. Tell Hannah I want to see her!" Maude turned her face to the wall, dismissing Laura.

"Maude, I'm sorry if I have offended you. That is not my intention. I love you." Laura left the room, trying to get down the hall, before she burst into tears. The tears were not for herself, but for her friend Maude. *Laura remembered last Thanksgiving when her friends were embarrassed, as she expressed her love for her Saviour. By their silence they rebuked her, but later the fruit of righteousness was bestowed upon Stella, as she submitted her life to Jesus Christ before her death.*

When Laura returned to the café, she said, "Hannah, Maude wants you to come to see her. I fear that I may have upset her. I didn't mean to be judgmental, but as we were talking about God and His Son, Jesus Christ, I have apparently offended her. I did apologize to her, but she soon dismissed me. Before you go, I will get the menu for tomorrow for her to determine a price for the meal. If you could wait for her to come up with the cost, then I will start to determine the kitchen needs for the Monday dinner. Also, ask how many people we need to prepare for dinner each day of the week. Maybe she has that written down someplace, or possibly, all those things are in her head."

Hannah said, "It sounds as if you did get approval for your one plate dinners. I will leave in about thirty minutes, so if you have something, I will take it to her. It would be great if you were to have all the menus for Maude to work on. It just might be that being confined to a hospital bed has made her testy. Don't worry about it if she is upset. I have learned that she soon gets over it."

Laura began to work on the menus:

Monday: Spaghetti with a hamburger base tomato sauce. (I thought of meatballs, but then, people begin to count meatballs and that is not good.) Two dinner rolls with grated cheese available at the table, and fruit cocktail. Coffee or tea is included with the price of the meal.

Tuesday: Hot ham and cheese sandwich with bean soup. Apple pie with tea or coffee.

Wednesday: Roast beef dinner, with mashed potatoes and gravy. Cooked carrots and peas mixed. Two dinner rolls. Two cookies with tea or coffee.

Thursday: Sauerkraut and wieners, with two dinner rolls. Cherry cobbler with whipped cream. Tea or coffee.

Friday: Vegetable beef soup (using the left over beef from Wednesday, planning to be heavy on the beef). Two dinner rolls. A brownie with a small scoop of ice cream. Tea or coffee.

Laura included a note to Maude along with the menus. "Look these over, and make whatever changes you think will work. Scrap an entire menu at your pleasure. However, if you do, be prepared to have one to replace it."

Hannah didn't return from the hospital until almost six o'clock. Laura was concerned, as it had been dark for some time. When she arrived, Laura asked her, "What took you so long,

Hannah? I was concerned that something might have happened to you. How was Maude?"

"She was fine after she saw me." Hannah put her arms around Laura. "She sends her love and to tell you that she was sorry that she dismissed you so abruptly. She admires your faith."

Hannah brought a paper from her coat pocket and showed it to Laura. "The only thing she suggested was to put the dinner rolls in a bowl on the table, an average of one and one-half per person. Each person will probably not eat two rolls."

Laura was excited and was up early Monday morning. She missed her alarm clock, hoping that it was at the railroad station. *When Hannah comes home from school, I will send her after the suitcases. Also, I need to go to the bank to see if I can reclaim my deposit boxes.* Laura brought Tylor downstairs with her and after he had nursed, he finished his sleep in the playpen. She was amazed that he was such a good baby.

Hannah came down to make the coffee and give what help she could before going to school. Vera came in right at seven and she and Laura kept busy until 8:30, when the crowd moved out, except for a few late coffee drinkers. Laura had started the dinner rolls, but had to go to the grocery store for a few herbs and additional spaghetti for the noon meal. Vera was excited about the one food, one plate and one price idea. Laura had printed on the blackboard the menu for each day and the price. Each day had been priced the same, as Maude had determined that it would even out and would be easy to remember. Maude anticipated that they would have 25 guests. They had served 26 by one o'clock. Laura had fixed for 30, so she had a little left. When she saw that they had all of the paying customers they would have, she brought out the remainder and offered seconds for those still there. That made them happy. Laura told them, "Now next week, don't come late expecting an extra helping, as

110

it might be gone by the time you show up." She had anticipated two dinner rolls per person. They ate all of that and probably would have had more if they hadn't run out.

While they were cleaning up, Vera said, "Laura, that was the easiest dinner crowd that I have ever served. I'm glad that I ate early. The spaghetti was great. Perhaps we are so beef oriented in the Sandhills that we forget that there are other foods. I'm looking forward to the Thursday menu when we serve the sauerkraut and wieners"

"Vera," Laura asked, "I know that you usually go home for a few hours before the supper trade, but could you watch things while I go to the bank? I shouldn't be gone long. Could I leave Tylor with you, as it would speed my task a great deal?"

"Of course, take your time, as he is no problem. I enjoy watching him, as he seems so content with life."

Laura left the café, but didn't go directly to the bank. Taking a side trip, she paid her respects to her beloved Dismal River, announcing to it, "I'm back. Did you miss me?" She was anxious to see it, as the heavy runoff was at its peak, as the results of the chinook that had moved into the Sandhills and melted the ice-crusted snow. Determined that she had tarried long enough, she made her way to the bank. As she was entering the bank, Ken followed her into the bank lobby. "Good afternoon, Laura," he said. "Do you have a moment to visit with me?"

"Certainly," Laura was pleased that he would take time for her. "How are things at the Holliday household? Is Mrs. Baker working out for you?"

"Oh, she is doing quite well. She is enjoying her new home here in Summit City. I imagine she would welcome a visit from you when you find it convenient. There is something that I want to ask you, if you don't mind," Ken said, as he started for his desk. Laura followed him and nodded to Mrs. Stahl as she passed her desk.

Ken indicated for her to have a seat. Laura noticed that he was somewhat ill at ease, so she started the conversation. "What did you wish to see me about?"

"Have I, or anyone at the bank offended you, Laura? I was somewhat puzzled by your note and the return of your deposit keys. What has happened?" Laura saw that he was concerned at the loss of a bank customer.

Laura laughed, "No, Ken, no one has offended me. If you had, I am not one to pout. I would have confronted you about the offense. In fact, I am here begging for your mercy. Last week, in one of my crazy moments, I decided to move back to Maine. Not wanting to make a scene, nor willing to give an explanation as to why I had emptied my deposit boxes, I thought it would be simpler to mail the keys to the bank. I never got out of town. Now, I am begging for my deposit boxes back. I am prepared to start over with a new lease. Only last month, I had renewed the lease on my first box. I need two deposit boxes and you are the only bank in town. I have no other choice than to start anew."

"I'm glad you had a change of heart and didn't leave. Summit County wouldn't be the same without Laura Martin and her son, Tylor." Standing up, he said, "Let me get your keys and we will start where you left off. If I might ask, why would you even think of leaving the Sandhills?"

"That is a good question, Ken." Laura said. "I wasn't thinking. Circumstances changed things. You probably know that Maude broke her leg and Tylor and I are staying there. I'm helping at the restaurant, but I'm no Maude. We hope to get her home by the end of the week, but she will be laid up for about three months. But tell me, how are Tara and Todd? Tell them I miss them and I do believe that Tylor misses them as well. The café is Maude's livelihood and we are trying so desperately to keep it solvent during the time that she is unable to work. Should you miss my cooking, stop in and eat with us. Today we started featuring only one item on the dinner menu. Today was spaghetti, a spin-off from my first night concoction at the Holliday house. It seemed to go well. Thanks for reinstating me as a bank customer."

Ken smiled, as it was good to see Laura again. *We have been through so much together. She doesn't realize how much I have missed her and her enthusiasm for life.* "I'm sure you realize that we were saddened when you returned the keys. We had lost our biggest challenge in trying to sign you up to a checking account."

"Of course," replied Laura. "Why else would I come back, but to renew the challenge? You don't know how difficult it is to refuse, time after time. I must go now, but thanks." Laura left to put her cash and documents in the deposit boxes and hurried back to the café so that Vera might spend a few moments at home.

Laura started cleaning the beans for the next day's soup. Hannah arrived from school. As soon as she had her milk and two cookies, Laura sent her for the suitcases. She was happy to have her possessions in custody, especially her treasured alarm clock. Laura asked Hannah, "We have a short time before the supper hour. Would you rather visit Maude before or after we are through with the cleanup? I know that she gets lonesome, so it is well if we each visit her every day."

"My intent is to visit her while you and Vera are cleaning up the kitchen," said Hannah. "I have homework when I return, so to avoid being late to bed, I will have an early start on the homework."

"That is quite logical, but better yet, go visit her now and all three of us will work on the cleanup. Then you can do your homework while I visit her. No matter who stays home, or when, that person will look after Tylor. It is too bad that he can't take a turn at some task as well."

Hannah started towards the door, when she turned. She said to Laura, "Living with you is a lot like a chess game. Every move I make, you are there with a checkmate. At least in chess, I win more than I lose." Before Laura could answer her, she was out the door.

By the time Hannah crossed the street, she was laughing. Now Laura won't know what to think, was I mad or not. If she thought that she had made me mad, she will be apologetic. Otherwise, she will just add fuel to the fire and chide me all the more.

Maude was looking forward to someone visiting her from the café. Two ladies that had dinner there, had stopped to see her after they had eaten. They had given a good report on the meal. They had mentioned however, that they could have had another dinner roll, had it been available. They were surprised how quickly they were served. Maude reported all this to Hannah, as they visited. "Hannah," Maude said, "sometimes Laura irritates me when she talks about how she looks to God for guidance. Do you think God cares about us mortals?"

"I don't know Maude," Hannah said, "but I'm sure that Laura does. I can't say that she has lived a charmed life, but her life has been interesting. What is a mystery to me is what brought her to the Sandhills? If God cares so much for her, why did she get pregnant, which resulted in her losing her job as a teacher? But, she sees the pregnancy as a joy, in that she has Tylor. I don't want to demean working in a café, but she is so much better suited in the classroom. I can still see her with Mrs. Holliday, covered with her blood as she continued to cough it up. Then she changed Stella's clothes and bathed her. She has a compassion for people. In my own case, my stepfather wouldn't let my mother give her anything for taking care of me. She bought me clothes and undergarments, but I mostly remember when I ran away from home. She was so big and heavy with child, but she was on the floor, washing my feet. They were dirty and bloody and her concern was that she was hurting me. I thought that someday she might marry Mr. Holliday, but now I'm not sure. We have talked about when you get well. I said it would be nice that we will all be together. She said 'no, that could not be, as it would mean that Vera would have to leave.' She wouldn't allow that to happen, as Vera probably needs this job. From time to time, she will tell me, Hannah, ask for God to bless you today and look for God's blessing. When you learn to look for and recognize the blessings of God, you will be blessed!"

"Perhaps there is something to it, as we don't recognize when we are blessed. We have her and she only has us. And yet, she would say that she is the one that has been blessed." Maude just shook her head in disbelief.

Hannah said, "I need to run. That is what I have been doing since I arrived home from school. Laura had me go to the railroad station to retrieve her suitcases. She was more concerned about her alarm clock than she was her clothes."

"Yes, that alarm clock. I was with her when she bought it at Shaw's Hardware. We laughed, as it was her top priority, even more than the clothes. She wanted to make sure that she didn't oversleep. Thanks for coming to visit me. I get lonesome away from the café. Good bye, Hannah."

Laura greeted Hannah at the door. "Oh, Hannah, I'm sorry that I spoke harshly to you. Vera and I will clean up and you can study. We will soon be through the supper hour. I want you to do well in school." Now Hannah felt bad the way she had acted towards Laura.

This was the third day that they had worked together and it was beginning to look like a team. Laura was picking up on the cooking side. There were fewer mistakes than the other two nights. Hannah helped with the cleanup, which was good as it afforded Vera the opportunity to go home to her children earlier. As soon as they finished, Laura left.

Maude was resting after her evening meal, thinking it would be good to be back at the café, relaxing at the close of the day. Neither Maude nor Laura mentioned their conflict of the day before. They were each embarrassed that they had hurt one another's feelings, but apparently too proud to bring it up.

Maude asked, "Well, Laura, how did the dinner debut go today?"

"I'm happy with the way things went, however, one day is still only one day. We will know better after a week of it. Vera was happy with it. She said it was the easiest dinner crowd that she has ever served. It was amazing, as there was no loss of time ordering off the menu. I know that I am guilty of spending too much time trying to decide what to order. We fed 26 today and you said that we would have 25. I did make enough for 30. We had a bit left over and I offered the extra spaghetti to the late comers. I thought, maybe that is taboo in the food business. If so, I won't do it again. The dinner rolls were wolfed down as if that was the first fresh baked bread they had ever tasted. Tomorrow I will make the rolls a bit larger and use that for the hot ham and cheese. I was thinking that two smaller sandwiches were better than one large sandwich. I'm sorry Maude, here I am rambling on about the café and I never asked you, how are you feeling?"

Maude paused, trying to compose herself. Reaching for her handkerchief, she dabbed at her eyes. "Laura, I have been trying to work the crutches and I am so awkward. Dr. Jessup maintains that I have to be able to use the crutches before he will dismiss me. He is concerned that I will reinjure that leg if I am unable to walk with the crutches. I miss the café and this food is not to my liking. There is a conspiracy to feed me bad food so that I will lose weight. Also a conspiracy for me to lose all of my money by keeping me here longer than the week he promised."

"Speaking of money, how do you want to handle the money that we are accumulating? Do you want us to put it under your mattress with the rest of your money?"

"Didn't Hannah say anything about that? I have turned over the finances to her. She pays Vera and the bills and puts the rest in the bank. She may have thought that I had put you in charge while I was away. She does a good job and I know she likes that responsibility. Listen! Do you hear that? That is Dr. Jessup, making his evening rounds. He is a bit late tonight. Laura, use your charm on him so that he will let me out on Friday."

Dr. Jessup came into the room accompanied by the night nurse that Laura had conned on her first visit with Maude. Dr. Jessup was surprised when he saw Laura there. "Good evening, Miss Martin. How is your son Tylor doing? Let me see, he must be about five months old by now. I would like to see him at about six months, just as a follow up." Laura saw the look of recognition on the night nurse's face. *I knew that I recognized that woman. Just got off the train did she?*

"Good evening, Dr. Jessup. Tylor is doing fine. I will call for an appointment as the time nears."

Turning to Maude, the doctor said, "Maude, I see that you are not doing well with the crutches. Are they comfortable, as far as the right size? I know that you are anxious to get out of here, but I don't want you to leave just yet. The nursing staff must be assured that you are capable of moving from place to place, as well as sitting in a chair and getting in and out of bed. I don't want you to fall again. It is just like dropping a plate. Each time it gets harder and harder to put it back together. Are you having any pain?"

"No, no pain, but I may die of boredom if I don't get out of here soon," Maude replied.

"I will leave now, so that I will no longer contribute to your boredom. Good night, ladies."

Laura left when the doctor and nurse left and followed them down the hall until they were where Maude couldn't hear them. Laura asked, "Is there anything that Hannah and I can do to get her home? We will fix her a room on the main floor of the café so that she will not have any stairs to navigate. She will want to be involved with the café, but it will only be running the cash register."

The nurse went down to the next room to wait for the doctor. Dr. Jessup said, "Let us take it one day at a time. I don't want her to stay any longer than necessary. Ideally, the patient heals much faster in the home."

"One other thing," asked Laura. "Would you permit me to bring one meal a day to her from the café? If I could bring the noon meal, it would mean a lot to her. That way, she could be criticizing my cooking, rather than the food at the hospital."

"You may bring her the noon meal. I will note her chart, but mind you, no banquet. She needs to eat in moderation."

Laura went back to the room with a big smile on her face. "I talked with Dr. Jessup and we are going to get you going. He wants you out of here as bad as you want out. Speaking of out of here, I need to get home. I have a boy waiting for me. Good night, Maude."

"Good night, Laura."

The next morning, thanks to her trusty alarm clock, Laura

was up early, preparing the food for the noon meal. She started on the apple pies, putting them together for baking later in the morning. She was surprised how much she could accomplish when she had the kitchen to herself. There was the dough to work for the hot ham and cheese sandwiches. She had the ham trimmed and ready for the oven. Fortunately, she had the beans soaking overnight for the soup. Laura was taking a few moments to enjoy her morning coffee when Hannah came down with Tylor clinging to her. "Laura, you get so engrossed with food preparation that you forget that this boy needs some love and nourishment."

"Come here, my son." Laura looked down at Tylor, as she nestled him against her breast. *These are the precious moments of the day, as he looks up into my eyes from time to time.* "I love you, Tylor Martin, I love you."

The breakfast regulars were fed. Even some of those that had eaten dinner yesterday were anticipating their dinner. Laura had already started the ham cooking. Its aroma would escape the kitchen as Vera moved from kitchen to dining room serving the guests.

As the twelve o'clock hour neared, Laura was in frenzy. She had a tray on the counter and was adding food to it. She placed a kitchen towel over it and told Vera, "Everything is set. I will be right back."

Laura was out the door on a run, crossing the street and moving as fast as possible while carrying the tray. Opening the door to the hospital lobby she slowed her pace as she neared Maude's room. Maude was sitting up as best she could when Laura entered the room. She exclaimed, "Laura Martin, what have you done now?" Laura flipped the cloth off the tray and there was Maude's dinner; two hot ham and cheese sandwiches, a bowl of bean soup and a slice of apple pie, complete with a cloth napkin and silverware.

"Your dinner, Madam. The hospital can furnish the coffee when you are ready. Enjoy your dinner." As quickly as she came, Laura was gone.

Before Maude could get settled, Dr. Jessup came into the room. "What smells so good? Let me take a look." Picking up one of the sandwiches, he said, "This is too much for you!" He started to eat the sandwich, commenting, "This is good." Leaving the room, he turned back and told Maude, "Don't eat the pie, I'll be back later." Maude thought, *if you are much later, there will be no pie.*

Midway through dinner, Laura was surprised to see Tag Taggat come in and sit down on one of the stools at the counter. Laura was shocked at his appearance on a workday. He was wearing what looked to be a new pair of boots. His hat was white, compared to his usual black crimped hat. Most noticeable was the absence of Jim McCann. Laura asked, "Where is Mr. McCann? Usually, if you see one, the other is close by."

"He stayed at home," Tag answered. "I'm on my way to Madden to pick up two fellows that are going to start working for me and there wasn't enough room in the pickup for all of us. We are ready to start calving, so we'll have the two hands to help us. Last year we just had yearlings and I contracted to have the hay put up. This year, we have all these heifers to calve out. And then, I can use the extra help to do the haying later this summer. The ranch is bigger than I expected when it comes to labor requirements. Why don't you give me a steak and I will be on my way?"

"I'm sorry Tag, but the best that I can offer you is our dinner special. It consists of two hot ham and cheese sandwiches, bean soup, apple pie and coffee. Maude is in the hospital and Vera and I are trying to keep it going until she recovers. So, at noon we only have the specials available. Stop by this evening and I can have a steak for you." Laura gave him her best smile, hoping to appease him.

"I guess I don't have much choice. I was tempted to eat before I left the ranch, but Jim isn't the best of cooks." When Laura heard him say, 'I don't have much choice,' she placed a plate before him and was pouring his coffee. Grabbing up a sandwich, he commented, "At least you are fast." As he took a bite, he grunted, "and good." Spooning up some of the soup, he nodded his head in approval. It was then that he asked Laura, "How about you coming to the 99 Ranch to be our cook? Jim has been cooking, but I need him to do ranch work. Besides, he can't cook anything like this."

Laura was unsure how to respond. She knew him to be a bit of a flirt, but she always thought he did that to impress Jim. As she was leaving to greet another guest, she asked Tag, "Is that a job offer or a proposal?"

Tag quickly laughed as he answered her, "Whichever is the cheapest!"

Hannah went to see Maude right from school on Tuesday afternoon. She reported to Laura that Maude was encouraged and had some success with the crutches earlier that afternoon. Laura laughed when she heard that Dr. Jessup had eaten one of the hot ham and cheese sandwiches. Of course, Maude was pleased that she had eaten the pie before he returned.

After supper Tuesday evening, Laura and Hannah cleared out a storage room off the kitchen and began to prepare a bedroom for Maude. The room had wooden floors, so their initial intent was to have throw rugs on the floor. But, they were of equal mind that it might be hazardous for Maude should she trip on the edge of the rugs. They opted for painting the walls and hanging new curtains. There was the potential for a small closet for her clothing. As far as bathroom facilities, she would have to use the café bathroom, which they decided would be good, as it would require her to move about a bit more. Until she could negotiate the stairs, Maude would have to be content with a sponge bath. It was getting late and they still had a few more days before Maude would be released. Laura asked, "Hannah, would you like to choose the paint for the room?"

Hannah was enthused that Laura entrusted her with that decision. "Oh, yes," she said. "I could get it tomorrow after school. If I visited Maude first and then bought the paint, do you think that we could paint it tomorrow evening?"

"That is a good idea! I saw some paintbrushes when we were cleaning the room. Get the yardstick and measure the room. Calculate the number of square feet of surface there is to cover, including the ceiling. Go to Shaw's Hardware and they will tell you how much paint it will take and what texture they recommend. Buy a good quality, as our biggest outlay in this project is the labor. Vera sews and perhaps she would be willing to make a curtain for the one window in the room. After that, there is the need of a bed. The room is rather small, so I am thinking a cot would be appropriate, with a nightstand. There would still be room for a chair and we will be in business. Won't Maude be surprised?"

"Laura," asked Hannah, "should I look for a cot while I am at Shaw's? After all, once Maude is able to sleep upstairs, you and Tylor can have my room and I can sleep downstairs."

"No, Hannah," said Laura. "No one will be taking your room. As soon as Maude is able to resume her duties of managing the café and doing the cooking, Tylor and I will leave. We will have fulfilled our mission. You will be out of school for the summer and will be able to help in the dining room. I know that the café is not large enough to support all of us. Vera is dependent upon working here. When the time comes, I will move on. I am trusting that the Lord will have something even greater than my experience here at Maude's café."

The tears welled up in Hannah's eyes. "Oh, Laura, I don't want you to leave. You don't know how much it has meant to me for you to be here, especially when Maude was still hurting."

"Hannah," Laura said, "who says that I will be leaving. I just might open a café next door and call it 'Laura's Fine Dining.' Then we would be close once again."

"Are you serious? That might even cause a food fight among friends. I think you are teasing me to make me feel good. I'm going to bed and dream about that dumpy little café next door to Maude's. What is that name again; 'Laura's Fine Dining,' the dumpy little café?"

"Remember tomorrow to get the paint. I will see to the cot, as I may need to use it occasionally. Good night, Hannah."

Wednesday was the roast beef dinner and the guests were more than happy with the meal. They thought they got more meal for their money than the previous days. Still, they had no complaints of the first two meals. Laura made her quick run to the hospital before she and Vera started serving at noon. Maude made sure that she started on her meal before Dr. Jessup came into the room.

After school, Hannah stopped in to see Maude. Maude told her, "Hannah, I made it down to the lobby with the crutches. I had to stop and rest before getting back to the bed. I do admit that I was tired from that much strain. Tell Laura, thanks for the meal, but I am concerned with the portion size. Tomorrow is the sauerkraut and wieners. Have her buy good wieners, but only two wieners on the plate. I see that she insists on giving two dinner rolls. She certainly is generous with my food."

"That is Laura's nature." Hannah moved closer to Maude's bed. "She can't help but be generous. Is that bad?"

Maude thought about Hannah's question. "No, being a philanthropist is a good thing, as long as it isn't with someone else's money."

Hannah asked, "What is a philanthropist?"

Maude had to think a moment. "You might want to look it up in the dictionary to get a more thorough meaning, but essentially, it is a person that is generous to others or a cause in order to provide a social benefit for that person or cause, like Laura."

Hannah spoke up. "Laura is a good philanthropist. She uses her own money. I have to leave now as she has sent me on a social cause that I need to complete before suppertime. Good bye, Maude." Hannah ran down the hall before Maude could bid her good bye.

Hannah arrived at the café with a gallon of paint. Laura asked, "What color did you choose? I'm anxious to get started. However, we should wait until after the guests have left after supper."

Hannah was excited as she started to describe the paint. "I chose a color of passion, a deep purple. Mr. Shaw said that I might need to give it two coats because of how dark it would be, but I know that Maude will love it. How fitting for a bedroom, the color of passion."

Hannah noticed that Laura was less than enthusiastic after she had described the paint. Laura reasoned; *I gave her the responsibility of choosing the color, I will live with it. Maude may have second thoughts, but we will wait until it is on the wall and we have a curtain for the window.*

After the evening cleanup, Laura said, "Vera, we want

to get started painting the room. After looking at the paint, you could have some idea of a curtain for the one window in the room. You are such a good seamstress; would you sew the curtain as you would know what material is easy to work with to complete the project?"

"I would be glad to do that for Maude. Perhaps after the breakfast serving I could go to the Mercantile and get the material. It shouldn't take long for one curtain."

"Good," said Laura. "Hannah, let's get started painting. Then Vera will have an idea of what material to get tomorrow. I found some old tarps and we can start on the ceiling and one wall. Which do you want to do Hannah, the ceiling or the wall, as we only have one ladder?"

"I will do the ceiling," said Hannah, "seeing that I am much younger than you."

"Fine with me," said Laura. "It isn't as far to fall when you are standing on the floor. Open the paint and we'll get started."

Hannah pried the lid from the paint can. Laura looked inside the can and said, "That is a good color, Hannah. Why did you tell me that it was a deep purple? That is the loveliest shade of blue I have ever seen. It has a calming effect on the emotions. Maude needs calm more than passion. Hannah, you wanted me to comment on your choice of color, but I fooled you. I was determined to live with whatever color you chose."

They had the room painted, with very little paint splattered on the floor and window. After the cleanup, they still had time for a late cup of tea and a time to chat. Laura didn't tell Hannah about Tag Taggat being in the café at dinnertime. For some reason, Hannah has a fear of him. Laura wasn't certain if it was what she had seen at the schoolyard or because her stepfather had remarked that he was mean.

Laura's morning went well. She opened the window to air out the newly painted room. When Vera came to work, she looked at the room even before removing her coat. "Hannah and Laura, I know just the material that I will get for that window. I may move in and abandon my husband and kids. It will be so cozy that Maude may want to keep this room. It will be handy for her. Except for bathing, she wouldn't need to climb those steps. That was an excellent choice of color for the room. Good job, Hannah."

Laura made her noon run of dinner to the hospital. When she went to Maude's room, Dr. Jessup was there, waiting for her. He said, "I missed you yesterday so I decided to come early today, strictly to monitor Maude's diet."

Laura set the tray down, "I will leave the dividing up of the dinner to the both of you. I need to get back to the café."

Hannah stopped to see Maude after school, but didn't stay long as she knew that Laura was planning to find a small bed or cot and also a nightstand for the room. She did have a message from Maude, which she delivered to Laura before she left. "Maude asked if you would have any leftovers from dinner. Dr. Jessup ate all of the sauerkraut and wieners, including the two dinner rolls. He remarked that it had been years since he had such a meal. He left her with the cherry cobbler. He did have the hospital kitchen take her a sandwich and coffee. I hope that there is some of the sauerkraut and wieners left."

"There is, fortunately. I imagine that Dr. Jessup may occasionally be eating dinner with us. He was upset that he missed robbing Maude yesterday. I could take extra, but maybe it is good for both of them to share." Laura was putting on her coat and scarf. "I won't be gone long. I need to find a nightstand. Should I get a cot, or a small bed?"

Vera and Hannah both thought a small bed would be

more beneficial, as they sensed that Maude might like the room for her permanent bedroom. Not only that, but it would probably be more comfortable.

Laura went to see Maude before the supper hour. She took her one wiener, some sauerkraut, and a dinner roll. Maude took one look at her plate and gave a look of disgust. "That bandit of a doctor got twice as much as the proprietor of the café."

"Maude, you will still get a meal from the hospital kitchen. I didn't want you to get overfilled with food. Against my better judgment, I will bring an extra bowl of the vegetable beef soup tomorrow. I hope this will be the last day, unless the doctor refuses to release you so that he can eat your lunch. Tomorrow, tell him he will have to start buying it when he comes to the café."

Friday, the furniture store delivered the bed and nightstand. Laura and Hannah brought down a number of Maude's things to make it homey for her return. Dr. Jessup was so happy with his dinner on Friday that he told Maude, "Against my better judgment, I am releasing you tomorrow morning. Just take it easy and let Laura and Hannah do the work so that you can mend. I will stop in from time to time to see how you are progressing." Laura had asked Ken Holliday if he would get Maude home from the hospital Saturday morning.

Maude was happy to be home and well pleased with her living arrangements. What excited her most was that all three of the ladies had contributed toward her comfort. Even though she was tired from checking out of the hospital and the struggle of getting in and out of the car, she still had strength to be at the cash register for the dinner crowd. Everyone remarked how good it was to see her back at the café.

Vera was needed at home, so it was Hannah and Laura running the café. It was good that Maude was able to run the

127

cash register, so it freed them up a bit. Laura had stepped out of the kitchen to bring a plate of food for the table that Hannah was serving, when she saw Tag Taggat heading for the counter. Oftentimes, the cook would wait on those at the counter if the table waitresses were behind with the serving. Hannah also saw Tag come into the café. She hesitated and whispered to Laura, "You wait on him, he is your friend."

Laura rounded the corner of the counter and welcomed him. "Good afternoon, Tag. Did you come to town by yourself and leave Jim to his own cooking? I know you came for that steak I promised you on Tuesday."

"Yes, and I don't want you telling me that I have to take the special of the day. That was good the other day, but there is nothing to compare to a steak, that is if it is cooked right."

Laura asked, "And, what do you consider as being right?" Laura noticed that he was dressed in almost new jeans and shirt today. She had earlier noted his new boots and his white hat from his previous trip to town. Most of the cowboys came in dressed as if they had traded their horse for a pickup truck for the ride to town.

Tag was in a jovial mood today, as he replied, "Medium rare; remember that the next time, so that you don't have to ask. Also, a baked potato with lots of butter and a plate of those dinner rolls. Coffee, too!"

Laura moved towards the coffee urn. As she filled the cup, she asked, "And how do you want your coffee?"

Tag laughed, as he told her, "Just like my women; hot and sweet."

Laura blushed, as she asked, "Did you want cream with that?" Not waiting for his answer, she moved towards the sugar bowl to place it before him, as she set the mug of coffee down.

She also reached for the creamer nearby. Reaching under the counter Laura brought up the silverware and a cloth napkin. "I will get that steak going and bring you some water when I return." Walking back to the kitchen, she was amazed at how that man fascinated her. He is like a lightning storm. You are intrigued by the display of the lightning, but still frightened as it strikes nearby.

Business was a bit slow today, so Laura watched the steak, making sure that it was just right. I fear that he could get nasty if it wasn't to his satisfaction. She had taken the dinner rolls and the water earlier. Placing the steak on a platter, she put the potato on another plate. Both of the plates were hot, as she used a hot pad on each hand. As she placed them down, he asked, "Didn't you forget the steak knife?"

"Mr. Taggat," as she looked him straight in the eye. "If you hadn't needed the knife to butter your bread, I wouldn't have given you any knife. All you need is a fork to cut that steak."

He looked shocked. I have offended her, or she wouldn't have addressed me as Mr. "I'm sorry, Miss Martin if I have offended your choice of steak and your cooking skills. I shall use my knife only for slicing my potato and the spreading of the butter." He picked up his fork and placed the first bite of steak in his mouth. "Miss Martin, come closer that I may reward you with a kiss for serving me this fine steak." He laughed, as Laura blushed and started to return to the kitchen.

As she started to push open the swinging doors, she turned to him, asking, "Does that mean I can be the cook at the 99 Ranch?" Before he had a chance to respond, she was in the kitchen, rattling the cookware so she was unable to hear his response.

Monday morning, Laura said to Maude, "Today we are serving spaghetti, so how many do you want to prepare for? Just

129

by the response, I estimate that we will have close to 35 guests today. This might be wishful thinking, but it is attainable, if not this week, then in the weeks to come. I have thought that we could advertise our menu in *The Sentinel*."

"Laura-- the eternal optimist." Maude smiled, as she looked at her friend. "You can't make money by wasting food. The one food, one plate and one price sounds good, but will it last? If we overestimate our numbers, our profit is gone, no matter how many we feed. Last week you made for 30, and fed 26, and gave away the extra. But, I will give you a chance to prove yourself. Make what you want, but we will figure the cost of the food, and see how you come out. Go ahead and make the 35. I'm willing to stand the loss to prove a point."

"Thank you, Maude," Laura said. "I'm willing to take the challenge."

Laura had started the dinner rolls and while the dough was rising, she went to the grocery store for the spaghetti and the hamburger for the sauce. She had previously stocked additional tins of the fruit cocktail as it was a good fill-in anytime she needed a quick dessert. She also asked the grocer for extra small paper bags.

By 11:45, the first guests began to arrive and Laura and Vera started serving, with Maude handling the cash register and keeping an eye on Tylor. At 12:10, Laura saw that Dr. Jessup came in and shortly afterwards, Ken Holliday arrived and they sat together. A few straggled in late and Laura had Vera wait on them, but instructed her to tell them it would be a few minutes longer before they could be served. By one o'clock, everyone had been served and Maude was all smiles. She hobbled on her crutches into the kitchen as the three of them hadn't eaten yet. As they sat down to eat, Maude said, "I must have lost count or made a mistake, as I counted 42 guests today. With the three of us, that would have made a total of 45. I thought that we had agreed on 35. What happened?" Maude looked at her figures again. Looking around the kitchen, she only saw empty pots.

Laura had a huge smile on her face. "Maude, with the response we had last Monday, I was confident that we would have 35 guests. I had water boiling, so when I saw that I needed more spaghetti, it was a matter of a few minutes to cook some more. I had extra sauce cooked, so I blended the two together and we met the demands of the moment. I had made eight dozen dinner rolls. When I was at the grocers, I had him get me some small paper sacks and I was prepared to sell what extra rolls we might have."

"Laura," Maude said, "I am a believer in your system now. And, I have never served that many people so easy in all my life."

"Maude," Vera said, "having you run the cash register made it easy, as all we had to do was serve."

****

The winter days had turned to spring. The snow that had moved from place to place had surrendered to the warmth of the sun and was now replaced by the immerging green grass. Even the cattle refused the hay that they had been eating all winter long for the tender sprigs of the grass that the Sandhills had produced for thousands of years. Not only the cattle welcomed the longer days, but also the hardy residents looked forward to the first flowers of spring. Each day, Laura was seen carrying Tylor on her hip, walking to the Dismal River. And each day, she praised God for rescuing her from the muddy waters. She knew that the days at Maude's café must come to an end. Hannah would be

131

finishing her first year of high school and she would be helping Maude and Vera. Maude was getting stronger each day and it appeared to Laura that Maude wasn't working to her potential. She sensed that Maude was relying on her assistance, with the sole purpose of delaying that time when she and Tylor would leave. Laura silently prayed for direction, but had been reluctant to beseech God as she had in the past for divine guidance. For she knew at that time, she would leave the comfort and companionship that she had enjoyed the last three months.

Returning to the café, she recognized the bright red pickup truck parked at the curb. Tag Taggat had been somewhat of a regular for Saturday dinner, requiring his usual steak. Laura hadn't seen Jim McCann since the day he and Tag had been in for pie and coffee. It had been that day that Tag had told about their wreck, when his vehicle ran into the train and caused it to be delayed. Laura was so happy that he had delayed the train, which afforded her to remain in Summit City, that she had kissed him on the cheek. It was the first time that this brash man had actually been embarrassed. Laura looked at her watch, thinking that she might have spent too much time at the Dismal River, as usually Tag came promptly at noon. Opening the door, she saw that Tag and Maude were at a table to the rear of the dining room and in a serious conversation. Laura placed Tylor in his playpen as she went to get herself a mug of coffee. As she looked over towards Maude, she lifted the coffeepot to indicate if they wanted a refill. Maude lifted her mug as a sign to bring the coffee over to refill their mugs. Laura set her coffee down and went over to pour the refills. Laura greeted Tag, saying, "You must have gotten up early this morning. Here you are in the middle of the morning, evidently wanting your steak." After she had filled their mugs, she turned to leave. Maude motioned for her to sit down. "Let me take this pot back. I will get my coffee and be right back."

When she returned, Maude started the conversation. "Tag has come to us needing our help. He has a branding next Saturday and wants us to fix the dinner for the branding crew. What do you think?" Evidently, Maude noticed a startled look on Laura's face, as she continued. "Tag said that you were at the Holler branding, so evidently you have some knowledge of how it is done."

"Are you kidding? My knowledge consisted of peeling potatoes, washing pots, pans and a ton of dinnerware. Also, I remember pouring gallons of coffee and iced tea. However, most memorable was observing the branding and throwing up in the grass. Not a good day!' Laura saw that Tag was laughing when she mentioned getting sick.

Maude was taking Tag's side in this argument. "Where is your compassion? He doesn't have a wife to cook the meal and it would certainly not be neighborly to send the branding crew home without feeding them. Don't you have some other idea?"

Laura took a sip of her coffee and setting the mug down, she said, "I certainly do have an idea. He has one week to find a wife. No man should be allowed to purchase a ranch if he doesn't have a wife!"

Laura started to get up to leave, as she wanted no part of putting together a branding dinner. Maude reached out and grabbing her arm, said, "Sit down. Don't go off in a huff. I have already given my word that we would help him out with the dinner. Right now, we are working on the details and that is where we need your help. I can see right now, the wheels are turning in that cute little head of yours, as you are forming a plan. Let's hear it!"

Laura said, "Maude, had you looked more closely at the wheels that you saw spinning, you would have noticed that they were spinning backwards, trying to find an exit. How many men and boys will be there and what do you want to feed them? I am presuming it would be beef, rather than my famous spaghetti dinner, or sauerkraut and wieners. It would be better to cook it there, but what do you have that would be suitable?"

Tag was enjoying the bantering back and forth between Maude and Laura, that he almost missed his cue. "There is a cook shack that we use. The Teasdale Ranch always had a large crew of single men working there when most of the haying was done with horses. That is where we do our cooking, even now."

Laura asked, "When I was at the Holler branding, there were about thirty men and boys that we served. Is that about the size of crew that you will have?"

"Figure on forty, as some of my relatives may show up." Tag was feeling good about this, as Laura was now asking questions instead of being so negative. "Laura, you and Maude know what to serve us men. I will leave it to you to come up with a menu. However, no surprises just for spite!"

Laura's eyes gleamed, "Maude, do you have a good recipe for mutton? If we order now, we should have it by Saturday." Returning to being serious, she asked Tag, "When could we look at the setup to determine what we might need ahead of time?"

"Do you have time this afternoon? If so, I can drive you out, and it will give me an opportunity to show off my new pickup truck. I was planning to eat dinner here anyway."

"Good," said Maude. "Vera and Hannah can clean up and run things this afternoon. Would it be alright if you left Tylor with them also?"

"That will be fine. It will give me a chance to look at the countryside." Maude noticed that Laura was almost ecstatic thinking about going back to the Good Hope community. "I haven't been to Good Hope since I was turkey hunting last

November. It will be good to see it again when it is green."

Tag took note of her reference to turkey hunting. "You are a turkey hunter, or did you mean you hunted to look at them? We occasionally see them along the river, but only a small flock. I don't want them close to the buildings. I like birds, but not big birds."

"You ask Toby Holler if I am a turkey hunter." Laura was more interested in the river he mentioned. "Do you have a river on the 99 Ranch? Is it the Dismal River?"

"It is the same river that flows past Summit City. In fact, if you could negotiate the fences that cross it, you float right near our ranch buildings. When the river is angry, it removes portions of those fences along its course." What a strange woman; a turkey hunter and a river rat! Tag was amused at Laura and yet he admired her zest for life.

Maude interrupted, "We are way off the track. Laura, fix this man his steak and let's get this show on the road." Laura started for the kitchen, as she knew that Maude was going to start talking price. Laura was excited to be going to see the 99 Ranch and get a new look at the Dismal River. *I wonder if the ranch is as neat and handsome as the owner. What is the matter with you Laura Martin, whoever heard of a handsome ranch?*

Tag had his usual Saturday steak and they were ready to leave Summit City. Maude made Laura sit in the middle. She felt like a thin slab of meat between two large slices of bread. Tag was a large man and Maude was still carrying an ample amount of flesh, despite the continual medical advice Dr. Jessup had heaped upon her.

As they crossed the Dismal River south of town, Laura tried to look at it, but most of her vision was limited to what she could see out of the windshield. Passing the Good Hope school and on to the church, they turned left and started up the hill. She remembered two things about this hill; *seeing two riders astride one horse on the day of the 'wreck,' and that Jim McCann rode down that hill on his way to church. That was a glorious day! That was the day that my burdens were lifted at Calvary!* As they crested the hill, Laura saw that it rimmed a valley and she could see the Dismal River. Cottonwood trees followed the course of the river, as well as the usual willows along its bank. It was then that she saw the ranch buildings that spread out, just above the river and the flood plain.

Tag stopped the truck. "There it is, the 99 Ranch." That is all he said, but just that statement showed forth the pride that he had in his ranch. Starting up again, they crossed the Dismal River and moved toward the buildings. Laura was disappointed that they didn't stop at the ranch house, but continued on to what was apparently referred to as the cook shack. Close by was another larger building, about the same width, but much longer. Laura imagined that was the bunkhouse. The cottonwood trees that shaded these buildings was not as impressive as those that grew near the river, but still large enough to give ample shade needed for cooling during the hot summer days. Tag got out and went around the truck to help Maude get to the ground. She still favored that leg with a slight limp. Dr. Jessup insisted that there was no need to limp, but to get out and walk at a steady pace and for a reasonable amount of time. Laura had tried walking with her, but Maude would beg off as being too busy. Maude had brought her cane to help steady herself. Laura sensed that Maude used the cane as if it was some symbol of dignity, but she didn't say that to Maude.

Entering the cook shack, a person first noticed the coolness, considering the heat of the day. Laura immediately was conscious of a man's touch when it came to housekeeping. She looked at Maude, but there was no communication between them. The room that served as a sort of dining room would seat about a dozen people. The presence of housekeeping was similar to that of the kitchen. Maude was the first to speak. "Do we need tables and chairs for the men when eating?"

"No," said Tag, "the men are used to squatting, or sitting on the ground under the shade trees. If you want, we can bring the tables from the dining room to set outside or leave them inside and have the men pass through, which might make it easier for you ladies. There is a room back here that was originally intended for the cook's quarters, if you need some privacy. We use it mostly for storage, even though there is a bed in there. If you have any questions about the appliances, Jim is the one to talk to as he has been doing the cooking. Do you want me to go find him?"

Laura asked, "Will it bother him if we come in and usurp his authority?"

"Uh," Tag stuttered, "Uh, I guess I don't know what that word means."

"I'm sorry," said Laura. "I mean, this is his territory, so will he object, or feel slighted if we prepare the branding dinner? Perhaps he considers that is his responsibility and will feel offended by our presence."

Tag laughed, "Not a bit; in fact, I have to threaten him with bodily harm each morning so that he will make the coffee and serve us with a miserable meal. Why do you suppose that I show up at the café every Saturday under the guise of going to Summit City for repairs? Do you want me to go get him to answer any question about the appliances?"

Maude said, "No."

"Yes," interrupted Laura. "We might need to know just how things work. Do you mind having him visit with us?" Maude gave her a strange look, as if to say, who are you to override my decision?

After Tag left, Laura said, "Maude, did you see the condition of that kitchen and dining room? It needs a good cleaning. How do you expect to fix a dinner in that filth?"

"Laura, there will not be one man in the whole bunch that will notice that the floor is dirty. We will sweep it and make sure that the plates and utensils are clean. Otherwise, it is good enough. Jim McCann may be offended if we clean it up like you want. We will leave it in better shape than we found it, but it is not going to pass any board of health inspection. Give those cowboys a hearty meal and forget the dirt. With the tables close by, it will be easy to put together a meal. I will check with Scott, you know that old-time cowboy that comes for breakfast every morning. I will see if he will bring us out early Saturday morning in his pickup. We can load all the food and prepare it here. Remind me, we may need to bring plates and utensils. Look around to see if there are sufficient pots and pans. Also a large enough coffeepot and iced tea pitchers. I will leave Vera to take care of the Saturday trade. Hannah, you and I will do this in fine shape. Scott will enjoy the day at the branding corrals. We can bring Tylor with us and put him on the bed in the back room. If it looks too bad, bring plenty of bedding to keep him clean. I intend to get a good check out of this cowboy. Can you imagine the cost of that fancy pickup truck? He doesn't use it to haul salt to the cows, that's for sure. Now go check that bed and have a look at the pots and pans. Here comes Tag and Jim around the corner of the bunk house now."

Jim and Laura checked the kitchen and Maude and Tag visited under the trees, haggling over the price. Laura made a few notes and then she was ready to return to Summit City. Maude and Tag shook hands, indicating that the deal had been sealed. Laura had tried to see what she could of the ranch, but was limited mostly to the bunkhouse and the cook shack. She was unable to see any evidence of flowers or a garden.

After they returned to Summit City, Maude and Laura talked about what they would have on the menu for the Taggat branding. Maude said, "Laura, you have a feel for the food that appeals to people's taste. Would you come up with a menu that will be tasty, but still be easy to prepare?"

"Quick and easy doesn't always mean tasty," Laura said. "However, if we fix what I call Swiss steak, I guarantee it will be tasty and the best part is that we can use the round steak which is more economical than other cuts of meat. For a branding, it has to be good. Usually, each rancher's wife has a specialty that she uses year after year. Try not to duplicate another woman's meal if you are in the same branding circle. I'm not aware of another recipe like this among the women. Prepare this in rich brown gravy, which includes some tomato products. Start it early to assure that it is tender. Separate the thick gravy to be ladled over mashed potatoes that have been mixed with butter and heavy cream. Be certain that sufficient salt and pepper have been added so that it is not necessary for the diner to add seasoning. Naturally, a lot of baked beans with bacon added should be served. A good potato salad may also work well. I don't know of any garden produce that is available at this time. Pie, coffee and iced tea should complete the menu. Leave enough of the gravy in the meat so that it is still coated. That will keep it from drying out. As for the pie, I am thinking nothing fancy other than apple and cherry. Don't give them too many choices or they will spend too much time in line, trying to make a decision. Did I miss anything?"

"No," said Maude, "it sounds good to me. I need a cup of coffee, how about you?"

Laura nodded. She took the mug from Maude and sat down. "Maude, I need to talk with you. It is time that I move

JOY AT THE DISMAL RIVER

on. This is the last week of school for Hannah and when that happens, you will have too much help. How would it be if I made this coming week my last week, with the Taggat branding my grand finale? I plan to run an ad in *The Sentinel* to announce my availability for work. I would be appreciative if Tylor and I could stay an extra week to see what comes up."

"Laura," Maude asked, "why do you have to make life so complicated? Do you have to leave so soon, or do you even have to leave? I need to pay you for all your work. Hannah said that she hasn't paid you one dime since you came here. Before you leave, you need to determine how much I owe you."

"Maude, you owe me nothing. I came as a friend to help a friend that was needy. I have very little need for money. You fed Tylor and me and we had a roof over our head. I sense that you might need all that you usually take in for expenses, including the doctor and hospital bills."

****

Saturday morning came all too early, particularly for Hannah. Scott was there at five o'clock as Maude had requested. They loaded the truck with all the food, plates and silverware. Laura remembered to get a large block of ice for the iced tea and had it wrapped in paper. Scott's truck cab was smaller than that of Tag's, so Laura and Hannah rode in the back, while Maude held Tylor in the front. Laura and Hannah enjoyed the morning breeze as it whipped their hair and blew into their face. It was amazing how well they worked together. Laura started with the meat and Maude had Hannah peeling potatoes, while she started the bread. At eight o'clock, they stopped for a quick breakfast and coffee. Laura was a bit disgusted that the men had left their breakfast dishes in the sink, but Maude explained to her that Tag was cracking the whip to get out and get the cattle rounded up for the branding. By eleven o'clock, the women were ready to

140

serve, as they were keeping an eye on the clock. Tag had assured Maude that they would be through before noon and that was when they would eat. Hannah had put out a tub of water for the men to use for washing. By setting it in the sun, it would hold its warmth. Hannah liked the excitement as it was different than her usual Saturdays. She was looking forward to seeing some of her former schoolmates of the Good Hope School.

When Maude saw the first of the cowboys come around the corner, she shouted at Hannah. "Direct them to the water, Hannah. Once they have found the food, start seeing to their needs of coffee or tea. I'm counting on you to keep the mugs and glasses full." Hannah nodded that she understood.

Maude had made the pies the day before, but she and Laura had slipped them into the oven for a few minutes to assure that they had a certain aroma and freshness to them. What surprised Laura the most after the pie was served, was three of the young cowboys came back in and took the rest of the Swiss steak off the serving platter. The last one grabbed one of the dinner rolls and mopped the last of the gravy on the platter. He told Laura, "This is the best meal that I have ever had. My mother would be ashamed of me, but I couldn't let that gravy go to waste." Laura smiled.

Those same three cowboys took a liking to Hannah and kept her busy filling their tea glasses. Laura remembered her first branding dinner and Tag Taggat had done the same thing with her. Maude talked to Jim and asked if he wanted the leftovers. Part of the deal with Tag was that he was to furnish the food. Fortunately the women had eaten early, except for the pie. Maude told Jim, "There will be two pies, a large bowl of beans, some potato salad and two dozen rolls. The meat and gravy are gone. I thought we made enough, but apparently not. I'm sorry."

"Don't worry, Ma'am," Jim said. "I saw those three go

back for the rest of the meat. They would have devoured another half of beef had you fixed it. They work for us and are never satisfied. If we could get them to work like they eat, we could run another ranch. Leave everything as nothing will go to waste."

The women cleaned up the kitchen and dining room. Laura gave the kitchen stove some extra care and made sure the floor was clean. Scott helped them load what few things they had to bring home, such as bowls and pans. Laura and Hannah were not as hilarious as they had been earlier that morning. It was a happy group, but also a tired group when they stopped in front of the café that late afternoon in May.

On Monday, Laura saw David Riggs at the post office. "David, it is now time to run my ad in *The Sentinel*." Handing him two dollars, she asked, "Is it still two dollars?"

"Yes," said David, "it is still two dollars, but I anticipate that you will have more success than your ad after the first of the year. Is Maude able to work the kitchen now? I noticed that she still limps about."

"It will be good for her to get in the kitchen," said Laura. "If she is busy, she forgets to limp. I need to leave so that she might fully recover. I'll look for the ad on Saturday. Oh, I forgot, use Maude's address as I no longer live in that little apartment. Good seeing you. Bye." David nodded.

It was Monday, mid-morning and things were slow at the café. Laura had held Tylor while he nursed and continuing to rock him, he had gone back to sleep. She had decided that this would be a good opportunity for a walk along the Dismal River. She began talking to herself, "What a coincidence! Tag lives as close to the river as I do. I had no idea that the river was that near to the Good Hope School. Should I need to leave Summit City, I will find a place near a large river. Here I am Lord, once again asking for your direction. You direct me for such a short time.

Perhaps, I need to ask for a place of permanence. Lord, Tylor needs a father so that he might have the stability of a father figure in the home. Even at Maude's he is surrounded by females. Even so, if it is your will, I desire to have a life companion. I desire other children. Forgive me for my impatience, but once again, I am faced with another move. Lord, Oh Lord, give me direction!"

Even as Laura was crying out to her Lord, another was seeking counsel of the Lord. Jim McCann was struggling with the meal preparation at the 99 Ranch. His struggle was with the need to be out in the pastures repairing fence along with the other hands, but only he is capable of fixing a decent meal. Tag was upset with Jim for asking for time to go to town to get some more groceries. He remembered Tag's bitter response to his request. "Fix the meals with what you have. We are behind with the fencing." In his bitterness, Jim went to the cook shack and took inventory of the food on hand. Those three renegades that Tag had hired had made short work of the branding leftovers, while complaining all of the time. They didn't see why Jim couldn't fix something like those women had fixed. Jim had three cans of beans, but the last time in town, he had bought two cases of eggs and three slabs of bacon, along with a sack of potatoes. He also had plenty of flour, but that was the extent of the food. He had hoped to find some canned fruit, but when he couldn't find any, he surmised that those three had been into the pantry late at night and now that too was gone.

Tuesday morning, Jim was up before the rest of the crew; making the coffee and fixing breakfast. Tag always joined the crew at mealtime, even though he lived in the house. Jim had fixed each person three eggs, making sure to cook them to their liking. Also, he served bacon, fried potatoes and biscuits. The men were happy with that, but no one stayed behind to help with the cleanup. At noon, everyone, including Tag came in for dinner. Jim had fixed bacon, fried potatoes, biscuits and three eggs. The supper menu was, fried potatoes, biscuits, three eggs, and bacon. While the rest of the crew was enjoying the cool evening, Jim was washing the dishes and pans.

Wednesday was a repeat of Tuesday and Thursday a repeat of Wednesday. Not only was the menu a repeat, but now the complaints about the food were repetitive as well. Thursday was the same, but Friday the menu had changed. No longer was bacon on the menu, as the supply of bacon was exhausted. The menu now consisted of three eggs, fried potatoes and biscuits for each meal. There was a slight modification of the Sunday menu which was expected, as there were no more potatoes. Fortunately, there appeared to be a never-ending supply of eggs and flour. It was now to the point that Jim McCann was actually enjoying his cooking duties. The madder the crew became, the happier the cook became. This is fun! We might even sell chances to see which will run out first, the eggs or the flour.

Monday morning! Tag and the crew came to the cook shack for breakfast, but only Tag showed up at the barn to start the workday. Jim was cleaning up the breakfast dishes when Tag came back to the cook shack and questioned Jim as to where the crew had gone. Jim knew nothing of their whereabouts, presuming that they had gone to the barn to start the day's work. Tag then went to the bunkhouse. They were lying on their bunks. Tag was furious and asked them, "What are you guys doing here? There is work to be done and it sure isn't in this bunk house."

Nick, the spokesman for the trio, got off his bunk and said, "Mr. Taggat, we have decided that we are not going to do any more work for you until we get some decent grub. We are tired of nothing but eggs and biscuits, three times a day. You fed us real good at branding time; why can't you feed us good now? I think that you are so driven to have each of us do the work of two men that you don't even know what we are eating."

144

"Well, what's the matter with the grub? You are getting enough of it, aren't you? Just remember; when you three fellows signed on, you were to get a $100.00 bonus at the end of the year. If you quit now there will be no bonus! Now, get back to work." Not looking back, Tag started for the door.

Jim was outside of the bunkhouse and could hear this taking place. He had come to the conclusion earlier that Tag was so intent on getting the work done that he had no idea what food and how much he was being served.

Nick hollered at him, "Tag Taggat! Either get us a decent cook or take us to town. We won't live long enough to collect that bonus!"

Tag looked back at the three men and paused a moment, trying to make a decision. "All right, you three whiners go back to work and I will go find a cook!"

This time, Tag got as far as the door when Nick said, "And tell the cook to bring some food with him."

Jim heard Tag's pickup start up. He spun dirt for thirty feet, as he headed for Summit City. Jim laughed to himself, as he thought, *dinner is the last time I cook eggs and biscuits for those three. It took longer than I thought to bring everything to a head. I may go open a can of beans, just for a change. Thank you, Lord. Nobody got hurt and I won't need to fix supper tonight!*

CHAPTER 5

I PICKED HER UP IN A PICKUP TRUCK

Previously that morning in Summit City, the same sun that had awakened Tag Taggat had also awakened Laura Martin. She looked across to the crib where her son Tylor was still sleeping. By the early morning light, she opened her Bible and began to read in the Book of Esther. As she saw how Esther had been used to affect the lives of other, she was compelled to pray. She quietly prayed, not wanting to awaken Tylor. "Lord, as I have asked in times past that you might touch me, this is my prayer today. Whether it is great or small, touch me, O Lord." She saw that Tylor was waking up, as he turned to look at his mother. She smiled, as she said, "Already, Lord, you have touched me by my son's smile. Thank you, Lord."

Laura changed her son and dressed him for the day. As she lifted him out of the crib, he began to paw at her bosom. He knew that his mother had established a ritual that he would be drawn to her breast as soon as he was taken from his crib. As he suckled at her breast, Laura was aware that she needed to be weaning him. As his dark eyes looked into her eyes, she was reluctant to make any change just yet. Tylor usually went back to sleep after he had nursed. She continued to rock him until she was assured that he was sleeping soundly. Returning him to his crib, Laura went downstairs. The aroma of the coffee, which indicated that Maude's Café was officially open for business, welcomed her.

Drawing a mug of coffee from the large urn, she greeted Maude and Hannah. They were busy meeting the needs of the early morning customers. Laura asked, "Do either one of you need any help?"

Maude was the first to respond. "Land sakes, girl, give

it a rest. You worked hard while I was sitting around with my broken leg, now it is your turn. You are so intent on leaving, I think that you should relax. The next job might be even more demanding."

Hannah spoke up, "Do you really have to go? It has been like living with a sister that I never had."

Finishing the last of her coffee, she set the empty coffee mug on the counter. Laura said, "Yes, I have had an ad in *The Sentinel* for several weeks now. I'm sure that the Lord has something for me. I enjoyed working here when I was needed, but you don't need me any longer. Tylor went back to sleep and I believe that I will walk to the Dismal River. It is such a beautiful morning that I am reminded of the verse, 'This is the day that the Lord hath made, we shall rejoice and be glad in it.' I shouldn't be gone long."

As she went out the door, Maude uttered, "Humpf, I haven't seen a whole lot in Laura's life for her to be rejoicing."

While Laura was making her way to the Dismal River, the mud caked red Ford pickup truck was making its way to Summit City. Tag Taggat was furious! He was furious at those snot-nosed kids that he had hired for refusing to go to work! He was furious at Jim McCann for not doing a better job of feeding his crew! He was furious that there was so much work to be done! By this time his fury had brought him to the outskirts of Summit City. He was surprised, as he didn't remember going by the Good Hope School. He slowed down as he crossed the Dismal River at the edge of town. Suddenly he realized that he had promised his crew a cook, but he had no idea where to look. He realized in his haste that he needed to look where he was driving, as he almost hit a gray sedan as it crossed in front of him at the intersection by the courthouse. Easing up to the next intersection, he looked to the right and then to the left. He thought he recognized a familiar figure a couple blocks to his left on the road that ended at the Dismal River. Checking the traffic once again, he turned left and after a time he was easing alongside of the woman that was walking towards the river. When he stopped, she turned and recognized Tag. Greeting him with a smile, she said, "Should I be concerned for my safety with you at the wheel?"

Tag grunted and told her, "Get in. I want to talk to you."

Opening the door, she remarked, "Perhaps I should have Maude here to chaperon me. She could sit on the seat next to the door."

Tag was impatient. "This doesn't concern Maude. Just get in and you can turn off your charm and witty little remarks. This is serious business."

She saw that Tag was in no mood for their usual bantering. Smoothing her dress over her knees, she said, "Tell me, what is so serious that you want nothing to do with my charm?"

Staring out the windshield of the truck, he blurted out, "I want you to come cook for me, and the crew." He added the last as an afterthought so she didn't get the wrong impression.

Unconsciously, she moved closer to the door, wedging herself in the corner as she turned to face him. "Tag, I saw those ruffians that you have working for you. They would be after me before the sun went down at night. I'm sure that you think you can handle them and maybe you can. I don't know what you think of me, but many in the community have an opinion of me as a loose woman because of Tylor. If I were to go to work at the 99 Ranch with five bachelors living there, they would certainly have a right to confirm their opinion. You undoubtedly saw my ad in *The Sentinel*. I no longer work at Maude's and I do need work, but not that bad." She started to open the door, but instead of opening it, she locked it. Struggling with the door handle, she began to panic. *Visions of the door at The Sentinel flashed through her mind. Why is it that when I try to escape, a door that won't open traps me?*

He reached out and touched her arm. "Don't be frightened. I won't harm you. I understand your concern and rightly so. I wouldn't want you to be harmed, but I am desperate and I know that you can do the job. What would it take for you to come to the ranch?"

Being unable to open the door of the truck, she had felt intimidated in the presence of Tag. Now she turned to him and boldly responded with only two words. "Marry me."

"What did you just say?" That is the only response that came from Tag's lips.

Laura repeated her words when she softly said, "Marry me. That is the only way that I would be safe if I were protected by your name. Your hired men wouldn't touch me and the community would be reasonably satisfied that Laura Martin finally got married. They may question your reasoning for marry me and others may question my sanity as well. You don't sound real enthused about being married to me. I am not clamoring for us to live as man and wife, but we will each get what we want; you a cook and I will have a wedding ring." Laura took a deep breath as she once again reached for the door handle. She remembered that last time, *pushing down didn't work, perhaps I need to pull up. It worked!* As the door started to swing out, she moved on the seat. Tag gripped her arm.

"Wait!" Those were his only words.

"What do you mean, wait?" As she moved closer to the open door she asked, "Why should I wait? Either I will be the cook at the 99 Ranch, or I won't. The moment that you let go of my arm, I want your answer. I have given mine and now you can give me yours. What will it be?"

Slowly he released his grip on her arm. In a tone of voice, which was unnatural of him, he said, "Yes, I will marry you."

As she gave him a smile, she said, "See, that wasn't so difficult. I know that you are anxious to get back to the ranch. I can have all of my stuff gathered up and be ready to go to the courthouse at one o'clock. I do want a ring. It doesn't have to be fancy, but I don't want one that will turn my finger green." Tag looked shocked at her remark. She instantly responded, "That's a joke, Tag. Is there anything that you need while we are in town?"

Nodding his head, he said, "Groceries. You'll need groceries for the crew as we ran out of food."

She questioned him. "Do you want me to buy the groceries? I can buy the groceries after we get married. Are you paying cash or do you have a charge account?" As Tag hadn't responded, she continued, "Tag, you need to talk to me. Loosen up, especially when we go before the Justice of the Peace. I want you to be able to at least say, 'I do.' If you hesitate, he may not marry us."

Finally he spoke as he said, "Laura, I want you to buy the ring. Then you will know if it fits." Reaching in his shirt pocket, he pulled out a $100.00. "Is this enough to buy the ring and the groceries? I will stay in the pickup while you deal with the grocer. The grocer and I don't get along. Is there anything else?"

Laura stepped out of the truck. As she held the handle before closing the door, she said, "Yes, yes there is. Go back home and get cleaned up. Right now, you look like a saddle tramp. If you fail to meet me at the courthouse, I will know that you got cold feet and I will keep the $100.00. Good bye." She closed the door and started back down the road towards the café. Tag sat there a few minutes before he started his truck and returned to the 99 Ranch and his ranch crew.

Laura hurried back to the café. As soon as she entered

she was greeted by the tinkle of the bell. She ran upstairs and lifting Tylor from his crib, she sat him on the floor. She began to pull the sheets off the bed and stuffing all the bed linens in Tylor's crib. Opening the closet, she found her best dress. It was a red linen dress with black trim. Hurriedly dressing, she stepped into her black shoes. She then fastened the gold chain that held the locket which had been her mother's. As she straightened the locket in the hollow of her neck, her thoughts turned to her mother this day. She put the rest of their clothes in her two suitcases. Hannah came to the door and asked, "What are you doing? Have you gone mad?"

Flinging out her arms as she danced around the room, she said, "Yes, Hannah, yes. I am mad, madly in love. My dear girl, I am getting married today and I am moving out." When Hannah heard this, she ran down the stairs and into the kitchen.

Trying to catch her breath, Hannah said, "Maude, Maude! Laura is getting married today. Isn't that exciting? She is upstairs packing and getting ready to leave."

Maude bounced off the stool that she was sitting on and pranced across the dining room to the stairs that led to the bedrooms. Hannah noticed that she hadn't bothered using her cane and knew that she was upset. Maude stopped in the doorway of Laura's room. "Hannah told me that you are getting married today. When were you going to tell me?"

Laura had been with Maude long enough to recognize that look of anger on her face. *My job is to use my charm and bring her back from her hostility.* "Why, Maude, I didn't see you in the dining room to tell you. And, I just knew that if I told you that I was getting married, you would struggle up those awful steps, helping me to pack. If I came down with all my packing done, then it would have saved you all the anguish of navigating the stairs with your poor leg. My goodness, who is going to look after you when I am gone from here?"

"Laura Martin, stop all that malarkey. Now, tell me who are you marrying and why?"

Patting the bed, she encouraged Maude to sit down on the mattress. Sitting down beside her, she took her hand as she said, "You do come right to the point. What, no congratulations, or I am happy for you, but who and why. The 'who' is, Tag Taggat, and the 'why' is because I asked him. Are you surprised?"

Jerking her hand loose from Laura's hand, she shook her head. She replied. "Coming from you, nothing surprises me anymore." Sitting up straighter, she asked, "Tell me, Laura, if your Grandma Martin were alive today, what would her reaction have been to such a union?"

"Grandma Martin would have said something like this; 'Laura Marie Martin, it appears that you are taking your pigs to a poor market.' That is what she would say!"

Maude replied rather sarcastically. "And, what would have been the response from Laura Marie Martin?"

Laura said, "She would have said, 'Grandma Martin, I respect your judgment, but when the pigs are ready for market, you take whichever market that will accept your pigs, whether good or bad.' That would have been Laura Marie Martin's response."

Maude got off the bed and hugged Laura. "I'm sorry that I am not more responsive. Congratulations, Laura. I know that you will make it work. I see that you are in a hurry, so what is your plan? You always have a plan."

"We are getting married at the courthouse at one. Maude, I sense that this wedding is painful for you, so I will not ask you to attend. However, if you would watch Tylor for me, I would appreciate it. It seems that a child resting on the hip of a bride takes some of the glamour out of a wedding ceremony. We will load up the suitcases and Tylor's crib. Our last stop is the grocery store to stock up on the groceries while we are in town." Turning to Hannah, she asked, "I would like you to stand up with me during the ceremony. Would you do that for me, please?"

"Oh, yes," Hannah cried out as she clutched her bosom. "Thank you for asking me. One o'clock at the courthouse."

Maude was still embittered, which was revealed in her final words to Laura. "Groceries, huh! You are the cook at the 99 Ranch! You are the cook!"

Laura wanted to be gracious. "Yes, Maude, that will be one of my responsibilities. You have trained me well. I intend to keep my man home for Saturday dinners." Laura continued her packing as Maude hobbled down the stairs.

Laura found a nice gold band for $20.00. She was waiting at the courthouse steps in her best dress and shoes. She had come early and had been looking at the clock above the door each minute. At five minutes till one, she saw Hannah coming up the courthouse steps with a bouquet of flowers tightly held in her hand. She handed them to Laura. "I know this wedding is rather sudden, but I felt that you needed a bouquet. I'm happy for you, Laura. I'll always love you."

Taking the flowers, she hugged Hanna and replied, "Thank you. I can always count on you being thoughtful. I just love these pink flowers."

Handing Laura a small white envelope, she said, "Maude sent this envelope and asked that you open it later when you are by yourself. She said that she wouldn't be at the café when you come for Tylor, as Vera or I will be watching him. It is too painful for her to say good bye to you. She knew that you would understand."

"It is difficult for me to understand, but I know how much of a disappointment I have been to her, but I will continue to love her." Looking up, she saw that familiar red Ford truck turn the corner and come to a stop at the courthouse.

Laura was proud of the way that Tag looked. She handed him the ring and he tucked it in his pocket. The ceremony was very simple and short. Tag placed the ring on Laura's finger. When the Justice told him 'you may kiss the bride' was rather an awkward moment, but he gently brushed her lips. Laura tossed the bouquet so that Hannah could catch it. Tag and Laura left the courthouse as Hannah waved at them.

Tag parked near the grocery store and Laura went in while Tag remained in the truck. She was unsure why Tag was at odds with the grocer, but tried to think what she might need while shopping without a list. Perhaps next time she would be better organized. A high school boy helped her take the groceries out to the truck and Tag stowed some in the cab and the remainder in the box of the truck. Laura was proud of her purchases and the fact that she still had almost twenty dollars left. *Do I give it back to Tag, or keep it for the next time? Those are some of the things that we will have to work out.*

Their next stop was at Maude's. Tag made room for Tylor's crib and the two suitcases as Vera brought Tylor out and gave Laura a hug and transferred Tylor to his mother. At the door was a highchair. Vera said, "Maude wanted Tylor to have this chair, as she thought you might need it as we won't be there to hold him." Vera then rushed back into the kitchen so that Laura wouldn't see her tears.

As they left the café, Laura reached out to touch Tag's arm. "Tag, I would like a few minutes to stop at the bank to check with Mrs. Stahl. It won't take long, but I do need to make this last stop." As they stopped at the bank, Laura picked up

Tylor and entered the building.

Seeing Mrs. Stahl at her desk, she asked to get into her safety deposit box. As she opened the box, Laura took the opportunity to reread the papers, which she had retrieved. This was something which she had written shortly after the birth of her son.

****

With Tylor resting on her hip, Laura hurriedly wrote the following as an addendum to the previous document:

Today is Monday, May 22, 1952. This is my wedding day to Tag Taggat, a man that I didn't love, nor did he love me. He wanted a cook and I wanted a husband. It is my desire to learn to love this man and he in return might love me as well. In the meantime, I will have removed the stigma of being an unwed mother and you will have a father. Subsequently, it is so that you might be able to take his name. Incidentally, your father and Tag Taggat were cousins.

****

Laura returned the papers to the safety deposit box, which she placed in the bank vault. As she left, Mrs. Stahl remarked, "Miss Martin, you certainly look nice today. Is this a special occasion?"

Laura paused a moment before hurrying out the door and said, "Thank you, Mrs. Stahl. It is my wedding day. Good day!"

Tag backed the truck from the curb and started for the edge of town. He reached across and touched Laura's hand and smiled. It was the first smile to come across his face since she had seen him at the courthouse. He said, "Mrs. Taggat, we are headed home to the 99 Ranch." Laura touched his massive hand as she smiled and nodded. It was the best that she could muster with the tears in her eyes.

Laura remembered her devotional time that morning as she had sought out the solitude of the Dismal River. She had been studying in the book of Esther. Esther had been chosen to please King Asheruerus of Persia. She had been chosen that she might save her people, the Israelites. The question that went through Laura's mind; *have I chose to please 'King Taggat of Summit County,' that I might have a father for my son Tylor and that he might bear the Taggat name?*

CHAPTER 6

BE CAREFUL OF YOUR BARGAIN

Arriving at the ranch, Tag pulled up close to the cook shack. He began to unload the crib, highchair and the suitcases. Laura asked, "What are you doing? Surely, this isn't where I will be staying."

Tag stopped and looked at Laura and said, "This is the cook shack and you are the cook. You said that we wouldn't live as man and wife. My bedroom is up there," as he pointed to the main house, "and yours is here. You got your wedding ring and I got a cook!" After unloading Laura's things, he started with the groceries, taking them in and placing them on the counter. Just before he got into the truck, he said, "Supper is at six and there will be five men to feed. After supper, you and I can plan your future trips to town for groceries. We are over six miles out so we need to plan ahead. You do know how to drive, don't you?"

"No," she said, "but I'm sure that if you could learn, I'm confident I will be able to do as well. After all, how hard can it be? Please help me get the crib inside and I will get started on the supper." He helped, but she sensed his disgust.

She had decided that if you don't know what to fix for supper and you are short of time, fix spaghetti. She cooked the meat and added the sauce. She remembered how to make baking powder biscuits and pulled some tins of fruit cocktail to put in the refrigerator to chill. She presumed that they would drink coffee, however, she had some tea mixed up if they wanted iced tea. She wanted the first meal to be edible, if nothing more.

As the men filed into the dining hall, they were pleased at the aroma that greeted them. The table was set for five, with the

159

plates and silverware in place. She had filled the water glasses and coffee mugs. Laura was still in the kitchen, but as she heard Tag's voice, she came out. "Fellas, we have a new cook tonight. This is Mrs. Laura Taggat. We got married this afternoon." Tag was blushing, but he continued with the introductions. "You may remember her as one of the ladies that helped with the branding dinner. The big fellow on the end is Nick. He is a ventriloquist, as he speaks for the others. Next to Nick is Jason, the shy one, and the curly haired fellow is Terry. And of course, there is Jim which you have known from the beginning." The young men's faces were a blur as she fixed her gaze on Jim. As soon as she stepped into the room, Jim's face had turned ashen. Evidently, Tag had not told him that they were married. Laura sensed the hostility in Jim's demeanor, which took her by surprise. The few times that they had both attended the Good Hope Community Church, they would often sit together. As Jim was probably 30 years her senior, she never considered anything romantic about sitting alongside one another. Tag continued to talk to the men, but Laura scarcely heard what he was saying as her eyes were riveted on Jim. "Laura runs the cook shack. When you are here, show her the respect she deserves as my wife and as the ranch cook. With all that said, we are ready to eat." Laura was aware of the silence, but didn't know why. It was then that she heard her name. "Laura, we are ready to eat, so you can bring the food."

"Oh, yes," Laura said. "I guess that I worked in a restaurant so long that I was waiting for you to order from the menu. Excuse me." She then went into the kitchen and began to bring out the food. Laura was amazed at the quantity of food the three young men consumed. She sensed that in order to fill them up, without bankrupting the food budget, fresh bread was the secret. More amazing was that after supper, each of them came to her and thanked her. They didn't realize that Laura would eat after the men, and there was very little left for her. She didn't find out until later what Jim McCann had been feeding them.

After supper, Tag and Laura met in the dining hall. He wanted to discuss the needs of the ranch, regarding her being the cook. Folding her hands on the table, she asked, "Do you have any preference as to what I feed the men?"

"No, just food! It doesn't need to be anything fancy, but I don't want them whining about your cooking." Tag didn't know what else to tell her.

"Tag," she said, with a bit of disgust in her voice, "I want to do a good job of cooking, so that they are not whining." She continued, "But also, I don't want you whining as well about the cost. Now that we have covered the topic of whiners, let me ask, do you have any of your own food? I was thinking, like a garden, a milk cow, or even your own beef?"

He looked at her as if she had no idea of the workings of a ranch! "Laura, I barely have enough help to run the ranch, without hoeing in the garden, or milking a cow. This isn't New England!" He paused, as he realized that he had been rather sharp with her. "I guess I could buy a beef and have it processed. Every bite of food we buy is from that highwayman at the grocery store."

Laura got up from the table where they were sitting and poured a mug of coffee for each of them. When she handed the mug to Tag, she deliberately let her hand touch his arm. "I didn't mean to upset you over the grocery menu or the cost of food. I sense at one time this ranch was quite independent of outside sources for its sustenance. That is, other than the staple items, such as flour and sugar. Would you mind if I put together a menu for each day of the week, for all three meals? I would then repeat the menu each week. For instance, what I feed the crew this Monday, I would feed them the same next Monday. That way, whatever the grocery bill is this week, would be about the same next week. Doing it this way, each week I would replace my inventory of groceries. You are the boss and I will do as you desire."

Tag drank the last of the coffee and got up to leave. "I like your plan, go ahead and put it into effect. Breakfast is at six so I will see you then. Good night." He let the screen door slam as he went out.

Laura sat at the table and wept. Rolling her wedding band around her finger, she thought, oh Tag, couldn't you have even touched me before leaving? I have a husband and now I am more miserable than when I was praying for a husband to hold me and cherish me. Finally, she got up and went to her room. Tylor was still sleeping. Laura sensed that even her son missed those that had shared their love toward him. Tomorrow I will have this room and the kitchen looking like a home. She went to bed, still clinging to the dream of a husband who would cherish her.

Thanks to her faithful alarm, Laura was up at five and was preparing breakfast. The brewing of coffee was first on her list, as she so enjoyed that initial cup from the pot. This morning, it was to be scrambled eggs with sausage links and pancakes. She set the table and as she was ahead of schedule, she took her coffee and strolled toward the Dismal River. She did enjoy the freshness of the morning. Even though Summit City was small compared to the other cities of the world, it couldn't match the morning dew and sounds of the ranch. As she walked around a large cottonwood, a man sitting on a stump of a tree startled her. Obviously, he was engrossed in his reading. "Oh," she said, "I didn't mean to interrupt." The man turned his head and she saw that it was Jim.

"Morning, Laura. I was having my quiet time," he said. "Apparently you were startled by my presence as I was by yours at supper last night." He stood up and said, "Why, Laura, why did you do it? Why did you marry Tag?" Laura saw that he was upset, and she was frightened by this gentle man as he hurled the accusations at her. She didn't answer, but threw the remainder of her coffee to the ground and fled to the cook shack.

Her heart was still pounding from the shock of his outburst, as she had thought him to be a friend!

A few minutes before six, Jason came and asked, "Mrs. Taggat, can I ring the bell?"

"Jason, what bell are you talking about? I don't see any bell," Laura said as she was puzzled by his question. "And, why would you want to ring a bell? I thought that was for schools."

"Nick said that you were from New England so now I understand why you don't know about the dinner bell. It is that iron triangle just outside the door. You hit it with an iron rod and it sounds like a bell. That is to let everyone know that it is time to eat." Jason felt proud of himself for explaining to Tag's wife about the dinner bell.

"Yes, Jason, you may ring the bell as breakfast is nearly ready."

Laura went out to watch. Evidently it is the cook's duty to ring the bell, or assign someone to ring it. After the ringing of the bell, the cowboys and Tag were at the table, devouring pancakes at a record pace. It was then that Laura determined to make pancakes as a staple food for the breakfast. Perhaps one day I will substitute biscuits and gravy.

While waiting for Tylor to awaken, she prepared a roast and had placed it in the refrigerator to wait for the time to put it into the oven. After a time, Tylor awakened and she fed him so that she would be ready to give her room a thorough cleaning. In a room to the side was the bathroom with a washing machine which had a clothes wringer for removing the excess water. There was also a clothesline behind the cook shack for hanging the clothes to dry. A tan colored shade, similar to the ones that Laura had used at the blackboard at the Good Hope School covered the window. She decided her next visit to Summit City would require looking for curtain material.

After dinner, as Laura had some time, she began to investigate the premises. She was curious about the main house, so that was her first destination. She desperately wanted to see inside but thought that would be improper. The front yard was overrun with grass. It obviously had been a place of beauty, as some iris flowers were blooming and the lilacs still thrived near the house. There was a birdbath that had been tipped over and the basin was cracked. The rock pathway was overgrown with weeds and grass so that the rocks were barely visible. Laura was saddened by the state of disrepair of the yard which seemed to include the house in the peeling paint of the porch pillars. Laura thought, *oh, if I could only have witnessed this in its splendor.* She left, saddened that she had seen enough neglect for the day.

Laura was enjoying her treasure hunt as she continued her exploration of the buildings. Wednesday was the day that she discovered the milking barn with its four stanchions and plank floor. She found the T-shaped, one-legged milk stool still hanging on the nails to the rear of the barn. Cautiously, she looked into the granary. To her surprise, there was a small feed cart. Instantly she reached out to retrieve the cart as she envisioned that Tylor could use this as Laura went from place to place on the ranch. *I can see him now, sitting in the cart as I milk the family cow. I need to find a cow! A cow that I can milk! How can I use my charm to get my husband to buy me a cow? I will ask Cindy Holler where they got their milk cows and how much a good cow would cost.*

Thursday morning, Laura washed up the feed cart and she

began to pad it. Now, Tylor could go with her as she continued her exploration of the grounds. Her fear of horses kept her away from the stables. She wanted to look inside this one building but the door was tightly closed and refused to budge. Laura was calm as she tried to reason why the door refused to open, even though it appeared to be loose enough. Stepping back a few steps she looked at the door, only then did she see the hook at the top that held the door closed. Reaching up, the door released and she pushed the door inward, only to be struck by an oppressive odor. As the sun had shone through the many windows on the south side, it had created an atmosphere comparable to that of an oven. Pushing the door further, Laura saw that this was the hen house. Unfortunately, when the last occupants had left the building, no one had bothered to clean the premises. She decided that this building was last on her list. A small building close by turned out to be the brooder house. This was for the rearing of the frying chickens and the pullets that would be a part of the laying flock.

Friday was the best day of all! Laura had found the vegetable garden which was overgrown with grass and weeds, but she recognized it as the garden. Along the north side was a long row of rhubarb. It was doing battle with the encroaching grass, but certainly not giving up. Close by was the asparagus, but it was having a more difficult time. Some of the stalks were going to seed, with others totally engulfed by grass. To test the battlefield waged in the garden, Laura began to pull the grass from the bed. With a bit of moisture and hard work, this bed can be productive by this time next year. Picking up Tylor, she went to where Tag had parked his red truck. She was certain that he had a spade in the box of the truck. Reaching in, she retrieved it and went back to the garden plot. She began to dig in the soil, turning over weeds, grass and dirt. As she ran her fingers through the soil, she was amazed at its texture. *Now I know why they are called the Sandhills! Had I been in White Oak Bay, I would have had a shovel full of rocks. It is great! I will grow a garden, but I can't do it alone.* Moving Tylor's cart to the rhubarb patch, she began to select the better, tender stalks from the bed and tucking them in beside Tylor. He thought it was funny to have the large leaves tickling his feet and legs. Laura was having so much fun that she almost forgot to get back to the cook shack to set the table for dinner.

As soon as dinner was over and the dishes put away, Laura started with the rhubarb. Washing it and dicing the stalks in small bits, she mixed sugar and flour in a baking dish with the rhubarb. Then on top of this, she added more flour, brown sugar and a bit of salt. Finally, she sprinkled bits of butter on the top. She set this aside, determined to start this in the oven a half-hour before she rang the bell for supper. She wanted to have whipped cream or ice cream to serve on top, but this was not possible. Her next solution was the canned milk that she had found on hand in the pantry. Putting three of the small cans in the refrigerator, it would work as a substitute for the whipped cream. *With this dessert, I may kill two birds with one stone. We will see, we will see.* Laura was excited. She could only pray that this dessert was as good as she remembered it to be when Grandma Martin made it years ago.

Before supper was finished, the aroma of the dessert was beginning to seep into the dining hall. The young cowboys were anxious to learn what Laura had made for their dessert. They had been excited to have her as a cook this week. After the dinner plates had been stacked, Laura brought bowls of the dessert to the table along with the canned milk. "Gentlemen, this dessert is quite warm as it has just come out of the oven. I have the cold canned milk that you may pour on top if you desire, or eat it alone. Interesting enough, the basic ingredient is growing on this ranch and can be had for the reaping and preparing. Ideally, this is better when it is topped with whipped cream, but unfortunately, we don't have a cow just yet." After that speech, she passed the bowls around the table. She decided that coffee would go well with the dessert so she had made extra coffee and filled their mugs again.

Jason, referred to as the shy one, was the first to speak. "Wow! Do you mean that this has been on the ranch all this time and this is the first time that it is being served to us?"

"That's right!" Laura said. "I have heard you young cowboys complain about being bored. I have a project for you that will guarantee good things on the dinner table. There is an abandoned garden plot that can be worked up, and it will produce a number of things that we can be eating until frost. This is rhubarb and grows in a bed that needs to be weeded. The garden needs to be plowed. This year, if we can get a small plot started, we will have garden produce. Do you want to give it a try?"

The three looked at one another and nodded, indicating that they would help Laura.

"All right," said Laura. "Find three shovels and a rake. By a shovel, I mean something to spade with. I will show you where to dig and then I will come back to clean up the kitchen. There is plenty of daylight left and three husky fellows like you can turn over a lot of sod in one evening." Laura picked up Tylor out of his highchair and started for the door. She turned and said, "Tag and Jim, if you are the least bit curious, you may come with us. You might enjoy yourself and perhaps be helpful while doing it."

When they arrived at the garden, Laura opened the gate and pointed out the area where she wanted the men to dig. Jim and Tag followed along, but brought no tools. Laura asked, "Tag, is there a garden hose and a place where we can get some water to this during the dry season? The asparagus bed needs weeding, but the grass has sapped the moisture from the bed. This makes it difficult to pull the grass."

Tag grumbled, "I can't figure why a fellow would want to spend all this time and work in a garden?"

"Why, Tag," said Laura. "You certainly ate your share of rhubarb cobbler. But, I will tell you why. There was a man in my hometown that was somewhat of a philosopher. He said, 'If a man wants to be happy for a day, get drunk. If a man wants to be happy for three days, get married. If a man wants to be happy for a season, plant a garden.' It is my goal for all of you to achieve happiness. Is there anyone that wants to do the dishes while I am being happy in the garden?" Not getting any response, Laura took Tylor and returned to the kitchen.

Laura came back later. The garden area that she had plotted out had been spaded. Jim had raked it, but there was still a lot of grass and weeds on the surface. Tag had found a hose and was soaking the asparagus bed.

"That's good for this evening," said Laura. "You have all done a great job. After the turned up weeds and grass have another day to dry down, another raking will give us a fine seed bed. When I go for supplies, I will get seeds and we will soon have a flourishing garden. Thank you for all of your hard work. It was too great of a task for me alone."

Saturday morning, Laura had her early morning stroll to the Dismal River before breakfast. She intended to avoid Jim after his outburst the first morning she was at the ranch, but she met him as he was returning from the river. Despite their strained relationship, she was polite and said, "Good morning, Jim," as she continued toward the Dismal River.

He blocked her path and prevented her from going any further. "Tell me something, Laura. Now that you are married, have you had your three days of happiness?" Undoubtedly he was referring to her remarks on 'happiness' the night before in the garden.

Laura replied as she walked around him to continue her walk to the river. "You should be asking that of Tag, as I was referring to the 'happiness of man,' not woman."

Jim grunted, to indicate his disgust and went toward the bunkhouse.

Laura returned in time to ring the triangular bell. This morning, Tylor was awake and she held him and rang the bell. He enjoyed hearing it and reached for the rod to ring it for himself. As he hit the edge, he dropped the rod and laughed when his mother had to reach to pick it up. He was now almost eight months old and was developing a personality of his own.

It was during breakfast that Tag spoke to the group. "We have accomplished a great deal this week. So those who want, we will eat early and go to Summit City and paint the town red." The three young men laughed, as you could see that they were all for the night out.

"By early, what time do you want your supper?" Laura asked. "This being my first Saturday night at the ranch, I am assuming that this is 'boys' night out and the ranch cook is excluded."

Tag laughed, "I fear that your presence would put a damper on the fun of the night."

Laura smiled, "Thank you for 'disinviting' me. You still need to tell me what time supper will be served. Also, what time for Sunday breakfast?"

"I'm sorry that you feel 'disinvited' to our party. Feel free at anytime to 'disinvite' us from your garden party. Breakfast will be at six. Sunday is another day." Tag got up to leave, indicating to the rest that the workday was ready to begin.

Before Tag got to the door, Laura asked, "Tag, do you have a minute? There are a few things that I need to get clear. Then tomorrow, it will be business as usual. I would like to go to church, but it doesn't dismiss until noon. Would you mind if I had the meal ready at, say 12:30, or 1:00 p.m.? I would put something in the oven that could cook while I was at church. I would certainly appreciate it."

Tag said, "No, I don't mind. Just ring the bell when it is ready. We will find something to do at the barn until you ring the bell. I feel that you have more to say, but can't it wait?"

"Just a minute, please. I need to get supplies on Monday. Is that possible? Also, Tuesday is Decoration Day. Do you do anything special that day, like visit the deceased relatives at the cemetery? I presume most of your ancestors are in the Madden cemetery. If you like, I could go with you."

Tag was irritated, as he was anxious to get to work. "Laura, why do you always have to ask two questions at a time? Yes, it is possible to pick up supplies on Monday. Unfortunately, it takes a man from the ranch to take you there and back. When are you going to learn to drive? In answer to the other question, no, I am not going to the cemetery. Tuesday will be another day of work at the ranch. Do you have any more questions for me, while I am stopped?"

"No! You don't like me to ask questions, but you have just asked me three questions!" Laura started to gather the morning dishes. Tag left the dining hall, letting the screen door bang as he went out.

Laura was finding that she was able to do the cooking with a reasonable amount of effort. This was in comparison to working in the kitchen at Maude's. She remembered that Hannah had given her an envelope from Maude, the day of her marriage. Opening it, she found a check for $100.00 that had been made payable to Maude's Café. Looking at it more closely, she saw that it had been signed by Tag Taggat and was endorsed by Maude. There was a note that it was for the branding dinner. Despite her opposition to the marriage, it was thoughtful of Maude to remember Laura in this special way. She decided that she would cash it and put it in her deposit box. She then would have it for a special need. Perhaps that special need might even be a cow. After the breakfast dishes were put away, Laura thought she might try her hand at running the washing machine. She wanted to do a few of the things of hers and Tylor's. Her first thought was, *I haven't seen anyone else doing any washing. Maybe they wash in the river. No telling what a cowboy might do.*

After dinner, Laura worked in the garden. She raked some more of that which had been dug up the night before and pulled the grass and weeds out of the overturned sod. It was beginning to look like a garden!

Supper was a wasted effort, as the men were as excited as a house full of kids at Christmas. They left in Tag's red truck with the three young men riding in the back, whooping and hollering, as they went over the hill. Laura hurried with the cleanup. She and Tylor spent the evening hours in the garden. She started cleaning out the asparagus bed, as it had loosened the soil with the watering the night before. It was starting to get dark as she finished. *She looked upon the garden and smiled with satisfaction. She remembered what she had seen earlier in the week when she first discovered the plot.*

As soon as they returned to the cook shack, Laura bathed Tylor and cuddled him for a time before putting him down for the night. She awakened at about two in the morning as the revelers drove into the yard. Laura was surprised at how the light of the moon bathed the ranch headquarters. It was almost as bright as day. She turned over and returned to her sleep. Tylor hadn't stirred at the noise made by the returning cowboys.

171

CHAPTER 7

THE INTRUDER!

Laura didn't know what had awakened her, but she knew fear that she had never experienced before. She sensed that someone was in her room, even before she heard or saw anyone. Her first concern was for the safety of Tylor. The only thing she heard was the pounding of her own heart. As she looked, she could see nothing. The room was dark in contrast to earlier when the moon had bathed the ranch headquarters. Silently she prayed for her son that she might have the strength and determination to protect him. *Then it came to her, it is not Tylor that they want, but I am the one! What am I to do? Do I fight, or do I submit? As I can't see the intruder, how will I fight? Lord, give me wisdom and your loving care.* Suddenly, despite that the shade was down, the room was lit up as the moon had passed behind the clouds in the sky, or else the clouds had moved on. Now Laura had her answer. She was now able to see the silhouette of a man, but she didn't know who it was. *Was it one of the men of the ranch, or a total stranger who might have followed them home?* As the intruder drew closer, Laura detected the strong smell of liquor and perspiration. Not moving, she thought that he might leave. When he came to the side of the bed and lay beside her, she remained still, but alert. She had kept her eyes narrowed to avoid revealing that she was awake. She waited and thought that he might even go to sleep or pass out. The intruder began to become aggressive. Laura lunged forward, sinking her teeth into the muscle at the junction of where the shoulder and the neck met. He pulled back and struck out, striking her on the side of her face as he yelled out, "You ugly wench!" As she was being struck, she reached to her nightstand. She clutched her alarm clock with her right hand, slamming it to the side of his head. He rolled off of the bed as she got out the other side. Laura rushed to Tylor's crib and scooping him up, she ran out of the cook shack, running toward the Dismal River. At the river's edge, she dropped to the ground. Her breath came in gasps, as she tried to listen to determine if she had been followed.

Laura's first thought *was to make her way to the bunkhouse to seek help. But, what if one of the men of the ranch was the intruder and she encountered him before she could get help. After a night of drinking, she was unsure how much help she could expect from the ranch hands. It was too far to the main house. As she waited, she began to shudder; a combination of the coolness of the night and the shock of the initial encounter.*

Her modesty also prevented her from going to the bunkhouse, as her nightgown was light and flimsy. She had chosen it, as her room was quite warm and she had trouble sleeping in the heat. Laura remained among the trees until it began to get light in the east. She had not seen her assailant come out of the cook shack. Her first thought was that she might have killed him when she struck him with her clock. She thought, *if I did, he deserved it for calling me 'ugly.'* She found Tylor's cart near the door of the cook shack. Pulling it off in the shelter of the trees, she placed him in the cart. Returning to the dining hall, she went to the gun cabinet, but knew that it was locked. As she ran her hand across the top of the cabinet, it was her hope that she might find the key. It was then that her hand brushed the key. Opening the cabinet, she pulled out a small caliber revolver, checking to see that it was loaded. Cautiously, Laura returned to her bedroom, prepared to shoot whatever moved, but the intruder was gone! She dressed hurriedly and was ready to leave, when she looked at her alarm clock. It had stopped at 3:22; more than an hour after the men had returned from Summit City. Who could it have been? She didn't recognize the voice of the man when she had bit him, but she wouldn't forget the taste of the sweat in her mouth immediately as her teeth sank into his neck. Touching her face where she had been hit, she could feel the soreness as she tried working her jaw.

Still clutching the revolver, Laura went back to where she had left Tylor. He was still sleeping, even though she had crunched him into an uncomfortable position in his cart. What a precious child! I have been blessed with a son that seems to bounce along with life, come what may.

Though it was early, Laura began making the morning coffee. She needed something to settle her nerves. Determined to not let this incident bring her to fear, she began to devise a plan. It was a plan that would let the assailant know that she was the one to be feared! Returning to the gun cabinet, she chose two other weapons; a Winchester rifle and a 20-gauge shotgun. A drawer provided the ammunition and she loaded each, being careful to check the safety on both of them. Laura looked through the items in the pantry and found what she needed for a target. Checking her watch, she still had time to set up her field of fire before it was time to prepare breakfast. Stepping off about 100 steps, she established her first target. Turning toward the cook shack; Laura retraced her steps, until she was 25 steps from the door, and the last target she placed 10 steps from the door. She had set the three weapons on a makeshift washstand that had been used at branding time.

It was now time to begin the breakfast preparation. Laura determined that after a night of drinking, perhaps she would prepare a meal heavy with grease. She had overheard how they detested the breakfast and dinner and supper as well that Jim had given them day after day. Instead of the bacon, she substituted sausage patties, but she remembered the fried potatoes and fried eggs! It was with some glee that she rang the dinner bell, not only early, but also extremely loud and long. Tyler had awakened earlier and he found great joy that the bell was ringing.

Laura greeted each man as they came into the dining hall, handing them a cup of coffee. There was no eagerness for the morning meal as there had been prior mornings. They had come to breakfast, more or less dragging in as if they would really have preferred to remain in bed. During the course of breakfast, Laura had taken the opportunity to carefully observe each man to see if there was any evidence of bruising to the head, and subtly she touched the shoulder of each where they might have been bitten. All had passed the test except for Nick. He hadn't come to breakfast. Laura filled the mugs with coffee and asked, "Where is Nick?"

Jason spoke up, "He said he wasn't feeling so good and he was staying in bed this morning." Tag had nothing to say. Normally, he would have been the first to notice his absence and would have routed him out of bed.

Laura said, "I have something to say and show all of you and I am only going to say it once. I don't care how many it takes, but I want Nick in this dining hall to see and hear what I have to say. Now go get him!"

Jason and Terry jumped up, and in a few minutes, Nick came into the dining hall. He came in with his shirt buttons mismatched and hanging outside of his trousers. His hair was rumpled and he was bare footed, but he was there.

"Thank you for coming to breakfast. Here, let me get your coffee for you." As she set the mug down, she clasped his shoulder, but he didn't flinch. Laura breathed a sigh of relief, as it was none of the men of the 99 Ranch.

"This morning is a good time to get a few things cleared up. I don't know if my life concerns any of you, nor were you too embarrassed to ask, 'Laura, what happened to your face?' Did you think that Tag and I had a marital argument and he put me in my place, or Tag, have you noticed that my face is bruised and I will have a black eye before the day is over? At 3:22 this morning, a man that is unknown to me at the present assaulted me. My first thought was that it was one of you. I would have been disappointed if that were the case, as this week has meant much to me as we have begun to work together and to trust one another."

Laura saw that the men were shocked to think that this could happen to Laura. She continued, "Fortunately, a punch to the face is the worst that I suffered physically. Emotionally, it is very traumatic to see a man approaching at that time of the morning. My first thought was to protect my son. I think one or more of you know this person. He might have been drinking with you last night. He certainly knew where I would be. We are going to step outside and I will show you what I intend to do, so this incident will not be repeated. I have no problem that what I am about to do is made known to your acquaintances. I fended him off by biting him on the shoulder and hitting him in the head with my alarm clock. That is how I knew what time the assault occurred. I don't know if you noticed this morning, but in my own subtle way, I squeezed your shoulder to see if you flinched. Let's go outside."

As soon as they were all outside, Laura grabbed up the rifle and bringing it to her shoulder, she fired. Off in the distance was a spray of red. Putting the rifle down, she took the 20-gauge shotgun and fired it, and a second spray of red was seen. Next she took the revolver. It was then that the men saw that she was aiming at a catsup bottle about 25 feet away. The first shot blew it away, and turning to the right, she hit another. All this took about 15 seconds.

Cradling the revolver in her hand, she said, "Let it be known, this revolver will be under my pillow tonight and I will use it. If I miss with the revolver, I still know how to hit a man with a shotgun or rifle. Keep in mind, I can also hit a moving target."

Unloading the weapons, she carefully handed them to Nick. "Nick," she said, "you were the last one to breakfast, therefore, it would be well if you would clean the weapons and go pick up the glass at the target sights. Also, keep in mind, the weapons will need to be cleaned for the next two days." She started for the kitchen. "Dinner will be ready at about half past twelve. Please excuse me, as I have dishes to take care of at this time."

Tag left with the men, not responding to anything Laura had said or done.

Laura had the table set for dinner and the beef roast ready to put into the oven at the appointed time. She had leftover rolls to warm up. Potatoes and carrots were to be cooked with the roast. The pies were baked yesterday.

Laura dressed for church and had Tylor ready. She estimated that it would require 20 minutes to walk to church. She absolutely refused to ask Tag to take her. Once I learn to drive, maybe he will let me drive his red truck to church. It was a beautiful morning, with a hint of rain in the air. She liked the walk, as it gave her time to thank God for His mercy in sparing her any further harm than that which she had received. She had been unsuccessful to cover up the bruise. As she got near the church, she saw that Jim had his horse tied to the fence.

Church was about to begin. The first person to greet her was Karen Barnes. "Miss Martin, I have missed you. I am going to be in the third grade." She took hold of Tylor's hand and kissed his little fist. "Miss Martin, Tylor is a pretty baby."

"Thank you, Karen." Laura touched Karen and told her. "Karen, I am married now and you may call me Mrs. Taggat. I have been married a week."

Karen's eyes got real big. "Did you really marry that mean Mr. Taggat? Is he the one with that bad horse?"

"Oh, Karen, he isn't mean. He is kind, but sometimes his horse is bad. He was especially bad when I hit him on the nose as he tried to bite me. That was a funny day when the horses were tangled up, wasn't it?"

Peggy Barnes came to Laura. It was an awkward moment until Peggy said, "Congratulations, Laura. We heard that you were married. Welcome once again to the community." She saw the bruise, but said nothing.

After church, Laura left as quickly as she could. As she shook Pastor Don's hand, he held it for a short time and asked, "Laura, are things all right? I want to be assured that you are safe. We heard gunfire earlier this morning. Tell me, how did you get that bruise?"

"Thank you for asking," Laura replied, "but everything is fine. There was an incident that caused the bruise, but I assure you, it wasn't as a result of a domestic problem. I was giving a demonstration of firearms to some of the young men that we have working for us at the ranch. Sorry for the disturbance."

Laura hurried back toward the ranch, carrying Tylor on her hip. As she tired, she shifted him to her shoulder. She heard Jim coming behind her on his horse. As he neared, he said, "Laura, let me take Tylor. It will be easier for you. I would have you ride, but I see that you are not dressed for riding horseback. Had I known that you were planning to go to church, we could have come in one of the trucks."

"No, I will carry him, as he is my son." Laura continued walking, as she kept her eyes looking straight ahead.

Jim pulled his horse in front of Laura, blocking her path. "Laura, quit being so stubborn. I know he is your son. I just want to help you. I'm sorry for my attitude earlier in the week, but Laura, I am concerned for your safety. You don't know Tag Taggat as I do. If he is angered, he is capable of killing you. I don't want that to happen. What happened to you early this morning is puzzling, but it is not coincidental. You were targeted, that is for sure. Now give me Tylor. I will make a cowboy out of him before you know it."

Laura handed Tylor to Jim. Her fears were soon eased, as she saw how careful Jim was as he nestled Tylor in front of him on the seat of the saddle. "Don't fret about Tylor. Bob here is a gentle horse, despite what you saw on that first day at the schoolyard. I'm certain that you saw Tag and me riding him double that day."

The walk to the ranch was in silence, except for Jim talking to Tylor and telling him what a good cowboy he was to ride Bob this far. When they arrived at the cook shack, Jim handed Tylor down to Laura. He began to kick and straighten his back, so that Laura had a struggle to even get a hold of him. Laura laughed, "Look what you have done! One ride and he turns his back on his mother and wants to be a cowboy. Thanks for giving him his first ride." Apparently this eased the tension between the two adults.

Jim smiled, "Next time, we will trot the horse and he will want to sleep in the bunkhouse." Tipping his hat, Jim said, "See you at dinnertime, and thanks for being the cook of this outfit. You are a good cook and I know all the boys appreciate it." Jim spurred his horse, as Bob started for the barn, looking forward to his dinner of a few oats.

It took a while, but Laura finally had Tylor settled down and was able to have the dinner ready for the men. She picked up Tylor and they rang the dinner bell. When the men came in, they had recovered very little from their night of painting the town red. Two of the men sat down at the table, wearing their hats. Before serving the food, Laura stood in the doorway of the kitchen and told the men. "Those of you that have your hat on, have the option of waiting until the others have been served. You may then fill your plate in the kitchen and go outside to eat, or remove your hat and eat with the rest of the crew. There will be no wearing of hats in my dining hall." Laura then returned to the kitchen and began to bring out the Sunday dinner to the men sitting at the table.

Terry and Nick got up from the table and went to the back of the room where the hooks were located to hang the coats and hats. Somewhat red faced, they returned and were ready to eat.

Monday, Laura was anxious, as this was market day in Summit City. She had her shopping list prepared and was looking forward to getting some curtain material. Also, she planned on going to the bank and cashing her $100.00 check that Maude had given her. That was the one that Tag had given to Maude for the branding dinner. The trip will give Tag and me an opportunity to talk. He is so subdued around me. Before we were married he was rather brash, but what a contrast! In all my anxiety, I do want to see Dr. Jessup. He might have a clue to the identity of my intruder and why he came here.

At noon, as the men were finishing their dessert, Tag looked at Jim and said, "Jim, will you see that Laura gets to town this afternoon to pick up supplies. And start giving her driving lessons. We can't have her being dependent on us to drive her around. We will soon be haying on the Everett meadow and she will have to bring us our dinner."

After the men had left the table, Laura asked, "Tag, do you have some money for me to buy the groceries for the week? Also, are you willing to pay for the replacing of my alarm clock, or is that my responsibility? Really, Tag, we do need to talk about finances and what you expect of me. I sense that you don't want to be bothered with all this, but someone needs to make these decisions and accept the responsibility!"

He responded to her sharply. "Quit hounding me about this! Just get it done! Charge the groceries at the store and I will take care of it later. Can't anybody do anything right around here? And hurry up and learn to drive, so we can quit wet nursing you all the time."

Laura put the dishes to soak, as she knew that Jim had heard the outburst of Tag, and he too was anxious to get to town. She had her list and was sitting in the truck when Jim came out of the bunkhouse after changing into better clothes. As Jim crawled into the truck, he waited a moment before starting the engine. He gazed through the windshield, not looking at Laura, but spoke with sincerity. "Laura," he said. She sensed that he was about to embark on a serious discussion by the tone of his voice. "This is the last time I will bring this up, so listen carefully and consider what I have to say before responding. Because of the common bond we have in Jesus Christ, you need to know about Tag Taggat. He is possessed by two personalities. The softer of the two shows gentleness, but it is devoid of love. The other personality, which you have witnessed, is one of anger and frustration, and I believe is capable of murder. Not premeditated murder but spontaneous because of his anger. He almost beat a young woman to death in Barton County about two years ago because of his anger. Laura, I have some money that I will give you. If you want to skip the country on the evening train, you can be far from here before Tag finds out. I owe that much to you as a brother in the faith. I will wait while you get your clothes together."

While Jim was telling Laura these things, she was trying to suppress her tears. Wiping her eyes, she asked, "But, what about you? If I ran away, what would happen to you? I don't think that Tag would take it very well if you let me get away. Would you consider running away with me?"

He quickly replied, "No, Laura, no, I couldn't! It wouldn't be right. I just couldn't!"

"Why is it all right for me, the woman that is legally married to Tag and not you, his foreman?"

He began, "I have been with the Taggat family since I was twelve years old. George Taggat, the patriarch of the family, on a trip to Omaha to sell cattle, found me living at the stockyards. I had neither father nor mother and was living by my wits as best as I could. George Taggat brought me to Barton County and he and his wife raised me. Mrs. Taggat was as fine a woman that ever lived. I am what I am today, because of that lady. I never knew her first name, as it was always Mrs. Taggat to me. George was a diamond in the rough, a true cowboy, but a square shooter. Interestingly enough, I believe that every one of George Taggat's grandsons, and he had a number of them that carries the middle name of George after their grandfather. Unfortunately, not a one is worthy of having that name. Tag's mother died when he was born. He had two older brothers. After a time, Tag's father remarried to a woman that was Tag's downfall from the beginning. I am a firm believer, that if you are a man, and desiring to have good children, then it is essential that they have a good mother. A child can overcome a rotten father and many of them have, but rarely does a child overcome being raised by a poor mother. And such was the case. George Taggat saw this in Tag and he wanted me to look after him. Shortly before George died, he asked if I would do my utmost to keep Tag from harm. He said, 'I don't want your promise, but if at all possible, help him.' I don't suppose that you noticed yesterday morning at your firearm exhibition, but Tag is fearful of guns. The middle brother accidentally shot his older brother when he was about 16 years of age. Two years later, while driving cattle during a summer storm, that middle brother was struck by lightning. Tag has not had an easy life. The family basically exiled Tag to Summit County and sent me along. That is why I cannot abandon Tag."

"And neither can I," said Laura. "When it was time for me to leave Maude's after her recovery, there were too many of us for what needed to be done. I asked God for direction in my life. I was seeking a father for Tylor and a companion for myself. I was desirous for more children. God opened the door for me to be the cook here and He did give me a husband. However, as of yet, I do not have a father for Tylor, nor a companion, or more children, but I see these to come in God's timing. What you have told me about Tag gives me a better understanding of how to conduct myself in Tag's presence. I shall make every endeavor to avoid antagonizing him. I seem to have the uncanny ability to needle people, solely for my enjoyment. I see that Tag has a pride of ownership in this ranch, but it appears to be falling down around his knees. I want to make a difference so that he can be proud of his accomplishment. Jim, let's go to town!"

The first stop was at Dr. Jessup's office. Laura went in while Jim stayed with Tylor. Laura was able to see Dr. Jessup, as he had just finished setting a cowboy's broken arm. "What can I do for you, Mrs. Taggat? Congratulations!"

"Doctor, this is an unusual request," said Laura, "but have you treated anyone who has experienced a blow to the head or a bite to the neck in the last 36 hours?"

She noticed that he was startled by her question. He asked, "That is strange. Why do you ask?"

"At 3:22 a.m. yesterday morning, a man entered my bedroom and tried to assault me. I bit him on the neck, at which time he struck me, as you can still see the bruising. I struck him on the head with my alarm clock and he rolled off the bed. I grabbed my son and fled to the river. I remained there until daylight, but the intruder was gone when I returned. Who did you treat that fit that description?"

"Laura, I can't reveal the name of a person that I treat to another individual. Between you and me, your story is much more interesting than his. His story is that he was bit by a horse, and to escape the biting horse, he threw his head back and cut it open. It was cut quite severely, as it required eleven stitches to close. The bite did break the skin, and I cautioned him to watch the horse, should there be any indication of rabies. I washed it out, but I was curious, as it didn't seem large enough for a horse, unless it was a colt. As I said, I can't tell you, but only an officer of the law might request this information if a complaint is filed. Does that answer your question? I have a question, that is really none of my business, but it may be asked in the course of an investigation. Where was your husband when all this was taking place?"

Laura blushed, "Thank you Doctor, you have been most helpful. Good day."

Laura told Jim what she had learned and they went to see Sheriff Morgan. She gave him the facts and what she had learned from Dr. Jessup. Laura filed a report and Sheriff Morgan said that he would go right away. He would let Laura know what he found out.

Laura wanted to go to *The Sentinel* office to order the paper, but was reluctant to see David Riggs so soon after her marriage to Tag. She decided to forgo the paper for the present.

The next stop was at the bank. Jim had business also, so Laura took Tylor, as she and Jim went in together. Mrs. Stahl waited on her as she presented her $100.00 check to cash. Mrs. Stahl was somewhat embarrassed as she told Laura, "I'm sorry, but that check can't be cashed as the funds are still insufficient. I recall Maude bringing that check about ten days ago and nothing has been added since that time."

Laura was furious and embarrassed. *Maude knew that the check was no good when she gave it to me! She had to have the last word. In essence, 'I told you so.'* Laura asked, "If I put $25.00 in the account would the check be good?" Mrs. Stahl said nothing, but shook her head, indicating no. "How about $50.00?" Mrs. Stahl nodded. Laura asked, "May I get to my deposit box?"

After Laura had been to her deposit box, she deposited $50.00 to Tag's account. She then cashed her check, putting the money in her purse. *Her thoughts were how many more checks are floating around?* Laura's thoughts were interrupted by Mrs. Stahl, "Laura, if you have a moment, Mr. Holliday would like to speak with you."

"Certainly, may I go in now?" She took her around to where Ken was sitting at his desk.

Ken stood up and greeted Laura. "I hear that congratulations are in order, but that is not why I wanted to see you. I will be direct with you. Are you all right? I didn't have the opportunity to talk with you at church, but I am concerned about the bruise to your face. Who hit you, and why?"

"Thank you for your concern, but it was not domestic. The sheriff is investigating the incident, but there was an intruder at the ranch early Sunday morning. But, I am confident it didn't involve anyone at the ranch. Let me be direct with you. Is Tag in financial trouble? Now that I am his wife, I need to know these things. I just had to add $50.00 to his account to make good his $100.00 check. And, I sense that he may be in trouble with the grocer, my next stop. I am cooking for five men and it takes a lot of food."

Ken hesitated, "Yes and no. How do you like that for an answer? He appears to have sufficient collateral, but it is essential that he hit a good cattle market this fall. I don't know if he is afraid of me, but he seems to be reluctant to come in to see me to get operating capital. I don't like to have our borrowers writing insufficient fund checks. It makes us look as if we are reluctant to finance our customers. You are persuasive. Can you get him to come in and get sufficient financing?"

"I'll give it a try. And thanks for being concerned for my welfare. Tell the children hello for me. Tell Tara, Tylor took his first horseback ride yesterday. He is a born cowboy. Bye." Ken flicked his hand to acknowledge her leaving.

When Laura returned to the truck, Jim was waiting. He looked over to her and giving Tylor a little tickle under the chin, he asked, "Where to next?"

"Jim, is there a place that I can buy meat in a larger quantity already packaged? If I'm to feed those young men, besides you and Tag, I need to economize. Not in quantity, but in price. Back in Maine, we had a locker plant that butchered and processed cattle and hogs."

Jim thought a minute before answering her. "I believe there is a place like that at the north end of town. Someone had told me that a veteran from the Second World War had started it up when he got out of the service. Do you want to check him out? The afternoon is spent, so there is no need of getting back too early. Tag would put me to work anyway."

"If you don't mind," Laura said. "I could at least get some prices and approach Tag with the figures. I am a firm believer in feeding the help well and then they don't mind the hard work that Tag heaps upon them. Did you notice how they attacked the garden project? I already have a rainy day project outlined, but it will take a good meal to see it through."

187

As they neared the locker plant, Laura was impressed by the white stucco structure surrounded by blooming flowers. The driveway was gravel, which was smooth and weed free, despite the recent rains. Jim went in with Laura and Tylor. A pleasant lady with red hair, wearing a white butcher's apron over her dress, met them at the door. After exchanging pleasantries, Laura asked, "I wanted to get prices on a side of beef and pork that has been processed. Is that available here?"

"It certainly is," she assured Laura. "I am Greta Carlson. My husband Swede does the butchering and I help with the processing. We can get grain fed beef and pork from a producer. Here are our prices. We do have fresh meat in our counter as well."

Laura took the price sheet offered to her, and she and Jim moved over to the counter to look at the fresh meat available. Laura said to Jim, "I think that we should get our meat here. We can see if that is the way to approach that part of the meal preparation. Tonight is spaghetti night at the 99 Ranch, so we will get hamburger. I do want to implement beefsteak in the meals. Jim, after your turn of cooking, do you think the men can tolerate bacon for breakfast?"

Jim laughed, "You heard about that, did you? Only one way to find out is to feed it to them and if they refuse to go to work, then you will know that it was too soon. I know I would welcome a good steak."

After purchasing the meat, Greta handed the package to Jim. Later she said to Laura, "My, you and your husband certainly have a handsome baby. He sure looks like his daddy. Good bye."

Jim had already gone out to the truck with the meat and didn't hear Greta's remarks. Laura was embarrassed for the lady. Now that I am a customer, I must clarify my relationship with Jim. "Mrs. Carlson, I don't want to embarrass you, and I understand how you might have mistaken us as husband and wife. Jim McCann is my husband's foreman and his purpose in being with me today is to teach me to drive. I am Laura Taggat and my husband is Tag. We live on the 99 Ranch in the Good Hope community. This is my error, as I should have introduced Jim and myself when you told us your name. You are correct as my son is handsome and there is a similarity to Mr. McCann, however, I was not acquainted with Mr. McCann at the time of Tylor's conception." Greta smiled, as Laura left the shop.

Laura said nothing to Jim about Greta's remarks. She told him, "Next stop is the grocery store. I'm not looking forward to this stop, as Tag wouldn't go in with me the last time we were here."

As Jim parked the truck at the curb, he said, "I'm not running out on you Laura, but I will look after Tylor if you want?"

"That would be a big help. I realize shopping is not a man's favorite pastime. I will hurry and thanks for looking after Tylor. We may have to refer to you as Tylor's, Uncle Jim."

Jim grinned, "I would be happy with that. Uncle Jim it is!" Laura went into the store and asked the lady that was stocking shelves, "Is the owner of the store in, as I need to ask him something?"

"Yes, usually you will find him at the meat counter. That is his specialty. He won't let anyone else do the meat cutting. He roams the store to keep an eye on things, but ends up cleaning and cutting, cleaning and cutting. His name is Cal Carter."

Laura thought, *oh, no, not him! Well, here goes. Unfortunately, he was there.* "Mr. Carter, I need to visit with you if you have a moment. You might remember me as Miss Laura Martin, the teacher last year at the Good Hope School. But now

I am married, and---.”

"Sure, I remember you, you’re the oyster lady.” He chuckled, as he saw that he had made Laura blush.

"What can I do for you? However, just don’t ask for oysters.”

Laura was trying to get control of the conversation. "As I was saying, I’m now married to Tag Taggat, and I want to buy groceries today. Does Mr. Taggat have a charge account with the store? If so, I would like to charge the groceries that I will be picking up today.”

"Mrs. Taggat, he has an account here which he has been ignoring to pay, despite my pleas and threats. No, you cannot charge another thing at this store!” He returned to his meat cutting, indicating the finality of his decision.

"Mr. Carter, I understand your frustration. I have only been married to Tag for a week, but I do have $50.00 to spend today. And, I do need supplies. If I gave you the money that I have, could I then charge what I purchase today? Or, would you prefer that I pay cash for those items which I purchase?” She stopped a moment before her next question. "Just how much does Mr. Taggat owe you?”

"As I recall, it is more than $140.00, and that is over the last six months. Weren’t you in here last week and bought a big order? I never remembered you spending more than five dollars at a time before. I was curious at why the big spender all of a sudden. You were buying supplies for that spread of his! At least you are forthright in your dealings. Give me the $50.00 and go ahead and charge today. Now, when will I get the rest of my money?”

Laura was delighted that she was able to buy the supplies, otherwise, the closest grocery store was at Madden.

Laura reached in her purse and took out the last of the $50.00 from cashing the $100.00 check and gave it to Mr. Carter. "Mr. Carter, I can't give you a definite answer, but I will do my utmost to get this paid up. If nothing more, I will at least be paying an equal amount as I have done today. I appreciate you doing this for me, as it is difficult to feed a large crew of men and not have a good supplier." Laura hurried with her shopping, as she knew that they needed to get home.

A young man helped Laura load the groceries in the back of the truck. "Thank you for being so patient," she said to Jim. "I don't know how I would have managed, had you not come along today."

Jim tipped his crumpled hat back on his head and laughed. "I'm afraid not very well. Do you realize that this was to be a lesson in learning to drive? Instead, you have had me drive you from one place after another. Have you been watching me, as I shift gears and apply the brakes?"

Laura was frustrated and a bit angry. "No, I haven't! It seems like the only thing that I have been watching are the dollars, particularly, not enough of them. Is he always like this, Tag I mean? He gave Maude a $100.00 check that was insufficient, and he owes the grocer a bill that is six months past due of $140.00. What's with him? He won't give the men a day off, not even Sunday?" She paused before continuing. "Jim, would you teach me to drive in the evening? I think that Jason might look after Tylor for a little while so that I might learn. Maybe I can learn to do one thing that will please Tag. And, is there an old truck that I could drive? I wouldn't want to put a scratch or dent on his new truck."

It was almost suppertime before they got back to the ranch. The men were hanging around the cook shack when they pulled up to unload the supplies. Tag came out and Laura saw that once again, he was furious. He started in on Jim. "What took you so long? I thought the two of you decided to run away together. Jim, you knew that I had things for you to do as soon as you got back. It is almost suppertime and nothing is done. Laura needs to be here to fix supper." Looking in the back of the truck, he spotted the bedding plants that Laura had purchased for planting in the garden. Then it was Laura's turn to be ridiculed. "Why in the world did you buy plants instead of corn and beans to eat? Has everyone gone crazy?"

"Mr. Taggat, no one has gone crazy! However, when you ridicule my purchases, I would appreciate that it is not done before the others. As far as getting home late, I take full responsibility. No matter how much coaxing, Jim refused to run off with me as he knew how angry you would be at the loss of your new truck. If someone will help unload the truck, I will get supper started. A word of caution, I will not tolerate anyone damaging the bedding plants, whether it be by accident or deliberate. They are to be planted tonight after supper should anyone care to help."

By ten minutes after six, Laura had her spaghetti ready to serve. Even though the men were sitting on benches in front of the cook shack, Laura stepped out and rang the bell as if they were still at the barn. Very little was said at the supper table, other than the polite pleasantries when someone asked for something to be passed.

Everyone but Tag was eager to help in the garden. The bedding plants were placed in the ground and watered. The evening light still lingered as the men planted the last of the seeds and the rows marked to indicate that this is where the seeds would sprout. Laura had made lemonade and brought it up from the cook shack, along with her special molasses cookies as the men lingered to talk of looking forward to harvest. Laura went to the main ranch house and knocked on the door. Tag

192

came to the door. She reached out and touched his arm. "Tag, I'm sorry for my anger. The men are in the garden and we are having refreshments. Would you please come? We can't be at war with one another. If you will come, it will indicate that we are united. Then they will have no reason to play one against the other. I love you, Tag. Please come with me. We can settle our differences in private at another time." He reached back and Laura thought he was going to close the door on her, but he was reaching for his hat. Pulling on his hat, he stepped out and they went to the garden together.

CHAPTER 8

A FOOT IN THE DOOR

Laura awakened this morning, realizing that today was Friday, May 30, 1952. It was Decoration Day. When she lived in Maine, she and Grandma Martin honored the day. Even though Laura's parents were never found when their boat capsized during the storm, Grandma Martin had erected headstones in their honor. Grandma Martin had been buried in the same cemetery at White Oak Bay.

Today, her thoughts were centered on the church cemetery in Madden and the soldier that had been laid to rest last November. Perhaps Tag will go there, as undoubtedly his mother and grandparents were buried in the same cemetery. Tag was a very personal individual, which surprised Laura. Prior to their marriage, he was somewhat of a flirt. She often thought of those fighting in Korea. It was a war that troubled Laura, and particularly the on again, off again peace talks. Laura thought, *men are prone to war, while women are prone to peace. Why didn't they have the women talking peace while the men were engaged in war?*

She served breakfast, using the bacon that had been purchased at the locker plant in Summit City. There had been no derogatory comments about the food and no rebellion among the men. Therefore, the choice of bacon, which she and Jim had decided upon, had been a good decision. As the men were finishing breakfast, Laura asked, "Tag, what are the plans for the day?"

He looked surprised and replied, "What do you mean; plans for the day? Today is like any other day. A day of work, or did you want us to hoe in the garden today? Or maybe clean the henhouse?"

Laura thought, *there I go, getting him riled up. I imagine that the crew wished that I would keep my mouth shut as he takes his frustration of me out on the men.* "Today is Decoration Day and I wondered if you were going to go to Madden to the cemetery. Maybe some of the others may wish to decorate the graves of their ancestors as well. I was asking to know how many to prepare dinner for at noon?" Laura was waiting for an answer when she added, "Speaking of the henhouse, I thought it could wait for a rainy day, but it would be well to get to it as soon as you can."

"No, I am not going to Madden. If any man wants the day off, it is a day without pay. And the same goes for you, Laura. Fix dinner and supper for every man here. This is like every other day, a day of work." Tag jumped up and headed for the door.

Before he cleared the door, she spoke up, "But Tag, this is the day that the Lord has made, we shall rejoice and be glad in it. It is not like every other day, it is unique!" Tag grunted, and went out the door. The men didn't move for a moment, as they took in what Laura had said.

After the men left, she began to clean up the morning dishes and make plans for dinner seeing that no one was exempt from work today. Today is a steak day, but I will save it for this evening. Tag's response and her outburst at him saddened her. *I keep telling myself that I need to be gentler with him, but I seem to fail.*

Laura had some free time, so she took Tylor and walked to the Dismal River. It was cool among the trees and she sat on an exposed tree stump. She prayed for those that had been killed in all wars, man's inhumanity upon mankind. She prayed for Tag and she prayed for herself that she might be the wife to honor and respect her husband. While she was praying, she heard a car drive up and park near the cook shack.

Laura took Tylor and left the coolness of the trees and the river and went to see who the visitors might be. She saw that it was two women who had left their car and were walking toward the garden. One in particular was walking quite slow, aided by a cane as she was taking the slight incline with care. The other, apparently her daughter, was trying to steady her. As Laura drew closer, she saw that the younger of the two was probably sixty five years of age and the lady with the cane must be near ninety. Laura called out to them, "Good morning, ladies; is there anything that I can help you with?"

They were somewhat startled by Laura's voice, as they were intent upon their journey, apparently to the garden. Turning around to see who had greeted them, the younger of the two said, "Good morning! I am Claire Beaumont and this is my mother, Viola Teasdale. We have come to visit the cemetery. We wondered if there were any iris blooming that we might pick to place on the graves?"

"They are at the main ranch house. Here we go, up there along this path." Laura stopped and said, "Teasdale, then you lived here, is that right?"

Viola said, "Yes, I came here as a new bride in 1880. I miss this old ranch. I now live with a caretaker in Summit City. Claire lives in Boston and she has come out for a visit. We wanted to come out to the ranch cemetery and place flowers on the graves."

Laura was surprised. "I didn't realize that there was a cemetery on the ranch. I am Laura Taggat and have only lived on the ranch a little over a week. Here we are. You can see that the iris have still survived and blooming. The rhubarb in the garden has done well and only last week we had a cobbler for dessert. Pick as many iris flowers as you want. I must apologize for the condition of the yard, as two bachelors have occupied the ranch since it was sold. I hope to make some changes as I can. The men on the ranch assisted me in planting a garden. But tell me more about the cemetery here on the ranch."

Claire asked, "Would you like to go with us? As I recall, it isn't too far from the headquarters."

"I would love to go with you. I was raised in Maine and I just love the history of the Sandhills." She was excited about meeting the former owner of the ranch.

After gathering the iris, they went back to the car. Laura and Tylor sat in the back. Claire was at home with the trail road. The cemetery was about one-half mile from the buildings. Laura saw that it was fenced with cedar posts and barbed wire. She could see the headstones as they neared the cemetery. She thought it a bit depressing, as she saw that the grass was rather tall and already growing through the prior year's growth. Viola said, "We will need to be careful as we walk in the grass that we don't scare up any snakes. We never had much problem, but we do need to be careful."

They opened a small wooden gate and entered the cemetery. It was small by most standards, measuring about 100 feet square and appeared to have about 10 headstones, scattered about the cemetery. "My husband Elmer," Viola said with a quivering voice, "established this plot when one of the young cowboys drowned in the Dismal River. It was a boggy spot where his horse floundered in the river. The water was high for that time of the year." As she pointed, she said, "He is buried in the far corner, as close to his home state of Tennessee as we could. He had ridden up from Texas with the herd that Elmer had purchased and stayed on in the Sandhills." She continued to reminisce. "Elmer knew that at some point in our life, we would bury one of our kin and he thought it would not be good to have the cemetery close to the headquarters. He feared that the sight of the burial would be a constant reminder of our loss. Elmer was a practical man, as he wanted us to get over our loss and go on with our life. Little did he realize that the next burial would be our stillborn son. I was only 17 at the time and it was difficult to bury my son away from the home. The last one buried was Elmer himself. That was 22 years ago. I will probably be the next, as I plan to rest beside him."

Viola and Claire took the iris that they had picked and distributed a few at each grave, pausing a moment to pray at each headstone. Laura and Tylor remained near the gate, not interrupting their special moments in the cemetery.

As they returned to the cook shack, Laura asked, "Would you care for some refreshments before you return to Summit City? It won't take me long to put something together."

Viola was pleased that Laura had invited them, as she wanted to take one last look at the ranch. "I would be glad to and become better acquainted with you, now that you are the mistress of the ranch. I understand that it is now known as the 99 Ranch. Do you mind Claire, if we spend a little time with this delightful lady?"

"Not at all, Mother. I would enjoy a walk down to the river before we leave. We have no reason to hurry back." Claire drove her car near the cook shack and they all got out, with Laura leading the way. She seated them in the dining hall.

After getting them settled, Laura asked, "I have iced tea, coffee, or hot tea. Which do you prefer?"

Viola spoke up, replying, "The Teasdale were English, as Elmer migrated to this country as a young man, so we had a lot of tea. I would prefer a cup of hot tea with a touch of milk, if you don't mind?"

"The same for me," said Claire.

Laura began preparing the tea, but continued to converse with her guests. "I was a caretaker for Stella Holliday for three months before her passing last December. She was also from England, so I made her a lot of tea, especially when we wanted to chat in those last few days." As Laura made the tea, she was reminded of Stella. *I trust that Ken and the children have gone to the cemetery in Summit City,*

As Laura poured the tea, she asked Mrs. Teasdale, "Do you have the history of the cemetery and those buried there? I would like to have that information, that is if you would care to share it with me. Also, I am ashamed that as caretakers of the land, we have neglected this small plot. If you don't mind, I would like to clean the dead grass out and mow the new grass. Perhaps, I could plant a few wild flowers and even some iris plants." Laura set out a plate of her molasses cookies and joined the ladies while Tylor mauled one of the cookies while sitting in his high chair.

Viola Teasdale was overwhelmed to think that Laura was interested in the cemetery as she replied to Laura's request. "I would be most happy to share that information with you. Were you aware that when we sold the ranch, we retained the cemetery and the access to it as well? Therefore, no one can be buried in that plot without the written consent of the cemetery administrator, which happens to be Claire and me as co-administrators. If you would clean it up, I would be glad to recompense you for your trouble." Sipping her tea, she commented, "Mrs. Taggat, you do make a fine cup of tea."

After Claire had returned from her visit to the Dismal River, she and Viola returned to Summit City. Laura was encouraged by their company and promised Viola that she would visit her one day in Summit City to learn more of the history of the Teasdale ranch.

Laura saw that it was time to begin the dinner for the men. While preparing cold roast beef sandwiches and potato salad, along with her choice of pie, she feared that it might not be enough to satisfy their hunger. However, tonight she was planning a big steak dinner with the mashed potatoes and gravy. She would make a cake this afternoon. The young men especially liked things that were sweet.

As the men were getting ready to return to work and loitering outside the dining hall, a car drove up and Sheriff Morgan got out. Approaching Tag, he said, "Tag, could I speak with you and Mrs. Taggat?"

"Sure," he said. "I will be with you in a minute." Turning to the men, he told them, "Go ahead to the barn. Jim, get them started repairing the haying equipment and I will be along shortly."

Walking back toward the sheriff, he asked, "Is there a problem, as I usually don't get a visit on the ranch from the sheriff?"

Laura asked Sheriff Morgan, "We still have some coffee and for some reason, the men didn't eat all of the pie. Could I encourage you to have some of each?"

The sheriff smiled, "I have never heard of a lawman yet that turned down a piece of pie and especially yours. Yes, ma'am, I will have that pie and coffee."

Laura said, "We can sit here in the dining hall, as it will give us some privacy. Is this in regard to the attack on me Sunday morning?"

"Yes it is, Mrs. Taggat. Dr. Jessup treated Charles Williams Sunday morning. He observed a strong odor of alcohol on his breath, even at that time. All indications are that he is the

201

one involved in the attack. Other than your involvement in the custody regarding his stepdaughter, is there any other reason for him targeting you?"

Tag spoke up, "He and I have tangled over the years. He was in the bar on Saturday night when my crew and I were in town. He may have talked with some of them during the evening and found out that Laura was home alone. What do you intend to do about it?"

Sheriff Morgan took a sip of coffee, indicating that he was not wanting to disclose the bad news that he was about to deliver to the Taggats. "I discussed this with the county attorney and his thinking was that the evidence was pretty much circumstantial. He has no doubt that Charles Williams is the culprit, but there is no positive identification. I just came from visiting with Charles and he is aware that we have him as a suspect. I don't think you have to worry about him coming back, as he knows that Mrs. Taggat is handy with most any firearm and is now sleeping with a revolver under her pillow."

When Tag heard that, he was surprised and asked, "How did he know that Laura has a revolver?"

"Why, I told him! He needs to know that if he is going to mess with her, he could get hurt. His only concern with her is to get close enough to her to inflict bodily harm. Alcohol gave him the courage. I have no idea if he has a beef with you. However, keep a close eye out for him and don't leave Laura alone at night. That is if he might find more courage in a bottle and pull the same thing again. He knows where to find her now." The sheriff finished his pie and stood up. "I will go now and I hope that is the last we hear from Charles Williams. I will stop at Maude's and let her and Hannah know that he is about. Just maybe, Maude will offer me some pie and coffee for the information. Thanks for the pie. It was good." He left after Tag and Laura thanked him for acting so promptly in Laura's behalf.

Laura saw that Tag was infuriated and she steeled herself for the outrage, which was sure to come as soon as the sheriff left the ranch.

Laura waited in the dining hall as Tag returned from seeing the sheriff to his vehicle. She had decided that it would be cooler in the dining hall and if she was to face Tag's anger, it might at least be in a comfortable setting. Tag started the conversation by asking Laura, "Why did you find it necessary to blab to the sheriff about our life here on the ranch? Poor Laura, there was nobody here to protect her while the men of the ranch are in town getting drunk. Not only that, but no one was in bed with her when the attack was made at 3:22 in the morning. Consequently, the sheriff tells me not to leave Laura alone at night. Am I to believe that he will come out to watch over her if I don't?"

What started as a beautiful day had come to this. Laura had deemed *'This is the day that the Lord hath made; we shall rejoice and be glad in it.'* However the inhabitants of the day were wreaking havoc with the day. Laura began, "Tag, don't be concerned about the welfare of the ranch cook. I am sure that you can drive down most any street in Summit City and find another to replace the previous one, should she be assaulted or killed. What do you want from me? You won't take the time to give me any direction in how you want me to feed the men, yet, if I do anything on my own, you criticize my intents and actions. The only emotions of yours that I have been able to stir up are those of anger towards me. When I was single, you would flirt with me and give me every indication that I was a woman of interest to you. Why did you think that I married you? Was it so that I would have the opportunity to prepare three meals a day, seven days a week for a bunch of men? Incidentally, when you criticized me for buying the garden seeds and plants, it was my money that paid for those things, along with the groceries. The day that we married, you refused to go into the grocery store because you owed him money. Yesterday I spent my money that I might be able to buy what supplies we needed." She paused, as she took a deep breath.

"You even tried to cheat Maude by giving her an insufficient fund check for $100.00 to cover the cost of the branding dinner. Maude tried to cash it and the bank refused to honor the check. In an effort to show me what a poor choice I had made, she then gave it to me as a wedding gift. You are not only a slave driver, but also a cheat. I have told you that I love you and touched you to show that I have affection for you, but you rebuff my overtures toward you. Do you hate me so for insisting that you marry me?" Laura was uncertain what she should do, as she continued. "If that is the case, let us have this marriage dissolved and I will keep my part of the bargain and continue as the cook. There will need to be some changes made in my responsibilities, as I will discontinue seeking your favor by touching you and telling you that I love you. I would ask that, as a divorcee, I retain the name of Laura Taggat. I will continue living in the cook shack and sleeping with the revolver under my pillow."

Laura wondered if anything she said had any impact on Tag, as he showed no emotion whatsoever. When she had nothing further to say, she went into the kitchen and started washing the dinner dishes. It was difficult to wash dishes when the eyes were moist with tears. Suddenly she broke down and leaning her head in her arms, as they rested on the edge of the sink, she cried out. "Oh, God, I am sorry for loving a man that does not love me. I was wrong for not waiting for your direction, as I know that you wouldn't lead me into a loveless marriage. You know my motives were not pure. Forgive me, Father, forgive me." With a last shuddered sob, Laura straightened up and reached for a tea towel to wipe her hands and dry the tears from her eyes. Turning to replace the towel, she looked into the eyes of Tag, as he stood behind her. *For how long, she didn't know.*

"How long have you been here?" Laura demanded.

Tag didn't answer her question, but ask one of his own. "Who were you talking to, and why are you crying? You get upset and you start bawling. Can't you control your emotions?"

Laura was defiant as she answered him. "I was talking to God and I was crying, not that I was upset, but those were tears of remorse as I have offended God because of my rebellion. Do you find my talking to God as being offensive? If so, I will only talk to God during my idle time."

"No, no, that is fine. I just thought that people talked to God silently or prayed publicly as a display of piety. But never out loud, as if He was in the room. Does God ever talk to you, like you talk to Him?" Tag was not asking mockingly, but out of curiosity.

Laura was glad for the opportunity to relate to Tag about her faith. She conveyed to God a quick prayer for guidance and wisdom. Before she could begin, Jason came into the dining hall.

"Jim sent me to tell you that we are ready to go repair the hay machinery in the lower meadow." Jason was out of breath, as he paused before going on with his message. "He wanted to know if we are to wait for you or go on to the meadow."

"Tell him to go on without me, as Laura and I have things to discuss." By Tag's instructions, Laura knew that their conversation wasn't over. Once again, she sought God's guidance and wisdom.

"Let's go back to the dining hall and sit down and I will try to control my emotions. You asked, 'does God talk to me?' He doesn't speak verbally to me, but through His written word the Bible, as well as the Holy Spirit, which dwells within me. That is what brings conviction to my soul when I have sinned against Him and others. That is why I was asking His forgiveness and shedding tears of remorse for sinning against His will for my life. How much did you hear of my conversation with God?"

Tag paused before answering her. "You were telling God that you were sorry for loving a man that doesn't love you. And there was something about your motives not being pure. What do you mean about your motives not being pure? Just what were your motives in marrying me?"

"Well, you heard it all." Laura decided to be open with Tag and answer his response to her frankness regarding her motives. "You were desperate for a cook and I was desperate for a man. Not just any man, but a man that would meet my criteria to be my husband and to be a father to my son, Tylor."

Tag was puzzled. "You hardly knew me. How did you know that I was to be the man of your choice?"

"A number of things seemed to mesh, to such an extent, that I mistook these as being a sign from God that you were to be my husband. The one thing that I didn't expect was that you don't love me. I was vain enough to expect any man that I said yes to, would be in love with me. Your first name, Taylor was a close match for my son's name of Tylor. You are somewhat of a rogue, in that people fear you. Face it, your reputation preceded you when you came to this community. People were somewhat hostile that an outsider purchased the Teasdale Ranch and then immediately changed the name to the 99 Ranch. In truth, I am also an outsider. The mystery surrounding Tylor's birth doesn't put me very high on the community's social list. As long as I remained in the community as a single mother; I was as nothing. However, once I am married, even if it is to that rascal Tag Taggat, my son and I begin to establish some semblance of respectability. Oh sure, a community of this size will still remember the single school teacher that had a son, but they will be more forgiving now that she is married. That is why I asked that if you divorced me, I wanted to retain your name. What I didn't count on was falling in love with you. I admit that I am a woman of passion and falling in love with you and your ignoring my advances are what have brought sorrow to my life. God has showed me that with all my scheming, I haven't found happiness. Let's face it! We are not compatible and should not be married. I was wrong to force you into this marriage. Being here on this ranch has given me new purpose. I enjoy cooking for the men and I know that given the opportunity, I can feed this crew well and save you money in doing it. I'm excited about the garden, but Tag, I can't do it with my own money or battle creditors every time I go for groceries. Give me a set amount of money each week and I will feed this crew. It will be one less worry for you. Let's forget about the marriage and make this ranch work for you. Is that fair enough?"

Tag was almost speechless. *Laura had said all that and never shed a tear. I will need to watch her, or she will be running the ranch and I will be working for her. He was surprised and glad, at least, I still have a cook.* He told her, "Laura that is a good idea. You come up with a dollar figure and we can work it out. You do need to work on learning to drive. One other thing; I want you to move to the main house until this thing with Charles Williams is solved. Otherwise, Sheriff Morgan will be out here again checking on your welfare. I shouldn't have had you staying down at the cook shack alone. Unfortunately, you may need to do some cleaning before getting settled. Get things together and we will move you after supper."

Reaching out to Laura, he covered her two hands that had been clasped on the table. He said, "I'm sorry for interrupting your talk with God, but Jim sent me back to the cook shack. He told me that I have not treated you fair, as I was always criticizing anything that you did. I guess he was right. I'm sorry. Now I need to get to the lower meadow to be with the crew." Tag left and Laura sat there for a time, pondering their conversation, realizing that they had more issues to cover, but this was a beginning.

Tylor was awake now, so Laura began to gather her belongings in anticipation of her move to the main house. She *was unsure of how the men would respond to her move, as they were certainly aware of her presence in the cook shack bedroom.* It wasn't long before she was starting on the evening meal, as she prepared the steak that she had purchased yesterday at the processing plant. She and Tylor made a quick run to the rhubarb patch so that she might make a cobbler. Fortunately, she had bought some heavy cream yesterday, so she would have whipped cream for a topping. She began to peel the potatoes for the mashed potatoes. She thought; *I like peeling potatoes as it gives me a time to reflect. The day started with my quote to Tag, 'This is the day that the Lord hath made; we shall rejoice and be glad in it.' Look what has happened already; the Teasdale ladies visited me and I was able to honor those that helped to make this a great ranch as we visited the ranch cemetery. And, how often does one get a visit from the county sheriff? Tag and I have come to some sort of an understanding, and best of all, today is moving day! Tylor and I are going to move to the main ranch house. I have wanted to get inside, but I have only been to the front door. I knew this day was unique!*

Supper was a huge success as the men continued to praise Laura for the meal. Jason, Terry and Nick were anxious to go to the garden, so Laura had them water the transplants and let Jason look after Tylor. Jim was going to give Laura her first driving lesson. It was well that Jim did the instruction rather than Tag, as there was a lot of grinding of gears and the popping of the clutch before the lesson was over. Jim was an encourager as he and Laura laughed at her inability to steer in a straight line. They had agreed that she would only drive the older truck when it was available.

While they were driving, Laura said, "Jim, I want to thank you for speaking to Tag about the unfair treatment he has shown to me, however, we have made some inroads in regard to our relationship with one another. Did he say anything about Tylor and me moving into the main house?"

"Yes," said Jim, as they continued on the road to where the mailbox was located. "He told me about the visit from the sheriff."

"Tag was very defensive about Sheriff Morgan telling him not to leave me alone at night." Laura hesitated before bringing up the next thing. "As I said, I appreciated your coming to my defense, but Tag is a proud man and he might not like anyone telling him what to do about me. I don't want to be the one to come between the two of you. I talked to Ken Holliday about Tag not paying his bills and giving a bad check to Maude. Apparently he has sufficient credit, but won't go into the bank to borrow the money. I suggested that he give me so much money each week to feed the crew, but I will have to get him in to see the banker before he writes anymore checks. I was hoping for a rainy day so he will take off work."

"Let's head back and get you moved in before it gets dark. Maybe we need to pray for rain so you can get your money. You need to understand, thatTag left school after the eighth grade. He would rather do an hour of hard work than take the time to write a check." Jim went on, "Among your other duties, perhaps you can help him with his bookkeeping."

When they got back to the cook shack, Jim had the young men help move Laura to the main house. She noticed the elbow jabbing and grinning they gave one another as they loaded the back of the truck with Laura's possessions.

CHAPTER 9
THE NIGHTMARE

When Laura entered the main house, she was speechless. She knew that it was large by looking at it from the outside. Now she realized that the shrubs and grass that had overgrown the front yard had dwarfed the house. The hall opened into a huge living room with a fireplace and the stone hearth stretching across the width of the room. Except for an upholstered chair and sofa, the room was empty of any large furniture. This made the room appear even larger. Off the living room was the dining room with a bay window that provided a view of the Dismal River and the numerous cottonwood trees. The kitchen was even bigger than the one at the cook shack. Immediately, as she saw the appliances, Laura knew that she would be able to store much of the frozen meat that she had planned to buy, right here in this kitchen. Tag directed the movers to the bedroom that Laura and Tylor would occupy. Here again, the furniture was a double bed, a nightstand and one chair. Tylor's crib was added and there was still ample room to move about. There was a dresser in an adjacent room that Tag had the men bring into the room. It appeared to have four bedrooms. Laura had learned that Jim occupied one of the bedrooms when the bunkhouse was empty. Otherwise, he bunked with the men. After surveying the house, the question that came to her mind, *who's responsible for the cleaning? Evidently, Tag was not doing any of the cleaning. Now that I am living in the main house, it will be my responsibility to keep it clean.*

Friday morning, a light drizzle of rain was falling and it looked as if it would set in all day. Jim was the first to come in for breakfast. Laura greeted him and said, "It appears as if our prayers have been answered. That reminds me of the verse, 'The effectual fervent prayer of a righteous man availth much.' Now I need your prayers that I can get Tag to the banker today and the hen house cleaned. If I can find any laying hens, we will soon have our own eggs. Living in the main house has its advantages, as I now have a phone for my use, so it will be easier to find what I need. If I can get Tag away from the ranch, can I persuade you to have the hen house cleaned today?"

He said, "Laura, if you can get Tag to take a day off to go see a banker, I will guarantee you the hen house will be cleaned and sprayed."

After breakfast, Laura asked Tag, "I have been practicing the driving, and as it is too wet to work outside, would you let me drive you to Summit City this morning? I have a number of things to buy and it will give us an opportunity to work out the details of buying the supplies."

"I don't think that this little drizzle will last long. We need to be working down at the lower meadow. Can it wait a few more days?" Tag pushed back from the table and dismissed Laura's request.

"No, it can't wait." Laura was emphatic. "With your permission, may I pray for the rain to persist all day?"

"Laura, if you can get it to rain through the dinner hour, I will go to town with you. If you want to pray, that is fine. Or if you are inclined to perform a rain dance, whichever you desire suits me. But it must rain through the dinner hour."

Laura said nothing, but when Jim looked at her, she gave a slight nod of the head. He grinned and returned the nod.

Laura spent the morning going over the supplies that she might need, as well as a few things she had need of in her bedroom. She still needed to replace her alarm clock, as she almost overslept this morning now that she was in different surroundings. From time to time, she would check the weather. The light drizzle had dwindled to a fine mist and by 11:30, bits of the sun would slip by the clouds. Laura rang the dinner bell as the first drops of rain began to fall. By the time the men were seated at the table, a steady rain had set in. Jim gave Laura a wink as he sat down at the dinner table. Tag was the last one at the table. No one said anything, as they knew that he did not like to be bested in any contest. Laura was praying that the rain would continue and this was not just a squall that was passing through.

Tag got up from the table and told Jim, "Find something for the men to do this afternoon, as I will be going to Summit City with the rain goddess." The men, still at the table, laughed at his joke.

"Don't worry," said Jim. "I will find something to keep them busy. A good boss always has a rainy day project in his hip pocket to pull out when needed."

Laura came out of the kitchen, offering the men a last cup of coffee. Tag looked at her and said, "All right, Laura, you can stop the rain dance. I will leave for town in twenty minutes. Just make sure you are sitting in the cab of the truck when I leave."

Laura bowed to him. "Ugh, Great White Chief. Not use rain dance. It takes too long. Use prayer. Answer right away. I go now to sit in iron pony." The others snickered at Laura's Indian maiden imitation.

When Tag came to his truck, Laura, with Tylor on her lap was waiting for him. It was still raining, but not as hard as it did during the noon hour. She said, "I had wanted to show you my driving skills, but I would prefer that you do the driving under these conditions. That is, if you don't mind?"

"Have it your way. Don't you always get your way?" Tag

was still miffed because the rain had interrupted his plans.

"I wouldn't say that I always get my way, but eventually I have my way, even if I see the need of altering it somewhat." Laura was trying to be pleasant. "Tag, I respect you for keeping your word and taking me to town. But, I would hope that you would rejoice over the fine bit of moisture that fell on the ranch. The Sandhills always needs rain. This will help the hay crop."

Nothing more was said as they rode in silence, listening to the mud and water squish under the wheels. Finally, Laura broached the subject of finances. "Tag, could I help you with your bookwork, like the paying of the bills each month. If you looked them over and approved their payment, I could write the check and you could sign it. I know that you carry a heavy burden of responsibility and if I can help, I would be happy to do that for you. We could certainly do it in the evening."

Tag looked at her out of the corner of his eye, not wanting to take his eyes off the rain-soaked road. Laura could tell that he didn't like that plan. "I don't need to have some woman knowing how I spend my money and how much money I have in the bank."

Now Laura was upset. At these times, Laura was inclined to be sarcastic in her reply. "But darling, after all, we are husband and wife. I will tell you how much I have in my checking account, if you tell me about yours. Shouldn't we be partners and not have secrets from one another?" She stopped; realizing what she had done. She then continued, "I'm sorry for being sarcastic. Discuss this with Ken Holliday and see if there is any merit to my suggestion of keeping your books for you. I will abide by his decision. Is that fair enough?"

"I'll do anything to keep you quiet. Where do you get all these ideas? You must lay awake nights to come up with all these weird schemes." He was nearing the bank when he noticed that the streets in Summit City were dry. He asked, "When did it quit raining? With all your jabbering, I didn't know when we ran out of the rain."

"About three miles back. But, we are here in town, so don't back out on me now. Besides, if we returned to the ranch, you might have to clean out the hen house."

"Laura Taggat, you got Jim to clean out the hen house while we are in town? What a waste of manpower!"

"Oh, Tag, I just love it when you call me by my married name. Laura Taggat sounds so domestic and charming. Thank you, Tag. You certainly are kind. Should I wait for you to open the door or do you just want me to jump out with Tylor in my arms?" Laura stepped down and was carrying Tylor toward the front door of the bank by the time Tag got out of the truck.

Ken was available to see them and as they went to see him in his office, Tag turned to Laura. "You can wait out here, as this won't take long."

She didn't stop, but continued on to where Ken was sitting. She seated herself on the nearest chair and answering back to Tag, she said, "This concerns me as much as it does you, so I will set in on this meeting should you overlook anything that needs to be brought up. We agreed to accept Mr. Holliday's recommendation."

Ken Holliday sensed a volatile situation was brewing, so he began the meeting by asking, "What can I do for the two of you?"

Tag was determined to have the first word and began, "Laura thinks that she can run the ranch better than I can, so it is her intent to take over the bill paying and buying the food supplies. That is my ranch and she has no business sitting in on this meeting."

Ken saw that this was a battle of wills. He knew of Tag's reputation and he was certainly familiar with Laura's disposition when she was distraught. "Tell me Tag, have you been keeping current with those that you owe money? I am aware of one returned check of $100.00, as well as your owing the grocery store for more than six months. Your credit is good here and when people know that we are financing someone and they are not paying their bills, they assume that this bank is not loaning them the money they need. This gives the bank a bad name as well. Tag, I sense that you are a good manager, but you need to make up your mind. Do you want to be a manager or a bookkeeper. It is difficult to be both. I'm well acquainted with Laura. She managed our household for three of the most difficult months in our life and she did it well. It was not our choice that she left. Laura is your wife now and you cannot leave her out. Let me ask you this Tag, is Laura doing a good job of cooking for the men?"

Tag stuttered a bit, as he knew the answer, but was reluctant to reveal it. "Well, yes, but she is always interfering. Like after supper one night, she had the men out planting a garden. And today, they are cleaning out the hen house."

Ken chuckled, "That is Laura for you! Did the men enjoy planting the garden? They may not enjoy cleaning out the hen house, but why do you think she wanted that hen house cleaned out? Some morning you will wake up to the crowing of a rooster. Right now she is planning to put hens in that house so that you will have your own eggs. On second thought, maybe you should stick to the bookkeeping and let Laura manage the ranch."

Laura cringed when she heard Ken say that about her. Tag spoke up, "She can't even drive a vehicle, so how can she manage a ranch? All right, Laura, go ahead and do the bookkeeping. But, I don't want her signing any checks. That is my job."

"That is fine, Tag," conceded Laura. "It is fitting that you know where every dollar goes. Now, do you owe anyone else beside the grocer and me for making a deposit to your account? And also buying the groceries and meat last Monday? Also, we need to arrive at a figure for the purchase of supplies each week."

Tag said, "I owe that bandit about $140.00 plus what I owe you. But, I will have you know, I am not buying any chickens!"

"That's fine, as I intend to buy the chickens, as they will help feed the crew. I will pay for their feed, but I was thinking that I should have $80.00 for supplies each week. Then you wouldn't have a grocery bill to pay, as it would be my responsibility out of the $80.00. This, incidentally, also includes the meat that they consume. Is that agreeable with you?"

Tag didn't like to give in, so he countered with an offer. "I think $70.00 a week would be more like it"

"Tag, let's not bicker before others. I will split the difference with you and make it $75.00 per week. Is that agreeable?" Tag nodded.

She then turned to Ken, "Now, with haying season beginning and repairs needed and the men to pay, I am thinking that we would probably need $1500.00 to start with. Then, each month, I will submit a list of expenditures and the needs for the following month. Is that satisfactory?"

Ken, trying to be diplomatic with the Taggats, turned to Tag and asked, "Does that sound about right, Tag? It seems logical to me. If so, I will make up a note and you will have money in the bank. I know the grocer will be happy to get his money." Ken quickly made out the note and handed it to Tag for his signature. He looked up the balance on the checking account and placed it on the desk. "You now have $1517.04 in the checking account." Tag reached for it and handed the paper to Laura.

Ken said to Laura, "I have been meaning to tell you Laura, we want you to have Stella's easel and artist supplies. You meant so much to her and only you are capable of carrying on her tradition of painting the portraits of people. When you have time, stop by the house and pick it up. Spend a little time each day working with the oils. Your time in our home was so special to all of us."

"Thank you, Ken." Laura hardly knew how to respond to the gift, as she remembered the times that she and Stella had spent together, each painting their respective portraits of the ones that they loved. "Those were special times that Stella and I looked forward to each day. Perhaps I can stop in on a Saturday and spend some time with the children. Thank you."

Laura and Tag left the bank. When they were seated in the truck, Tag looked over to Laura and asked, "What did he mean about special times in the home?"

Laura was surprised by his question! "Why, I believe you are actually jealous. Tag, I believe when two people marry, they should forget the past of their mate. It is comparable to the new birth in Christ. II Corinthians 5:17 tells us, 'Therefore if any man be in Christ, he is a new creature: old things are passed away; behold, all things are become new.' Unfortunately, we married one another for the wrong reasons, but I am willing to start anew. I think we have made progress today. To put your mind at ease regarding Ken Holliday and myself, you may question if I loved him. I don't know. Had I remained in the home after Stella's death, it would have put him in a bad light in the community. Therefore, I chose to move out and to assist in finding a replacement for me. Of course we had feelings for one another, as we watched the woman we both loved die slowly each day. As far as anything immoral between us, no, there wasn't anything, nor did he ever make any advances toward me. My intent is to be faithful to you and you only."

Tag still had his hand on the ignition switch, but had not started the motor. It was almost as if he had a question in mind, but unable to formulate it into words. Finally, it came forth. "Laura, why do you seem to spiritualize so much of your conversation?"

"Tag, I never thought of it that way. I didn't realize that is what I have been doing, but perhaps you are right. Probably because I am as much spiritual as I am physical. I have spiritual needs, as I do physical needs. We understand the physical because we can see and touch those needs. The spiritual needs are real, but not visible to the eye. Because of the demands of the physical, which are not always met to our satisfaction, we have the need of the spiritual to bring satisfaction to our life. You undoubtedly think of me as a fighter and being aggressive. The adult years of my life have not been easy, particularly the last year and a half, or since I came to Summit County. The physical brought me to a point of despair when I found out that I was pregnant and unmarried. The physical brought me to the place that the solution to the pregnancy was suicide. Tag, only a few people today are aware that I was going to drown myself in the Dismal River." Laura paused as she hugged her son. Taking her handkerchief, she wiped the tears in her eyes. "It was right over there, at the edge of town. I was in the water up to my waist, when the child within my womb seemed to beckon me to go back to the shore. I collapsed on the bank and that is where the Wes Schooley family found me and took me home. The next day, I made my peace with God, and now I am not only physical, but also spiritual. One day the physical shall die, but the spiritual will live on. It is not what I have done, but what God has done. I'm sorry, but there I go again, shedding more tears, but they are tears of joy."

Tag started the truck. As he backed away from the curb, he said, "You are an amazing woman, Laura Taggat, an amazing woman. I don't understand you, but you are amazing."

Before they left town, they stopped at the grocery store. Laura said, "If you want, I will go in and get what few items that I need and find out the total, including the old account. Then I will come out and get the check from you and we will be clear with him. Do you want to watch Tylor while I am in the store?"

"Really, I'd rather not. I'm not very good with kids. Can you handle him all right?"

Laura stepped from the truck and took Tylor with her. The thought went through her mind; *Mr. Taggat, you had better get used to kids, as I intend to have a whole bunch. None of this raising an only child!*

When Laura returned, she was planning to ask Tag to let her drive. But, she knew that he was intent on getting back to work, so she sat back and enjoyed the fresh countryside that had been washed by the rain. *As she looked over the Sandhills, she thought the rain was so cleansing! It is like tears that cleanse the soul. Even as I think about these things, it causes the tears to well up in my eyes. And thank you Father, for this day. Tag talked with me more today than all the time that we have been married. Yes, Father, it has truly been a good day!*

When they drove up to the cook shack to unload the groceries, Jason came running. When he got near to Laura, he exclaimed, "Mrs. Taggat, we got the hen house all cleaned out and Jim found some spray and I even washed the windows. When do we get some chickens?" Laura hadn't heard so many words from Jason since she first met him.

"We need to look at this hen house! Come on, Tag, let's see how the crew has spent their afternoon." Laura was carrying Tylor up the slope to the hen house. Tag was following reluctantly. Jason opened the door, as if he was ushering them into his home. Laura could smell the spray to kill the mites and lice that may have lingered from the previous inhabitants. "Jason, surely this can't be the same hen house that I looked into a week ago. Oh, and the windows just sparkle. Just think of how much sunlight they will let in for the chickens this winter. I think a touch of exterior paint, and we will have the prettiest and cleanest hen house in the Sandhills. Thank you, Jason, and tell the rest of the crew thank you as well. Where are the rest of the men?"

"They are at the barn, working on harnesses and sharpening sickles. I took off when I saw you driving to the cook shack."

Laura looked at her watch. "It is now 3:30, and if you will give me a minute, I will have some iced tea and coffee and maybe even a few cookies set out in the dining hall. If you want, you may invite them as a celebration of the cleaning of the hen house."

Jason left for the barn on a run. Laura turned to go to the cook shack when she encountered Tag and she sensed that he was not happy. "What business do you have taking the men from their work to drink tea and eat cookies? Give you a little authority and you are thinking that you run the place. Ken Holliday was right. I keep the books and you manage the ranch. That is what you want! Well, it isn't going to happen!"

Laura was saddened by what she had done. "Tag, I'm sorry. I should have cleared it with you first. I saw how elated that Jason was that he had accomplished a task that he took pride in. I assure you that the next time the hen house needs cleaning, he will be just as eager to volunteer for the job. Please give the men this moment. Then, when you need something extra from them, they will not begrudge the extra work. I want to work with you, not against you. Tag, I have worked at many menial jobs while going to college. I assure you, that when I was shown kindness, I was a much better employee than when I was driven. Excuse me, as I will now go fix the refreshments and I would encourage you to join us. Then they will think that it was your idea as well as mine." Laura left, still carrying Tylor on her hip as she made her way to the cook shack.

Laura noticed that when the men came to the dining hall, they were unsure if Jason had given them the right message. Tag was there and had taken Laura's advice and praised the men for cleaning the hen house. Traditionally, on a ranch of this size, there would be one employee designated as the 'chore boy' that would be responsible for the chickens, milking the cows and maintenance and upkeep of the buildings and grounds. It was beneath a cowboy to clean the chicken house or milk a cow.

Nick asked, "Now that we have the chicken house cleaned, when are we going to get some fried chicken?"

"Well, Nick," Laura smiled at his request, "I don't want to discourage you, but what was cleaned today was for the laying hens. Right now, we are a bit late in the season for raising chickens to eat. Did you notice the smaller building close by? That is the brooder house and it is used for raising the baby chicks in the early spring that would eventually be the fried chicken you so desire. Come back next year and I will raise the frying chickens at that time." Laura in her enthusiasm failed to see Tag sitting at the end of the table. Had she been able to read his thoughts, she would have witnessed that she would not be here next spring to raise any baby chickens!

The men didn't tarry and were intent on returning to their

work. Laura noticed that Tylor was fussy. With all the excitement, he hadn't been able to get his full afternoon nap. She took him to the house and while he napped, she had an idea. Still not comfortable in using the phone, she called Cindy Holler. After exchanging the pleasantries of phone etiquette, she asked Cindy, "I am thinking of buying a milk cow. To avoid embarrassing my husband, since you are aware that I am prone to an occasional faux pas; where might I go to find one? I'm not aware of anyone else having cows that are milking, so I am asking you for your assistance. Tag isn't into anything that might make him look like a farmer. He is content to use canned milk, but Tylor needs fresh milk and we have some young men working for us that I am sure would enjoy it as well. Would you believe it, with the rain today, I even got them to clean out the hen house. So now I am looking for some laying hens to occupy it and provide us with eggs. The hens and the cow will come out of the money that I have saved since moving to Summit County. It is truly the land of opportunity."

Cindy laughed, "Laura, the eternal optimist! I think that I may help you with both purchases, but I need to clear it with Grant. When we bought our last heifer from a shorthorn breeder about 50 miles north of here, she was bred and had a roan heifer calf. She is now ready to calve and Grant said that we don't need any more milk cows at this time. You would need to talk with him about the heifer. I know that she is gentle, but Laura, do you know anything about milking cows?"

"I would hope so. How hard could it be? After all, surely I am smarter than a calf, and they can milk a cow. Now, concerning the laying hens, what is the story on them?"

"Before we start in on the hens, what is this about the rain? We didn't get any rain. We didn't have any clouds to give us rain."

Laura said, "Cindy, it was of the Lord. I wanted to go to the bank to get some things cleared up and Tag refused, as he wanted to work. It was overcast this morning with a light mist and he promised that if it rained during the dinner hour and he was unable to work, we would go to town. Jim and I agreed to pray and it started to rain at noon, and we had a good rain. The men couldn't work, so Jim agreed to clean out the hen house and it was a mess to say the least. He sprayed it with disinfectant and Jason washed the windows. Now I need some hens. How can you help me?"

"Laura, I'm glad for you. You need to be blessed by the Lord. Peggy Barnes always raises chickens in the spring so that they will have fried chicken in the summer. She always orders day old cockerels, as she has no interest in having laying hens. As the chicks got older, she began to see that they had sent her straight run, that is, about half of them were pullets. They are later maturing than the cockerels. She gets them quite early, so they should soon be laying eggs. She was reluctant to butcher them, as they are real nice pullets. You might give her a call to see if she still has them. I didn't realize that you were such an enthusiast about the ranch life. I am impressed! But, I have always been impressed with you. I do have one concern and you can tell me if it is none of my business, but Sunday I noticed the bruise on your face. Is Tag abusing you? You don't have to put up with that and I will help you any way that I can."

Laura replied, "Thank you for your concern. Other than being frightened, the black eye was the extent of the damage to me. We have a pretty good idea who the assailant was, but have no definite proof. As to why, we are uncertain if it was because of me, or someone wanting to get even with Tag. The person had a heavy odor of alcohol about them. We are presuming that is where the courage came from to provoke such an attack. I was able to afflict some damage on the person, so it gave us some clue as to whom it was that came to the ranch. Please tell Grant that I am interested in the heifer if he wants to part with her. Bye, and thanks for the information on the pullets. I will give Peggy a call." Laura hung up the phone and looked at the time, and saw that she had time to call Peggy.

Dialing the number, Peggy answered the phone. Laura said, "Hello, Peggy, this is Laura Taggat." Before she could say anything more, Peggy broke in.

"Oh, Laura," she said. "I'm so glad that you called. I was concerned about you. I called the ranch, but never got an answer. Are you all right? I'm ashamed that I didn't say anything Sunday, but I was shocked that you had married Tag. And then I saw the bruise. Is Tag hurting you?"

Laura interrupted. "No, everything is all right. The bruise came from a person that attacked me early last Sunday morning. We are not certain who it was, nor why; but we do have a pretty good idea as to their identity, but cannot prove anything. I'm sure my appearance came as a shock to you, but I am doing better. I do thank you for your concern. I just talked with Cindy and she said that you had some pullets that you might want to sell. We just got the hen house cleaned out and I wanted us to have our own eggs, with maybe a few to sell. Are the pullets available?"

"Laura, I'm glad that you are all right. I have been praying for you, as you have always been so special to our family. I'm happy that you called about the pullets. They are nice and I didn't have the heart to butcher them. I guess it is a woman thing. The hatchery did make an adjustment on the order, so if you want them, I will give them to you. That way I don't have to make a decision as to their fate. I think there are about 40 of them. Just come and get them any time, as I am tired of chickens at this point. In fact, there are three roosters in the bunch and you might as well take them also. Laura, you may consider it as a wedding gift. That will make you a real pioneer woman, as oftentimes the early women received such items as they were needed more than fancy dishes. Incidentally, we have a chicken crate that you can use to take them home in and you might look around the buildings there at the ranch and find feeders and waterers. That way, all you will need is the feed and a little straw for the nests, as they will soon start laying eggs. I have been getting the feed for them at the feed store in Summit City. Be sure to ask for a laying mash. Give me a call when you are ready to get them and I will have them shut up so that they will be easy to catch. Is there anything else I can help you with at this time?"

"Peggy, how can I ever thank you? This is most generous of you and thank you for praying for me. When I get things sorted out a bit, perhaps you and the girls can come over some afternoon. I hear Tylor waking up from his nap, so I will go. Bye."

While the men were eating supper, Laura asked, "Have any of you seen any chicken waterers or feeders in any of the buildings? I will need to locate some before we can get the laying hens home."

Terry spoke up, "Mrs. Taggat, I think there are some in one of the empty box stalls at the far end of the barn. I could look for you. My mother raised chickens, so I would know what to look for. If you don't mind waiting I would go now, but I don't want to miss the dessert."

Before Laura could acknowledge Terry's offer, Tag spoke up. "What do you mean before we can get the laying hens home? Have you already bought some chickens? We never agreed that you could buy any chickens. Furthermore, we don't need any chickens on this ranch."

Laura thought, *all right Tag Taggat, if you want to do battle with me in front of the help, be sure that you have chosen the right battleground.* Laura began, "But darling, now that the hen house is cleaned, wouldn't it be a waste of manpower if we left it empty and didn't put chickens in it? Besides, I have 40 pullets that were given to us as a wedding gift. Surely, we couldn't refuse this token of good will from one of our neighbors. That would be rude and disrespectful."

Jim was taken aback by the conversation between the two of them. It appeared as a contest of the wills and whenever Laura started a sentence with 'but darling,' he knew that she was going to put him down. Tag said nothing, but Jim knew that he was seething.

Before Tag could say anything, Laura started in again. "Oh, also, Grant Holler may call about a milk cow. I had talked to Cindy and if he should call of a cow for sale, it would be nice if you would go with me, as I know very little about cows."

"Have you gone mad?" Jim saw that Tag was fuming, as he lit into Laura. "Who do you think is going to milk the cow? If you wanted to be a farmer's wife, then you should have married a farmer. We don't have that much use for a cow. I'm not spending any money for a cow or the grain to feed her. And don't tell me that Grant Holler is going to give you a cow for a wedding present. Laura, just forget it. The chickens are already too much, without adding a cow to the mix. Quit your dreaming."

"But darling," said Laura. Jim winced at those words. *If that woman doesn't shut up, she is going to get herself killed.* "You have asked me a series of questions and I will try to answer them. No, I have not gone mad. In regard to milking the cow, Cindy Holler asked me the same question and I have the same answer for you. What is so difficult about milking a cow? If a calf can do it, surely I can do it, as I am smarter than a calf. The reason that I never married a farmer is because no farmer ever asked me. I have the money for a cow, but I thought that buying a cow is something that we could do together, like a romantic interlude, just the two of us. I have nursed Tylor since day one and as he is getting bigger, he is requiring more milk than I am able to produce. It would also be nice to have cream and butter for the table. As for Grant Holler giving me the cow for a wedding gift, I think not. Cindy might, but not Grant. I sense that he is one of those tight-fisted ranchers that will squeeze every dollar out of you they can."

Jim had heard enough and decided that the men didn't need to be exposed to any more of the feuding between Tag and Laura. He got up from the table and told Terry, "Let's go look for the poultry equipment. I imagine that it will need some cleaning before it is ready to use. So, you think it is in the barn, do you?" The men all left and Tag and Laura were alone.

Laura gathered the dishes and carried them into the kitchen. Tag continued to sit at the table in the dining room. Laura began washing the dishes. She heard Tag push back from the table.

Tag came into the kitchen as Laura continued to wash the dishes with her back to him.

With anger in his voice, Tag said, "Laura, I have had enough of your smart talk. Maybe it is time that I taught you a lesson or two in marital manners."

Laura swung around from the sink. As she brought her hands out of the water, she was clutching a butcher knife in her right hand. She was in a slight crouch when she told him, "You lay a hand on me and you will be scooping your guts off the kitchen floor!"

Tag laughed. "You know that I can take that knife away from you. Then how tough will you be?" He took one step toward her.

Laura moved from the sink. "You heard what happened to Charles Williams. I might get lucky and open you up. Possibly you might take a lesson or two in marital manners as well. Should you treat your wife with respect, then she shall reciprocate by treating you with respect. However, should you resort to violence; you can expect violence in return." Laura laid the knife aside and returned to washing the dishes in the sink.

Tag left the kitchen and walked toward the main house.

Laura finished in the kitchen and was leaving to go take a look at the garden. Terry came and told her, "We found what you needed. We are washing the equipment with the hose up at the garden. It looks like you won't need to buy anything. There is a large barrel for storing the feed, complete with a lid. Do you want to come and see what we have found?"

"Let me get Tylor and I will be right up. Thank you for remembering where you had seen the equipment. I can hardly wait until we get the hens!"

Laura awakened Tylor and they made their way to the garden. Jim was there and he motioned to Laura. She went to meet him. "Laura," he said, "I want you to pretend that you are looking at this row of beans. If you will look closely, you will see that one of them is ready to break through the soil. Now, I want you to listen to what I have to say and I mean listen. Stop needling Tag! You seem to enjoy it. I wince every time that you start a sentence of 'but darling'. You scored two points with the chickens and the milk cow. Don't run up the score on him. Let him score a point now and then. You are in the main house; is that what you want? If it is, then count that as a point. What I am telling you, back off and give it a rest. There is only so much that I can do. Now look down and point out to the boys that the beans they planted are ready to come up."

"Thank you, fellows, for cleaning up the poultry

equipment. Now watch where you walk and come over to where you planted the beans and see what is taking place." All three of the young men were excited at what they saw. Laura explained to them, "Beans are a warm weather crop and they sprout rapidly in this kind of soil, as they also prefer the sand. Good job. Soon we will have green beans for the table!"

Laura took Tylor to the house and bathed him before putting him to bed. He enjoyed his bath, but he has always been reluctant to play in the Dismal River, even with Laura holding him. She rocked him for a while and after a time, he was asleep. Laura went to the living room to bid Tag good night and try to make some attempt to make peace for her actions, but he had gone to his room.

She went to bed, but couldn't sleep as she rehearsed the words of wisdom that Jim had graciously conveyed to her. The living room clock struck ten and she was not asleep. She prayed for Tag and asked God for His forgiveness. What had been a good day ended on a bad note with their war of words and threatening one another? When the clock struck eleven, Laura thought that surely she would sleep, now that she had asked forgiveness. It was as if God was punishing her by giving her a sleepless night. At twelve o'clock, Laura sat up in bed, as she heard something, almost like a dog whining. She put on her robe and went out into the hall. The noise came from Tag's bedroom. She heard voices, and as she opened the door, she saw Tag flailing the covers and shouting over and over, "Don't shoot, don't shoot, you are going to kill him! Don't shoot." And then he sobbed and sobbed. Laura was frightened, as she had never seen a person have a nightmare. She tried to awaken him by calling his name and to touch him. When she touched him, he reached out to her and said, "Momma, Momma, you have come for me. Hold me, Momma." Laura crawled into the bed and took him into her arms and patting his cheek, she said, "It's all right now, I'm here.

Go back to sleep." Then she began to hum a lullaby and after a time, Tag was sleeping soundly. Laura carefully crawled out of the bed and returned to her own room. Now she knew why God had not let her sleep. Sleep came to Laura, but only after she had shed tears for Tag. This was not to be the last of terror filled nights.

CHAPTER 10

NORA, COME BACK

Laura awakened, feeling sluggish after her sleepless night. She anticipated that Tag would have no recollection of his nightmare. She started the day with the men's breakfast. Everyone seemed somewhat solemn. Tag had announced that Monday morning they would start the haying season. He made no mention of going to Summit City on Saturday night, but said that they would only work Sunday mornings. At 10:00 o'clock, Jim came in and said that he was going to Summit City for repairs, as they found that a casting on one of the mowers was cracked and wouldn't hold oil. Laura asked if he would go to the feed store and get four bags of laying mash for the hens, as she expected to get them in the next day or so. She went to her room and gave him sufficient money to what she expected that she would have to pay. She wanted to get the hens on Sunday afternoon if Peggy didn't mind them coming on Sunday. She hoped that she could persuade Tag to go with her. She was not sure if Jim was going to go to church on Sunday morning or not, but she planned to go.

Laura went to the house and called Peggy. "Good morning, Peggy. We are ready for the pullets and would it be all right if we came over Sunday afternoon. If you would rather I not come at that time, just say so. I could find some time on Monday, but all my chicken catchers will be in the hay field."

"Sunday afternoon will be fine. I'm glad that you are going to take them. They are quite tame and not flighty like some pullets might be. I will have the crate down and we should be able to get all of them in it. Then we'll see you on Sunday. Bye."

As Laura had not heard from Grant, she decided to give the Hollers a call. Cindy answered the phone. "Cindy, this is

Laura. I thought I would give you a call and see what Grant had decided about the heifer."

There was a long pause on the other end. Finally, Cindy came on the line. "This is a bit awkward, Laura, and maybe I shouldn't say anything, but Grant talked with Tag. He said that the two of you decided not to buy the heifer, as you didn't use that much milk to afford a cow. Evidently the two of you are not in agreement in this matter."

"Of course he doesn't think we need a cow, but he doesn't have an eight month old baby tugging at him all day long, wanting more milk. What did Grant want for the heifer originally? Grant needs to keep in mind that it wasn't Tag buying the heifer, it was me. It is my money and it is me that will do the milking. Tag is miffed because I am getting the pullets from Peggy. If I didn't hate the smell of pigs so much, I would be tempted to buy a sow and a litter of pigs!"

Cindy laughed, "Now calm down, Laura. Grant said that he would take $150.00 for the heifer and would throw in either two kittens, or a mother cat. In fact, you would have no option. You had to take the cats."

"Is that heifer halter broke?" asked Laura.

"The boys broke her to the halter when she was quite young and she leads well. Why do you ask?"

"Tell Grant, I will give him the $150.00 and take the mother cat. I will add another $5.00 if one of the boys wants to lead her over here. Also, I will handle Tag at this end. With the men in the hay field starting Monday, I wouldn't be able to get her home. Grant can let me know tomorrow at church. I'm sorry to get you involved in our family problems, but right now, each of us are trying to establish our own territory. Once I get that heifer home, I will have all the territory I want. For now, that is. Bye for now and I will see you tomorrow." Laura was feeling good with her purchases, as she had set aside $200.00 for the purchase of a cow and the chickens. Once the pullets start laying eggs and the heifer has her calf and they have milk, cream and butter, the grocery bill will be smaller. That means that she will be able to set more aside in the bank.

Sunday morning, Laura walked to church as Tag had both trucks busy. Jim rode and took Tylor with him, as they rode the horse Bob to church.

After church, Laura saw Grant. Reaching in her purse, she handed him the money. "Here is the money for the heifer. I'm sorry to get you involved in the family feud, but I need that heifer if I am going to survive. Is five dollars sufficient for bringing her to the ranch? Oh, I forgot to ask when she is to have her calf. And what is her name? You can tell, I'm not much of a cattle buyer, but I trust you."

Grant paused, "Now let me see if I can answer those questions in the order they were asked. Yes, five dollars is plenty. In fact, for five dollars, I might deliver her. She will have her calf in about two weeks and she is bred to a Hereford bull, so you will have a fine calf. We called her 'Roanie' which isn't very original, but she likes it. As to the mother cat, I will arrange delivery at a later date. Once you get your heifer home, if you are not satisfied with her, I will refund your money and take her back, but you'll like her." Grant paused, as he changed subjects. ""I see that you are making a cowboy out of that son of yours. Jim is a gentle man. He will be good for Tylor." Grant Holler was able to sense the relationship of Jim and Tylor that it would take Laura several years to realize.

Laura walked home after church and within thirty minutes had dinner for the men. She was able to talk with Tag before they ate. "Peggy Barnes said that we could get the pullets this afternoon. Would you please go with me? I would greatly appreciate it. I was thinking that maybe some of the men might like to go along, as they have been involved in this project. It will be an outing for them as well. I sense that once you start haying, it will be full steam ahead." Laura awaited his answer; praying that he might say yes.

He surprised Laura, as he seemed quite receptive to going along with her to the Barnes Ranch. "That is a good idea. If we take those three young guys along, then I won't need to catch any chickens. You can ask them after dinner."

Laura was pleased that he had agreed, as she knew that he was not enthused over the chickens on the ranch. Fortunately, there was an enclosure in the front of the chicken house, so the chickens wouldn't be running loose. Laura had heard what a cowboy detests most, is to step in chicken manure. "If you were to invite them, I think they would appreciate it and be more likely to go with us. Tag, they like me because I feed them, but they respect you."

"All right, I'll do the asking," said Tag. Laura realized that she had made the right suggestion, as Tag enjoyed being in control. Now, the next hurdle to get over is approaching him about buying the heifer. That can wait, as we take one hurdle at a time.

Terry, Jason and Nick were eager to get off the ranch for the afternoon, especially when Laura told them that the Barnes family consisted of three beautiful daughters. She failed to tell them that the two oldest girls were eight years old. They rode in the back of the truck. Jim didn't go with the group, but chose to remain at the ranch. Tag decided to take the older truck, as he couldn't imagine hauling chickens in his new red truck. After catching the pullets, Peggy had refreshments for everyone and Karen and Sharon entertained the young men with their chatter. Carol Baker, Peggy's mother was spending the afternoon with the family and Laura had a good visit with her regarding the Holliday family. Laura was pleased, as Tag and Carl had the opportunity to visit as well. After returning home, the young men turned the pullets loose and in a short time, they had them fed and watered while Laura went to the cook shack to fix supper.

After supper, Laura walked through the garden. She was surprised to see that the men were sitting in the shade of the trees, visiting during the cool of the evening. They were sitting on benches. She asked, "I didn't remember any benches in the garden. Where did they come from?"

Tag said, "Jim built them out of scrap lumber this afternoon. He had the idea that we might like to sit in the garden. Here, Laura, you and Tylor can sit here with me. Now what is that nursery rhyme; Mary, Mary, quite contrary---that won't do. 'Laura, Laura, quite contrary, how does your garden grow?' I don't remember the rest, but that is enough to give you an idea." Laura blushed, as she knew that the nursery rhyme was fitting for her. *I am contrary and I don't know why Tag puts with me. And now I have bought a dumb old cow against his wishes. When will I ever learn to be a submissive wife? As she thought of all this, the tears started to well in her eyes.* She jumped up, leaving Tylor sitting with Tag and ran to the house. As soon as she opened the door, she began to sob. She went to her bedroom and was still sobbing when Tag came in and sat down beside her. He put his arm around her and said, "I'm sorry, Laura, I thought I was being cute and I didn't mean to offend you. Please forgive me." He continued to hold her.

She put her face into his chest and still sobbing, said, "It isn't you, it is me. I went ahead and bought that heifer this morning from Grant Holler against your wishes. I am the contrary one. Please forgive me. Grant said if I wasn't happy with the heifer, he would take her back. I'll call him and tell him that I made a mistake and can't take the heifer. I'm sorry that I disobeyed you. It seems that all I do is disobey you and bawl." Laura began sobbing again.

Tag pulled a handkerchief from his pocket and started to dry her eyes. "Laura Taggat, I have heard about you in the community and your 'cowboy contract.' You made a deal with Grant Holler and don't you back out of it! I would think less of you if you did. The other thing I like about you is that you don't bawl in public. I was wrong in not telling you that Grant called. I told him that we changed our mind. That was wrong, as I didn't ask you. I'm sorry."

Laura got off the bed and went to the bathroom to bathe her eyes. Coming out, she remarked, "I guess we need to see what Tylor is up to, or else they will have him sleeping in the bunk house."

As they returned, Jason said, "Mrs. Taggat, have you seen how those beans have grown? Now I know how Jack got his beanstalk to grow so fast, as he must have planted it in the Sandhills."

Laura laughed at Jason's remark. "It has been almost a week since we put out the bedding plants and they are trying to peek out of their protective containers. Jim, it was thoughtful of you to make the benches for all of us. We spent the afternoon drinking iced tea at the Barnes Ranch and you were working away, but we do enjoy sitting here."

"Speaking of sitting here," Tag said, "Laura, I failed to tell you, but you will need to bring our lunch to the hayfield tomorrow and probably for the next two weeks. I will have you ride with the first load of repair equipment so that you will know where to come at noon. There will be two gates for you to go through, so you will need to allow yourself plenty of time. This will be like a picnic, so adjust your meals accordingly." Laura began to make a mental note of what she planned to prepare, so she was oblivious of any further conversation that evening. Tag got up, and said, "We have a big day tomorrow, so I guess that I will turn in. Are you coming Laura?"

Laura bid the men good night and taking Tylor as he rested on her hip, followed Tag to the house.

As Laura was ready to go to her room, she touched Tag's arm, and said, "Thank you for seeing that we got the pullets home. I enjoyed the afternoon visiting with our neighbors and the evening in the garden." She lingered a moment, aching for some response from Tag. When she got none, she said, "Good night." Going to her room, she looked in the mirror to see if she was so unattractive that she was unable to trigger any interest from Tag. That night she slept with her door open, so that she might hear him should he have another nightmare.

The next day was likened to a daytime nightmare. Tag was a bundle of nerves, getting everyone lined out. Jim and Laura left early to get out of Tag's way. Jim had Laura drive, as it was the first time that she had driven on a trail road. After going from side to side for a short distance, Laura was able to maneuver the truck quite well. At the first gate, she was unable to stop in time and ran into the wire gate. She didn't breaking anything, but she did stretch the wires. Jim had told her that makes the gate easier to open. At the next gate, she stopped all right and he had Laura get out so that she might see how it was to open a wire gate. She struggled until she understood the principles of how it worked. Arriving at the hay camp, they unloaded the equipment and returned to the ranch. Laura was glad to have Jim as her instructor. He pointed out various landmarks so that she might not get lost. He left her at the cook shack and he went on to the barn to start taking some of the horses to the hay camp.

Laura took the opportunity to go to the hen house to look in at the chickens. Everything was fine and they seemed to be adapting to their new surroundings. Laura started putting together her lunch after she had cleaned up the morning dishes. She had started a roast and was going to have warm meat for sandwiches, along with large dinner rolls that she would be baking. Potato salad, canned peaches and iced tea would complete the menu. She thought that it sounded good!

Laura loaded the food in the truck and managed to wedge Tylor in among some of the boxes so he didn't fall on the floor. She went through the first gate with no problem. That was the one that she had stretched out. She became confused and was unable to locate the second gate. Laura then returned to the first gate and tried to retrace her route to locate the second gate. Now she understood why the early settlers feared the Sandhills. There were so few landmarks that they feared getting lost. It was now almost noon and she didn't know what to do. Rather than wander around, she began to honk the horn. Three short blasts every couple of minutes. She also prayed to be found when she wasn't honking the horn. After about ten minutes, she saw Tag's red truck appear in the distance. Her prayer then turned to thanksgiving for being rescued, but also that she hadn't angered Tag. Her prayer also was that the driver of the red truck might be Jim, as she had no desire to exchange harsh words with her husband. As the vehicle drew closer, she saw that it was Tag and he drove up alongside. He stuck his head out of the window and said, "Hey, lady, are you going my way?"

Laura was relieved that he wasn't angry. She replied, "Only if I can buy you lunch. How lost was I?"

"Only about a half mile. That was good thinking to honk the horn. It helped to find you. Follow me and don't get lost."

When she arrived at the hay camp, she saw that they had mowed a large patch of hay. The men were hungry and happy for the iced tea, as the day was quite warm. Nick said, "Mrs. Taggat,

I was worried when you didn't show up on time. I know you like to be on time and I was afraid that we had lost the best cook in Summit County. I like Jim, but I don't want him to ever do any cooking for this outfit again."

Laura asked Tag, "How can I be assured that I won't get lost going home? I am really confused."

"I will take you back to the second gate. Actually, you can see it from here. After you go through the gate, stay on the trail to the first gate and on to home. Tomorrow, when you go through the first gate, there is only one trail until you go about a quarter of a mile where the trail forks. Take the left fork and you will have to turn left a little bit to stay on it. That trail will bring you to the second gate, where you will see the hay camp. Can you make it home all right, as I don't want you to get lost?"

Laura nodded her head. "Now I understand. I'm sorry that I was late and thank you for rescuing me." Laura had packed things and was ready to go home, as she left in a cloud of dust.

When Laura arrived back at the ranch, Timmy Holler was coming up the road on his horse, leading a roan heifer. Laura exclaimed to Tylor, "Look, Son, our cow has come home. Isn't she beautiful?" She picked up Tylor and got out of the truck to meet Timmy. "Oh, Timmy, thank you for bringing Roanie to us. She is beautiful. Let's take her to the corral so she can drink and rest a bit. Do you need to water your horse?" Timmy nodded. "When you finish, stop down at the cook shack and I will have some iced tea and cookies for you."

Laura hurried and set out the cookies and tea and waited for Timmy to stop at the cook shack.

After Timmy had consumed a quantity of iced tea and three cookies, Laura gave him the five dollars that she had promised. She asked him, "Would you boys mind if I changed the name of the heifer? Roanie is kind of plain for such a thing of beauty. I thought that I might call her 'Macaroni.' That way, the Roanie sound is still there, but this would be a name with class. I doubt if there is another cow in this whole world with a name like that. What do you think?"

"Mrs. Taggat, I do believe that you are right about that. There probably isn't another cow named Macaroni." Timmy smiled as he got up to leave. "Thank you for the five dollars and I hope that you like her. She is a fine heifer and a fine name as well." He got on his horse and kicked him into a gallop, as he went down the road toward home.

Laura reminisced about the Holler family. *I failed to ask Timmy about his plans, but I am sure that he will be going to high school this year. I suppose that the boys are still playing ball with that softball that hit me in the stomach last year. Cindy and I have had some great moments together. In fact, I have been in the Sandhills for 18 months. What an exciting—or is it an adventure— time in my life! A lot of tears and a lot of laughs have crossed my path in these 18 months. It seems that I have lived a lifetime in the Sandhills, but I know that there is more to come. Thank you, Lord. I have been touched!*

Laura went back out to look at Macaroni. As she was holding Tylor, she pointed and told him, "Cow, cow." Macaroni came to the fence and sniffed Tylor. He was bare-footed and she reached through the fence and licked his feet. He laughed, as her rough tongue had also rubbed against Laura's arm and she could see why it had tickled Tylor. It was then that he said his first word; other than 'Momma' when he said, "C-c-cow." Laura noticed that even at that age, he had a tendency to stutter, but was sure that he would outgrow it.

Going over to the hen house, she peeked in and saw that things looked good, except that the three roosters were constantly fighting and stirring up the pullets. All at once, she knew what she would take to the hay field for dinner tomorrow. *Nick wanted fried chicken. Nick will have fried chicken! All I need is one rooster to crow in the morning. The winner will survive!* She found the—*I guess you would call it a 'chicken catcher' that looked like a miniature shepherd's crook. Tomorrow morning, two of you will be in the frying pan. To go with the fried chicken, I will have baked beans and I still have some potato salad and, oh yes, olives. I will think of a dessert later. Won't Nick be surprised! I enjoy cooking for the men. If it is good, they will praise you. If it is not so good, they will eat it any way.*

The men arrived for supper in good spirits and hungry. The first day had gone well, which is normally unusual. Laura presumed the cook getting lost was usual, so that didn't count. After supper, they all went out to admire Macaroni. Tag offered some of his horse oats for her until Laura could buy her own cow feed. Tag said, "Laura, the small pasture next to the corral can be her pasture, as it is close by. Normally it is used for a saddle horse or two, but there is plenty of grass and can be shared if needed. The feed store sells a grain mixture called 'COB' that is a combination of corn, oats and barley that is ground or rolled. A lot of it is sold for the 4-H livestock. For her, you might want to top-dress it with some protein supplement such as soybean meal. You made a fine choice Laura. Do you really think that you can milk her? Yeah, I know, I have heard you say, 'how hard can it be?' I don't think you know how hard it can be." Laura smiled, as she knew how hard it could be. She had learned that as an early teen-ager. It was one of those things where you struggle and struggle and then all of a sudden it is there.

The men spent some time in the garden, as it was cool. Later, Tag and Laura went to the house where they worked on the ranch books for a while before going to bed. Again, Laura slept with her bedroom door open, to listen for Tag, should he have a nightmare. Maybe the one was an isolated instance.

The next morning after the dishes were washed and put away, Laura went to the ranch machine shop to look for a hatchet. After putting one foot inside, she was amazed at the clutter. Her first thought was how do they find anything in here? Looking around, she located it hanging on the wall near the door. It was one of the few tools which was hanging. She tested to see if it was sharp and it was reasonably sharp. She and Tylor then went to the hen house. She located the first rooster and snagged him by one leg. Taking him outside, she chopped his head off and left him to flop around while she found the other loser, who promptly lost his head. She returned the hatchet to the shop and came back to clean the birds. Things were going well, as the last item of the dinner was to prepare the chicken. As soon as the chicken was out of the skillet, she had everything packed and ready to go. She prayed that she would not get lost and that everything would ride well, including Tylor. The aroma of the chicken permeated the cab of the truck. Laura was tempted to stop and have her lunch before she got to the hay camp. She had tasted the baked beans and the taste was even better than their aroma.

The men were washed and waiting when she drove into the camp. Nick helped Laura unpack the cab while she was getting Tylor out of his seat. Nick grinned, and said, "Mrs. Taggat, if this is what I think it is, I may faint from sheer joy. This has to be fried chicken."

Laura laughed as she saw his delight. "Unfortunately, I only had two roosters to eat, as I wanted one just to hear him crow. Please respect your fellow workers when you help yourself, as the number of pieces is limited. If this goes well, I may have to find another source for obtaining roosters to eat."

Laura was busy, seeing that the men were fed and their glasses were filled. She noticed that Jim was slow eating and when the rest of the crew had started on their dessert of cherry pie, he still hadn't finished the main course. Laura usually ate after the men were fed. She started to fill her plate and noticed that the chicken was gone, even the necks which she anticipated were to be hers. Jim came over to where she was sitting and motioned to a thigh still on his plate. "I knew you wouldn't save any for yourself, so I have held this back. You need to know how good it was. I have tasted chicken before, but none better than this. Thank you, Laura."

Her first thought was to refuse it, but she realized that this was as dear as a gift, and was thankful that Jim remembered her. "Thank you, Jim. I consider this the best piece of all, because you thought of me." Once again, her eyes clouded with tears of happiness, as she realized the close bond there was between Jim and her. It was delicious and even now, she was planning to raise chickens for next year. It was an easy way to feed the men. Ideally, had she been setting the table at the ranch, she would have had mashed potatoes and gravy to go with the chicken. Gathering the dirty dishes, she realized that she had nothing to take home as leftovers!

The routine of each day was such that one scarcely realized what day of the week it was. Laura crossed each day off the calendar as she went to bed. Friday was not a good day. Terry was raking hay with the team of horses when they encountered a nest of ground wasps. The frightened horses ran away, throwing Terry off the rake. Fortunately, he was not hurt, but there was considerable damage to the rake. Laura sensed the tension as the men came to the dining hall for supper. Tag was not in a good mood and was short with everyone, including Laura. He was given a wide berth and everyone breathed a sigh of relief when he went to the house. As the men sat in the garden that evening watching the sun go down, Jim tried to ease the situation. "Terry, don't take this personal. These things happen and it is no one's fault. I'm thankful that you were not thrown under the rake. I am of the opinion that if you can walk away from a wreck and a few dollars can fix it, it was a good wreck. Tomorrow is another day. It may be good and it may be bad, but we will get through it. Now, enjoy the evening and see if the garden was growing while we were haying. I'm sure it was." As it started to darken, the group broke up and each went their own way. It was Laura's prayer that Tag had gone to bed before she entered the house.

The house was silent as she and Tylor entered the living room. Tag's bedroom door was closed and she tried to be as quiet as possible as she put Tylor to bed. Laura was tired, but sleep would not overtake her. The feeding of the crew at the hay camp was a lot of extra work. She missed the coolness of the dining hall at mid-day as compared to the noon time heat of the hay camp. Laura tossed and turned and it seemed that she had just dozed off, when she heard the wailing from Tag's room. She put on her robe and looked at the clock and saw that it was a little after eleven. Once again, Tag was crying out and Laura thought he was calling for her, but as she listened, it sounded as if he was calling for 'Nora.' Then he began to sob and called out, "Nora, Nora, don't run away from me. Come back! Come back! Nora, come back!" Once again, as the previous time, Laura tried to console him by touching him and calling his name. And as before, he reached out to her, and said, "Momma, you are here. Hold me, Momma, hold me!" Laura rubbed his face and neck and climbed in beside him and once again, as she held him, she consoled him with a lullaby. After a time, he was sleeping peacefully and Laura returned to her room.

Sleep wouldn't come to Laura however. She prayed for Tag, but was uncertain as how to pray. And, who was this Nora? Perhaps Jim had some answers, but she was reluctant to reveal to Jim what she had witnessed on these occasions. Maybe Jim is unaware of his nightmares. Laura questioned if there was a pattern developing, as each evening the nightmare occurred, Tag had been angry. Was he capable of physical violence? Jim seemed to think that he might be. I pray that neither Tylor nor I are being in danger.

Tag showed up at breakfast as if nothing had happened the previous day. He certainly looked as if he had experienced a good night's sleep. Such was not the case with Laura. The nightmares were a fearful thing and then she was unable to obtain a sound night of sleep.

At breakfast, Tag informed her that he was going to town for the repairs to the rake and not to expect to take lunch to the men. She was to have sandwiches made up when he returned from Summit City and he would take it to them. They were short a vehicle and couldn't spare the running around. As he left the table, he said, "I don't know what time I will be back, but have it ready to load when I arrive. However, be sure that they have a full meal. I will leave now. Jim, you know what to do. Let's get some hay put up today!"

The men were still eating their breakfast when Tag left. Jason, in his slow way said, "I do believe that if Mr. Taggat had created the world, he would have it done by the second day and still enough daylight left to sit in the garden for a spell." The men laughed in agreement.

As the men left, Jim was the last to leave the table. Laura asked him, "Jim, who is Nora?"

Jim gave a startled look. "Laura, you don't need to know!" He hurried out of the dining hall before Laura could ask any further.

Laura shouted after him, "I do need to know! And, I will find out!"

Laura hurried with the morning dishes and began to prepare the noon meal, as if Tag would be here any minute. She had taken out some hamburger from the freezer portion of the refrigerator. She had purchased it from the locker plant. That reminded her that she needed to get back to town and stock up on supplies again. She had anticipated going this afternoon, but that would not happen, as she wouldn't have a vehicle. She was looking forward to testing her driving skills on her trip to Summit City. She had hoped to stop in and see Maude and Hannah if time permitted. Laura wanted to get the feed for Macaroni so that they would be better acquainted when the time came for her to start milking her. Though she dreaded it, she also wanted to subscribe to *The Sentinel* once again. All the time she was planning her trip, she was mixing the dough for a batch of baking soda biscuits. *Also, while the oven is hot, I will make some more cookies for the men, especially for those three young ones. I do believe that they don't chew them, but simply inhale them.* Tylor was happily playing on the floor and from time to time, he would call to his mother, with his m-m-m-momma way of saying it. He should soon be walking in the next month or so. Laura set out two cans of canned peaches, along with the can opener, so that the men could have peaches and cookies for dessert. Laura had planned to break up the hamburger and cook it, adding catsup and spices. This could be ladled over the biscuits and eaten with a fork, similar to biscuits and gravy. She would keep it simmering so that it would be hot when Tag came for it. She made the iced tea and had it in the refrigerator, as she awaited Tag's return. Laura questioned her fear of Tag. *If I am going to live with a man, I cannot be a prisoner of fear. I sense that this Nora is the key to his nightmares. Jim McCann is not going to get off so easy by brushing me off. I will find out and put an end to these senseless nightmares.*

Laura kept a close eye on the clock. At five minutes until noon, Tag drove up to the cook shack in a flurry of dust. Immediately he started shouting orders, as if the men were going to die if they were not fed at once. Laura stopped him. "Tag, the men had a good breakfast and if you will relax, they will have a good lunch, but a few minutes late. This is what I have, so someone can figure out how to put it together."

"No, no, no," he affirmed. "It is too late, so you can go with me and bring a vehicle back. It took longer than it should have. That is the slowest town I have ever seen. I bet the sun comes up an hour later than anywhere else. Get in and get the stuff together." Laura was methodical in loading the truck with the dinner. Despite Tag's urging, she remembered the philosophy of Grandma Martin that proclaimed 'haste makes waste' and she wasn't about to waste any portion of the meal to please Tag's impatience.

As soon as the truck was loaded, she had Tylor sitting on her lap while she was trying to keep everything from spilling, as Tag left in a hurry. At the first gate, he told Laura to get out and open the gate. "Nobody opened the gates for me. I am holding a child and trying to keep the rest of the food from upsetting. And, now you expect me to open the gate? You could have it opened in the time that we have been arguing over this."

Tag jumped out and opened the gate, drove through, then back out to close the gate and then back into the truck. He repeated the same process through the second gate as well. After a time, they pulled into the hay camp and Laura began to feed the men. They were pleased with the meal. Tag scarcely ate anything; he was wound so tight. Laura ate after the men had their fill and began to put things together to return to the ranch. She asked Tag, "I am going to town for supplies, which truck do you want me to drive to town? I prefer the older truck, as I am familiar with the operation of it. Also, I wouldn't want anything to happen to your new truck while it was in my care."

"No," said Tag, "I don't want you to go to town today. You can go next week. It won't hurt you to stay at home once in a while."

"Why do you say such a ridiculous thing, as if I am on the road all the time? If I am to feed these men, then I will go to town this afternoon. Stop trying to control me. I am a mature woman and make mature decisions. I asked you a simple question regarding which truck to take. I didn't ask if I could go, but how. Answer my question! Is that so hard?"

"Take the old one and be back in time for supper." Tag left in a huff, thinking he had the last word by telling her when to come back.

Nick helped Laura put the things in the truck and she secured Tylor in the seat. Laura said to Nick, "Thank you for helping me. I'm sorry that you men have to be a witness to our war of words. I do have a number of things to get done and I am getting a late start. Should I be late, don't be alarmed, as I haven't abandoned you."

Laura returned to the ranch. She enjoyed driving the trails in the pastures and seeing the various wild flowers. Sometimes she would come upon small bunches of cattle. The cows and their calves, lifted their heads to acknowledge her presence, but afterwards returned to their grazing. Once she spotted a doe with her twin fawns as they bounced along, heading for the cover along a small creek. Laura determined that she needed a few turkeys, like the Hollers had, to give a balance to the wildlife. Perhaps, she could get Toby to trap some for her, as he was adept at calling them in last Thanksgiving when they went turkey hunting. *Lord, I have been touched by your splendor exhibited in the Sandhills.* She pulled up to the cook shack and unloaded what was left of the dinner. Stopping at the house, she retrieved her purse and started for Summit City. Her first stop was at the feed store where she purchased four bags of COB and one bag of soybean meal. She was running short of cash and realized that she needed to get settled up with the ranch account, but for the time being she would withdraw money from her safety deposit box. While in the bank, she met Sheriff Morgan. He greeted her and asked, "Mrs. Taggat, do you have a Nebraska driver's license?"

Laura looked at the sheriff rather quizzically. Then she went over to the window and looked out at her truck. "Sure, I do. See, it is fastened to the bumper."

The Sheriff laughed, "Are you funning me? That is for the vehicle. Do you have a license that says you know the laws of the state and have had your eyes tested, and that shows you are capable to drive? How about a license from back east, or wherever you came from? Did they issue you a license?"

Laura hiked Tylor to a more comfortable spot on her hip. "Sheriff, I just learned to drive this past week, why would I need a license from Maine?"

"Mrs. Taggat, because of the law in this state, you must have a license if you drive that vehicle. I will have to arrest you for driving without a license. I don't want to do that, but the law says that is my responsibility."

Laura asked, "Would you throw me in jail, like, over the week-end?"

"I might do that, if you were uncooperative," he said.

"Sheriff, I really need a rest and I am not appreciated. I warn you, I am going to start up that vehicle so that you will arrest me and throw me in jail. May I keep my boy with me? He is still nursing, so he would miss me."

Ken Holliday came out, and asked, "What is the problem?"

The sheriff was flustered to say the least. "Ken, can you talk some sense into this woman's head. She is driving around town without a license. She says that she is going to drive so that I will throw her in jail, so that she can have some rest. Not only that, because she is nursing her son, she wants him with her. I don't want to do that, but I will."

Ken tried to reason with her. "Laura, if you are arrested, it will be on your record. It will not only be with the state, but the insurance company as well. Tag will have to pay a higher premium on the insurance. Sheriff Morgan has been real understanding by not arresting you. He has given you an option to get a license next week and everything will be all right. I will drive you around town and get all of your shopping done. I'll then drive you home and someone can bring me back to town. Doesn't that seem the most logical thing to do?"

Laura was disgusted. "Yes, the most logical, but I was counting on a few days of rest while being in jail."

Sheriff Morgan told Ken, "Thanks, I was afraid I was going to have to lock her up. Can you imagine *The Sentinel* printing that I had arrested a nursing mother and baby? Laura, come back this winter and I will give you two free days in jail with no publicity." Laura accepted his decision with a shrug of her shoulders.

Ken said, "Come on, Laura, let's get your shopping done and get you out of town."

Ken was very tolerant, as he escorted Laura around town, picking up her groceries and the meat at the locker plant. Laura was having second thoughts about feeding the crew for a flat rate instead of actual costs. Laura noticed that the better she fed the men, the more they ate. That heifer better hurry with that calf and the same goes for the pullets. I am buying feed, but not getting any return. Laura was disappointed that she was unable to visit Maude and Hannah, but she decided that after she gets her license, she could run to and fro throughout the state.

252

As they left Summit City and crossed the Dismal River, Laura asked, "Ken, how are things going with you? Unfortunately, I don't see much of you at church, as I am needed at the ranch to prepare the noon meal. Then too, at the bank, it is always business. Thank you for playing the role of mediator when Tag and I were in the other day. We have our good days and our bad days, but we are gaining ground." Remembering Ken's offer, she said, "I appreciate the gift of Stella's easel, but I cannot paint now. Perhaps, when the snow is flying, I can get back to it. I did so enjoy the painting." Changing the subject to a lighter note, she asked, "But tell me, how is Todd and Tara? They are such lovely children and I do miss them."

"Tara is taking swimming lessons and Todd has a job this summer at the school helping the custodian with the resealing of floors and general outdoor maintenance. Mrs. Baker is doing fine, but she is no Laura Martin." Ken looked over at Laura when he said that, and smiled.

Laura said, "Probably that is just as well. One is enough. Thank you, Ken, for rescuing me from Sheriff Morgan. Otherwise, I would probably be spending the evening in jail. Why am I so obstinate? My mother wasn't, but I must take after my Grandma Martin. What is it you told me? That I was 'gutsy,' or maybe just plain stubborn is more like it."

Ken laughed, "I will never forget my first encounter with you. I wasn't sure when you pulled off your coat and threw it on the desk just how many clothes you were going to take off. I went home that night and told Stella that the school board from Good Hope had a wildcat for a teacher. After you came to live with us and was so good with Stella, she constantly reminded me about making rash judgments about people, as she regarded you as a jewel."

"Ken," said Laura, with tears in her eyes, "those three

months that Tylor and I spent in your home were the most heart rendering and the most precious times of our lives." The rest of the trip to the ranch was spent in silence.

As Ken drove to the cook shack, it was after six and the men were waiting outside, presumably waiting for the cook to show up. Laura turned to Ken, "Won't you stay for supper? This calls for emergency rations, as I need to prepare a meal fast, so you know what that means don't you?"

Ken said only one word, "Spaghetti!" He laughed and said, "I will stay, which means that the one that drives me back will not miss their meal."

When the truck came to a stop, Laura got out and handed Tylor to Jim, saying to Tag, "Save your snide remarks until later. I will start supper and will have it as quickly as I can. Should you have any questions, Mr. Holliday will handle those. Nick, please see to unloading the groceries. Terry, there are five sacks of feed for the cow. See that it is put away."

Jason said, "Oh, boy, spaghetti!"

Laura knew how to hustle and hustle she did. She soon had the traditional spaghetti dinner, with the fruit cocktail for dessert. Tag was silent during the meal. Laura was embarrassed, as if he was ignoring Ken. Jim tried to carry the conversation and later agreed to drive him back to Summit City.

As they were preparing to leave, Laura went to Ken, "Thank you, Ken, for bringing me home. I fear that I took most of your afternoon. When you see Sheriff Morgan, tell him I have had second thoughts about the two free days this winter, so not to hold the cell for me. I fear that if he ever got me in a cell, he might keep me. He and I have had other confrontations in the past. Good night."

"Good night, Laura, and thank you for the dinner. Your

spaghetti is still as good as ever."

As Laura returned to the cook shack, she met Tag. He grabbed her by the wrist, and asked, "What is that all about?" She struggled to free herself, but he continued to hold her wrist.

She pleaded, "Please let me go! You are hurting my wrist."

The tone of Tag's voice indicated that he was furious. "I will let go when you tell me what this is all about. A thousand people in Summit City and he is the one to bring you home and to bring you home late. What is there between you two?" He was still holding her wrist. By now, she ceased to struggle, as she learned that by struggling, he gripped harder.

Now, Laura was angry. "Tag, I have told you before; there is nothing between us. I have been faithful to you and I was faithful to you today. I don't know why, but I am. If you were so concerned with my fidelity, why didn't you ask him? You were so angry and jealous, that you hardly said two words to him. He is my friend and he did what friends do, they help people." She tried to pry his fingers from her wrist, but he held on. "Please let me go. Tell me what you want, but please let me go." Only then did he release her. She held her wrist to her stomach, as she ran into the cook shack, sobbing as she went.

When she entered the kitchen, Nick was washing the dishes. Tylor was crawling on the floor and Laura knelt and hugged him. Nick said, "I'm sorry, Mrs. Taggat. I don't know what to do to help you. I will finish with the dishes. Thank you for the supper. It was real good, as always. Please don't leave. You mean a lot to us and you treat us good."

"Thank you, Nick. I need to go to the house now. I will take Tylor with me. Please close up. You mean a lot to me, also. I won't leave you, as I am not a quitter." Laura was thankful for Nick. In all his simplicity, he knew right from wrong. Laura hugged Tylor and hurried to the house. Her wrist pained her and she wanted to put ice on it. She knew that Tag didn't realize his own strength when he was angry.

Laura bathed Tylor, as he was restless. It had been a big day for him and he was tired. Laura had trouble lifting him into his bed because of her wrist. She kissed him and left the room.

Laura went to the kitchen and fixed an ice pack for her wrist. Returning to her bedroom, she looked for an aspirin among the medications that she had brought with her when she left Maude and the café. These were things that she had accumulated while in her own apartment. She began to reflect over her life. *Is it getting better, or am I falling deeper and deeper, into what, I don't know? Just when I think I am making progress with Tag, then this incident bursts forth. Is he capable of murder? Am I always the one to trigger these attacks? Is it because I am a woman? What is the answer?* These were the questions running through her head, when she dropped off to sleep.

Evidently these things were instilled in her mind when someone softly calling her name and touching her shoulder awakened her. In one swift motion, she brought up the revolver and had it pointed in the intruder's face. Laura screamed, "Stop! Stop right there, or I will shoot! I mean it!" When the intruder heard the cocking of the gun, he yelled, "Don't shoot, Laura, it is me, Tag! Don't shoot!" Laura kept the gun in his face, as she reached for the light on the nightstand. Turning it on, she saw that it was Tag and he was shaking with fear, as he looked at the gun pointed in his face. Once again, he said, "Please don't shoot. I won't harm you."

With both hands holding the revolver, Laura asked, "What do you want?" She didn't waver, as the end of the barrel of the gun was just inches from his nose.

"It is Jason. He is terribly sick. Can you help him? Jim

came and woke me up. He is in the hallway. Laura, I didn't mean to scare you, but do you have to keep a gun under your pillow? I thought you were going to shoot me. Put that thing down, please, please, put it away. I won't hurt you. Jim is out in the hallway. Say something, Jim. She has a gun pointed at me and won't put it down. Say something!"

"It's all right, Laura. Jason is sick and I came here to see if you know what to do for him, or if we need to take him to the hospital. It is one o'clock in the morning, but he is moaning something awful." Jim had never seen Tag so scared in all the time they had been together. With all the shouting, Jim thought that Laura was going to shoot Tag, as he sensed that she was reliving the attack on her just a couple of weeks ago.

Laura released the hammer on the revolver and placed it under her pillow. She reached for her robe that was on the chair close by, as her sheer nightgown revealed the outline of her body. Tag thought, *I didn't realize how thin she has become. The nursing of Tylor and the demands of cooking for the crew have taken a toll on her body.* Putting on her robe and finding a pair of shoes, she grabbed the bag that she had been rummaging through earlier in the evening. As she grabbed the bag, she winced in pain, as she had used the arm that had been gripped earlier in the evening by Tag. Tucking the bag under the good arm, she looked over at Tylor and saw that he was still sleeping, despite the shouting. *Perhaps, had I pulled the trigger, he would have awakened. Had the intrusion happened earlier when I was suffering from pain in the arm, I might have pulled the trigger. Well, only if I had moved the gun to the side. Not hurt Tag, but give him a good scare.*

Accompanied by Tag and Jim, Laura cut across through the garden to the bunkhouse. The lights were on and everyone was up, except for Jason, who was lying on his bunk, moaning.

Laura asked, "Have any of the others had any problems tonight?" Everyone shook their head, indicating no. *I believe they all think that he is going to die and they are afraid to say anything.* "Jason, have you had any diarrhea with this?" Jason shook his head no. "How about vomiting? Have you vomited tonight?" He nodded his head. "All right, how many times have you vomited?" He held up two fingers. "All right; this next question is a little tougher, but how many helpings of spaghetti did you have?" Jason held up four fingers. "And fruit cocktail?" Jason held up two fingers and said, "Big ones." Laura smiled, "My diagnosis is that he is suffering from gluttony." Reaching into her bag, she pulled out a bottle. "Someone get me a tablespoon from the kitchen." Terry hurried, and came back with the spoon. Laura measured out a spoonful from a bottle and gave it to Jason. He made a face as he swallowed it. Laura held up two fingers in front of his face and gave him another spoonful. That face was even worse than the first. "That should ease the pain. Now stop the moaning, as the rest of the crew need their rest. Good night!"

The next morning, everyone was at breakfast, except for Jason. They said that he was up, but didn't feel like coming to eat. Once again, Tag insisted that the crew put in a half day on Sunday. Laura, Tylor and Jim went to church, in their usual procession, with Laura walking and Jim and Tylor riding Bob. Laura was glad that she didn't have to carry Tylor, as her wrist was still experiencing some pain. She chose to wear a long sleeved blouse to hide the discoloration. Evidently, because of the heat of the day, Pastor Don had cut the sermon short and Laura and Jim arrived at the ranch before the hay crew. Laura sensed that the crew would be late, as she expected Tag would work them as late as he could get by with, without too much complaining.

When Laura reached up to take Tylor from Jim, he

258

did his usual stiffening of the body and kicking to indicate his displeasure. This time he howled. Laura gave him a swat on his bottom and scolded him. "That is enough of that! When I say it is time to get down, that is what I mean!" Tylor was surprised at his mother's action, but by the tone of her voice, even though he was nearing nine months of age, he understood that his mother meant business. Laura looked up at Jim to see his reaction. Jim was noncommittal. Laura asked, "I imagine that dinner will be a bit late. I can heat up some morning coffee and find a cookie or two. That way, it will tide you over until dinner."

Jim stepped down from Bob and let the reins fall to the ground as he followed Laura into the kitchen. Laura asked, "Won't Bob run away?"

"No, he has been trained, when the reins are on the ground that is where he is to stay."

Laura was amazed. "Will it work with children?" Laura started to heat the coffee and she sat out a plate of cookies, giving one to Tylor to slobber over, as he was cutting his teeth again.

Jim laughed, "Not that I am aware of, but I rather doubt if it would work. They are too independent." Jim sat down on a chair, and pulled himself to the worktable that was in the center of the kitchen. "Laura, you didn't specifically invite me in for coffee and cookies. What is on your mind?"

"You know me pretty well, don't you? Tell me! Who is Nora? I want to know. Who is she?"

"I told you before, you don't want to know, and you don't need to know!" Jim was standing firm on this matter.

She was just as determined as Jim was in this matter. "Does Tag have a history of nightmares?"

"I am not aware of Tag having such a problem. Surely a big, tough fellow like him wouldn't have nightmares."

Laura set coffee before Jim and pulled her chair to the table before she spoke. "He has had two of them in the past week. The first one I could hear him cry out, even though both of our doors were closed. He kept crying out, 'don't shoot, don't shoot, you are going to kill him.' When I touched him and talked to him, he called me 'momma.' It was frightening."

"I'm not surprised after that episode with the gun last night. He has known that you sleep with a gun under your pillow since that shooting gallery display two weeks ago." She had never seen Jim worked up like he was this morning.

Laura countered, "I don't think so. Since the first one, I have been sleeping with my door open, so that I might detect if it was a one-time thing. The latest was when he called for Nora. He said, 'Nora, Nora, don't run away from me. Come back! Come back! Nora, come back!' Then when I touched him and talked to him, he thought it was his mother. Now, are you going to tell me, who is Nora?"

Jim was silent. It was almost as if he was mute. Finally he spoke. "Nora was a woman that he met in a bar in Madden. She came in alone. Before the evening was over, Tag and she had become quite chummy. Her beauty took him and they began to meet at the bar. What he didn't know was that she was married to a cattle buyer that had come into the area. Tag was talking marriage when he found out that she had been playing him for a fool. Despite all this, he still loved her and wanted her to leave her husband and marry him. When she refused is when he beat her and beat her savagely. As soon as she recovered enough to leave, that is when she ran away, as she feared for her life. No one knows where she went, but when she left, she left with a huge sum of money, presumably not to press charges against Tag. I know who paid her off and how much she was paid. However, it wasn't Tag."

260

Laura spoke in a whisper that was barely audible. "Then she won't be back?"

"Let me assure you," said Jim. "She won't be back."

She got up from the table. "Thank you, Jim. That is what I needed to know."

Jim went out to his horse, still standing where he had left him. Laura went to her child, his face covered with the remnants of a cookie.

It was almost one o'clock before the men came to dinner. Evidently, Tag had worked them hard in the heat. Fortunately, Laura had a beef roast cooking and plenty of iced tea. Jason ate some, but was moderate in how much he ate. Later, Terry, Nick and Jason had gone down to the Dismal River to swim. Laura had been informed not to show up at the river, as none of them had swimsuits. Tag was repairing some mower sickles and Jim was riding out to check one of the windmills on the ranch. It had been hot and he was not sure how much wind had blown to pump water for the cattle. Laura had decided that she and Tylor would take a nap, as it had been a strenuous week.

When Laura had awakened from her nap, she saw that she needed to begin fixing supper for the men. She decided that since they had not worked hard in the afternoon, she would fix them roast beef sandwiches to eat along with a potato salad. She had made Jell-O by adding the left over fruit cocktail to the mix and setting it aside. At six, she rang the dinner bell, with no response. It appeared to Laura that something had come up and the men had left the ranch headquarters. *Well, Tylor and I will go to the garden and see how it has grown. Perhaps we will water a few of the bedding plants.* The sun was setting low in the sky and the air was beginning to cool, when the men rode in and went to the horse barn. Laura presumed that they had been working cattle was the reason that they were late. Laura quickly

JOY AT THE DISMAL RIVER

sensed that Tag was in one of his moods, as evidently things had not gone as well as he had wanted. After they came to the dining hall and washed up, she began to serve them. No one said anything, until Jason asked for the potato salad. Tag piped up, "Kid, if you could work cows like you eat, you would be a whale of a cowboy. I swear, I have seen farmers' wives shoo cattle with their aprons better than the three of you did this afternoon. I don't believe you know which end of the cow the tail is on!" No one said anything and no one passed the potato salad to Jason.

Laura went to the end of the table where the potato salad was setting. She picked it up and took it to Jason. He took the bowl and set it on the table, but didn't take anything. Laura had seen and heard enough. "Gentlemen, when you are at my table, I would appreciate it if you kept the conversation pleasant, as eating should be a pleasant experience. Jason, please help yourself to some potato salad and ask the person next to you if they would like some as well. I will not tolerate derogatory remarks to others while at the table."

"Laura, you may be the cook here, but you will not interfere when I am speaking to any of the men. This is between me and the men, so go back to the kitchen where you belong!" Laura saw that this was going nowhere, with Tag in his present state of mind.

"I will leave, but remember Tag, you called them men, but you are treating them as little boys. They are men and deserve to be treated as men!" Laura picked up an empty platter and returned to the kitchen.

Laura cleaned up the kitchen and dining room and turned off the lights, as it was now getting dark. As she prepared for bed, her thoughts went to Tag. *Will this be the night for one of his nightmares? The scenario would indicate so, as he was experiencing stress. Something happened with the cattle and it had taken most of the afternoon to get it straightened out. The other factor was that he and I had a confrontation. No one will stand up to him, right or wrong!*

Tylor was fussy, as his teeth were bothering him and it had been a long day. Laura bathed him and put him down for the night. She especially took time to pray before going to bed. Foremost was her relationship to Tag. *How long must we go on, how long?*

Laura's sleep was interrupted by sounds from Tag's room. In her hurry to hear what he was saying, she neglected to grab her robe from the back of the chair. The moonlight was shining through the large window and was casting its light on the floor. As she entered the room she could hear Tag calling over and over, "Nora, Nora, come back. Don't run away from me. I love you, Nora. Come back." Laura was startled; partially from hearing his pleas and partially remembering what Jim had told her about Tag's attack upon Nora. Laura went to him as she had done previously to console him and to touch him and to call his name, so that he might be released from the nightmare. He asked, "Is that you, Nora? You came back, you came back!" As he spoke those words, he engulfed Laura in his arms. As she struggled, his grasp was so tight that she could only whisper, "No, this is Laura, it is Laura." Whether the names were so similar, or he was so sure that it was Nora and unable to comprehend the difference, she was unsure, but she knew that there was no escape from Tag. Her heart beat so fast that she thought her chest would break. This is not the way she wanted it to happen, but she also knew that if the marriage was to be consummated, this was the opportunity. Later, as she relaxed in Tag's arms and his soul was at rest, the tears rolled down her cheeks in remorse for how she had deceived Tag.

Laura was unaware when she went to sleep, but it was Tag that awakened first in the morning. When he saw that Laura

263

was in his arms, he sensed that they had been intimate and in his anger, he was not to be denied. Once again, Laura was at his mercy, but she determined that in the future, she would teach him gentleness in his passion. Laura smiled to herself, *for she realized that now I have a husband!*

That night was the last night that Tag Taggat had a nightmare!

CHAPTER 11
HAPPY BIRTHDAY!

Without asking, Laura moved her things into Tag's bedroom. Tylor now had a room of his own. She came to the conclusion that marriage was good for Tag, as he had fewer and fewer outbursts over the everyday events which take place on a Sandhills ranch.

Sometimes, good things happen as well, as they are times for rejoicing. Macaroni, the roan heifer had a freckle-faced bull calf with roan hairs along the top of his back. As Laura had bought the heifer from Grant Holler, she decided to call the calf General Lee. The men made fun of Laura for her choice of names, except for the one given to Tylor.

Laura called Cindy Holler one evening. Laura chatted about the weather, and told Cindy about the new calf. She then asked, "Cindy, I have a request of you, but feel free to say no if you don't feel comfortable about doing it. I have learned to drive and I think that I am doing quite well. However, the state requires a license and I have none. In fact, I barely escaped jail time. I was insisting to drive myself home after the sheriff found out that I didn't have a license. Cooler heads prevailed and Ken Holliday drove me home. I can drive that dumb old pickup truck all over the ranch, hauling food and running errands, but I cannot drive the streets of Summit City! Tag doesn't think that they have time to take me in for the license. The only opportunity I have to buy supplies is to catch a ride if Jim goes for repairs. What I am asking is, would you be so kind as to take me in when they are holding the exam for the licensing? I would have use of the truck at the time when they are open in the afternoons on Monday and Friday. Afternoons are best for me anyway. The time that I had the run in with the sheriff, I had wanted to visit Maude and

Hannah. I haven't seen them since I got married and Maude and I left on a bit of a sour note. I do want to make amends and see if Hannah has need of anything before she goes to school." Laura paused, and started in again. "Wow, my conversation has flowed like an artesian well. I hope that I am not boring you, but I have had very little opportunity to talk with another woman. Is this what they call as being stir-crazy?"

Cindy laughed, "Laura, your conversations are never boring, but your antics are entertaining. Someone in the bank, but not Ken, overheard you and Sheriff Morgan. It is all over town to your asking to go to jail in order to get a few days of rest. I sympathize with you, as sometimes a woman's day on the ranch can be rather demanding. Laura, you pick the day and time and I will be there for you. We women need to stick together. In fact, Grant is standing here right now with a rake part in his hand. Call back anytime. Bye."

After hanging up the phone, Laura paused before going back to the cook shack to start dinner. She thanked God for a dear friend like Cindy. Laura tried to recall the women in the Bible that had a mentor or a friend to go to. *The first to come to her mind were Ruth and Naomi in the Old Testament. Then there was Mary and her cousin Elisabeth. As Laura considered other possibilities of friendship among women, she thought of Rachel and her sister Leah. Add in their handmaidens that bore children of Jacob and the household was filled with jealousy, just by adding one man, Jacob to the mix. Even two women and one man created chaos in the household of Abraham, with Sarah and her handmaiden Hagar.* Laura remembered other men in the Bible, but especially, she remembered that she needed to pray for Tag, the man in her own household. She prayed that he might be a father to Tylor, who has none. Also that he might be a father to those children she desires to bear.

The taking of the driving test was uneventful. Laura,

being familiar with the older truck of the ranch, maneuvered it to the satisfaction of the examiner. She treated Cindy to ice cream at the local drug store. Normally, she would have patronized Maude, but she was uncertain how she would be received. She would wait until another time and also when she could spend more time with Maude and Hannah.

On the way home, Laura said, "I'm rather disappointed with Grant."

Trying to keep her eyes on the road, Cindy glanced over at Laura and asked, "Why is that, what has he done now?"

Laura said, "He has done nothing. That is the problem. He said that as a part of the purchase of Macaroni, I had to take a mother cat and he still has not delivered her. Now that I have milk to feed her and mice for her to catch, that man owes me a cat!"

"Laura," Cindy replied, "I will inform him of your disappointment. I assure you that he will make it right. He will be pleased that you have not forgotten that part of the deal."

When they arrived at the ranch, Laura insisted that Cindy look in on General Lee. When Cindy saw that the calf was with the cow, she asked, "Aren't you milking her? I see that the calf is still with Macaroni. Incidentally, that is a strange name for a cow. Timmy laughed when he was telling the family about the name. He said, I imagine that she looked the cow in the eye and said, 'your name is Macaroni; that is spelled M-a-c-a-r-o-n-i.' The boys will be pleased to know that you named her calf 'General Lee.' I won't tell them if you spelled it to him or not."

"I am milking Macaroni, but on my schedule. Normally, I would milk her morning and night, but with the feeding of five men and a child, somebody has to be slighted. She being female, she is more tolerant than the males. When I want milk, I pen the calf away from the cow. Then when I have time, I milk the cow and turn the calf back with his mother and everyone is happy. We love the whole milk and now I want to find a small cream separator so that I can have some cream and even enough that I might make my own butter. Now, I want you to see my pullets before you leave and then my garden. Or, I should say the ranch garden, as the young men are very good in helping me with it. I think it is doing well, despite getting it in late."

Cindy was getting ready to leave. "Laura, this has been fun, just the two of us to chat with one another. I have always been puzzled by this marriage and also concerned with your well being. Is everything all right?"

Laura paused before answering. Cindy took note of her hesitation. Laura repeated the question "Is everything all right? I don't know if there is ever a time that everything is all right, but things are going well. There was a time that I was about to give up had he told me to leave, as I was not getting out of the marriage what I expected. I was unable to prompt a desire for me that I thought there should be. That has now been met, as we are now sharing the same bed. I wanted a father for my son. I see Tylor as an adorable little boy, which everyone should cherish. He is not whiny and he rarely cries. Yet, Tag will not pick him up, nor will he hold him just to help me out. I sense that he sees Tylor as another man's progeny and not worthy to be loved. Jim is much better with Tylor. Each Sunday, Jim takes him to church on his horse and Tylor reciprocates at how he reacts to Jim. My concern is, how will Tag react to children of his own? The ranch has been neglected for several years, particularly the headquarters. I am reclaiming it, piece by piece. First there was the garden and then the hen house and the milk barn and now the front yard of the main house. Were you aware that there is a cemetery on the ranch? I met Mrs. Teasdale and her daughter Claire Beaumont on Decoration Day when they came out to the ranch. Claire lives in Boston and she was out visiting her mother. I had a good visit with Mrs. Teasdale and I want to put together the history of the cemetery and those buried there. Mrs. Teasdale is in her nineties and a delightful lady. She still lives in Summit City. Oh, I forgot to tell you, Ken Holliday wants me to have Stella's easel and paints. This winter, when the snow is blowing and the winds are howling, I will be in my cozy home, painting a picture. I haven't painted any landscape, but I do enjoy capturing the soul of an individual. Oh, my! There I go again, my mouth gushing like an artesian well. I'm sorry for controlling the conversation."

"Laura, never apologize for your enthusiasm." Cindy hugged Laura. "I do need to go, but I see that things are going well for you and I will continue to pray for you."

"Thank you for taking me to Summit City. I have treasured your friendship since I first met you at the Good Hope School. Just think, I have committed no faux pas today. That must be a record for me when I am with you. Bye, Cindy."

After Cindy left, Laura took Tylor and they went to seek shade among the cottonwood trees along the Dismal River. Tylor and she sat on an old cottonwood stump and watched the river flow by, bringing its coolness to the seated spectators. Laura had been on the move most of the afternoon and Tylor was feeling neglected. He began to paw at her dress, as he desired to nurse. Laura enjoyed these moments with her son. She knew that he was getting very little milk, as she was getting thinner and the milk flow was undoubtedly dwindling. *I need to be weaning him was her thought, as he is drinking from a cup and the milk from Macaroni is more nutritious than that from his mother. However, I know that I would miss these moments.*

Looking down at Tylor, she was unaware that Tag had approached them from the direction of the cook shack. "Here you are!" His voice had startled Laura and in turn frightened

269

Tylor, who started to cry at the sight of Tag.

Laura tried to soothe Tylor. "That's all right, as it is only your father. There is nothing to worry about. He just caught us enjoying the coolness of the Dismal River." She started to button up her dress. "Come and join us. It is so pleasant here. Guess what? I passed my driver test, so now I am no longer a pedestrian. When can we go look for a convertible for me to drive to town when you are in need of parts for the machinery?"

"Congratulations, Laura, but that is no reason to be lazing in the shade. The rest of us have to work in the sun and endure the heat of the day." She didn't know what Tag was getting at by that remark, but she didn't like it.

"I know that I am the envy of all the big strong men at the ranch. I have this beautiful tan, which I acquired by lolling on the beach and drinking mint juleps. What's your point, Tag?"

"My point is, the men need to eat early as we are moving equipment after supper and they need to be fed and I find you down here in the shade." Tag was shuffling his feet, indicating for Laura to get up and get to work.

"I was feeding the number one man in my life, but I saw no reason for us to be in the sun while he nursed. I don't need that much tan. Tag, couldn't you have asked me to feed the men early, instead of this discourse about my being lazy and seeking the comfort of the shade? I started at five o'clock this morning fixing the men's breakfast, so don't begrudge me a few moments as a mother to spend time feeding my son. Give me a few minutes, as I will slice some cold roast and fix sandwiches. I will try to figure out something to go with it. It would have helped if you had forewarned me. You know that I don't like this spur of the moment decisions. I will ring the bell when it is ready." Laura trudged up the bank of the river and made her way to the cook shack, which she knew would be hot at this time of the day. In all probability, I will be driving a truck when they move the equipment.

Laura fried some potatoes to serve with the cold roast beef sandwiches. She also opened some tuna and cut up pickles and mixed with the tuna. She sliced the apple pie that she had planned to feed them tomorrow. Fixing the iced tea, she stepped outside to ring the bell. As she looked toward the river, she saw the men sauntering up the slope toward the cook shack. As they got closer, she asked, "Would you men prefer to eat down by the river? If so, just fill your plate and I will bring the iced tea and pie. Keep in mind, should you want seconds, you will have to expose yourself to the sun to come back to the kitchen." As the men began to fill their plates, Laura loaded the iced tea and pie in the cart that she used to transport Tylor around the ranch. He managed to fit in and she pushed the cart back to the shade of the trees.

After the men were fed, Laura kept herself busy and Tag didn't ask her to help with the move, nor did he thank her for the supper. After supper, the men saw that the plates and utensils were returned to the kitchen and Nick helped get Tylor back to the cook shack. He thanked Laura for the meal. He asked Laura, "How do you come up with something to feed us without prior warning? I would like to be a cook, but I don't know if I could think that far ahead."

"Sure you can." Laura looked at him, "Nick, you thought far enough ahead to thank me and to help me get things back to the cook shack. No one else did and I appreciate your recognizing my efforts. Always thank the cook. Would you like me to teach you a few things about cooking? I don't always plan on being the cook here. Once day I hope to have so many babies that I can only cook for them." Nick laughed at Laura. *She comes up with some funny ideas.*

271

The next morning at breakfast, Tag told the crew, "We will not be working on the fourth of July. Summit City has a big parade in the morning and a rodeo in the afternoon. After sundown there will be fireworks and after those are over, there will be a street dance at about ten in the evening. We will take two pickups into town. One will come home early and the other will stay until the last dog is hung. Remember that the next day is a workday, so choose wisely. Those of you who want to draw some of your pay, let me know so that I can have the money ready for you the night before. We will leave here at nine in the morning. Our beloved cook will have a picnic lunch for us in the park at noon, but supper is on your own. Any questions?"

Laura wanted to go to town to stock up on supplies and get what she needed for the picnic on the fourth. She took the opportunity to stop in at Maude's in the afternoon when business was slow. The first thing Maude said, "Well, well, once again the prodigal daughter has returned. What is it? Is he a wife beater, a philanderer; or just too tight to feed you? Good heavens girl, you are nothing but skin and bones."

"Maude," Laura began, "the last time I saw you, we were scarcely speaking over my choice of a husband. I have returned to make amends, as I have missed you immensely. Just give me a hug and let us forget those harsh words and hurt feelings."

Maude hugged her. "I missed you too. Welcome back and how is that boy? My goodness, he certainly has grown. He even has teeth. Come here and let me hold you." She took Tylor from Laura and gave him a kiss in the crook of his neck, so that he giggled.

Laura asked, "Is Hannah around?"

"Her class in school is working on a float for the parade. They have been working every minute that I can spare her. She will be sorry that she missed you. By the way, are you coming to the big celebration?"

"Yes," said Laura, "I came in to get supplies for our ranch picnic. This is the first trip to town since I received my driver license. I suppose you heard about that. Cindy Holler was telling me that she had heard about it, so it must be all over the county. I was ready to go to jail, but Ken Holliday saved my reputation by taking me home. I did want to check with you regarding Hannah's needs for the school year. Do I owe you anything for her medical and such? I can't remember what I said I would pay for, but surely, I must owe you something."

"I can't think of anything, as that girl is pretty independent. You must have taught her well. She does rather well earning tips when she is waiting tables. She does much better than I do. I don't suppose age and looks has anything to do with it." Maude went to the counter and brought the coffeepot and two mugs. "I know you always want free coffee, so here is your opportunity. Tell me and I want you to be honest. Is Tag being good to you?"

Laura was shocked at the question! But, she was more shocked at herself, when she paused to formulate an answer to Maude's question. "Maude," Laura stalled for time before answering. "Maude, I'm not sure that I can appropriately answer you. Is he being good to me? He doesn't beat me, but I don't believe that he loves me. Is he good for me? To that I would have to say yes. There was quite some time before our marriage was consummated, but we are now sharing the same bedroom in the main ranch house. I now have the passion that I so yearned for, but now I am yearning for compassion. Passion is fueled by lust, while compassion is fueled by love. In some respect we are much alike; in that we are both strong willed, so there is the constant clashing of the wills. Oftentimes the men that work on the ranch are caught in the middle of our conflicts. I desired a father for Tylor; whether Tag agrees to give Tylor his name remains to be seen. I must be patient; however, you are aware that patience is not one of my virtues. Did I make a poor choice? That remains to be seen. I do believe that if this marriage is to continue, it is dependent upon me to make it work. I have a vested interest in this, and I cannot make any more mistakes. You saw how one mistake in my life was so detrimental. Now I am a married woman, married to one of larger landowners in the county and I have a father for my son. Also, I have a cadre of friends that have stood by me when things were the bleakest."

"You always have a plan, Laura, you always have a plan." Maude continued, "I can see it now, even as we talk, you are formulating a plan. When others around are asking, what will we do? Laura is working out a plan, perfecting it down to the last detail. Your plan for that ranch began the moment that Tag Taggat said he needed a cook. I later learned that his crew had rebelled and refused to work as long as Jim McCann was the cook. What have you accomplished since moving to the 99 Ranch?"

"Let me see," Laura began. "I'm not sure if I have done so much, but I have enlisted the aid of the crew in a number of ways. They are pleased with the food. The menu is standardized. I now know how much to order each week, almost like an inventory system of replacing the same amount of ingredients each week. We have planted a garden, bought a milk cow and 40 pullets that will soon be laying eggs. I have learned to drive and have my license. One of my major deeds was to convince Tag that I could keep the ranch books and pay the bills. That is how I got my money from the insufficient funds check that I received as a wedding gift. Thank you, Maude. I had a few choice words for my friend Maude, thinking that she had the last laugh on her friend Laura. You will be happy to know that I did have to deposit $50.00 to the account so that the check would clear."

"All right," Maude interrupted, "so much for your accomplishments, but what are your plans for the future?"

"The ranch house!" Laura was enthusiastic in revealing her plans for the house. "The main house has been occupied by two bachelors for the past year and a resident manager for the last ten years. Incidentally, it is devoid of furniture and in need of painting and new floor covering. I have plans, but they are dependent on extricating the funds from a man that has no interest in making a house presentable. I just need to keep a sharp eye out for some good used furniture. Paint is relatively economical, considering the benefits derived from its application. Then, there are the grounds around the house that have been neglected. The men are good about helping me after supper with various projects. They have learned to keep on the good side of the cook. The other project I have is cleaning up the cemetery."

"The cemetery? What cemetery?" Maude was confused by Laura's latest project.

Laura went into great detail, explaining to Maude about the cemetery and its history. Also, Laura related about her visit with Viola Teasdale and her daughter Claire. Maude was fascinated that there was a cemetery on the ranch.

It was then that the conversation turned to Charles Williams. Laura asked, "Did Sheriff Morgan warn you and Hannah about Charles Williams? I'm sure that he is the man that assaulted me in the night. I'm hoping that the attack was the result of contention between him and Tag, rather than of his jealousy over Hannah and her leaving. I have been sleeping with a gun under my pillow ever since that attack."

"Yes, the sheriff was here," said Maude, "but Hannah sees no threat to herself, as she sees that the conflict is between Charles and you. She viewed her role in all this as a pawn. You were the aggressor in getting her away from Charles. She is sorry all this has happened because of her. She has always appreciated what you have done for her. She was grieved because of the rift between you and me and she will be glad to hear that we have mended our fences."

Laura asked, "Maude, are you open on the fourth of July?"

Maude shook her head, "No, different organizations have food booths for fund raising, so I will just enjoy the day and be a lady of leisure. I'm not sure of Hannah's plans. As I said, she is certainly independent and rightly so, as she is now seventeen. Sometimes we tend to push the children through the school system too soon. They attain the education, but lack the maturity. Hannah wants to go to college and she will be almost twenty by the time that she graduates from high school. Laura, had you not intervened, she would have never graduated, nor been mature at age twenty. Unfortunately, people dwell on a person's misdeeds, rather than their deeds. Not Hannah however, as she knows that what she is today, much is through your efforts and money that you invested in her."

Laura blushed, "Why, thank you, Maude. That was kind of you to tell me, but I do want to invite you to join us for the celebration and share our picnic dinner in the park. Hannah too, if she cares to come. Don't worry about bringing anything, as you said, you would be a lady of leisure. We are bringing two vehicles, with the intent that some of us will return to the ranch after the fireworks and the rest will return whenever they have had enough of the celebration. I need to get back to the ranch. Thank you Maude, I have enjoyed this time with you. Before I forget it, I want you to know that I am extending an invitation to you and Hannah to spend Thanksgiving Day with us. Put that down on your social calendar. Bye." She gave Maude a hug, and leaving the café, the bell at the door gave its familiar ring.

Independence Day indicated that it would be hot, as the early morning sun seemed to hurry above the horizon.

Apparently, it wanted to get an early start, even as the celebrants were preparing to go to Summit City. Laura had arrived at the cook shack in the predawn morning and began to prepare the picnic dinner. She was surprised as Nick came to the kitchen and asked, "Mrs. Taggat, how can I help you?"

"Oh, Nick, it was thoughtful of you to come here to help me this morning. Yes, I can use help, but also, let us make this a training session as well. Have you ever made potato salad?" Nick shook his head, indicating that he had not. "Very well, I will take you from the beginning to end, so by the time you have finished, you can say that you can make potato salad. Let's start with the least glamorous part of the potato salad and that is the peeling of the potatoes."

Nick seemed to enjoy the tasks as Laura explained each phase of the process. Once that was completed, they set it aside to cool and she started him on the baked beans, while she continued to prepare the men's breakfast. Terry and Jason had fun ribbing Nick about his attire, as he had wound a dishtowel around his waist to keep clean, but he stayed in the kitchen and helped Laura cut up and fry the chicken that she had bought in town. She explained why it was necessary to pack some things in ice to keep them cool. Fortunately she had been accumulating extra ice for such an occasion. By nine o'clock they had the one truck packed and the 99 Ranch employees were ready to go to town. As Tag had explained earlier, those who wanted to come home after the fireworks could do so, and the rest could stay for the festivities that ran until two in the morning. Laura enjoyed the parade and she was able to wave at Hannah as her school float passed by. Maude had joined Laura and Tylor, as the men found themselves a separate spot to view the parade. They had made arrangements to meet in the park for the picnic. Hannah had declined the offer to eat with them, as she was meeting her classmates and eating together. Laura was content with that, deciding that a girl of seventeen, as pretty as Hannah, would be a distraction to the three young cowhands. Nick had helped set out the food. It was a pleasant time under the huge cottonwood trees in the park. Everyone relaxed, waiting for the rodeo to start at two in the afternoon. Laura was excited, as this would be her first rodeo. Maude said, "Laura, if you would like, I will look after Tylor right here among the shade trees and green grass, while you take in the rodeo. It will be hot for him there in the grandstands. This way, Tag can explain the various events and you won't have Tylor to look after. Besides, I need an excuse to stay here in the shade." Maude had a motive to her offer, as now Tag will have to sit with Laura instead of him sitting with his drinking buddies.

"Oh, Maude," Laura said, "I would like that very much. I have heard so much about rodeos, but know very little about them. Thank you, Maude. I have bottles fixed for Tylor and I know that he will be more comfortable in the shade. Then he will be rested for the fireworks."

Laura enjoyed the afternoon, particularly being with Tag. She was careful not to be asking too many questions of the events. She loved her son, but it was good to have a little free time with her husband. That Maude Dunham is a crafty lady when she set this all in motion. Tag was not given the opportunity to refuse!

The events went well and nothing disastrous happened to mar the day. After the fireworks, a summer thunderstorm moved in which cancelled the street dance, so those expecting to party late into the night went home early.

Laura rose early the next morning and was greeted by the freshness left by the evening thunderstorm. It was still too early to start breakfast, so she went down to the Dismal River and walked among the trees. More water was flowing as a result of the rain, but nothing violent, since so much of the rain remained in the ground. As she was seated on a tree stump, she thanked God for the moisture and the relief from the heat. It had been a day free of conflict. How pleasant it was to be with Tag for the afternoon. Dear Maude, she and I had such a joyous day having made our peace with one another. God, I thank you for the people that have blessed me so much. My precious Tylor; what have you in store for his life? I thank you for him.

The summer rushed by fast and the first days of fall were welcome. The men had completed the haying season and preparations were being made for the winter. Tag would not reveal to Laura how long he would be keeping the three young men employed, but she sensed that they would not be there through the winter.

September 30, 1952—Tylor's first birthday was a joyous occasion on the ranch. Laura had baked him a cake and Nick asked if he could decorate it for Tylor. As the men had been anticipating the celebration, they each had contributed to buying him a rocking horse. They were pleased as Jim set him up on it and he was able to rock it after a little persuasion.

As Laura handed him a stuffed cow, she said, "Here, Tylor, see what Mama and Daddy got for you." As she looked to Tag for his approval, it was evident that he was not pleased, but Laura was unsure of what had upset him.

Tylor recognized the stuffed toy and said, "C-c-cow," and took the toy and hugged it. Laura was concerned that he continued to stutter, even calling her 'M-m-mama.' His vocabulary was beginning to develop, but was hampered by his stuttering. She had made an appointment to see Dr. Jessup on Tuesday afternoon regarding his stuttering. Also, he was making no attempt to walk.

Nick had decorated the cake with little animals and had included Tylor's name, along with 'Birthday Wishes.' Laura

279

was amazed at the culinary skills that Nick was developing. The birthday party had been held at the cook shack after the evening meal. After the party, Tag left and went to the main house while Laura stayed to finish cleaning up. Laura had a few preparations to complete for the morning meal. She had been in the habit of filling the coffeepot and having it ready to start first thing in the morning. Laura soon had things to her liking, so she took Tylor and went to the house. Tag was reading the paper and going through the mail when Laura came in with Tylor. She said, "I will put Tylor to bed and be out shortly. Would you care for a cup of coffee? I thought that it might get the sweetness of the birthday cake out of my mouth."

"That would be fine," was Tag's response. "I'm going through the mail, and there are some things we need to discuss while we have the coffee."

Laura had fixed Tylor a bottle and he was eager to go to his bed. She kissed him good night and he gave his mother a grin and gripped his bottle, happy to be in his bed.

Laura went to the kitchen, and was fixing the coffee, when Tag said, "Laura, I don't feel comfortable when you refer to me as 'Daddy' when you talk to Tylor. I am not his daddy!"

Laura thought, *so that is what upset him!* "Tylor is learning to talk. How do you want him to address you? When we married, didn't it occur to you that one day; he was going to have to call you something? What suggestions do you have?"

"Well, I don't know, but Daddy seems too personal when I am really not his Dad." Tag was unsure what he wanted, *but he certainly didn't want that kid calling him Daddy!*

Laura was unsure how to handle this, when even Tag didn't know what he wanted. She began, "Well, let us consider the alternatives to Daddy, as there is Papa, or Dad, or Tag, or Mr. Taggat, or Taylor, or Uncle Tag, or Father. And then he could call you, 'Hey You,' until such time that he leaves home. You pick the name, and I will train him to use that title. Or would you prefer to have him address you as 'Sir?' The choice is yours."

"I knew that this would happen if I brought it up! You would make a mockery of the whole idea."

"I am glad that you brought it up," said Laura. "What I see from this is that you are rejecting my son. You really don't want him in the house. He is a reminder that I was intimate with another man and you can't handle that. But, you are also realizing that you cannot handle this ranch without me. You may not admit it, but you cannot deny it. The men that are working for you see it. Jim McCann is so loyal to you, that he would die for you, but should you ask him, he would have to admit that you need me! Incidentally, Tylor is a part of the package. In fact, he is the whole package. I have witnessed your rejection from the first day that I was here. Most people, men and women, can't help but admire a small child, but you won't touch him nor do you help me with him whatsoever. Already, Tylor is aware of that, even at one year of age. You tell me what you want him to call you and as I said, that is how I will train him." Laura paused, but she was not finished. "I was hoping for the sake of uniformity, that he would be able to take the name of Taggat, but perhaps that is asking too much at this time."

The very thought was a shock to Tag! *He had no idea that Laura had ever considered Tylor taking the Taggat name.* "That is one thing that I will not allow. He is not a Taggat; and will not be called as such. Why would you ever think of such a thing?"

"As I said," Laura replied, "I was hoping for the sake of uniformity. I expect to have other children and it would be rather awkward to introduce our children as Taggats and then there is one with the last name of Martin. That would certainly raise a red flag to the uninformed as to why the one maverick in the bunch. Do you understand my thinking?"

Tag asked, "Laura, how could I possibly understand your thinking? It is as if we are from two different worlds. In fact, we are from two different cultures. You have the mindset of the Yankee from New England, while mine is of the Sandhills. Here the family name is esteemed, not tarnished by outsiders. The family name is synonymous with pedigree, or purebred. It is almost likened to being undefiled. Do you understand what I mean?"

"Of course, darling," said Laura, smiling as she took a moment to gather her thoughts. "I believe the Bible speaks of it in Proverbs 22: 1—'A good name is rather to be chosen than great riches, and loving favour rather than silver and gold.' See we are on common ground. That is why, as a mother, I desire that my son have a good name. Sometime soon, we need to see what needs to be done legally to change his name from Martin to Taggat. It has been a big day and I believe that I will turn in. Darling, are you coming to bed soon?"

"I am right behind you," said Tag. *Why does she turn things around to make you think it was your idea, when actually, it was what she wanted all along? Her days are numbered on this ranch!*

Laura learned that night, it is not well to have a clashing of the wills before going to bed. She must choose her place and time more carefully next time.

Laura had taken pictures of Tylor on his birthday. She sent them away to be developed and the day that they returned, she chose one of the best. It was the one showing him smiling with his hands outstretched. With a heavy heart, she wrote on the back, 'Tylor Martin, one year old, taken at his birthday party, September 30, 1952.'

Two days later, that same small frail woman that one year earlier had walked down the dusty lane, made the same trek to the mailbox beside the county road. Her step was a bit slower, as the year had not been kind to her. The hair was no grayer, but perhaps thinner. The bandanna was the same that she had worn a year ago. Once again, her clothes were clean, but plain. The rusty mailbox had not changed. As she tugged at the door, it rubbed on the edge, causing it to squeak, even as it had a year ago. Reaching in, she pulled a small envelope from the interior. Slamming the door shut, so that it might remain closed, the woman noticed that there was no return address on the upper left hand of the envelope. However, the postmark indicated that it was mailed in Summit City. Sliding a small, wrinkled finger under the flap, she tore the envelope open, pulling one small sheet of folded paper from the envelope. She noticed that nestled in the fold was a photograph. Feeling into her apron pocket, she pulled her glasses out and fitting them to her face, she recognized the writing of a year ago. It was the same feminine hand. On the back of the photograph was written, 'Tylor Martin, one year old, taken at his birthday party, September 30, 1952.' On the folded paper was written; 'his favorite word is Mama, and his favorite toy is a stuffed cow.' Once again, in a rather non-committal manner, she returned the paper to the envelope and placed it in her apron pocket. The photograph, she held in her hand and looked at it from time to time. Slowly, returning to the ranch house, she reached for the rope that held the front gate shut. She remembered that it was at this spot one year ago, that she had received the telegram telling of her son Tylor being killed in Korea on September 30, 1951. Going inside, she crumpled the envelope and the single sheet of paper and threw them in the trash. Passing by the table with the two plates that had been set there in preparation for the noon meal, she went to a closet. Opening the door, she reached up to a shelf and pulling down a worn cardboard shoebox she removed the lid and carefully placed the photograph to the rear of the box. Replacing the lid, she returned the box to its original place and closed the door. She then took her place at the table, waiting for her husband.

CHAPTER 12

THE INHERITANCE

Tuesday morning, Laura awakened to the sound of rain dripping from the eaves. It was the changing of the seasons. She was not yet ready for the late summer to come to a close. The fear of the unknown often troubles us more than that which we see and experience. Today was the day that she was taking Tylor into the doctor. Laura was troubled with the stuttering and the fact that he made no effort to stand on his feet, let alone walk. Peggy Barnes' daughter, Rebecca had walked at ten months. Why wasn't Tylor making some effort? Perhaps, if he were more robust, Tag would take a liking to him. As Laura listened to the rain, she rebuked herself for being of little faith. Lord, I have committed my son into your hands; why am I fretting so? Suddenly, a verse came to her mind; 'This is the day that the Lord hath made; we shall rejoice and be glad in it.' A rain in the Sandhills is always worthy of rejoicing! And, Tylor is to be seen by Dr. Jessup, a gentle man that Laura has utmost confidence in to make the right diagnosis. With the rain, perhaps Tag will go with me today, if nothing more than to see me safely over the muddy roads.

Breakfast was a solemn affair. Tag had planned to sort some of the cattle and put them on fresh pasture. What he had wanted to do was to put the cows with heifer calves in the south pasture and those cows with the steer calves in what he called the Butte pasture. Then when he was ready to sell either steers or heifers, they were already sorted except for their mothers. After breakfast, when the men were having their second cup of coffee, Tag looked up at Laura. He then turned to Jim, saying, "Jim, when the weather lets up, you can bring those late calves that have not been worked and throw them in the meadow near the house. Then, when they dry off, we can brand them and work them. We will include Laura's General Lee in the bunch. I don't want a young freckled faced bull running around with the cows. Is it all right, Laura, if we put the 99 brand on that young 'feller?' We should really brand Macaroni as well."

"Oh, no! Not Macaroni! It would be too much of a shock for her and she would cut down on her milk and we need that milk. If anything, we should be looking for another cow so that we will have milk when she is dry. As to General Lee, now that I am a cattle baroness, I think it would be well if I had my own brand. What do I have to do to get a brand?"

"Laura, it is ridiculous for you to have your own brand for two head of livestock and not rebrand one of those." Tag was trying to discourage her, but he sensed that would not happen. "However, if you insist, I have the forms to submit to the Brand Board. I think the fee is $20.00. Then you have to buy the branding irons for your brand once it is approved. What brand were you considering? Remember, be practical and keep it short. After all, a cow is only so big."

"I can be practical, if needed." Laura smiled to herself; *I will show him what practical is.* "Now your brand is 99, on the left ribs. Therefore, mine will be 66, on the left ribs. That way I can use your irons, and I won't need to buy any." The men around the table laughed at Laura's practicality. Tag blushed. *Why does she do this to me, especially in front of the men?*

Tag agreed to take Laura and Tylor to town. It would give him an opportunity to stop at the bank and visit with Ken Holliday, regarding the sale of his cattle.

After dinner, Laura was getting Tylor ready, when she asked, "Tag, do you have that form for the Brand Board?"

He quickly answered, "I wasn't able to locate it. We may have to write for a form. I will look up their address this evening."

"That is fine." answered Laura. "I was planning to fatten General Lee and have him processed at the locker plant. That way, we will have our own beef. I guess we are ready, anytime you are."

Laura was glad that Tag was driving. "Thank you, Tag, for bringing us to town today. I was dreading the drive in the rain and with the muddy roads. I feared that I might slide off into the ditch. Do you think that they will ever pave this road, at least to Good Hope?"

"It is all about politics," said Tag. "The only way to get any paving out this way is to elect a county commissioner from this end of the county. That is what commissioners do, they pave the road to their ranch."

"Then maybe you should run for commissioner," Laura replied. "That way, we would have a good road."

"Laura, I fear that I have enough enemies without being a county commissioner." Tag laughed at his own joke.

Laura got out at the doctor's office. Before she closed the door, she said, "Will you come for us?"Tag nodded. "I'm hoping that it doesn't take too long. Bye."

Carrying Tylor on her hip, Laura entered the office. The nurse was at the receptionist desk, and said, "You are early, but Dr. Jessup will see you now. Just follow me."

Entering the office, Dr. Jessup smiled and held out his arms to Tylor. Taking Tylor, he set him on the examining table. "Hey, here is the birthday boy. One year old and what a handsome lad! Didn't I tell you when he was born, that I only delivered handsome boys and beautiful girls? He seems to be of normal weight. Let me hear how things are sounding in his chest." As he applied the stethoscope, Tylor giggled, as he was being tickled. "Sounds good in there and he has a hearty laugh. You said you had some concerns. What are they?"

Laura said, "He is learning to talk, but he stutters. I brought his favorite soft toy, so you could hear him." Picking up his toy cow, she asked, "Tylor, what is this?"

Tylor reached out for it, and said, "C-c-cow."

Then she pointed to herself, and once again asked, "Who is this?"

Tylor pointed at his mother and saying, "M-m-mama." Laura hugged him and giving Tylor a kiss, she shed a few tears.

"Laura, I understand your concern. Most often children will outgrow the stuttering, unless, in an older child they have suffered something traumatic in their life. Just be gentle and don't rush him to speak too rapidly. If you determine that he has difficulty with certain words, try to avoid them until he has an opportunity to practice saying those words. I am aware of the patience that you exhibited in working with Karen Barnes, and I know that you will do the same with Tylor. If later on there is no improvement, then a speech therapist would be helpful. You mentioned concerns in the plural, what else do you have?"

"He hasn't walked, nor does he care to stand on his feet, as if they hurt or something. Also, he rarely crawls. I sit him on the floor and he stays there. Is there something wrong with his legs?"

Dr. Jessup pulled off Tylor's shoes and examined his feet, applying pressure to the sole of the foot. Tylor didn't draw back. He then tried to stand him up and he pulled his feet up to a point that his legs were parallel to the examining table. "Laura, he will be slow to walk. He will be a great cowboy, as he would rather sit on a horse than walk. I have seen you around town, packing him on your hip. Why walk when you can be carried?

Get him some pants to where his legs are covered, so that the floor doesn't scratch his legs. Let's get him crawling before we work on the walking. Put things just out of his reach and don't jump to his every whim. Make him work a little. Does that cover your concerns?" Laura nodded. "All right, I have some concerns that you can help me with at this time. Laura, you are too thin, much too thin. Is Tylor still nursing? If so, I think that now is a good time to stop."

"But, Dr. Jessup, this is such a special time for both of us. It is such a joy, just to hold him in my arms and watch him suckle." Laura shed another tear at the thought of discontinuing their special time.

"Will you allow me to give you a thorough exam at this time? I want to weigh you to start with. The nurse has a gown for you if you will remove your clothes behind this screen." Dr. Jessup went to the front to get Laura's file.

Laura asked the nurse, "What am I to do with Tylor? I don't want to undress in front of him. I know that he is just a little boy, but I don't feel right about doing that."

The nurse said, "Here, I will take him just around this file cabinet and set him on the floor. He will be all right there. Now, let's get you ready for the doctor. Step on this scale and I will weigh you and then check your blood pressure." She had her weighed, the blood pressure and pulse taken by the time the doctor returned. She showed him the figures. He studied them before he began to examine Laura.

The doctor walked over to where a full-length mirror was attached to the wall. "Come over here, Laura." She stepped across the room to stand beside him. "Do not be embarrassed, but I want you to face the mirror. Now I am going to remove your gown. Do you recognize that body? Right now you weigh 101 pounds. Notice the ribs that are visible; there is very little flesh covering your body and the arms and legs are like matchsticks. Turn to a side view, and notice the absence of the flesh on the buttocks. The breasts are almost non-existent. Except for the cuddling, Tylor is not going to miss his mother's milk. Put your gown back on and tell me what is happening that you have lost so much weight. Your blood pressure is low. These things are not good, but what I saw that was most frightening, were the bruises. How did you come by those? Is Tag abusing you?"

Laura was sitting on the examination table and was unsure how to answer the doctor, in a delicate manner. "I don't quite know how to answer that question without causing doubt in your mind. Is he intentionally abusing me, I would say no. I try not to irritate him before we go to bed at night, but you are aware, that at times I tend to be abrasive. At those times, he tends to be a bit rough with me, so I try to avoid those confrontations late at night. I love my husband and I don't want to cause any trouble for him." Tears entered her eyes. Her first thought was, here I go again, getting weepy and nothing to wipe the tears away. She reached down and took the corner of the gown and tried to wipe away the tears. Doctor Jessup picked up a box of tissues and handed it to Laura.

"Don't worry about that," said the doctor. "I won't cause him any trouble, but I do want to talk with him when he comes to pick you up. Laura, I want to get some weight on you. My concern is that if any illness or accident should strike you in your present condition, you don't have enough resistance to ward off anything major. I have prescribed some vitamins for you and I'll have the nurse give you a diet that I want you to adhere to as close as you can. Usually, when we think of a diet, it is for the purpose of losing weight. This is for you to gain weight. Get more rest. When Tylor lays down for his afternoon nap, I want you to take a nap also. As a suggestion, I know that you are cooking for the men and you are serving them and then eating afterwards. Either, eat before they eat, or eat with them. They have been literally, taking the food from your mouth. I hear that you have a cow by the name of Macaroni. Drink all the milk that you want. It will be good for you! Are there any questions?" Laura shook her head, thinking, *what have I started?* Doctor Jessup got up from his stool. "Laura, I want to see you in two weeks. And, I want to see Tag before you leave town today." He patted her on the shoulder and left for her to get dressed.

Laura told the receptionist that she was going over to the sheriff's office and to tell Tag that she would be right back. Arriving at the courthouse, she met Sheriff Morgan in the hallway. Laura asked, "Sheriff, do you have any brand application forms?"

"Why, yes I do. Come to the office and I will give you one. Have you seen anything of Charles Williams?"

"No," said Laura, "I hope that I don't either. As far as I'm concerned, he is history. Thanks for the brand application. I need to run, as I am to meet Tag."

"Wait just a minute!" The sheriff asked, "Are you still sleeping with a gun under your pillow?"

"Absolutely," she said, "and it is loaded. I check it every night. I am prepared. Good bye."

Laura hurried back to the clinic and was seated and breathing normally when Tag came in the door.

Doctor Jessup came into the waiting room about the time that Tag came into the office. "Good afternoon, Tag. Could I see you for a minute or so? It won't take long, as I know that you are busy." As he ushered Tag into a small conference room, he motioned to a chair, as he asked, "Are you getting a good rain out your way?"

Tag settled into a chair and grunted, "Yes, but I don't

think you asked me in to talk about the rain. What do you want?"

Dr. Jessup smiled, "Well, I guess you get right to the point. No, I see patients whether it rains or not. It is Laura. She is much too thin and I have made some changes in her life in order to have her health and weight restored to a normal level. She understands what I expect of her and I see no reason for her not to get back on her feet. I am most perturbed about the bruises on her body and I am presuming that they have been caused by you!"

Tag jumped up. "Did she tell you that? It is none of your business!"

The doctor leaned back in his chair, trying to bring some calm to the conversation. "Mr. Taggat, when a person comes to see me and they have bruises on their body such as those that Laura has, it becomes my business. Please sit down and I will explain to you why it is my business. I realize that perhaps these bruises occurred at a time of intimacy. However, Laura is a woman weighing 101 pounds and I would guess that you are over 225 pounds. Laura is defenseless against a man of your size. I am suggesting that you consider a more tender approach on these occasions. I will see Laura in two weeks and I expect those bruises to be healed and no new ones present on her body. Are we clear on that matter?"

Tag was furious! "You old quack. Some woman comes in and tells you a pack of lies and you believe her over her husband. I don't know how she got them, but it sure wasn't me. She outright lied to you."

"Mr. Taggat, I first met Laura when she came to me and asked how much it would cost to deliver her baby. I gave her a price and within thirty minutes, she had the money, paid up front. She did the same with the hospital. I consider her a woman of integrity. She does what she says she will do. You are not.

Last fall, I treated you for stepping on a rusty nail. I cleaned the wound and gave you the tetanus shot, but you have yet to give me a dime on that bill. Tell me, who has the integrity? Tag, you have a woman that obviously loves you. I have heard how hard she has worked on that ranch. That is why she is in the condition she is in today. You should be cherishing her instead of roughing her up. Now get out of my office and pay for the visit today and the services rendered a year ago." The doctor got up and went out and told the receptionist what Tag was going to pay.

Laura had heard the shouting between the two men. When Tag came out, he did pay the receptionist and went out the door. Laura came along, carrying Tylor. Tag never said anything, but started the truck and started to leave town. Laura spoke up, "Tag, I need to go to the drugstore to get some medicine. It shouldn't take long." At the drugstore, she took Tylor with her. They weren't busy, so it didn't take very long to fill the prescription. She had wanted to do some shopping, but thought it best, not to ask Tag to wait. She would come back later in the week. The trip home was quiet, neither of them speaking.

That night at bedtime, Tag had still not spoken to her. As she crawled into bed, she feared what might take place, as she knew that the visit with the doctor was unsettling and she wasn't sure what Dr. Jessup had said to Tag. Tag came to bed and turned his back to Laura. She tried to touch him, but he brushed her off. Laura wept in her pillow. The progress that they had made appeared to be undone by the visit that afternoon.

Laura had sensed that Tag didn't want her to file a brand application when he had told her he couldn't find it. Two weeks later she received verification of her owning the 66 brand. *Now, how do I tell him?* The crew had been busy, so they hadn't been able to work the group of late calves, of which General Lee would be a part. She would bide her time.

Laura returned to the doctor's office after the two weeks. When he came into the examining room he said to Laura, "Let's see how you have done. Remember last time, you had only the gown. To get an accurate check, let us weigh you in the same manner." Laura removed her clothes and put the gown on. She stepped on the scales, her heart pounding. She wasn't sure if she had gained or not, but she was feeling better and had more energy. She did miss holding Tylor to her breast, but she understood why it must be. The doctor eyed the scale. He said, "I'm not sure, but you may have lost a pound or so." Laura's heart sank. *I tried to do everything right.* The nurse looked at it and pointed to the indicator. "Well, I declare, you have gained three pounds. Congratulations!"

Laura stepped down and started to put on her clothes. "Just a minute," Dr. Jessup said. "I want to look at the bruises." As he examined Laura, he nodded his head. "They look like they are healing nicely and no evidence of any new bruises. It looks good. I am pleased."

"What did you say to him?" Laura demanded. "He hasn't touched me since my last visit. That isn't what I wanted, but you had to interfere."

"Laura," began the doctor, "what I said, had to be said. It has stopped the abuse. Laura, I know that you are capable of jumpstarting the romance and it will be better without the rough stuff. I will see you in the conference room after you have dressed."

When Laura came in, Dr. Jessup said, "Mrs. Viola Teasdale was in on Monday and we had quite a visit. She was my first patient when I came to Summit City. She said that she had a delightful visit with you on Decoration Day at the ranch. She remembered your enthusiasm regarding the restoration of the ranch. She was pleased that you are living in the main house, but she remembered your saying that two bachelors had occupied it. Laura, she wants to sell her furniture and wants to give you first chance at it. It is the original furniture that came out of the house when she moved to Summit City."

"That would be great, but did she say how much she wanted for it? Tag is not real great on house furnishings. Do you know where she lives? I would at least like to take a look at it and maybe I would buy a few pieces. I do have some of my own money, but I'm afraid that most of the things that she has would be classified as antiques." Laura paused. "But, what is she going to do? Is she moving away? I'm sorry, but I have neglected to go visit her, as I wanted the history of the ranch cemetery."

"Laura, I have a few minutes until my next patient. Why don't I lead the way and you can follow. Then I can leave when I need to be back here." The doctor was as excited as Laura was about the furniture.

Laura and Tylor followed Dr. Jessup's black Buick as he wound around the streets of the better homes of the city. Arriving at the house, Mrs. Teasdale was thrilled to see Laura. She invited them for tea and the doctor stayed longer than he had planned. Laura was waiting for Viola to mention the furniture. She brought out the history of the cemetery, along with the documents stating who the overseers were. Mrs. Teasdale took Laura by the hand and said, "Claire and I want you to have this book of the history of the cemetery and we want you to replace me as the co-administrator with Claire. I sense that you will see that it is well kept. We have faith in you."

"Oh, Viola," Laura said, "I would count it as an honor. Thank you very much."

Mrs. Teasdale looked out the window, as if she was trying to see someone, or remember something. "Did Dr. Jessup tell you about the furniture? You know, he is quite taken with you. He told me that you are a woman of integrity and to be trusted. Dr. Jessup has been a good doctor to me and I respect his judgment."

"I understand what you mean, as I have learned to trust him as well." Laura paused, not sure of what Mrs. Teasdale was working toward. "He seems to have an insight as he doctors the people; trying to minister to their emotional needs as well as the physical. He has helped me a great deal. Mrs. Teasdale, what are your plans?"

"I have decided to spend my last years with Claire." Once again, she looked out of the window and then she turned to Laura. "I want you to have the furniture."

"I understand, but what price have you set on the various pieces? I realize that the collection is quite valuable, but if you would part with some of it as individual items, I would like to invest in what I could to preserve the history of the ranch. Also, I am sure there are some of the older pieces that Claire would want." Laura was wishing that Claire was here, as she would feel more comfortable if they both were present.

"No, I want you to have the furniture. Claire doesn't need any of it. I asked her and she said that she has a house full." Laura thought that Mrs. Teasdale was a bit confused. I wish that Dr. Jessup had remained a bit longer.

Laura took Mrs. Teasdale's hand and said, "All right, how much do you want for all of the furniture in the house, seeing that Claire doesn't want any of it?"

"I don't want to sell it. I want to give it to you, so that you can furnish the ranch house as it once was furnished. Everything in the house is yours, except for my clothes and various pictures. That includes this tea set we are drinking from even now. My only stipulation is that you may not sell any of it. You may give it away, but you are not to profit from the sale of any item. It needs to be returned to the ranch." Mrs. Teasdale was emphatic in her decision. Laura had no doubt that it was a decision of a woman who was aware of the impact of what she had done.

Laura was almost breathless when she realized what Mrs. Teasdale had said. "Mrs. Teasdale, you have made me the happiest woman in the Sandhills. What a generous gift you have bestowed upon me. When do you want me to take it out of the house?"

Mrs. Teasdale thought a moment. "I will be leaving in about ten days. Once I am gone, you may remove the contents. Colby Realty will handle the sale of the house after you have removed the furniture. Is that satisfactory?"

"Absolutely! Be assured I will take excellent care of it. When I drink from this tea set, I will think of my generous friend and say a prayer for her. Thank you so much. I need to go now, but may I stop by Dr. Jessup's office and tell him of my good fortune?"

Mrs. Teasdale laughed, "You may, but he already knows. We discussed this to great lengths. But there is one other thing that I must show you that is part of the deal." She took Laura to the garage. As she opened the overhead door, Laura gasped at what she saw. There was a black antique horse drawn hearse. Mrs. Teasdale smiled at the look on Laura's face. She said, "About the time of the first World War, the undertaker in town had purchased a gas powered hearse and no longer intended to use the horse drawn one. Elmer said, 'I will not have any of my family or my cowboys be hauled to the cemetery in one of those noise, smelly machines.' So, Elmer bought the hearse from the undertaker. Whenever it was used, it was pulled by two black geldings. Elmer's body was the last one to ride in it. It belongs at the ranch. I expect to be the next one to ride in it. Take it Laura, as it as much a part of the history of the ranch as the furniture and dishes." Laura was shocked, but yet she was mesmerized by its beauty. It was a glistening black which shone as if it had been polished that morning. The large glass sides were clean, and the bright red wheels accentuated the hearse. Despite its beauty, Laura experienced the eerie feeling of impending death. Mrs. Teasdale closed the garage door and as she said, "Good bye, Laura," she returned to her home.

Laura bid her good bye. She stopped at the locker plant and purchased T-bone steaks for supper to celebrate her good fortune. Her next thought was how do I explain my good fortune to Tag? I pray that he will be happy for me, or rather us. Now we will have the house furnished. I will need to start with the paintbrush, because in ten days, it will be moving day!

Laura had also purchased apples, so as soon as she was home, she fixed a dessert that she called apple crisp. She had whipped the thick cream as a topping. She knew that the men would enjoy that, along with the mashed potatoes and gravy. It had surprisingly not frosted as yet and she was able to pick a few late green beans for a vegetable. It pleased the young men when she had something from the garden. Supper was a joyous occasion as the men relished the steak and especially the rich dessert. Laura was surprised when Tag commented about the delicious supper that had been served. She hurried and cleaned the kitchen. Before leaving, she took the dessert that was left over, along with the whipped cream and took it to the ranch house. *This will go good with a late cup of coffee. That is the time to tell Tag about my good fortune.*

Laura bathed Tylor and got him to bed and then decided to bathe as well. She felt refreshed and excited. I do believe that the vitamins that the doctor prescribed have helped me. Putting on her robe, she started the coffee and served up the leftover dessert. Tag was at his desk, looking over the mail when she went in to invite him to the kitchen for a cup of coffee. He turned in his chair and looked at Laura as if she was an intruder in the household. "I see by the livestock report that a brand application was approved for Laura Martin Taggat. The brand is to read 66." He turned back to his desk. "Why did you do that and how did you know how to file it, as I never gave you an application?"

"Tag, I knew that you were pulling a delaying tactic with me. You thought that this is one of Laura's whims and it will pass, so I won't give her an application form. I went to the sheriff's office and picked up a form. As far as knowing how to file it, you forget that I am not just a dumb ranch cook. I do have a college education! Oh, darn, darn, darn! I wanted to tell you my good news and you have to bring up a stupid $20.00 brand application. If it will make you happy, I will write them to cancel the application and they can keep their $20.00. Tag, why can't we be happy with one another? Is this how marriage is supposed to be?"

Tag stood up. Laura feared that he would strike her. "You asked two questions. Which one do you want me to answer first? Are you saying that you are not happy?"

Laura responded, "I didn't say that I wasn't happy, but I believe that we are not happy with one another. Tell me, what can I do, that will make you happy with me? Or better yet, tell me what I have done that makes you happy. Do I have one good quality that pleases you? Just name one!"

Tag took his time to answer Laura. He thought, *I can probably name a dozen things about her that displeases me, but I can't think of one good thing without sounding ridiculous.* Laura waited and still he said nothing. Finally she said, "Evidently, I have no good qualities." She turned to go into the kitchen.

Suddenly he said, "You make a great cup of coffee!"

Laura looked back at Tag and laughed. "Why, thank you. That is complimentary enough to ask you to share a cup with me, along with the remains of the apple crisp. I don't want to fight. I want to be more of a lover than a fighter." She reached out to him and taking his hand, she led him to the kitchen.

"And, you have the softest hands." Tag looked down at her. He didn't realize how small she seemed. "Also, I like it when you caress my arm with your hands." Tag was like a little boy, walking with his mother.

As they drank their coffee, Laura set her cup down. "Tag, you are right, I do make a great cup of coffee." They both laughed.

Tag touched Laura's hand. "Somewhere along the line of our bickering, you mentioned that you wanted to tell me about your good news. Now that we are settled down, what is this good news?"

"Today, I received an inheritance. It will benefit you, as well as me, but I am particularly pleased with it." Laura looked around at her sparsely furnished home. The furniture they had was a collection of mismatched items. "Mrs. Teasdale is moving to Boston to be with her daughter Claire. She is selling her house and she wants me to have her furniture. It is a collection of what she had when she lived here. The furniture has returned! Not only that, but the chinaware as well. I am thrilled. It is almost like inheriting a museum. Think of the history in all this!" She purposely omitted the gift of the hearse.

"I'm happy for you, Laura." Tag showed that he was happy for her, as he continued. "I know that you like things to be neat and proper and I could see it in your face how much you wanted this ranch house to exhibit what it had been in the past. This furniture we have was sufficient for a couple of bachelors, but not for a lady. Tell me, what are your plans and what are the timelines for getting the furniture home?"

They talked well into the night with the   planning of

possible colors to paint the walls and how it would be possible to do some entertaining. After they had gone to bed, Laura was happy. She remembered the words of Dr. Jessup, when she had accused him of interfering with her marital relationship. 'Laura, I know that you are capable of jumpstarting the romance.' She had!

CHAPTER 13
THE OUTLAW IN-LAWS

To Laura, the changing of the fall colors wasn't nearly as dramatic as the changing of the colors on the walls of the ranch house. Laura was excited and her enthusiasm had carried over to the men of the ranch as well. Nick, Terry and Jason would come to the house after supper and paint for a few hours. Laura always managed to have refreshments for them to encourage them to come back. Tag had rented a furniture van from the Mercantile to haul the furniture after Mrs. Teasdale had vacated the house and traveled to Boston to live. Laura was impressed at how careful the ranch hands handled the move. The hardwood floors had been refinished, so it was as if moving into a new house. Tag had not been real enthralled with the horse drawn hearse. However, at Laura's insistence, he had cleared out the things stored in a carriage barn that was near the garage. After pushing it into the barn, he covered it with a tarp. As he closed the door, he shuddered at the very thought of that vehicle of death. The Saturday night after the completion of the move, Laura entertained the men in her dining room with a meal featuring roast beef and all the trimmings. After supper they went to the living room, where Terry entertained them with a number of songs on the piano. It was a joyous occasion. Now Laura was planning the Thanksgiving dinner. She had already invited Maude and Hannah. She would also include the men of the ranch. She had wanted to include Dr. Jessup, but was unsure if that would be wise at this time because of the conflict between him and Tag. She had considered inviting Ken Holliday and his family. *Last year at the Hollidays had been a joyous occasion. Not really! I remember sharing around the table and the embarrassing moment when I had professed my faith in Jesus Christ. Then there was my conflict with Todd when I had struck him not once, but twice. But, God had worked it out to His glory. Through that embarrassing moment, Stella had asked me about my faith and then she came to know Jesus Christ as her Savior, just prior to her death. Todd had apologized for his behavior and was now on his way to becoming a fine young man. Perhaps I will approach Tag about adding to our guest list. If I invited the Hollidays, then Mrs. Baker could have the day with her daughter and family, the Barnes family.*

It was now the first of November and Laura needed to finalize her plans for Thanksgiving. After supper, she asked, "Tag, I would like to celebrate Thanksgiving here at the ranch with a few guests. Last summer, I had invited Maude and Hannah and I am presuming that they will come. However, I will call her to ask if she plans to attend. Of course, the ranch help will be here and I wanted to know if you would mind if we asked Ken Holliday and his family. Last year, Tara and I went turkey hunting at Grant Hollers and we had a lot of fun. If we had the Holliday family, I may ask Tara to go hunting with me again. What are your thoughts on that?"

Tag grinned, as he began to answer Laura. "It won't hurt to be on the good side of the banker, as long as you don't shoot his kid while on the turkey hunt."

"You have seen me shoot," she replied. "I shoot only what I aim at, and nothing more. Which reminds me, is there a bluff nearby where I could do some target practice? I really have the desire to do some pistol shooting and familiarize myself with the 22-caliber rifle, if that is what I will use to shoot the turkey."

"Sure, just down from the cemetery there is a bluff that is protected from the wind and will give you a clear shot and should be out of range of any buildings or livestock. Why do you like guns and shooting turkeys? I was surprised how handy you were with a weapon and how quick you were to shove the revolver to my face when I awakened you the night that Jason was ill. I really feared for my life. Laura, must you keep that revolver under your pillow?"

"Tag, I have no intention of shooting you, but I feel more comfortable when I am armed. I wouldn't be able to sleep well, if I wasn't armed." She reached out and touched him, saying, "I am careful not to fire at an unknown target. You are safe with me, but until Charles Williams is behind bars or moves out of the country, he is my greatest fear."

Tag asked, "Then, are you going to call Ken and invite them?"

Laura asked, "On second thought, instead of the Hollidays, maybe you would like to invite your parents? I have never met them and now that our house is furnished, perhaps Thanksgiving would be a good time for us to get acquainted. We would still have our other guests, but not the Hollidays."

Tag turned so pale that Laura thought he might faint. "No! Absolutely not! You can meet them at another time, but not now!"

Laura answered quickly, "That is fine. I will wait for another time that you think will be best. I will go now and call Ken to invite them." Immediately, she left the room. *She wondered why Tag was so upset at the mention of his parents.*

She rang the Holliday number and Ken answered the phone. "Hello, Ken. This is Laura Taggat, and as Thanksgiving is fast approaching, Tag and I are extending an invitation to you and your family to join us. I had earlier extended an invitation to Maude and Hannah and I will call them to remind them as well. If Mrs. Baker wants to join us, she is quite welcome, but I thought that she might be visiting Peggy and her family."

"How thoughtful it is of you and Tag to invite us." Ken sounded sincere in his reply. "Yes, Mrs. Baker had indicated that she would like to be with Peggy, but she had agreed to fix our dinner ahead of time, but this will work out just fine. One question, may I bring a guest?"

"Of course! On second thought Ken, please none of my old boyfriends. Do I know this guest?"

Ken said, "No, but I need to confirm that there will be a guest before revealing who it is. I will call you back when I am sure. Is that fair enough?"

"It works for me. I'm planning to ask Cindy Holler for permission to go turkey hunting on their ranch. Tara had so much fun last year that I would like her to join me on the hunt if she cares to go along."

Laura could tell by the sound of Ken's voice that he was pleased by the invitation for Tara to join the hunt. "She is in bed now, but I will tell her in the morning. I know that she will be happy about the 'annual turkey safari.' It is thoughtful of you to include her. She still talks about the fun that she had. Even now at this age, I think that she is somewhat smitten with Toby Holler, all because of that one event."

"Tell her I will let her know more of the details as it gets closer to the time of the hunt, but I am thinking the Saturday before Thanksgiving Day will be hunting day. Bye for now."

The Saturday before Thanksgiving, Tara and Laura went hunting. Laura had agreed to go to Summit City to get Tara in exchange for Mrs. Baker babysitting Tylor. It was almost a repetition of the previous year. The morning was brisk with a light snow falling. Toby knew where the turkeys would be and he called them closer than the previous year. Laura shot three hens, as she had promised Cindy a bird and she thought that she would need two hens this year, considering the number of guests she had invited. Tara was well prepared as what to expect and she cleaned one all by herself. Laura thought that it might have been to impress Toby Holler as to her capabilities of being a hunter. On the way back to Summit City, Tara said, "Daddy has a lady friend and her name is Mrs. Hunter. She is real pretty, just like you. I think that you are pretty, Mrs. Taggat."

"Thank you for the compliment, Tara," said Laura. "It is nice that your father has a lady friend."

"Daddy doesn't want us to call her his girl friend, so we call her his lady friend." Tara seemed pleased to have shared the family secret with Laura.

Laura wondered if she is the lady that Ken referred to when he asked if he could bring a guest. I need to find out more about this lady friend. "Does Mrs. Hunter have a job?"

"Oh, yes." Tara was excited. "She is a school teacher and she teaches Todd. I don't know if Todd likes her, but I do. She doesn't have a husband, as he got killed. I think in the war. She is sad sometimes, but Daddy makes her laugh and then she isn't sad. Did I tell you I like her? She is nice to me. Her name is Natalie, but we call her Mrs. Hunter."

"That is good that you show her respect. Do you remember when I lived with you? I had you call me, Miss Martin. When I have more time, I will need to meet Mrs. Hunter. She sounds like a nice lady. You may want to tell her about our annual turkey hunt and how much fun we have." Laura drove in the driveway and went in to get Tylor. As she was ready to leave, she said to Tara, "Should we plan on hunting turkeys next year on the Saturday before Thanksgiving?" Tara nodded her head and went in to tell everyone about the turkey hunt. Laura wrapped up Tylor and they were off to the 99 Ranch.

After two days of continual light snow, Thanksgiving morning dawned bright with a full sun to lighten the day. The temperature was near zero, but was ideal so that everyone would enjoy being inside. Tag had started a fire in the fireplace. Laura had decorated the living room with fall colors. Ken was bringing a guest and he had consented to give Maude and Hannah a ride. Laura had asked Tag to have the men come to the ranch house by eleven that morning. Nick had agreed to help Laura in the kitchen in lieu of taking care of the cattle, as the others would be doing. She was glad for his help, as he had a sixth sense in knowing what needed to be done. Laura had wanted to instruct him on setting the table, but she would save that for another time, as she was saving that task for Hannah, Todd and Tara. Now, if she could keep Tara from sampling the olives as they put the dinnerware on the table, she would indeed be fortunate.

As the guests drove into the yard, Laura was eager to meet them at the front door. First in was Tara, as she brought a gift of candy for Laura. She handed it to Laura and immediately went to Tylor who was sitting on the floor. Next to enter was Maude and Hannah. Hannah gave Laura a hug and commented that she missed her. Ken escorted in his 'lady friend.' Laura was dumbfounded when she saw her! It was almost as if Laura was looking into the future and could see herself fifteen years from now. Ken introduced her, "Laura, this is Mrs. Hunter; Natalie, Mrs. Taggat."

"Welcome to our home, Mrs. Hunter. Please call me, Laura. I'm glad that you could be with us at this time. Let me take your coat. Yours also, Ken. I will hang them in this closet. Come into the living room. I had Tag start a fire in the fire place, as it seems to make the place glow if a fire is burning."

"What a lovely home, Laura. Please call me, Natalie. I have been anxious to meet you; Ken has told me so much about you. Thank you for inviting us. I have heard so much about these turkeys that I can scarcely wait to view them. It made Tara's week to go hunting with you."

Laura had to control her eyes. Natalie was an attractive woman in her late 30's, with dark hair, and about the same stature of Laura. *When she saw Natalie with Ken, a stab of jealousy pierced her soul. She made an effort to curb her thoughts.* To create a distraction, she called to Hannah. "Hannah, would you, Todd and Tara please set the table for twelve. Tylor will sit in his highchair. Hannah, you are in charge and I am counting on you to assign someone other than Tara to put the olives on the table. The dinnerware that we will be using is on the counter in the kitchen. Plan on having it completed by 12:30, as that is the time we plan to eat. Nick is in charge in the kitchen and I will be the lady of the house and entertain our guests. Do not disturb me, unless it is absolutely necessary. Any questions?"

Hannah came to the doorway, and making a face at Laura, she replied, "No Laura, no questions."

Laura was unsure how to get the conversation going, so she turned to Maude, "Maude, I have been so busy, what is the latest news in Summit City?"

With a sly look on her face, she said, "It seems that the banker has shown an interest in one of the school teachers at the high school. However, we don't get much news at the café." Ken blushed and Natalie said nothing, but smiled proudly.

Laura was embarrassed that she had created an awkward situation, but was determined to correct it. "I presume that you have heard of my good fortune when Mrs. Teasdale gave me her furniture. Much of it was what she had furnished this house with, so I was happy to have it returned to the ranch. It is almost as if we are living in a museum. It took us several days to move all of it and clean her house for selling. Tag had the good fortune to rent a furniture truck from the Mercantile, which protected these old pieces quite well. I am especially happy to have the piano in the living room. I have played some over the years, but really not that good. Terry, one of our hands played for us the first night we had it set up. I am hoping for the Christmas carols in the next month. Tell me, Natalie, do you play?"

"No, unfortunately, I never had the opportunity to learn, but I wish I had."

"I thought," Laura began, "that you might be the music teacher, but evidently not. What subjects do you teach?" Laura was hoping to smooth over the awkward start to the conversation. *Am I vain or is it that this woman looks so much like me, it is almost eerie?*

"I am the English teacher and some of the Social Studies, as well as the girls Physical Education. I'm not really well qualified in that, but in a smaller school you help where you can. Previously, I taught in eastern Nebraska and it was English only, but it was a much larger school. Ken tells me that I rented your former apartment in town."

"Really? I loved that apartment as it was close to the Dismal River. I lived in it during the summer months and it was rather confining, however, each evening I would wade along the edge of the river to cool off. I was expecting at that time, so the heat was oppressive at times."

"Excuse me, Laura," asked Natalie, "could you please show me to the bathroom."

Laura stood up, "Certainly, just follow me and we will go into our bedroom."

As they entered the bedroom, Natalie closed the door and confronted Laura. "What is this all about?" Grabbing Laura by the arm, she turned her around, as they stood facing the large mirror on the dresser. "This is what I mean."

Laura calmly replied, "Natalie, I see two beautiful women. What do you see?"

Laura was seeing a different side of Natalie. She first saw her as charming, but now there was a viciousness about her that was frightening. "I see two women who look alike, but what disturbs me, is why Ken chose a woman to date that looks so much like his former mistress?"

Now it was Laura's turn to do some arm grabbing. She set Natalie on the edge of the bed. "Let me put your fears at ease. I was never Ken's mistress. Did I love him? I probably did, but Ken and I were not compatible socially. That is why I left when I did. Had I chosen to do so, I could have manipulated Ken into marriage. He was vulnerable at that time. I doubt that Ken realizes that two women in his life look so much alike. I rather imagine that Ken looks at us, as two women that are different in their mannerisms, characteristics and background. It is interesting, as Tara told me that Daddy had a lady friend. She never once mentioned that we looked alike. She did say that you were nice. Perhaps, it is just you and me that notice the similarity. Natalie, you seem to be knowledgeable of my background, why don't you fill me in on yours?" Laura sat down on the edge of the bed beside Natalie.

Natalie stared at Laura as if she was uncertain as to what she had asked. "I grew up in central Iowa, the only child of a college professor and a stay at home mom. I am a widow, as my husband Gordon was killed in Korea about 18 months ago. I was teaching in eastern Nebraska, but I just had to get away, as there were too many memories. That is why I chose to come to Summit City. I have no children." Natalie paused. She reached out and clasped Laura's hand. "I'm sorry for my doubts and fears. I have come to cherish Ken very much, and when I saw you with your youth and beauty, and when I had heard how close you were to the family, jealousy gripped my soul." She paused before continuing. "I feared that I couldn't measure up to you in Ken's eyes." It was then that she began to sob and clutched

Laura. She repeated, "I'm sorry, Laura, so sorry. Please forgive me. I shouldn't have listened to the gossips. I believe you."

"Let's get the eyes dried and cooled off and rejoin the rest. I'm glad that you came today."

Dinner went off without a hitch and Laura played it cautious by asking Jim McCann to ask the blessing on the food. The three young cowboys and Todd and Hannah agreed to do the dishes. Later they went to the garage that was heated, as the men had rigged a makeshift Ping-Pong table in the center and the young people were involved in the activities there.

The adults became involved with a game of bridge, as Maude and Natalie partnered against Ken and Laura, while Tag and Jim had a checker game going near the fireplace. Only Tylor had chosen to sleep the afternoon away. Everyone enjoyed Laura's pumpkin pie with the heavy whipped cream for a topping. After an early supper, the party broke up, and the people from Summit City left, declining Laura's offer of some of the leftover turkey. Ken said he remembered how much turkey they ate last Thanksgiving from the leftovers. Tara insisted that she wanted some, so Laura fixed her a package of the turkey.

Nick started back to the bunkhouse ahead of the other two. Laura told him, "Thank you for the help today. I do appreciate your assistance. Take one of the pies to the cook shack, as you men may want some more before going to bed tonight. I'll have the others take the turkey with them and I will teach you how to use the leftovers in our meals for the next few days. Good night."

The weather was chilly as the sun had dropped over the western horizon. Tag put another log on the fireplace and backed up to the flame to warm his backside. He commented to Laura, "I enjoyed the day and it has been a long time since I have eaten turkey. Thanksgiving was not one of the holidays that we celebrated at home. I wouldn't mind having a few turkeys on the river, just as a part of the wildlife scene. Do you think that it is possible that we could get some from the Hollers, to just give us a start?"

Laura had wanted turkeys ever since she came to the ranch, but was not sure how to approach Tag about having them. She knew that Grant Holler didn't like them around the buildings, as they were messy, but he tolerated them in the wild. Laura said, "I imagine if you were to give Toby Holler a few dollars per turkey, he could trap some of them for you. If we were to get four hens and a gobbler, it would give us a start. Cindy said that they were beneficial, in that the coyotes would hunt turkeys and were prone to leave the baby calves alone in the spring. You might check with them, as they have plenty to spare. A person wouldn't have to wait until Thanksgiving to have an occasional turkey to eat. I enjoy shooting them, as they are a challenge."

"I might just do that," said Tag. Changing the subject, he asked, "What did you think of Ken's girl friend. You know, there is something familiar about that woman, as if I have seen her before, but I just can't place her. She certainly is attractive and smart too. I think that she is smart enough to catch herself a banker for a husband."

Laura smiled to herself, as she sensed that Tag was confused by the fact that Natalie and she were so similar in size and looks, except for the age difference. Let him try to figure it out, as it will keep him occupied for some time. "Tag, Tara informed me that she is not Ken's girl friend, but rather his lady friend. Maybe there is a difference, but I think you are right in that there is a wedding in the making." Laura was happy for the both of them. She was saddened that Natalie had lost her husband in the war. She could sympathize for her loss.

"So that you will know," Tag said, "the end of the month

will be the last day of work for Terry, Jason and Nick. We will take them to town and settle up with them at that time. Jim will be moving into the spare bedroom here at the house and all the meals will be cooked here. If by chance we need extra help during the winter, we still have the bunkhouse, but will eat here."

"But, Tag, isn't it cruel to let them go at this time of the year?" Laura knew what it was like to be without work. "Can't you keep them on at a reduced pay? What will they do during the winter?"

"They knew this when they hired on. Terry likes to spend the winter on the ski slopes and the other two said that they could find work at the sale barn, or feed store. If they need a place to sleep, they can always come back here. If they do a little bit of work, I will still feed them. In the years of open range, it was called 'riding the grub line.' They will do all right and come spring, they will be at the door, wanting to help with the spring calving." Tag thought, *Laura is just too softhearted to make tough decisions.* "Incidentally, you said that you wanted to meet my parents. Well, you will have the opportunity, as they will be at the attorney's at the time that we settle up. John is what I call my father and Mavis is my stepmother. They helped me with the financing of the place, so they are coming for a loan payment and to oversee how I am doing. It isn't pleasant to have to do some things, but some things just have to be done, like it or not!"

Laura wondered what he meant by that last statement? "Tag, will you have money for all of this, or will you need to borrow from the bank?"

"The calves will be sold on Monday while we still have help for the roundup. I'm expecting a good check, as the calves should have a good weight and the market is good, thanks to the war in Korea. I should be able to make a payment to John and Mavis, clear the notes at the bank and have a good start for next year. It has been a good year. I will need you there at the attorney's office to help write the checks and do the figuring. Last year I was just getting started and only had some yearlings to sell, so this year is a chance to catch up. Each year that the war goes on, it means money in the pocket!"

It grieved Laura to hear those words. *People profiting because of the war! Why must it continue? Today, Natalie told of her husband being killed there and it has been a little over a year since Tylor's father was buried, as the result of that horrible war. And all of this took place in a part of the world that most people wouldn't be able to find on a map. Was it so that others might profit? Oh, Lord, how long must we suffer?*

Laura turned her thoughts back to what would happen on the day of settlement. "Tag, who is your attorney that you go to and what time is this settlement? I am scheduled for an appointment with Dr. Jessup that day and perhaps I could have it finished by the time I go to the attorney's. If I have continued to gain weight and get my blood pressure stabilized, this should be my last appointment."

At the mention of Dr. Jessup, Tag had a tendency to become upset. He was still angry over their earlier confrontation. "I would think so, as he has milked this malnutrition thing long enough. Incidentally, the attorney is Karl Larson and we will meet with him at three in the afternoon. We will eat at the ranch. That should give you time to see that old pill pusher."

Laura went to the kitchen to make a note on the calendar of those facts, so that she could set up the appointment after dinner. Calling back to Tag, "Darling, would you like pie and coffee before we go to bed? It won't take long to warm up the coffee."

He was at the kitchen by the time she finished the sentence. "Laura, I like the two kinds of pie that you make, hot and cold. Get that coffee hot, as it is a cold night."

Now that the weather turned cold, Jim no longer rode his horse to church and Laura drove the pickup. Usually Jim rode with her, but he was feeling ill, so had opted to remain home so that he might be fit the next day for the roundup of the calves. As she arrived at home, she saw that the men had not returned from moving the cattle on fresh grass near the headquarters. She and Tylor changed clothes and returned to the cook shack to prepare the dinner for the men. She had started the coffee and was making sandwiches from the roast she had started before leaving for church. Jim came in and sat down on a stool in the kitchen. "Laura," he asked, "I don't want to be a bother, but would it be all right if I had my dinner now? I will eat, and then go back to my bunk and try to feel better for tomorrow."

"I'm sorry that you aren't feeling well, but sure, let me get your coffee and I have the sandwiches ready. Let me fix you a bit of broth to go with that as well. We need to get you well for the big day! Is it as exciting as branding?" Laura was always curious as to the workings of a Sandhills cattle ranch, and particularly the 99 Ranch.

Jim spooned his broth, over and over. He was not putting it to his mouth, but filling the spoon and then spilling it back into the bowl. Laura was uncertain if he knew that he was doing it, or was he preparing to say something to her? Finally he spoke, "Laura, are you acquainted with an attorney?" Laura thought that was an odd question that Jim had asked her.

"Yes, but why do you ask? Leon Kelly in town handled the guardianship of Hannah that I was involved in." Laura was curious.

"You might want to make him aware of your status at this time. John and Mavis Taggat are not to be reckoned with. That is all I can tell you, but watch your step when all of you meet at Karl Larson's office the end of the month. I'm not disloyal to Tag, but I do have a loyalty to you. Also, I don't want you to get hurt." Jim started to spoon his broth again. After a time, he had his dinner consumed and back to his bunk before the others had come in for dinner. Laura pondered what Jim had said and was determined to call Leon Kelly on Monday.

On Monday, Laura called the doctor's office to make an appointment at 2:00 p.m. She informed the receptionist that it was a routine visit to check what progress she had been making. She then called Leon Kelly. It had been over a year since she had talked with him, so when he came on the line, she identified herself. "This is Laura Taggat. I was in your office about a year ago regarding the Hannah Williams guardianship. My name at that time was Laura Martin, but has since changed when I married Tag Taggat. This may seem a little strange, but a confidant warned me that I might need an attorney when the family of my husband meets with us on the 30th of this month. This person told me nothing more, but I deem them to be a reliable source. We are to meet at 3:00 p.m. with Karl Larson at his office. Would you be available if anything develops?"

"Oh, yes, I remember you. You were the lady that paid up front on the guardianship case. I never heard anything more, so I am presuming that everything worked out for you. Do you have any idea what might take place? The Taggats have somewhat of a reputation, but as you have apparently married into the family, it must be somewhat of a family matter if you need representation. I am free that afternoon, so if you need me, I will be available. The Larson firm is close by, so I can be there in a matter of minutes." Leon put the phone down. *That is a strange call, but I remember Laura as a bit of a feisty girl. She was pregnant at the time and I thought that it was to be a paternity case, which turned out to be the guardianship of a teenage girl. These Taggats might make for an interesting case.*

The cattle sold well and Tag was in a festive mood. "Laura, you have been a big help in making this a good year. What is it that you would like me to buy you to show that I appreciate all of your hard work? Just name it!"

Laura's first thought was a new car, but decided against it. *If I reach too high in the sky, he will reject it and I will get nothing. She realized that had she not asked Tag to marry her, she would have received wages for the past six months. I know what I need and he will see it as a practical request.* "Tag, I want a milk cow, like Macaroni. In fact, a red cow at this time would be perfect, as Macaroni is with calf now and will be drying up in a few months. We should always have a cow to milk. That way, I can rotate them in such a manner to have milk and cream continually. I even know what I would call her. I would call her 'Cheese.' Did you get that? Cheese and Macaroni would be the cow's names. How clever of me."

Laura's request caught Tag by surprise. *He expected that she would ask for something expensive and he could deny it as costing too much. He anticipated a car, or even a diamond ring as a request. He had given her money for her wedding ring, which had cost $20.00 for a simple wedding band.* "I guess we could look for another cow, but one due to calve now might be hard to find, as most of them are bred for spring calving. We have all winter to look for a cow, so no need of getting excited just yet." He thought, *timing is important to allay the evidence of generosity, which will cost me nothing in the end.*

Laura sensed the tactic that Tag was deploying. But she knew that Nebraska was a big state, and surely at this moment, there is a red cow due to calve within the next six weeks. I will find her!

Laura was dreading the last day of the month. It was the date that Nick, Jason and Terry would be leaving the ranch. I will miss them, as they have been like family. More so, there was the impending doom of the meeting with John and Mavis Taggat. The unpleasantness of what was to take place was no match for the weather. The sun failed to make its presence in the early morning hours. And a bitter cold wind was blowing in from the northwest, promising a cold December awaiting the residents of the Sandhills. Because of the cold temperatures, both trucks were driven to town. Jim, Terry, Laura and Tylor were crowded in the older truck and came in earlier because of Laura's appointment with Dr. Jessup. The others would follow later. Jim promised Laura that he would return a little before three, so that she wouldn't have to brave the cold wind.

Laura went into the office and immediately the nurse handed her a questionnaire to complete.

After completing the questionnaire, she returned it to the nurse and asked, "Will I be able to see the doctor now? I need to be at the attorney's office by three."

"Laura," the nurse said, "Dr. Jessup is with another patient right now, but he will see you next. You should be out of here before then. Let's go back and weigh you and check out a few other things while the doctor looks over your chart and the questionnaire."

After a few minutes, Dr. Jessup entered the examining room. "Laura, you have made great progress in the last two months. I want you to keep on the same diet and continue with the vitamins. Also, come back in two weeks and I will check you again."

Laura was surprised, "But, Doctor, this was to be my last time. Tag was hoping that we could stop these office calls. He won't be very happy with me coming in so often."

Dr. Jessup smiled, "I know Tag doesn't want to part with a dollar, but do you think that he will be happy to know that you are pregnant? I'm not sure you should tell him just yet, as I am not 100% positive, but I am confident it is true. You were so thin that you had ceased to ovulate. Once you started to gain weight, the body regained its ability to function. I venture to say that the Fourth of July will be an exciting day for the Taggats. That is why I need to keep tabs on you. We do need to stabilize the blood pressure, but that should be no problem." He paused before continuing. "Laura, you are extremely quiet for having received this news. Aren't you happy about this pregnancy?"

Laura didn't answer right away. "Yes and no. I have always wanted a lot of children. At the present, I'm not sure of Tylor's condition. I had hoped that he would be less work when the next one came along, but we will manage. Thank you, Doctor. I'm sorry for not being more responsive, but I have a lot on my mind and the day isn't over." Laura left, and looking out the reception room window, she saw that Jim was waiting for her. She picked up Tylor and prepared to go out the door into the cold. A young man held the door for her as he was entering the office at the same time that she was leaving. *There was a familiarity about him, as if she had seen him before.* Chase Adams had the same thought about this woman holding the child in her arms. *He recognized the red coat from their first meeting on the train near Madden, as well as the fear mirrored in her brown eyes. He recalled the rapid beating of her heart was exhibited by the throbbing of the pulse in her neck. The fear in her eyes had left him with an eerie feeling. And, so it was today. Who is this woman?*

Entering the attorney's office, Laura was impressed with the richness of the furnishings.

Evidently, Mr. Larson's practice has done quite well. He was in the outer office when Laura came in from the cold. He approached her and sticking out his hand, he said, "Good afternoon, I presume that you are Mrs. Taggat. The others are here and when you are ready, we can begin."

Laura was ushered into the conference room and it was even more exquisite than the waiting room. The walnut table and the upholstered chairs filled the room. Seated at the head of the table as if he was in charge of the meeting was a man every bit as large as Tag. His white hair topped a wrinkled face that had experienced the harsh climate of the Sandhills. He had folded his hands in front of him. As they rested on the table, they were gnarled and huge.

Seated by him was a large woman that complemented his demeanor. There was a harshness about her that was hard to define, but its presence was evident.

Still clutching Tylor, who was resting on her hip, she advanced toward them. I will take the contest of the wills to them and go and introduce myself. Rounding the table, she said, "Mr. and Mrs. Taggat, it is good to finally meet you. I am Laura, and this is my son, Tylor. I feared that I might be late, but I see by the clock that I am five minutes early. I will set him down and then I will be ready when the rest of you are." She had sent in the checkbook and the ledgers with Tag, so she delved into them and placed them in front of her, giving the others a view of her competency.

John Taggat continued to have his hands in front of him and asked, "Have the men been paid and told that they no longer have a job?" His voice was such, that Laura expected the water glasses on the table to vibrate.

Laura said, "I have figured each man's wages due and deducted for the social security. I didn't include the proposed bonus of $100.00, as I didn't have an opportunity to verify this with Tag, but it will be easy to make an additional check."

John and Tag spoke simultaneously, "They get no bonus!"

Laura was as quick to speak up. "And, why not? They stayed to the bitter end! They have earned their bonus!"

Tag replied, "They refused to go to work. That is the same as quitting!"

Laura couldn't believe what she was hearing. "Tag, they refused because Jim McCann was feeding them a diet of eggs, bacon and potatoes three times a day, seven days a week. No wonder they refused to go to work. When I went to work, you were wound so tight that you had no idea what you were eating. Besides, if you back down on the bonuses now, they will not be back in the spring. Think about that. For a measly $300.00 you will lose your next year's help."

John pounded the table, "Shut that woman up, Tag! She has no business being in this meeting!"

Laura responded. "Mr. Taggat, I have a vested interest in this meeting and in this ranch. I am his wife."

Once again John pounded the table. He turned to Karl Larson. "Pay that woman off, but get her off that ranch." Turning to Laura, he continued, "You just married him for his money. I know your kind. It's true, isn't it? You wanted his money."

Laura spoke softly, "No, Mr. Taggat, I wanted his name. The Taggat name is likened to an English Coat of Arms. The Taggat name in the Sandhills has such prestige." Karl Larson took note of the sarcasm in her reply.

Laura then turned to the attorney. "Mr. Larson, this meeting was set up with the express purpose of getting me out of this marriage. Am I so wicked that the Taggats, including Tag, want me gone?" Next she turned to Tag. "Is this what you want, or are you caving into your parents' wishes? Tell me, Tag, did the marriage bed mean nothing to you?"

Tag said nothing, but stared at the table. His silence and

demeanor caused Laura's heart to pound. She instantly breathed a silent prayer! *'Oh God, help me! Give me wisdom, as this is almost a repeat of what happened nearly two years ago. I can't go through the same thing again!'*

Karl Larson, seeing that the meeting was going nowhere, intervened. "Mrs. Taggat, you are correct. In visiting with Tag and his parents, we see that it is in the best interest of all, that this marriage should be terminated and they are willing to compensate you for your part in it."

Laura said, "I see that I have no say in whether I stay or leave. It is all about money. Well, how much money and what if I refuse?"

Karl Larson said, "The amount is $3,000.00, and it would be well if you didn't refuse. A divorce like this could be messy and I don't think you want us delving too deeply into your past."

Laura looked at Tag. "Is this what you want? Can you tell me that it is what you want? Just say something!" Tag just stared at her, showing no emotion whatsoever, as if he was in a trance.

Laura spoke to the group. "Let me get this straight. You will pay me $3,000.00 to leave. Now I have accumulated some assets while there. Do I retain them, or must I forfeit my rights to those as well?"

Karl Larson continued to be the spokesman for the group. "I see no reason for you giving them up, but perhaps you could tell us what they are and we could include them when drafting the agreement."

"Let me see," began Laura. "There is my son Tylor, but I am sure no Taggat would want him. Then there is what cash I have in the bank under my name. Forty pullets and a rooster and a cow and her calf and the furniture received as a gift from Mrs.

Teasdale rounds out my assets acquired while at the 99 Ranch. Oh, I almost forgot. There is also Tag's child that I am carrying. I will take that child with me. I just learned this afternoon that I am pregnant. After I have seen my attorney, I will get back to you."

Laura got up and putting on her coat, she heard someone at the table clear their throat. Turning around, she heard Tag whisper, "Laura, don't go. Please don't go. I'm sorry." Getting up from the table, he gripped her arms and pulled her to him.

Laura returned his embrace, as she said, "Tag, I love you." As she nestled her head in the hollow of his shoulder, she began to weep silently. As the tears began to flow down her cheeks, she thought, *this is one of those times that my tears are tears of joy. I am unsure if Tag's response is his love for me, or the child that I am carrying, but I rejoice that my marriage is still intact.*

John and Mavis left the office, saying nothing to Tag.

That night, as Laura placed Tylor in his bed, he hugged his mother, telling her, "I l-l-love you, M-M-Mama." Later, as she went to her own bed, she began to reflect upon the events of the day. *I remember Galatians 5: 22, 23 'But the fruit of the Spirit is love, joy, peace, longsuffering, gentleness, goodness, faith, meekness, temperance.' A year ago, I had experienced 'Faith, Faith at the Dismal River.' I can now lay claim to having found 'Joy, Joy at the Dismal River,' as I rejoice that my husband has been freed from the dominance of his parents. And the three young cowboys received their bonus. I am anxious to see what the Spirit of God has for me, as I look forward to the birth of our child. Will it be 'hope,' or perhaps 'love?*

Sleep came to Laura, as Tag lay by her side with his arm around her, giving her comfort, assurance and joy.

As Laura slept in her husband's arms, a troubled young

man pondered his chance meeting of the lady in the red coat. As he sat on the edge of his hotel bed in Summit City, he began to write in his journal.

The troubled dove flew to her nest

She pulled her young, close to her breast

Suddenly she flew away, she flew away

Will she return another day?

Will she return another day?

THE END

ABOUT THE AUTHOR

In my first book, Faith at the Dismal River, I went into great detail as to my credentials. In this book, let me tell you why I write in the unconventional manner in which I have chosen to write. My life has been rather unconventional as well. Let me cite a few examples. I didn't learn to walk until I was twenty-two months old, nor did I learn to ride a bicycle until I was thirty-eight years of age. So it was not surprising, at least it wasn't to me, to begin my first romantic novel when I was seventy-eight.

You will find that I use few adjectives to describe my characters, or the scenery as well. As an example, in the first book, I described Maude Dunham, the café owner as a plump woman in her late fifties. I rely upon the reader to provide a mental image of this character based upon those two clues. I also use a lot of interaction between the characters, so that you will pick up on their emotional characteristics as well as their physical attributes.

I first started writing by following all of dos and don'ts of the industry, but I found it rather stifling. Consequently, I began to write what I deemed as a natural flow of the story, with the purpose of having brought the book to a close, but the reader looking forward to the next book in the series. I enjoy including scenes of irony, as well as emotional scenes that bring the reader to tears. I am presuming that will be the occasion, as I am brought to tears when I initially write it, as well as each time it is edited.

Many of the scenes are based upon my personal experiences with some tweaking, which provides a greater degree of authenticity. Enjoy the read!